ESCAPING CONVICTION

Conviction Series Book One

GREER RIVERS

Copyright © 2021 by Greer Rivers

All rights reserved.

No part of this book may be reproduced or used in any form without written permission from the author, except for the use of brief quotations in a book review. For more information, contact greerriverswriting@gmail.com.

This is a work of fiction. Names, characters, businesses, places, events, locales, and incidents are either the products of the author's imagination or used in a fictitious manner. Any resemblance to actual persons, living or dead, or actual events is purely coincidental.

The legal terminology and themes discussed in this work of fiction are written to exemplify the judicial system to the best of the author's capability and interpretation. Please note she has taken authorial license over some ideas and interactions for storytelling purposes.

Cover Design: Jodielocks Designs

Editing and Proofreading: My Brother's Editor

ASIN: B08NF7XRZK / ISBN: 9798564154246

❀ Created with Vellum

ESCAPING CONVICTION

Jason

I'm not letting her go after this.
I left the love of my life when she needed me most. I thought I was saving the world, but instead I lost everything.
Now I need *her*.
My sister is missing and I'm suspect #1. Without Jules as my defense attorney, I would be locked in a cell instead of saving my sister. Once I find Ellie, I'm never letting either of them out of my sight.
I'm never making that mistake again.

Jules

He's just like every other client.
The man I thought was the love of my life, ghosted me when I needed him most. But he's not the one that got away. No, he's the bullet I dodged.
Now he needs *me*.
His sister is missing and he's been charged with her kidnapping. He thinks we can mend what he broke. But I can't trust him.
I'm never making that mistake again.

A NOTE FROM THE AUTHOR

Escaping Conviction is a second chance romantic suspense with legal, military, and mature themes. It is the first in the Conviction series of interconnected standalones, all of which contribute to an overarching plot. Don't worry, there's no cliffhanger for the couple in their respective story. HEA guaranteed.

This series takes place in Ashland County, a small, fictional, southern county somewhere in the mountains of the Carolinas. Ashland County is full of steamy, legal intrigue, so some characters may appear in other stories written in the same universe.

The Conviction series should only be read by mature readers (18+) and contains sexually explicit scenes, along with descriptions of human trafficking, drugs, strong language, and physical and sexual violence.

Reader discretion is advised.

*For all those who are waiting for their sign.
This is it.*

CHAPTER ONE

Click-clack.

Her red-bottom heels resounded like shots fired in an indoor shooting range. With each step, conversations hushed and laughter quieted inside the bustling police station. She smirked and kept her focus straight ahead. Inside a building that's eighty-eight percent male, anything walking in with tits and ass is going to get a second—or third—glance. But it was the other looks she craved. Awe meant she'd impressed them, even though she was technically one of "the bad guys." Disgust meant she'd bested them.

"Hey, Juliet," a timid rookie had the nerve to call out.

Jules smiled and winked at him, enjoying the blush that crept up his neck. He immediately turned around and pretended to organize papers on the small desk he shared with other new officers. She had a case not too long ago where shy Officer Henry Brown screwed up royally. It was a benefit for her client, the suspect at the time, but it nearly got the poor guy fired. After the charge was dismissed, she'd stepped in and spoken with the district attorney to convince the sheriff to give the guy a break. Everybody deserves a second chance…

She felt the vibration of her phone up the handle of her white Prada tote for the umpteenth time.

...Almost everybody.

Although she already knew who it was, she opened the bag just enough to confirm the name on the screen. She swallowed a groan but never missed a step as she continued on to her destination.

She didn't have time for that particular asshole and hadn't since the day he cheated on her. Not that you could call it that, since they never really dated—in her mind anyway. But the fact that *he* thought they'd been dating was enough for her to write him off. It was a technicality, but she snatched the excuse and waved it around every time he insisted she hear him out. It didn't help his case that he'd slept with a certain woman in particular. At the time, he knew what he was doing and who he was doing it with. Jules could guess what he'd aimed to make her feel. Sucks for him that all she felt was relief.

But at that moment, relief was the last thing she felt. Past the deputy desks, the hallway seemed to cave in on the sides, making her lightheaded and queasy. The faux-granite tiling underneath her Louboutins stretched endlessly. Did the lights usually flicker that ominously? Damned government buildings and their shitty maintenance.

Lock it down, Jules.

What she was about to do was normally a piece of cake. Second nature by now, even after only a few years. She was used to having the law eating out of the palm of her hand, but each step closer to the interrogation room at the end of the hall made her nausea that much stronger.

After an eternity, she finally stood outside the faded green door with its frosted window. She could see shadowy figures, one of which looked like it was pacing. The other somehow looked bored, even through the distorted glass, but that had to be her imagination. She glanced around, dipped her hand underneath her coat, and wiped her sweaty palm on the skirt of her dress, thankful that she'd worn a darker color. After a steadying breath, she allowed her fingertips to hover over the doorknob. She tried to clear her mind, to get in the zone. But this wasn't a regular client.

This was *Jason*.

The man she'd thought was the love of her life until he'd ghosted her when she'd needed him most. He was the one that got away.

No. She shook her head slightly.

He's the bullet I dodged.

Any man who could do what he'd done wasn't worth the dirt under her stilettos.

He's just like every other client.

The words whispered across her mind like a prayer, and she hoped it would be answered. Jules took another breath and tilted the handle down, shoving into the room. Just as swiftly as she walked in, it hit her.

He wasn't like every other client. Only one half-second look into those painfully familiar stormy eyes told her it was different this time. She moved her gaze to the handcuffs around his wrists before looking away entirely and glared at the officer who'd locked her client up.

"Jason, let's go. This interrogation is over."

CHAPTER TWO

Fuck me.

That was the first thing Jason thought when Juliet Bellerose barreled through the door, like a goddamn Valkyrie, choosing who in the room she'd take to Valhalla and who she would spare. The others in the room seemed surprised, but he'd heard her heels clicking down the hallway long before the door opened.

It'd been seven years, but he'd been dreaming of that walk since the first day he saw her. Her sexy, confident swagger always made him want to scoop her up and hold her, never letting go until her pleasure was his own. Before his mind could follow that thought down into the gutter, he relaxed in his seat and took her in.

Jules's honey-brown hair loosely curled down the lapels of the long white coat that covered her dark knee-length garnet dress. Her matching heels were sky high on already long legs. A memory flashed of faint pressure on his hips as she wrapped around him. Damn, he'd tried to relax, but his mind was not cooperating. Instead, he felt himself already getting hard within seconds of her entering the room. He absentmindedly wondered if she also felt the room get warmer as Jason's gaze traveled along her figure, all the way up until he caught a glimpse of her dispassionate glance at him.

Despite the initial hope that bubbled up when he realized she was coming to his rescue, his heart tanked into his stomach. That beautiful face told him everything he needed to know. She'd already decided his fate. One way or another, he was doomed.

"What's the meaning of this?" The pudgy, unkempt investigator hadn't been able to keep still since he'd entered the interrogation room. His graying blond, receding hairline was quickly developing beads of sweat that dripped down his red face and furrowed brow. Not even the occasional dabbing of his yellowed handkerchief at his forehead was enough to stave off the perspiration.

"Burgess, he told you he wanted a lawyer. Ms. Bellerose is obviously it."

The investigator gaped at the assistant district attorney as the calmer, younger man eased out of his nonchalant pose in the corner of the room. His comment took Jules's focus off the investigator and a flicker of surprise passed over her face before a sly smile emerged.

"Marco, what are you doing here? Isn't an interrogation a little hands-on for an ADA?"

His arms crossed and his lips ticked up slightly. "It's been a while, Jules."

She shrugged a shoulder and her smile grew. "Not since the MC gang case, I don't think."

The ADA's eyes sparked and Jason thought he detected a hint of nostalgia in his accompanying chuckle. "Oh, you don't think. You *know*. It's hard to forget how your cross-examination of my main witness single-handedly destroyed my case."

He continued to meander toward Jules until he was barely a foot away from her. Way too comfortable for Jason's liking, but to his immense satisfaction, she politely stepped back and schooled her expression to reflect the seriousness of her tone.

"Well, I *know* you know why I'm here. Why the hell is my client being interrogated without his attorney present?"

Getting the message, the ADA took a step back to match hers and dove his hands in his pockets, only looking slightly chastised before he cleared his throat.

"This is no interrogation. But you are indeed Mr. Stone's attorney? He failed to mention you by name."

She stood with her feet wide and her arms crossed, never once looking Jason's way. "You know the drill, Marco. Why is my client in handcuffs if this isn't an interrogation? Is he under arrest?"

"Just a precaution. He's only in investigative detention, *not* under arrest. You have to understand, this is a potential missing persons case and we have nothing of evidentiary value besides the phones he brought in. Phones belonging to both of the missing girls."

"Exactly! 'Nothing of evidentiary value.' And one of those girls is his *sister*. You're grasping at straws here. He's obviously trying to help."

"That may be the case, but considering Mr. Stone's history, the precinct had to consider his training and the fact that he's a potential danger to officers should he... overreact. This is just an informal investigation. He knows that."

"The fuck it is," Jason grumbled under his breath. This whole thing was pissing him off. If what they'd been questioning him over was true, he was losing precious time and he needed to get the hell out of there.

"Be quiet, Jason. Nothing else from you," Jules gritted out before her perfect bow lips slipped back into a Cheshire smile.

"Mr. Stone's 'history,' as you put it, includes being a Night Stalker in our great nation's Army. He flew helicopters into battle and risked his life to protect our freedoms countless times. Precaution or not, Marco, the media here in Ashland County will have a field day once they realize this is the way our government treats our veterans." The ADA's lips thinned while

Jules went on. "Interrogation while in custody is a violation of his Fifth Amendment rights, especially if he's invoked his right to an attorney. Unless you want a pretty solid Section 1983 suit on this precinct, I suggest you uncuff him and let him go. Right. *The hell.* Now."

The ADA recovered with a stiff smile and nodded toward Investigator Burgess. "You heard the woman. Let him go." He winked at her. "Right. *The hell.* Now."

Investigator Burgess trudged toward Jason with his cuff key in hand, grumbling with every step. The heavyset officer grunted and crossed his arms after the cuffs fell to the table, purposely positioning himself between Jason and potential escape.

Even though his wrists didn't hurt, Jason caught himself rubbing them like he'd seen "perps" do in the movies. He was technically free to leave, but considering the ever-increasing tightness in his jeans, he couldn't get up just yet. It always made him hard whenever Jules took control. He loved it as long as he could take it back where it counted. The bed. A wall. A counter. Really just any surface they could find.

As she sparred with the prosecutor, he used the moment to calm himself down—so to speak—to his advantage and watched her shine. She'd toned down her southern twang, but her voice was still music to his ears. He liked that she wore less makeup now, accentuating her natural beauty. Her face was a bit thinner, proof that she'd grown up while he was away. Her figure, however, was the same outline he remembered, even if it was a little more than it used to be. That was fine by him. More to hold on to. He couldn't help but smile a little at his cock's pulse of anticipation.

One thing that remained the same were those deep cerulean eyes. Damn, he could get lost in those.

But as he kept watching, he noticed a darkness that wasn't there before. Those piercing eyes now seemed tense around the edges and her brow and mouth were too quick to frown. Weariness affected her posture. He wanted to lift whatever burdens were weighing her down to carry them as his own and shield her from any threat.

He'd been that for her once. Her protector. He'd assumed she needed him, until he feared she needed him too much. What a crock of shit that was. It looked like she'd thrived without him.

Considering the way he left, he still couldn't believe he'd actually had the nerve to ask for her help. Aside from their history, she had to be swamped with clients begging her to defend them. From what he'd gathered, she was a savant in her field. Only a few years out of law school and somehow, she was already the best defense attorney in the state. Hell, he'd only called her about twenty minutes ago, but here she was, completely prepared. Hot and ready to do her job.

At the turn of phrase in his mind, he couldn't help reminiscing. His train of thought was no help in quelling his unintentional erection—the one still keeping him in his chair. Memories surfaced with Jules upside down on a chrome pole, in barely anything. Her bright blue-green gaze luring him in, hypnotizing him. In his mind, it was just them. No nasty pricks in the room wishing their dicks were in their hands as they salivated over her body.

No, if this was his fantasy, then she was still only his. Body and soul, they'd been meant for each other. If only he'd learned that sooner. Time and regret were cruel teachers.

He concentrated hard to make the vision go away, but when he heard his devilish angel laughing the ADA's name again, realization hit and all control went out the window.

"*Marco?* Oh, it's like that, huh?" Whoops. He hadn't meant to yell that.

Jules's eyes narrowed toward him and the prosecutor's brow raised as he waited for her to respond.

"I told you. Zip it if you know what's good for you," she hissed before miming the gesture.

Damn, if that tone didn't turn him on. Even though she'd looked in his direction, she maddeningly still hadn't looked directly at him. Good to know he still affected her. Even if she hated him, that was better than nothing at all.

Fuck, he felt insane. Or maybe, he was just pussy-starved. It had been a long time. But even as he thought it, he knew his dry spell wasn't the issue. In any case, something had to be wrong with him since he couldn't stop thinking about her, even in a fucking police interrogation room.

"Cuffs or not, Marco, this interrogation is over. We're leaving."

The investigator's reddening face made him look like he was about to detonate. He puffed up his short stature and stood his ground between Jason and the door. Jules and the ADA looked at each other sternly once more, holding their cards close to their chest. Jules's right eyebrow lifted up just a hair.

The ADA folded. He rubbed his hand down his goatee and sighed, looking toward the investigator. "Alright, let him go," he said, conceding a victory that Jules hid behind a stoic half-smile.

The investigator had no such poker face as he stumbled over his words and stepped in front of Jules to argue with her and the ADA. "But... but... the girls?"

"Burgess, you know we need more than what we've got to arrest him. With, or without, Ms. Bellerose as his attorney, he's a free man in the eyes of the law." The ADA's stare bore into Jason's patience. "For now."

"This is bullshit!" Investigator Burgess rose on his toes to get into the ADA's face and pointed wildly around the room. "We have forty-eight hours before the odds are against us. Hell, it still might be too late. They've been missing since at least this morning. He had their phones in his possession. He has to be the last one who saw them!"

Jason smacked his hand on the table and stood up. "I don't know anything! I've said that, over and over! When my sister didn't respond to my text message, I thought that was odd, but I figured she was just being a teenager. Then I found Ellie and Sasha's phones outside my apartment. My aunt told me they weren't at school this morning, so I was the one who called *you*. And I agreed to come here with you guys! Now you're wasting all this goddamn time you're talking about by questioning *me* instead of being out there, looking for them!"

"And oh, how convenient it was that you had *both* of their phones—"

"You mother—"

Soft pressure on Jason's chest made the fog of his rage dissipate. At some point, he and the incompetent cop had gotten within feet of one another. All that was between them was Jules, and with one small touch, she'd silently brought him back to the moment.

"Chill, Jay... just relax. You're going home now. We'll figure this out." Her hand calmed him even as it pressed more fervently against him. He backed up slowly until the back of his legs touched the table.

"*Mierda.*"

He heard the soft curse behind him and turned abruptly to stare at the forgotten ADA. His tan face quickly shuttered, but not before Jason recognized the regret and acceptance there.

"What?" Jules asked, her hand still on Jason, and he fought everything in him not to press into it harder. He was afraid once she realized what she was doing, she'd stop.

"Nothing. It's just... it's him, isn't it?"

Jules actively avoided looking at Jason as she kept her focus on the prosecutor. An enticing dark pink blush warmed her cheeks and she cleared her throat.

"I don't know what you're talking about, Marco. But if I did, you'd zip it, too."

Marco reverted back to an easy smile and chuckled. "Ah, *mi sirenita.*" Turning toward Jason, his expression cooled significantly. "You better not fuck her over this time, *cabron*. There are better men than you who would take good care of her."

Jason opened his mouth to respond, but Jules beat him to the punch. "Don't call him that, *cabron*. It seems you've forgotten who taught me all the 'important' Spanish words." She gave him a death glare and pointed her finger at him. Despite her height, the ADA still had a good half a foot on her. Hell, he might even be as tall as Jason. "You know I don't need takin' care of. I take care of shit my own damn self." Her angry twang broke through, but instead of cowering—like a sensible person—the ADA's shoulders shook lightly with silent laughter.

"Wouldn't expect anything less, *sirenita*."

It was as if he were in on an inside joke, one that made Jules hide a smile as she led Jason by the arm, finally walking out of that godforsaken interrogation room.

While they were walking down the hall, Inv. Burgess finally found some balls and started yelling. "We'll be watching you, Jason Stone! We know what you did!"

Ignoring the eyes on them, Jules hurried past all the officers' desks with an impressive grip on his arm. They may be watching him, but he was innocent of whatever they *thought* he'd done.

What he *hadn't* done was much worse.

CHAPTER THREE

"I swear to God, Jason, you can't do that male posturing bullshit with a public official. In a freaking police station, for crying out loud! That alone might've gotten you arrested, you know that, right?"

They were out of the precinct and Jason was fuming as he hustled down the concrete steps. He hated that he'd been interrogated by a bunch of idiots. He hated that he had been interrogated at all. He hated that this had been such a goddamn waste of time and a distraction from what was important. And he really hated that the first time Jules had seen him in years, he was in fucking handcuffs.

"You're lucky that Marco and I are friends. You could've spent the night in jail, and what good would that have done? Hm? How are we gonna find Ellie with you behind bars?"

At hearing his sister's name, Jason felt lightheaded as his rage skyrocketed and just as quickly plummeted during Jules's real talk. What the fuck was wrong with him? He'd thought that the prosecutor was an alright guy until Jules came in. Then all he wanted to do was take the asshole out back. The mention of his baby sister was a splash of cold water on his hot anger. It'd been a while since he'd let himself give a shit, and the rush made him feel like he was being waterboarded with the sudden emotions.

"Look, I know this has to be stressful and you're worried as all get out about her..."

Jason laced his fingers on top of his head and paced to calm down and not fall out on the concrete. Careful not to meander into precinct traffic, the sidewalk restricted his movements and he ended up turning in a slow circle. Jules's gentle tug on his shirt brought him back to their conversation. Her usually bright eyes were dark with worry, and he found it impossible to look away. Air released from his chest and whooshed out on a deep breath.

"You gotta phone?"

"Yeah, I've got yours, here." She dug around the inside of her purse to pull out a clear plastic bag containing his belongings from the jail inventory stash. The officers had taken his personal items "just in case" before interrogating him. That had been his major clue he needed to call for backup. Jules carefully plopped the bag into his hand, as if to make sure their fingertips didn't touch. He tilted his head to the side, tempted to confront her about her hesitance around him, but decided it would have to wait. He fished his phone out from the bag and thumbed through his contacts to make a call.

"Jason? Oh, thank God. I was worried when you didn't call back. Have they found Ellie?" Aunt Rachel's warbly voice came over the speaker. Ellie lived with Aunt Rachel ever since their parents died in a car crash when Ellie was an infant. Their quirky old great-aunt was a regular mother hen when it came to Jason's sister, and Aunt Rachel hardly ever let Ellie out of her sight.

"No, they haven't. But remember, we talked about this before I got to the precinct. Ellie and Sasha are teenagers. They're probably just playing hooky. God knows Ellie could use the vacation." He forced a laugh, but the lies coming out of his mouth made him feel nauseous. Aunt Rachel needed to hear something positive though, so he was giving his best shot at sincerity.

"That girl has never missed a day of school in her life. You really think she'd play hooky now? In her senior year?"

"It's called senior skip day, Aunt Rach. Let the girl live it up for once. We'll find her, but I bet she's on her way home as we speak." He hoped she was more gullible than the sassy lie detector in front of him. Jules's raised brow told him she disapproved of his tactics, but Aunt Rachel was nearly seventy-five years old and practically senile. If he didn't assuage her paranoia, she might go walking around Ashland in her muumuu to look for Ellie herself and then forget why she left the house at all.

"I hope we weren't acting too rashly by calling the police. It's just, when she didn't show up for school, I panicked. And then you found her phone…" Aunt Rachel sighed. "But, yes. You're probably right. I hope you're right. I'll let you know if she comes home." Her voice caught at the end.

Jason swallowed hard. "Thanks Rach. I'll keep you in the loop. Love you."

"Love you too. Be safe out there."

Jason hung up and tried to convince himself that Ellie was fine. He tucked his phone into his pocket and turned back to Jules. "Listen, I gotta go… do something. Anything to try to find El. I'd like for you to come with me." He hated the lilt in his voice at the end, but maybe the vulnerability would convince her to stay with him. He didn't know if it was because Ellie was missing, but he had a strong urge to never let Jules out of his sight again.

Jules's fingertips brushed against his forearm, the heat of them a stark contrast against the cool winter air seeping through his thin pullover. "We'll find her, alright? We just need to be smart and figure this out. Together." Jason could see the moment she realized what she was doing—what she was saying. When she did, she snatched her hand back, as if her skin burned as much as he did for her. She stood ramrod straight, gathering her purse close to her like a shield. "They haven't made a formal accusation or arrest because there's no probable cause to any of this. Hell, there's not even been a crime that we know of yet. But, if we don't get ahead of it all, or some other shit hits the fan, you're one lazy officer away from a jail cell."

He shook his head. Jason knew what was at stake, but he couldn't help still being frustrated at the cops. They'd wasted time questioning him like a criminal while his sister was missing, and it was utter bull—

She snapped her fingers in his face. "Hey! I'm your defense attorney now, do you understand that, Jason? Are you gonna listen to me, for once?"

"Don't you have to be paid before you can be my lawyer?" he asked stupidly.

Jules snatched the plastic bag from his hand and grabbed his wallet from inside. She extracted a fiver before shoving the bag into his chest. "Here, that should cover it. You gonna listen to me now?"

"Damn, you work for cheap these days, don't—*Oof.*" The punch was quick and since he'd turned away from her, it hit square in his kidney. Just like he taught her. He was even a little proud she'd managed to get a lick in. No one had snuck up on him like that since he'd play-fought with Ellie when she was little.

A memory of belly laughs and adorable screeches during a tickle fight knifed through him, the slice to his heart more painful than any physical strike.

"Trust me. It's just a formality. I don't need your money. Never have, never will. Now let's go." She stepped off the sidewalk to the parking lot with quick strides.

"Where are you going?"

She looked at him like he was an idiot. "I'm assuming you had a black and white limo that got you here?" He gave a single nod. "So, I'll take you home."

"Aw, hell, Jules. You don't have to do that. I'll get an Uber or—"

The chirp of a car unlocking drew his attention toward the

back of the parking lot. He stopped mid-stride on the last step and almost busted his ass.

"*That's* your car?"

She giggled, causing an ache in his chest again. "I thought 'jaw-dropping' was only an expression. Are you going to drool, too?" Jules nonchalantly continued to the far corner of the lot, well away from any potential threat of a crappy parking job or scratched paint.

"Hey, give me a break." As he got closer, his fingers twitched at the prospect of gliding down the sleek black McLaren 720S Spider. "It's not every day a guy gets to see a quarter-million-dollar car, let alone ride in one. Bounty hunting pays the bills, but not like this."

She tilted her head and smirked. "Aren't you a trust fund baby?"

Jason rolled his eyes. "All that goes to Ellie and Aunt Rachel... you know that. That was always the plan. I barely touch the stuff."

Jules nodded. "Well, it's more than a quarter-million actually... so that's a 'no' on the Uber then?"

"Hell no. Are you kidding?" He followed her lead and slid his hand reverently along the middle of the door, activating it to pull up like a butterfly wing. He was a little surprised he *didn't* drool when he saw the black carbon fiber seats and garnet trimming. An homage to her alma mater, no doubt. "This is a long way from the Pontiac. What happened? Was the Bonneville not sophisticated enough for a high-powered attorney?"

She gathered her skirt to get in. "Bonnie was a good ol' girl but she died only a few months after you, uh, left." Her voice cracked on the last word. Jason stopped stroking the car interior and reached for her, but she cleared her throat and buckled in, breaking the moment.

"Actually, this was payment from the first case I ever won. One of my clients—I won't say who—was definitely *not* selling drugs, and the jury agreed with me. I got this as payment. My client said he's got seven hundred and ten horsepower. I've never been in enough of a hurry to try it, but he's supposed to be able to get up to two hundred miles per hour."

"Hell of a payment, here."

"Yeah, let's just say my client was also not very good at doing his own taxes, so he had a lot of expendable income. It was hard for him to have an honest conversation with the government about all the money he made *not* selling drugs."

Jason narrowed his eyes at her explanation.

"What?" She shrugged. "The underlying reasonable suspicion to search him was fabricated, there was no consent or probable cause to search the vehicle, and the traffic stop itself was suspect! The so-called 'reliable' confidential informant was even *high* at the time the information was given! Even from the in-car camera there was no reason—"

Jason chuckled at her lawyer-speak. It was all nonsense to him, but he was damn proud of her new lingo. "It's always about technicalities with you, isn't it?"

"Hey, laws are made for a reason. It's not my fault when the reasons are stupid or the statute is so convoluted the government can't even follow it."

He shook his head. *She's still feisty, I'll give her that.*

Trying to keep his cool, he settled into the passenger seat and automatically reached for the START button. He felt the sting before he saw the slap on his hand.

"No touching Larry." Her eyes meant business as she pressed a few buttons causing a satisfying pop and roar of the engine as it came alive.

"*Larry?*" Despite his best efforts, Jason's smile widened and couldn't resist teasing her. "Let me get this straight. You've decided that this beauty is of the *male* gender? And I know you've always had a thing for naming inanimate objects, but you're gonna call one of the most revered sports cars in history... *Larry?*"

Jules whipped the car around the parking lot and made for

the exit. Her forehead was scrunched as she replied, "Um, yeah? Sexist much? What else would you call him?"

Jason huffed out a chuckle and shook his head. "I wouldn't call *him* anything..."

The McLaren—*Larry*—gathered speed as Jules tore down the road.

"He's got a British accent, too." She winked at him and slammed her foot on the gas, powering up every one of the seven hundred and ten horses. Jason grabbed the "oh shit" handle and busted out laughing before a terrifying thought crossed his mind.

"You sure you know how to drive this thing?"

"Of course. What? You think I can't drive a sports car because I'm a girl?"

He huffed and wanted to roll his eyes but refused to take them off the road. "You know me better than that. Supercars are really easy to crash for anyone. Did you take lessons?"

"Guess you're going to find out." She smirked. She drove at breakneck speed around the town, whizzing through yellow lights and rolling through stop signs. By the time people blared their horns, Larry was already off in the distance. It would've turned him on if he wasn't imagining his death waiting around every corner. At least when he jumped out of helicopters, he had a parachute.

"For fuck's sake, slow down! I can't find my sister if I'm dead!"

Jules sobered and lifted her foot off the gas so they were driving just above speed limit. Jason pushed out a breath and waited. After a few law-abiding and unexciting moments of riding, he loosened his grip and took in the view. Watching Jules navigate such a powerful beast was hot, but her wide smile back at him took his breath away.

She seemed... happy. It sounded creepy, and maybe it was, but he'd been keeping tabs on her ever since he got back from overseas. The town gossip said she landed herself Andrew Ascot, "the most eligible bachelor in Ashland County." Not that Jason paid much attention to that shit, but recon is recon even if it is just from loudmouthed socialites in the local coffee shop.

They were jealous. Andrew Asshat was more likely holding on to her by the tips of his manicured fingers. But what could Jason do about it? Who was he to judge? Maybe not all pompous assholes are pompous assholes. Maybe, for once in his life, Jason did the right thing when he left all those years ago. Granted, it was most certainly the wrong choice for *him*.

"Okay, time to get down to business. Lies?" she asked, her eyebrow perfectly arched.

"No lies." And just like that, Jason fell back into the familiar. He saw her grin from the corner of his eyes, no doubt remembering how many times they'd said that to each other. Inevitably, he winced at the memory of that last conversation. Jules squirmed in her seat, probably trying to forget the same thing.

"Okay, well, it seems these days I have more standards for my clients than I do in my love life—"

Ouch.

"—lie to me and I'll drop you" —she snapped her fingers— "like that. I never fire clients unless they're disrespectful or lie to me. And believe me when I say I have no problem with firing a client." She looked straight at him but—like the coward he was —he kept staring at the road. "Even you. So, now's the time to explain to me how you ended up in a police station."

Jason's good mood went sour real quick. He didn't want to talk about any of this, but he knew that Jules was probably his best bet at getting any answers. He had a sick feeling deep in his gut that something was wrong with his sister.

"Ellie's missing."

"Yeah, I know at least that much. Aside from that fiasco at the station, your Aunt Rachel called me. I tried to call Ellie but it went straight to voicemail." She tapped her long fake nude nails. Back in the old days, they'd been all sorts of wild colors.

"What can you tell me about it? Cops don't usually take people in for no reason." He whipped his head to glare at her and she held her hand up. "No judgments, but no lies. Obviously, I don't think you did anything. But now's the time to spill. Spill."

The buildings beyond his window faded into a blur and he sighed before he spoke. "Ellie and I were supposed to go to dinner last night, but I—" He swallowed and he felt Jules's sharp attention on him. He wouldn't lie, but she didn't need to know the whole truth, did she? "I couldn't make it. She never responded when I called her to cancel, which I thought was strange, but I chalked it up to her having a life. Anyway, I got a call from Aunt Rachel this morning. She said Ellie had told her she went out to meet me, but she never came back home. She hadn't called sooner because she thought Ellie stayed the night with me. But then the school called. Aunt Rach was worried, but she freaked-out when Ellie still wasn't answering her phone." He barked out a dark laugh. "You know her generation and phones. They substitute technology in place of thinking for themselves. If she went without it for too long, she'd go crazy."

He felt like an old man saying that, but Ellie was sixteen years younger than him. His mom hadn't met Ellie's dad, Greg Stone, until Jason had been a teenager. After their parents' car accident, his whole world turned on its axis to revolve around his baby sister. Unfortunately, their age gap showed nowhere better than her techno-dependence and his techno-aversion. His own phone was a cracked-up piece of shit that couldn't even install new updates.

"I tried calling her, too," he continued. "I wondered if Ellie had screened Aunt Rachel's calls." The thought had been grounded in hope more than probability. All the other little shits her age were out partying or not giving a fuck about the world. Ellie was the type who listened intently to her senile great-aunt's overly long stories about her weird-eyed figurines. She'd never screen Aunt Rachel's calls.

Jason was beyond proud of the young woman his sister had become. But knowing he'd had absolutely nothing to do with that outcome was a knife to the heart. Aunt Rachel loved Ellie, but she was already batty when Ellie went to live with her as a baby, and the poor woman grew more eccentric by the day. Even though Jason left Jules and Ellie to go back into the military, Jules had stayed close with his sister. She was the one who'd been there during El's formative years. When Ellie had needed him most.

Jason glanced at the woman responsible for raising his sister and his self-inflicted wound didn't hurt as much. At least they'd had each other when he couldn't get his shit together. He cleared his throat of the lump of emotion welling up.

"I couldn't get her. I tried her best friend, Sasha's, phone number. El gave it to me a while back…" He recounted to Jules how he'd tried to call Sasha and the terrible pit in his stomach that formed when he'd heard a phone ringing outside. There, he'd found both Sasha's and Ellie's phones on the welcome mat outside his apartment door. He had been too concerned and confused to think straight and immediately called the police. When he was "invited" to ride back to the station with the cops, he wasn't in his right mind and agreed. At the time, learning what was going on with Ellie was forefront in his mind.

He shook his head. "Immediately, I was suspect number one." Sasha's parents had already reported her missing. The police hadn't done anything because at eighteen, Sasha was technically an adult. But when he found the girls' phones, the cops had tried to connect whatever dots were in front of them. Ellie was only seventeen and since it seemed both of them were missing, the cops held on to the one and only clue they had.

Jason.

When officers *suggested* they chat in a back room, being a suspect hadn't yet crossed his mind. When that shitty investigator came at him with handcuffs for no reason, he'd demanded an attorney. Before any questioning began, Jason made a quick phone call to the best in town… and nearly threw his phone when Jules never picked up.

"I remembered you used to screen your calls way back when

so I shouldn't have expected you to pick up the phone, but it still hurt." He chuckled and slapped his hand to his chest, mimicking a knife twisting motion.

"Hey now, don't let your ego get all offended. I don't answer anyone's calls unless they're Ellie or my assistant, Nora."

"Damn. Not even Cyn or Rose get the privilege?" He asked, referring to her former boss and best friend. He leaned closer and grinned. "You used to answer *my* calls."

She laughed. "I don't know your number anymore!"

He sat back smugly because what he'd heard was, *I'd have answered if I'd known it was you.*

He could tell she realized her mistake when her cheeks took on an achingly familiar rosy blush. Jason propped his elbow on the window to hide his smile behind his hand, trying not to imagine how far down the blush went. No need to piss her off. He couldn't believe she was even being *nice* to him. He'd expected her to be irritated, yet professional. It was still more than he deserved. He hadn't allowed "nice" to even be a fantasy.

What did that mean? Were there still feelings there? Or no feelings at all? Did she really have a thing for that asshat, Andrew Ascot? He was about to test the waters when the shrill of an old-time telephone rang through the car's audio system.

CHAPTER FOUR

"Hey, will you ignore that call for me? It'll keep going until you swipe it."

Jason dug through the purse hoisted into his lap and found the culprit.

Andy.

Speak of the devil. To his consternation, he accidentally swiped in the wrong direction.

"Juliet?" An adenoidal voice resounded over the car speakers, making Jason grimace.

"*Shit*... Shit. Shit. Shit..." Jules whispered and tried to grab the phone from his hands. It slipped between their fingers and fell underneath her seat.

"Juliet, sweetheart, are you there?" She glared at Jason and he shrugged apologetically, bewildered at her response. She frantically searched under her seat while trying to keep her eyes on the road, and Jason realized she didn't want to hear Ascot's voice any more than he did.

"Juliet? Are you at that dance studio again? Is this not a good time?" After almost swerving off the road, she heaved a sigh and gave up the search. She trained her eyes back to the road, noticeably off Jason.

"No, Andy, I'm not at the *strip club*, and you're right, it's not a good time. Can I call you later? I've got a client in the car."

"Oh, you know I don't like to call it that. I'm trying to respect you and your, you know, feminine morals, or whatever. And I've told you a thousand times to call me Andrew now. Father says that that nickname is too banal for a future partner. Make sure your friends call me that, too. Having to remind everyone all the time is growing tedious." He sighed. "Juliet, sweetheart, you never call me back. Please, we need to talk. I was hoping we could meet for dinner? Tonight, perhaps? Can't you take a five-minute break from work for once?" Jason's lip curled at the pathetic whimper echoing through the speaker.

"You can call it what it is, Andy. Original Sin is a strip club. OS has paid my bills for years and is one of my best clients. No need to coat it with fake sugar for my sake." She turned on her blinker. "And I think we've said everything we need to say already. I thought you'd understand that after I sent your first hundred calls to voicemail."

"Really, Juliet?" There was some mumbling on the line accompanied by the sound of a door closing. "I'm in the office, so I can't very well shout to the rooftops that you work for a—" his voice lowered further "—a titty bar," he tsked. "I guess your upbringing makes you incapable of having even the pretense of class. I, myself, try incredibly hard at Father's firm not to reveal that my fiancé used to dance naked back in her slutty days. I'll never make partner with a whore as a wife."

"Fiancé? What the fuck? You're actually gonna marry this asshat?"

"The fuck I am. He's delusional." Jules grunted as she returned to digging for her phone, this time with more determination.

Asshat hissed a forced whisper. "It's AsCOT. And you can't talk to me that way! Who even are you? Juliet, you're going to let your client speak to me that way? Am I on speakerphone?" he stammered as if he couldn't think and breathe at the same time. "Since when do you drive random men around town? I'd thought you'd given up being a *prostitute*."

"Watch it, Asshat." Jason growled.

"It's AsCOT—"

"Okay, okay. That's enough testosterone for one phone call, thank you very much." She put her hand on Jason's thigh to settle him and by God, it worked. A little bit. "Andy, seriously, I'm with a client. Which is *literally* none of your business. Not that any of my life is your business anymore."

Jason reached his arm through Jules's legs and grabbed the phone from the floor. Even though he was ready to tear the guy limb from limb, he couldn't resist stroking Jules's bare inner thigh as he brought the phone back up.

"Jesus," she whispered. Unable to hide her shiver, she tugged her dress further down her leg and blushed when he winked at her.

"Yeah, Asshat. Hang the fuck up already. She doesn't need your bullshit." Oh yeah, even with his mind in the gutter he was still pissed.

"I don't need your help, Jay."

"Wait... who is your new client, Juliet?"

Jules's eyes pled to the heavens before she rolled them back to Jason's. "Andy, you know as well as I do that I won't tell you. We learned about attorney-client confidentiality from the same damn professor."

"Okay, then. How recently did you *acquire* this client?"

"Still none of your business."

"OH MY GOD, JULIET. IS YOUR FUCKING EX IN THE CAR RIGHT NOW?"

Even though he knew technology didn't require it, Jason held the phone speaker close when he spoke. "That's right, motherfucker! I'm in the car, so watch your fuckin' mouth."

Jules tried to grab the phone from his hands but he kept it

out of reach. The sigh that escaped rattled the McLaren-Larry and Jason couldn't help but chuckle silently. Her frustration was funny at this point. Yeah, the guy was a first-rate prick, but it made Jason's black heart all mushy inside that she seemed to hate Asshat as much as he did right then. She glared at him and he finally had mercy on her and gave her the phone.

"Oh, that's rich, Juliet. You try to break up with me for one small indiscretion, but how long have you been fucking your ex behind my back? Even though he allegedly 'broke your heart'?" He scoffed. "I didn't realize you were taking *those* types of clients again—"

Jason was about to rip into him again after seeing Jules's flush of embarrassment, but the guy wasn't finished.

"—And to think! You've had *me* in your bed, but you've gone back to that lowlife kidnapper you met at a strip club. Lie with the pigs, Juliet, and you're bound to get filthy."

"For God's sake, give it a rest already. I never 'fucked anyone behind your back,' not that we were together in the first place!" She went to hang up on him, but her thumb halted just above the 'end' button. Her brow furrowed.

"Wait... what do you mean kidnapper?"

Larry's steady hum reverberated in the car as Jules rolled to a stop at the sign. The route required several more turns to get to Jason's apartment and they rode quite a few of them silently before she asked again.

"Andrew Wilton Ascot, *the Fourth*. That should've been classified information, so what the fuck are you talking about?"

"Everyone at the firm is talking about it. Of course, I know about it. You think *anything* happens in Ashland without Father's firm knowing about it? We practically run this place. Jason Stone kidnapped a couple of young women and refused to tell the police where they are. Truly, Juliet, does your moral compass know no bounds? He might've been a fling, but to represent someone who could do that?"

Jules sent Jason a worried look and spoke low. "Shit, Jay, I didn't know it was on the news already. I'll make sure to get Nora on that."

"Stop talking to him! You're on the phone with your fiancé! How could you want him back?!"

Jules's face clouded until it became devoid of all emotion in a way Jason hadn't seen from her in a very long time. It hurt his heart to watch the transformation, but he couldn't look away.

"Andy. Shut. Up. First of all, I am not *with* him. He's a *client*. So back off. Second, I never broke up with you—"

Jason's eyebrow lifted and his breath froze in his lungs. What did that mean? Were they still together? *Is she actually marrying this guy?*

"—I never thought we were actually serious enough that I needed to break up with you. I don't know when you universally decided that I was your fiancé, but I was there all those times you asked me and I distinctly remember saying no. Every. Single. Time. Then I explained to you—*in detail*—how we weren't even dating. I told you all that repeatedly. You were basically something to pass the time and blow off steam." Jason winced but Jules kept going. "Yeah, sure, you and I were friends in the beginning. But somewhere along the way, you went batshit. I'm concerned for you at this point, which is why I've kept my mouth shut for so long. I've been upfront this entire time. I told you a million and a half ways that you and I were just having fun, but boy let me tell you, I sure do regret having 'fun' now. It totally wasn't worth it."

If a childish pout could be heard, that was exactly what resonated over the speakers. "Well, I was only calling to have dinner tonight but I just checked my schedule and it looks like I'm busy after all. I'll have to rain check—"

"I told you I don't want—"

"Just so you know, Father has invited me to participate in an extremely important project. He's sure I'll be an asset to the firm. I better go work on it. Besides, you're saying things you don't mean right now and I don't want you to say anything you'll regret. I know I made you upset when I went behind your back with that girl—"

"I wouldn't have given two shits who you fucked, if it was anyone besides one of the Original Sinners. But you know my history—"

Leaning his head against the headrest, Jason closed his eyes and shook his head slowly.

"—and even though you *knew* that was a personal deal breaker for me, you did it anyway. Like I said, I don't care, but sleeping with a Sinner means no more sex with me. Simple. Hoes over bros and all that."

Jason's stomach tightened, accentuating the feeling that he'd been punched in the gut while trying to fist bump in the air.

"B-but... you barely even know that whore now. And you haven't worked there in years! You were distant, and cold, and an ungrateful bitch. And now? It's like you don't even know who you're talking to. I'm Andrew Wilton Ascot the Fourth. You should be down on your knees, begging forgiveness for me even having to turn to that rancid bimbo. Granted, she was way better on *her* knees than you ever were. I'm sure there's a certain *someone* who would agree with me. Maybe you should ask your *client*—"

The car weaved on the road as Jules tried to hang up with her left hand and Jason instinctively put his hand over her right to help guide the steering wheel.

"I'll put him on his knees if he doesn't shut the fuck up," she mumbled loud enough for them to hear.

"Watch out, Juliet. You know who I am and you know what I'm capable of. I don't have time for your immature games. Answer my phone calls in the future, sweetheart. I'd hate for you to lose me forever and see what regret really feels li—"

The steady hum of the car filled the silence once Jules hung up on the lunatic. Almost immediately, the phone rang again with Andy's name on the screen. She silenced the call and dropped it in her lap. *Ding*, a short note indicated a voicemail.

Ring-silence...Ding.

Ring-silence...Ding.

Soon, all Jason could focus on was the digital cadence of a desperate man begging to be heard. Jules groaned from somewhere deep inside before she finally pressed the button to turn the whole damn thing off, tossing it at Jason's feet.

"Man, he sure does like to hear himself talk, right?"

"Jules..."

"Usually he stops calling after a few times, but I guess he's in rare form today."

"How often does he do this? Does he always speak to you like that?"

"He didn't used to. He's always been somewhat of a pompous jerk. A long time ago, believe it or not, he was kind of sweet. Working for his father has done a real number on him."

"Is that why y'all broke up?"

"What?" Jules huffed. "No, no, no. Like I said, he's delusional. We never even dated. Literally, never went on a real date. Sure, we had fun and sometimes we'd even end up at the same restaurant or bar. I even thought he was following me around at one point." She forced a rough laugh.

"Do you still 'have fun' together?" He focused hard on the upcoming yield sign like he'd never seen one before.

"Not you, too." She groaned again. "I haven't 'had fun' with anyone in a long-ass time. Not that it's any of your business. I don't make it a habit to talk to my clients about my sex life... or lack thereof." She sighed. "I'm not going to apologize for anything. I've made it clear with everyone I've been with, especially Andy, that casual is all it will ever be. I'm focused on building my practice and I don't need distractions."

"Is that all I ever was? A distraction?"

She stopped too abruptly at the light. Cars laid on the horn angrily behind her, but she ignored them. She glanced at him before tightening her grip on the steering wheel and tapping the gas again after the light changed.

"It doesn't matter what you were. It only matters what you are now. And now, you're a client." She fixed her stare on him until he looked away. "Just a client."

Jason was beginning to hate that phrase. Being around her, laughing with her, made the air around him lighter and he could breathe deeper. It'd only been an hour or so, but already he knew he didn't want to be 'just a client.'

There was a time, forever ago, where he'd thought that he was her everything, and she was his. He wanted to go back to that. He knew that their relationship's collapse was completely his fault. He'd thought he'd been doing her a favor leaving all those years ago. Now that he'd had just a moment more with her, the thought of going back to that loneliness made his heart tank to his stomach. Maybe it was selfish of him, but at this point, he didn't care. If she was hanging out with guys like Asshat, she obviously didn't know what was good for her and he'd be happy to show her.

The past seven years they'd both been missing out on what they could've had, all because of his own damn insecurities. She'd still been with jerks and if she was gonna go slumming, it might as well be with him. The only question was, would she forgive him? Jason had a lot of atoning to do, that's for sure. Did he deserve her? Hell no. But he would make himself worthy of her. At least he knew what was in front of him now and this time, he wasn't going to let her slip away.

Jason was going to cherish her. Show her what she deserved. He would worship her until Jules wanted to forgive him as badly as he needed to be forgiven. He'd get on his knees if he had to.

Out of long-forgotten habit, Jason put his hand on the back of her neck and massaged. Jules sank into his fingers and the hum she let out made his lower half wake up again. He moved slightly to hide the soon-to-be obvious erection, snapping her out of her trance.

"What the hell do you think you're doing?" She rolled her

shoulders and slapped his arm away. "You can't touch me that way, Jason. Not anymore."

He laughed softly. "Baby, if you purr when I pet you, I ain't gonna stop."

She looked him up and down slowly, and he counted it as a win that she didn't look mad anymore. Jason would've suffered blue balls a thousand times just to know what she was thinking.

The car stopped and he shook himself from his hopes to find they were inside the gated grounds of his apartment. While some parts of the ride had made him want to take a tuck and roll outside of the moving car, the last few minutes felt like a tease. He wanted to invite Jules in, but the idling car wasn't even in 'park.' Jason was gripping the car handle when he paused, eyes narrowing. They weren't just inside the apartment complex. She'd driven him up to his exact building.

"How did you know where I live?"

After a moment, Jules unlocked the door and reached over him to push his open. She sighed heavily as she sat upright.

"I have my ways." Jules rubbed her eyes, obviously exhausted from the stressful car ride. Even still, he noted the shadow of a smile and felt his own grin form. Hers ghosted from her lips as soon as she caught him staring.

"So, my idea is you get your car and whatever you need, come to my place, and we'll brainstorm ways to find Ellie there. I'll text you my address and make a list of potential leads. Although I gotta say, I'm not sure we have much." She shook her head. "What Investigator Burgess said about the forty-eight-hour timeline is something to be concerned about, but it's not over if we don't find her in that time frame. The forty-eight-hour guideline just means that all the easy leads are usually explored by then. After that, it's harder to find the answers, but that doesn't mean those answers won't be found. That doesn't mean *Ellie* won't be found."

Anxiety slithered up his spine, but he took her hand in his and squeezed it. "Together."

Her gaze caught his and she lightly squeezed back before hastily retreating. She averted her gaze straight ahead.

Jason smiled to himself as he got out. The circumstances were fucking terrible, but Jules was going to help. Once they found Ellie, he would never let either of them out of his sight.

There was no way he was making that mistake again.

CHAPTER FIVE

This has to be a mistake.

That's all Ellie's foggy mind could repeat as she willed the nausea to settle in her stomach. She'd woken up to darkness—if you could call the slow fade into the hazy fog she was in "awake"—just moments ago, her body compactly huddled and cramped in the corner of what appeared to be a hotel bathroom. The floor was cold through her cotton panties and the realization helped her focus as she struggled to slide her hands down her body. Skin on skin confirmed her fears.

When did I take off my clothes?

A clammy, sweaty arm rubbed against hers and only Ellie's sense of self-preservation in the midst of uncertainty kept her from crying out. She forced herself to focus in the darkness and saw that the arm belonged to an unconscious woman leaning near the toilet. Confused, she tried to scoot over, only accomplishing a pathetic lean to the left and nearly yelped when her bare skin came in contact with yet another body.

"Sasha?" She felt a small puff of breath through her chapped lips, but she couldn't tell if her best friend's name actually came out. Her head felt like it did after she'd had too much of Sasha's red Solo cup concoctions.

Outside the bathroom, a door shut, and the displaced air caused the one next to her to crack open a fraction. Ellie used the sliver of light to become familiar with her surroundings.

There were several women in the bathroom with her. Some were laying down and some were propped up against one another, like the women to her right and left. All of them looked young. Each one was in varying stages of undress. A few were wearing T-shirts, but most were in just their bra and underwear, like Ellie. One or two looked completely naked. She peered closer at the darker-skinned girl next to her. Her distinctively curly hair was covering her face but Ellie was positive it was her friend.

At least I've got Sasha...

Ellie relaxed a little until she heard deep voices outside the door. Panic set in when she couldn't make out what they were saying.

"Will you buffoons speak in English for once? No one outside of your fucked-up country speaks Russian, you know that right? I don't know why the firm keeps you on." His upper-class dialect was vaguely familiar. *Where have I heard that voice?* She couldn't concentrate with the not so gentle pulse in her head.

"Sorry."

"I think you mean, 'Sorry, *sir*.'"

There was a deep grumble with more harsh consonants. "Sorry, *ser*... new product is good money. It... fresh. One is used and no as good. We sell the no as good until we get to auction. Fresh sell better there."

Fancy man's haughty laugh grated on Ellie's nerves. "Product, huh? That's what we call escorts these days? A little gauche, don't you think? I was just informed this morning that I'm to head up this new enterprise. I would like to take a look-see at our latest recruits. Where are the lovely ladies? Are they in the adjoining room?" The susurrus of hands rubbing together punctuated the question. "Maybe I'll get an employee discount."

"In there. They sleep."

"Sleep? What do you mean, sleep? In the bathroom?" The door opened slightly and Ellie blinked behind her long blonde hair, unable to see the face in the silhouette before the door slammed shut. Even though the voices were now muffled, Ellie was still able to make out the yelling.

"H-Holy *shit*! What the fuck? Are they *drugged*? I thought we were just recruiting whores, not kidnapping them!"

"Boss say do this thing. We do this thing." Another series of knocks preceded the opening of the hotel door.

"Ah, gentlemen. I'm sure everything is ready?" Although the first American sounded like he was fancy and posh, the new voice sounded even more pompous.

"*Da, ser*. The product in bathroom. They still sleep."

"Excellent!" Pompous said with a loud hand clap. "I would like to sample the two acquisitions we managed to collect from the soiree last night. Am I correct that one of them has been tasted before? Bring that one out. We can't bruise the unbitten fruits, can we, gentlemen?" Pompous laughed heartily in the silence.

"You knew about this? This is fucked-up. Aren't you afraid the firm will get caught?" Fancy hissed.

"As I understand it, the new ones won't be missed," Pompous explained. "I assure you that they were carefully vetted and chosen at the party. And Vlad, here, can tell you that their attachments will soon be taken care of. There will be no connection with this project and the firm. In fact, we've already suggested another culprit be explored by authorities. Nikolai has proven to be most adept at finding out pertinent information and capitalizing on it. He'll be a great asset to the firm."

While they talked, the bathroom door opened again and two men stood in the light of the doorway. They reached as if to grab her. She'd been trying to act like she was still sleeping, but Ellie couldn't help flinching.

"This one waking up."

"That's alright, gentlemen. Dose them again before the next

location. You can't stay here long. We need to get as far as possible from where the function was held. Though, I don't see the harm in having a little fun before you go."

A foot kicked her to the side and Ellie grunted against the paralysis. Instead of grabbing her, the two took Sasha by the arms and dragged her out the door, leaving it ajar.

Ellie bit her knee, too afraid to even scream as she saw her best friend's limp legs drag across the carpet floor. She wanted to help, but not only were her own limbs not working properly, she was petrified of finding out what getting picked meant.

"Oh, yes. She's perfect. I like them with a little meat on their bones. How long until she wakes up?"

"Dunno. She smaller than others. She may not wake."

"Hm, probably for the best we weed her out since she's defective."

"What the fuck?" Fancy screeched.

"Such vulgarity! You would do best to be quiet."

"I never signed up for this. We were supposed to enlist whores, not slaves. I thought we'd be giving these women ways to make easy money on their backs. Unsavory, but still their *choice*. Not drugging them and leaving them to die."

"Come now, the partners speak so highly of you. You can't be this daft." Pompous's voice was strained from exertion. "Help me, will you?"

"Absolutely not. I won't be a part of this."

Pompous gave a frustrated sigh. "It doesn't matter what you've convinced yourself. What matters is the law, and in the eyes of the law, you are just as culpable as anyone else in this room."

"What do you mean?"

"You orchestrated their attendance to the party—"

"What? I did no such—"

"—*You* supplied them drugged drinks—"

"You're lying! They weren't—"

"The *truth*... doesn't... matter. All that matters is what's supported by the facts that make sense to someone too lazy to learn the whole story. According to anyone at the party downstairs last night, it was *you*. *You* escorted them to the interview room. For all intents and purposes, *you* are the one who drugged and kidnapped them. So maybe *you* should keep your entitled mouth *shut*."

Just like that, it all came back to her.

CHAPTER SIX

Neither Ellie nor Sasha knew the handsome older boy with dark black hair at their high school college fair. Benjamin, as he'd introduced himself, approached them on the quad amidst all the hubbub with the opportunity of a freaking lifetime, an invite to the prestigious annual scholarship fundraiser held by influential law firms and companies in Ashland and the surrounding counties.

To be considered for a scholarship, all they had to do was submit their information and schmooze at a party. Ellie had heard whispers of such a yearly gathering, but she'd always assumed it was something akin to a secret society party. The invitation gave her a thrill of anxiety at the excitement and fear of being judged by the upper echelon of society.

"Who can you say you're with to make sure no one knows?" Benjamin leaned in conspiratorially as Sasha and Ellie finished filling out the questionnaires he'd given them. Ellie glanced up at them from her phone but continued to scroll. She was having a hard time paying attention to the conversation as she wrote down the numbers and addresses for Aunt Rachel and Jason in the emergency contact section.

"I can say I'm staying at Ellie's," Sasha suggested, her voice low to match his. She always did have a flair for the dramatic. "My parents work so much, they hardly even know I'm around. Besides, they'll forgive me for fibbing if one of us wins. And Ellie's aunt won't let her have a sleepover somewhere outside of family, so El, you can just say you're staying with Jason. That's her brother," Sasha provided helpfully.

"Aunt, huh?" Benjamin asked. "What would your parents think?"

Ellie signed her name at the bottom of the sheet and stood up from the table they'd used nearby. "My parents died when I was a baby. Now it's just me and my aunt. My brother pops by sometimes, but I don't see him too much," she answered absent-mindedly. If she never had to fill out another stupid information sheet for colleges and scholarships, it would still be too soon. It always included way more details than necessary.

"Jason's a freakin' loner and her aunt is batshit—"

"Sash!"

"What, El? Sorry, but she is." She turned to Benjamin. "She won't be checking up as long as Ellie tells her she's with Jason."

"But hold up. I can't even tell Aunt Rachel?" Ellie gave a tentative laugh. Benjamin hadn't explained that part yet, and if all this was for a scholarship, it didn't make sense to her that she couldn't tell anyone. She wanted to point that last part out but she was afraid of coming off rude or ungrateful.

"I know it sounds crazy, but everything until after the winners are announced is hush-hush so no one can crash the party or trick their way into the running for a scholarship. The sponsoring firms and companies are really picky about who they get involved with. It's a verbal invitation only. I think you guys have a real shot at it, though. I mean, that's my job, to recruit eligible scholarship recipients. The one catch is that no one can know about it. Not until after you win, of course." He'd winked at Sasha, who'd eaten it up and giggled like a child.

"Come on Ellie, please! This could be our shot at getting to go to the same college together. Hell, this isn't even half as bad as some of the hoops we've had to jump through to get scholarships."

Sasha and Ellie had talked about going to college together since they were kids, but as they grew older, it became more apparent that a university might've been out of the question for Sasha. Her parents were hard workers, but unless Sasha got some financial help, it was community college for her. So, when her best friend's hazel puppy dog eyes fixed on Ellie, she couldn't say no.

She quickly wrote out a text to her brother. If habit played out, he'd say yes, but cancel with some dumb excuse within a few hours. She could honestly tell Aunt Rachel she had plans with Jason, and neither would ever check the story out.

She looked up from her phone. "Okay. I guess we're going to a party."

Sasha squealed and Benjamin's jaw ticced into a scowl. As if realizing he was being watched, his mouth relaxed into a brilliant smile instead, and Ellie waved away the thought, turning back to her overly excited best friend tugging at her arm.

"Oh my God, Ellie, we can totally pretend like this is your pre-birthday-party party! It'll be your best one ever!" Sasha squeezed Ellie's arm and held tight.

Ellie laughed at her joke since her friend knew it would be the only birthday party ever. Sasha always wanted to throw a party, but inevitably gave in when Ellie insisted all she wanted was their traditional birthday donuts in their childhood treehouse.

"Birthday, huh?" When the boy smiled, he seemed older than she originally thought.

"Yep! Eighteen. This will be perfect." Sasha squealed.

Benjamin's olive features blanched and he took a step back. Sasha was still chattering away, trying to talk to him more. When he seemed to finally snap out of it, he took out some business cards and handed them one each.

"Great. Okay, well, I'll see you ladies around. Hap-happy birthday."

"Wait!" Sasha grabbed him. "You're not gonna be at the party?"

He gently extracted his arm from Sasha's grasp. "Uh, I usually don't go. Firm parties are kind of a drag. I've been to so many. So, um, tell me how it goes, alright?" He winked again and hurried off.

"Oh no, you don't." Sasha grabbed him by his elbow. "You have to come! Please! Pleasepleasepleaseplease—"

"Alright!" Benjamin's growl made Ellie jump, but Sasha was obliviously undeterred. "I'll see what I can do... no promises though." He mumbled a goodbye and hurried off.

"That was weird," Ellie noted under her breath.

"Oh my *God*, El. He was so fine. I'd eat him up with a baby spoon so I could savor each delicious bite."

"Ew, Sasha. That's just gross." Ellie ignored her friend drooling after the complete stranger and turned over the business card. "Hmm... 'The Ambrosia Room?' Is that all we get?"

"What?" She snatched the card and stared at it, as if more words would appear. She slapped her hand with it back and forth, muttering the name of the room before pausing, "Wait... doesn't that hotel on Main have apple-themed conference rooms?"

"How the heck should I know? What made you think of apples?" Ellie's eyes narrowed, but Sasha was typing on her phone.

"Ambrosia is a type of apple. Also, the food of the gods in Greek mythology." Sasha's mind was like the sun and shined on its own terms. Most of the time it was clouded with Top 50 Music Hits or what happened on her favorite TV show's last rose ceremony. Occasionally, though, a bright spot revealed random, yet useful, knowledge. She was a heck of a trivia player.

"Yes! Remember last year we had junior prom in 'The Gala Room?'" She tapped her phone, which displayed a nearby high-end hotel. "This is the same place! I knew I remembered it from somewhere."

"You didn't even go to prom." Ellie's eyebrow went up while the other eyebrow narrowed. A trick her brother taught her.

"Well, no. But this guy I know blew off his date and got a room there that night and—" She cleared her throat at Ellie's side-eye. "It doesn't matter. Do you know what this means?"

"That my friend should stop sleeping with other people's prom dates?" Ellie laughed but Sasha just rolled her eyes.

"Har-har. Very funny. Probably true. But whatever. This means that we're going to one of those rich people parties. The ones in big hotel conference rooms where you can wine and dine with the fancy-pants crowd. What are we going to wear? We obvi have to skip last period and figure it out. Your closet or mine?"

∼

Later, at the party, Ellie covertly wiped her sweaty palms on the pleats of the repurposed remnants of her junior year prom dress. She couldn't believe Sasha had completely taken it apart and made it over in only a matter of hours. The two snuck illegal sips of champagne and chatted with a bunch of old white guys in suits. The party might have been exclusive and verbal invitation only but the large, opulently decorated room was packed with young people her age and the who's who of Ashland.

Ellie had been nervous, but she and Sasha tried their best to seem sophisticated. Still, she couldn't escape the feeling they were being paraded around like cattle. Not knowing how parties like that worked, Ellie shrugged it off and focused on making sure she sounded intelligent to the men in charge of choosing the winners. She couldn't tell which ones those were, so they'd spoken to everyone.

Ellie's parents left their children an inheritance, but her half was locked up in trusts until she turned twenty-two and she didn't want to use Jason's. Besides, she wanted to get into college and pay for it on her own merit. Poor Sasha had no choice. She desperately needed the money. Ellie had already decided that if she got it and Sasha didn't, she'd find a way to halve it with her. If she had to, she'd take Jason's money, not that he used it, anyway. There was no way she was going to school without her best friend. If she had to suck up to a bunch of old guys for an hour and a half to achieve their dream, then so be it.

"It's amazing how there can be so many dang people at a party and still have it be considered 'exclusive.' There's nothing but old guys and pretty women." Ellie was exaggerating, of course, but the ratio of men and women, old and young, was definitely off.

"Ugh, El, stop whining. This is totally the chance of a lifetime right now. We snag the *right* rich old white guy here and Benjamin said we could get a full ride from one of these firms or companies. Speaking of... where is that beautiful bastard?" Sasha strained her neck to try to see past the crowd, but at just barely five feet, it was no use.

"He said he probably wasn't gonna be here," Ellie reminded her.

"I know... but a girl can dream, right?" After a breath, her friend squealed. "Oh my God, Benjamin! I'm so glad you came!"

The 'beautiful bastard' in question was walking toward the bar despite Sasha calling for him loud enough to quiet nearby conversations. She stalked up to him and tugged him by the shoulder.

"There you are!" She threw her entire body at him for an embrace. An unwelcome one, if the curling of his lip was any indication.

"Whoa there, Sasha." He chuckled as he extricated himself from her.

"I called for you! Did you not hear me?"

"Sorry, it's so crowded I must not have noticed." He turned

to the bartender. "Two glasses of champagne for the ladies as well."

The bartender nodded before serving a glass of whiskey and two flutes of champagne.

"Drinks for us? You shouldn't have!" Sasha grabbed and downed hers in one fell swoop.

"How are you finding the party?" His voice was halting and stilted, and Ellie noticed him fidgeting with his own whiskey glass. Knowing that even smooth talking Benjamin had nerves in that type of atmosphere made her relax a little, helping her realize her anxiety was normal.

"It's a-maz-ing. We are so honored to be here. Thank you so much for the invite." Sasha beamed with sincerity.

"Of course, of course. Have you, um. Have you talked to any firm members or partners yet?" His eyes flitted around the room as Sasha spoke.

"No, not yet. But since we know a partner's son..." She winked and sidled up to him. "You think you can get us an in? Honestly, we don't even know who we're supposed to be impressing over here. Where did you say your father worked?"

Keeping his eyes trained away from Sasha's face, he stepped away from her a fraction until they no longer touched.

"Hold on. Let me, uh... let me go get—" He turned and walked away mid-sentence.

"Why does he always have to be so mysterious! Give a girl a little somethin' to go off, sheesh!"

Ellie chuckled at her friend's bottom lip sticking out and watched Benjamin to see where he was headed. She had her brother's height and tried to use it for her friend before she saw perfectly coiffed blond hair on a familiar face. She caught the man's eyes and his head tilted to the side at her, just before he stopped Benjamin as he passed.

"Oh great. Just freakin' great."

"What? Who is Benjamin talking to?" Sasha hopped to try to see. The crowd parted enough for them to see him perfectly.

"Oh God. Is that Andrew Ascot? The one and only? The guy that dates your friend, Jules?"

"The one of four, actually, but who's counting... and they don't date."

Andy turned to a man who looked an awful lot like him and pointed to Ellie and Sasha. Benjamin was nodding as he spoke to the older man. The older man—Andy's father, Ellie realized—gave her a slow smirk and tipped his head toward them. He turned to Andy and Benjamin and they spoke another moment before Andy turned to her.

"Please don't come over here..." Ellie whispered.

Andy didn't used to be so bad, just a smidge puppy-doggish following Jules around. After he started working for his father, the guy became a grade A douchebag and Ellie couldn't stand him. He'd also upped the ante on his stalker vibe and teetered on the line of completely nuts. Ellie had been wholeheartedly supportive of Jules's decision to cut him loose.

With the absence of the Ascots' stare, Ellie tugged Sasha's arm and led her to the side of the room. "Come on, let's go."

Sasha jerked her arm away. "Are you kidding me? They were looking right at us! I've been around Jules plenty of times and I've still never met him! He's practically royalty to this town. If you think I'm gonna pass that up, you're outta your mind, girl."

Ellie geared up to argue when she felt a tap on her shoulder. Sasha's starstruck expression focused past her, and Ellie stifled a groan and turned around.

"Hey there, Ellie. It's been so long since we've spoken. How are you?"

She adopted a stiff smile and resisted the urge to mock his overarticulated speech.

"Very well, thank you. And, how are you?" She wasn't the best at the whole not-mocking thing.

But if Andy noticed he didn't let on. In fact, his smile brightened. "I am marvelous. Thank you for asking. Is Juliet with you?"

"Nope." The 'p' popped at the end.

He sighed and pouted. "Oh, that's too bad. When I noticed you, I was hoping to see her."

"You're Andy Ascot! Oh my God, it's so great to meet you. I'm—"

"It's Andrew," Andy interrupted with a scowl and turned back to Ellie. He tilted his head again. "If Juliet isn't here, why are you? No offense. I'm not surprised to see other lawyers and businessmen, but I'm perplexed as to your attendance. Were you sponsored by a firm? I didn't see your names on the list."

"We're here for the scholarship! Benjamin invited today as contenders for a scholarship from one of these firms," Sasha answered, her smile wide despite Andy's furrowed brow.

"Benjamin? Who—wait, really? I thought the scholarship donors had already submitted their candidates. I bet Juliet is proud, huh?"

A shiver of confusion was quickly replaced by a shock of fear at the thought of getting caught.

"Um... can you please not tell Jules you saw me? We were invited, I swear. But I didn't exactly tell Aunt Rachel where I was going. I don't want to get her hopes up if we don't get chosen."

Andy's eyebrows raised but he chuckled while he mimed locking his lips and throwing away the key. She gave him a shy grin. *See? Not so bad.*

He rolled his shoulders back. "Say, how's your brother?" He spat out the last word.

Never mind, there's the douchebag.

Ellie restrained her sass behind a tight-lipped smile. "Fine."

And she'd leave it at that. Andy's hatred of her brother was confusing at best and pathetic at worst. He'd always been overconscious of Jules's relationship with Jason, and despite the fact it'd happened years ago, it was probably for good reason. Ellie always hoped Jules and Jason would get back together, but the dummy had been back in the States for months and still refused to go see Jules. Ellie knew it was meant to be, if Jason just got his head outta his butt. Andy probably knew that too and hated Jason for having what he never could. Jules's heart.

He looked like he was going to say more, but thought better of it. "That's good... good."

The din of party goers filled the air between them. Ellie looked around for anyone else to talk to, but she and Sasha knew no one besides Benjamin and Andy. It dawned on her that if they were there to get a scholarship, Andy would be the best person to shake down about who they should talk to.

"So, um, about the scholarship—"

"Ah, Andrew, I see you've met some of our guests of honor." Andy's older carbon copy appeared beside him, juggling two glasses of whiskey and two of champagne in his hands. He was rounder all over than Andy, with aged white-blond hair, and his red face and slurred words suggested he was already deep in his cups.

"Well, don't just stand there, boy. Are you daft? Give these young ladies their drinks."

"Father they're only teen—"

"Do as I say, Andrew," Mr. Ascot growled under his breath. "I will not tolerate insubordination—no, no, not those two, you fool. These two." He maneuvered his grip so that Andy could grab the two champagne glasses. "Real men drink whiskey, Andrew."

Andy's brow furrowed but he complied and gave Sasha and Ellie the champagne flutes. "Yes, Father."

Mr. Ascot turned to them. "Ah, sorry ladies for my son's behavior. It would appear he's still learning his manners and to mind his elders. He didn't have a feminine example growing up to teach him the subtle art of etiquette. He killed his poor mother in childbirth, you understand."

"Father!"

Ellie coughed at the statement, and Sasha choked on her champagne.

"Oh my, it looks like you already need a refill my dear." He snapped and turned to one of the waiters. At least, Ellie thought he was a waiter. He was wearing all black, but he looked much rougher around the edges and was missing an apron and a tray. "Get these women some of our special champagne." The waiter gave a slow smile. Ellie saw a gold molar peek out and shivered as unease slithered up her spine.

"Oh, that's not necessary." Ellie tried to say on Sasha's behalf, but the man had already disappeared in the throng of people.

"Nonsense. He'll be right back. Now tell me a bit about yourselves, ladies."

Sasha lit up. "Yes, I'd love to. I make straight As... with the occasional B, but I have a 3.8 GPA overall. I'm class vice president, and I've been in several different clubs throughout high school—"

"Yes, yes. That's nice, dear. I'm sure all that is in your application. Oh look, your drinks. Andrew, why don't you make yourself useful again, hm?"

Andy's jaw tensed and he turned to get the champagne out of the man in black's hands. He handed the glasses to Ellie and Sasha, and Ellie tried not to feel self-conscious about being an underaged girl double-fisting champagne flutes at a cocktail party. They were talking to a partner of the firm. How bad could they look?

Mr. Ascot gave a stage whisper, "Ladies, it pays to have a sycophant as a son. He'd do anything for dear ol' dad's approval." He guffawed and slapped Andy on the back, hard enough for the younger Ascot to jolt forward. "Isn't that right son?"

Andy grimaced and opened his mouth, as if to object.

"Now, now. Don't be shy. That kind of ambition is going to help get you a promotion someday."

Andy went slack-jawed. "Really? Are you serious?"

Mr. Ascot slapped him on the back again, rougher still, and his ruddy face shook with laughter.

"Well, ladies, it was a pleasure getting to know you. I think it's time you go to the interview room now—"

"Interview room? Already? I thought donors agreed before choosing which recipients needed to advance to the interview phase. We haven't heard from Ellie and we don't even know where they want to go to school or what they want to major in—"

"Be quiet, Andrew. Why don't you go off with that girlfriend of yours? I'm not sure why you insisted on coming tonight if you were going to be rude and interrupt perfectly fine conversation." He rolled his eyes and pointed to Andy behind a raised hand, as if to hide it from him in one of those bad jokes that only old people told. "Can't bring him anywhere, am I right?" Sasha and Ellie winced, but Mr. Ascot continued to laugh at his son's expense.

Andy sighed heavily and turned to Ellie.

"It was good to see you, Ellie. Can we um... here, follow me." He leaned forward and tugged her to the side so he could speak to her more privately, but still not far away from the party.

"Ellie, can you do something for me? Juliet, she's uh, she's not answering my calls. I'm getting a little desperate here." He laughed roughly. Ellie tried to ignore the pang of compassion at the defeated sadness behind his eyes. When she didn't say anything, he cleared his throat. "Just, please... talk to her. For me? I need to speak with her. Tell her it's urgent."

"Urgent?" Ellie felt her brow furrow.

"Yeah, yeah. Or just something... I'll do anything at this point to get her attention." At the look on her face he gave a nervous laugh. "What? A little white lie never hurt anyone."

"Jules hates liars, Andy. You know that."

His fair skin pinkened and he pulled at his collar. "Right. Well, just think about it, will you? I think I'll, um, mingle now. Hope you ladies have a good time. And good luck. You must've impressed the donors significantly if they're granting interviews to you already." He clinked his whiskey glass to her champagne flute in a cheers. He smiled wide, nodding to her before heading to the bar.

"Finally, I thought we'd never get rid of him." Mr. Ascot's joke fell flat, but he didn't seem to notice. "Ladies, why don't you go on to the interview room," he repeated, pointing behind them and placing his hands on their shoulders to guide them. Ellie tried not to flinch at the unwelcome weight on her shoulder, but it lifted soon enough.

"Alright, ladies. Off you go. I think you both will be excellent candidates. I only hope that I may be able to appreciate your talents someday." He laughed wildly as if he had told a joke and winked as he turned to walk away.

"God, that An-*drew* guy was so rude. Is Jules all he talks about?"

"Yeah, so awkward, right?" Ellie asked, but Sasha was already on the move.

"Oh my God, Ellie, look! There's a chocolate fountain in here. Chocolate. Fountain. Let's go!"

Ellie rolled her eyes and followed her into the "interview room." She hoped they could talk to the right people and leave already. At some point, Jason and Aunt Rachel may talk to each other and then Ellie's little plan would be exposed. She'd never lied to them before, and it felt weird that she'd had to start for something as important as competing for a scholarship. But if it all worked out in the end, then they'd forgive her. Besides, she was a little annoyed at the conversations so far. They hadn't been riveting, to say the least, and it seemed as though some attendees were being treated differently than others.

To Ellie's disappointment, inside the interview room was no different than the outside. The conference room was decorated to look like a cozy parlor, although Ellie was anything but comfortable. Several of the nervous kids her age were surrounded by influential people in what looked like fascinating conversation. Others were left to fend for themselves, as if they held no interest to the donors. Ellie couldn't help but feel discouraged at the thought that the first group were most assuredly contenders for scholarships, while the second group seemed to be the one she and Sasha were stuck in. With the looks she and Sasha kept getting, and the open leers the other young women received, Ellie was starting to itch with discomfort.

"Maybe we should just go, Sash."

"No! Please? Pretty please? I know you're tired, I am too. Let's sit on that sofa over in the corner there for a little while and then try again, okay?"

"Fine," Ellie sighed. She barely had enough energy left to even argue, but her friend was right. This was their shot, especially Sasha's.

A few more men stopped by to chat. Still, they only asked very surface level questions like what school they went to, their ages, their families. They didn't even take the time to ask the important stuff, like extracurriculars or GPAs.

Ellie eventually felt her eyelids droop closed and it became harder and harder to keep them open. With the lag in conversation, she couldn't escape how tired she was. School had been hectic with college application deadlines and looming midterms and she hadn't gotten much shuteye recently. Still, falling asleep at an upscale party was embarrassing.

Not that Sasha seemed to mind. She'd passed out fifteen minutes ago.

Maybe I'll just rest my eyes for a minute. No one will notice.

CHAPTER SEVEN

The next thing Ellie remembered was being carried and a flash of gold glinting back at her from above. She closed her eyes against the memory. She and Sasha had done this to themselves. Who gets so wasted at a high-class function that they pass out?

Then she remembered what Pompous had said. They'd been drugged.

"What're you going to do with an unconscious girl?" Fancy's voice kept breaking as he yelled. "Your goons said she's had too much of whatever shit you gave her. She needs to go to a hospital!"

"Oh, I don't mind bruising a little fruit every now and then. She's just the way I like. Especially after a long hard day."

"I'll have no part in this. I-I'll call the authorities!"

"You can't get out now. You're culpable, remember? Like I said, don't forget who gave the little slut her drinks. You're in too deep." He chuckled low. The sound of a zipper grated against Ellie's eardrums.

"But I didn't—Stop! You can't do this!"

"He's getting tedious. Take him to the next room. And don't let him leave. I won't be disturbed and I don't want to be worried about him acting rashly."

"Sir, we go to next room, but one of us stays."

"Like hell—"

"Policy from boss." Ellie's heart pounded in the brief silence.

"Fine. But take him to the adjoining room with you. And if you must stay, at least stand at the entry. I may have certain tastes, but I draw the line at voyeurism."

Ellie heard objections and a struggle but the adjoining room door eventually *snicked* shut. A shadow passed by the bathroom door. The draft caused it to open a sliver more.

A metallic *clink* of a belt hitting the floor made Ellie break into a sweat. She closed her eyes roughly against her knees, the pressure causing dark shapes to form behind her eyelids.

The first sound of the man's pleasure made her swallow back bile. The rhythmic thumping and squeaking of bedsprings continued against the backdrop of stifled groans. The sound of retching brought it all to a stop.

"Stupid bitch!" A sharp slap on skin resounded through the door. The man rumbled more curses and an object hit the outer wall of the bathroom, connected to the bedroom. Ellie caught a glance in the adjacent mirror and gagged.

Her best friend was being held up by her throat, her face nearly purple despite her dark skin tone, and her eyes glazed over until they partially closed. Sasha's body spasmed and grew limp. The hand holding her threw her onto the bed and out of view. Ellie wanted to help, but she was paralyzed by fear. All she could do was watch the mirror.

There's nothing I can do to save her. There's nothing I can do to save her. There's nothing I can do to save her.

The mantra only went so far to ease her conscience. She became devoid of any thought at all when, to her horror, more grunting and the squeak of the bedsprings resumed, with more fervor. Ellie was so afraid and disgusted she couldn't move, but she still felt tears burn her face. Her eyes closed and she let hot streams run freely, biting her tongue to keep from screaming.

Eventually, the heavy breathing ended with the man's

perverted moans. The clink of the monster's belt buckle as he raised his pants and the metal teeth of the zipper replayed in reverse, as if the scene had rewound and the rape of her best friend hadn't happened feet away from her.

The door connecting the two rooms opened and shut abruptly, causing the bathroom door to open more as it responded to the change in air pressure.

"Wait until my father—" Fancy's voice choked up until Ellie heard more vomiting.

"Not you, too. I already had to deal with her rancid bile."

The gagging continued despite the complaint. More footsteps entered the room.

"Gentlemen, it seems the fruit has expired. You'll need to clean this mess up."

Ellie watched the shadow pass the bathroom door, straining to lift her head to try and catch a glimpse of her friend's rapist. But he walked too quickly and before she knew it, he'd already left.

Once he was gone, what sounded like Russian cursing and slang barraged the bedroom before Fancy finally quit puking his brains out.

"How could he do this? Is she dead? Oh God, what are we going to do?" Fancy's high-pitched rambling masked Ellie's sob as her worst fears were confirmed. Her best friend was gone, and she'd done absolutely nothing to stop it.

"We clean up. You make mess, too, *da*?"

Ellie watched through the widened sliver of light as one of the men pulled a large canvas duffel bag from a stack of many, stowed in the opposing closet.

"Me? Clean up? Y-you can't seriously think I'll do that. My father—"

"*Da*, we know who is your father, okay? You clean still."

There was a mumble of protest but after some curse words in both Russian and English— and more dry heaving—Ellie heard the bag zip. A low thud on the floor revealed a man collapsed against the wall across from the mirror. The adrenaline that had broken through her drug-induced haze as Sasha was being tortured, had calmed slightly, making it hard for her to focus again. But Ellie's brief view of Fancy's red and blotchy face activated a faint niggle of recognition in her mind, although it was too foggy to grasp.

"What have I done," he sobbed. "What have I done? Did I do this? Oh God, did I kill that girl?" The wailing alternated between that and more gagging. A large man stood by and awkwardly patted his shoulder.

"It is alright, *durak*. If not so much drugs, what he did would have killed her, okay? But then she be awake for it. This is much better."

"What about the other one? Was there another girl?"

"Other one? Yes, we have more in bathroom—"

"No, there was another girl, with *this* girl."

"You know this girl? Does boss know this thing?"

Fancy sputtered. "Oh, um, no I don't *know* her—"

"I think boss must know this—"

"NO! No, it's nothing. I just, I just remember her at the party, is all. I'm just—oh God, I'm so confused. This was only supposed to be recruiting for escorts. Not this. Never this. I don't want to be a part of *this*." Fancy wept, his face in his lap, and grabbed his hair in a painful grip, rocking against the wall back and forth.

One of the Russians hauled the now full bag... Sasha... onto his shoulder. The weight of guilt sank deep in her gut and became a low wail that erupted from her throat. The louder she got, the more energy depleted from her already low reserves. A stab of fear shot through her as she realized crying could get her in trouble, but there was nothing she could do to stop herself and deep sobs continued to wrack her body.

In between sobs, she heard one of the Russians curse. "I go do this thing. Take where it supposed to go, okay?" But the wreck on the floor didn't respond. "You should go, *durak*. There is nothing here to do tonight."

"Yeah... yeah... I should go."

"Remember what boss say. You did this thing."

More dry heaving and sobbing.

The Russian sighed and indicated with his head for the other to follow him. They met at the bathroom door, and the one with the bag, the head honcho it seemed, nodded his head toward the mess of a man and spoke in harsh Russian consonants. The sidekick looked back and nodded one quick jerk of the chin. Honcho then pulled out a suitcase from the closet and opened it. Sidekick bent low, took a vial and needle from the case, and closed it.

Ellie's heart palpitated strongly and she tried to choke back her cries. She felt her labored breathing as her body tried to hyperventilate against the drugs in her system. The Russians spoke again, this time nodding and pointing toward the bathroom. Honcho left and Sidekick prepared the syringe. It was only seconds, but Ellie tried to formulate a plan as quickly as possible. She was the closest to the door now that Sasha had been taken. She could fight him off, her brother had taught her the basics. She would kick the guy in the nuts, hard enough for Jason to be proud, and then run as fast as she could to the nearest person and call the cops. She felt her body tighten as she prepared it to flee.

But when Sidekick opened the door and lifted her left arm, Ellie willed her body to kick up and toward him, only to have her leg gently glide over the man's shin. Her other leg was much more sluggish and still stuck in fetal position. He grabbed her arm more forcefully and she hardly felt the prick as the syringe's contents emptied into her bloodstream.

He moved on to the next girl, and the next. Ellie all the while tried to get her muscles to respond to her commands. But the room felt hot and her eyelids grew heavy. It was too familiar to how she felt at the party and she tried to fight it with all the strength she had left. She reached out toward the bathroom door, trying to escape. Her mind was crying out with the need to get help, find safety any way possible before the dark haze in her brain took over. Maybe she could even appeal to the pathetic man still sobbing in the corner. She'd have done anything to save her life and the lives of the other women in the bathroom. Anything to keep them from Sasha's fate.

The Russian man who'd casually poisoned them, nonchalantly stepped over her, the bottom of the door scraping her fingers as it shut. The desperate screaming in her head reverberated around her skull until she finally succumbed to the black.

Before being shot up with God-knows-what, she'd been terrified, determined, enraged. Through the drug-induced confusion, she tried desperately to cling to the vestiges of those emotions.

But she didn't feel a thing.

CHAPTER EIGHT

Jules pressed her hand to her chest as she felt her heart pulse in time with the vibrating bass. It didn't help that well over six feet of solid muscle was flush behind her, close enough that not only could she feel him, she could almost taste campfire smoke and pine.

She took a deliberate step forward and to the left, away from the intoxicating aroma before she got drunk off his scent. Jules scanned the busy club again. The room was packed and even though the air felt hot and heavy, she shivered once she left his heat.

Although Jason wasn't bothering her, per se, he was distracting her from searching the crowd. Every few minutes, he checked his watch or swirled ice around in his glass, oddly fixated on its contents, as if he was trying to read his fortune from tea leaves. Every now and then he'd wince and glance around.

Since Jason was a borderline suspect, the cops weren't talking to them, so Jules and Jason turned to any and every idea they had to try to find Ellie. They poured over the messages from Ellie's iPad, brainstormed areas she might go, talked to classmates, checked the local hospital, and came up with nothing. Nada.

Absolutely no leads. Jules was mindful that a quarter of their forty-eight-hour clock had ticked by, but without anything to go off of, they'd decided to go to Original Sin. It was a longshot, but OS was where Jules always got her best intel. Nobody knew more secrets than the dirty little secrets themselves.

They'd already asked Jules's friends and former coworkers, or Sinners, if they knew anything, with no luck. Before calling it a night, Jules wanted to make one final effort and speak with Original Sin's owner and namesake, Cyn Turner. Nothing in Ashland happened without her knowledge, so Jules had sent a text asking her go-to informant and friend if she had time to talk.

After Cyn agreed to come out on the floor and meet with her, Jules and Jason waited. Sinners floated around in their sexy angel uniforms as they stopped to flirt with customers at their tables and booths. Unfortunately, there was no sign of the short, fiery redhead Jules was waiting for. She hoped Cyn wasn't in one of the other areas of the strip club. Jules wanted to avoid going any deeper into OS with Jason nearby, if she could help it.

Original Sin was built with three main areas, each space separated by thick, gauzy curtains resembling clouds. There was the lobby, called The Fall. The client would then walk through the cloud curtains to Eden, the bar area where the women interacted and flirted one-on-one with the customers. The final section of the club, or Heaven, also had a bar and tables, but minimal interaction from the women. Heaven was still the most popular because the seating gave the perfect view of the dancers as they performed on their stages. If clients wanted to get handsy, within reason and consent, they or their party could go to a Confessional, or private room, for a dance.

Jules had chosen to wait at the bar in Eden, but she could tell Jason was getting impatient. He'd gone very still and hadn't said anything in a while. He kept wiping his hand over his forehead, ending to trace the new scar above his left ear. It was a pale divot about three inches long and half an inch wide without any of his short dark brown hair growing over it. It looked like whatever happened had been painful, and she'd briefly wondered in the car ride over how he got it. She'd thought about asking, but didn't want to get too invested in knowing any more than she needed to for his case.

She slid her gaze over Jason again and watched him swirl his glass as they awkwardly waited at the bar together.

A flash of bright red hair caught her vision and Jules hopped off her barstool to run toward it.

"Cyn!" Jules called over the blaring music before she realized the short red hair she was looking for was actually long and flowing over angel wings.

Rose.

Jules's former best friend turned around with a pasted smile, only to have it fall into a grimace. "Oh, it's you."

Jules and Rose had become best friends working at OS together until Rose got into drugs in a bad way. Jules had tried to help her best friend get clean, but Rose's sobriety had required twenty-four seven care. At the time, Jules was neck deep in reading assignments for her senior year of college and foolishly deciding whether to forego law school in order to blindly follow the frustrating man behind her. Not to mention taking care of Rose brought back painful memories Jules had tried desperately to suppress.

Jules thrived while pursuing her legal dreams, but things went from bad to rock bottom for Rose. She'd only recently been released from prison for serving time on drug charges and Jules would've much rather had their first meeting in the real world be more private. Rose was finally free, but Jules had been patiently waiting to see her on her friend's terms.

Unable to help herself, Jules ran up for a hug, but Rose put her hands up in defense.

"Rose, what the—"

"I know I've been blowing you off, but cornering me at work is a bitch move. Even for you, Jules."

Jules's heart stuttered to a halt, and she felt her mouth fall open in protest. "Rose, I'm not—"

"Listen..." Rose blew out a harsh breath. "You've got to stop, okay?" Rose kept her hands up as her glance darted around the club behind Jules.

"'Stop?' What do you mean, 'stop?' I haven't done anything! This is the first time I've even seen you in years!"

Rose's shoulders raised and fell on a sigh. "I can't-I just can't be around you right now, okay?"

"No. Not okay." Jules grabbed Rose's arm and tugged her across the room, through the cloudy curtains into Heaven and into the closest empty Confessional. She shut the door before turning to Rose. "Tell me what the hell is going on," Jules demanded. She watched as her friend's hands started to tremble and panic shot down Jules's spine. "Rose, are you using again?" She asked in hushed tones and tried to hide the disappointment in her voice. By the time Jules had graduated law school, Rose was in heavy legal trouble thanks to her addiction and putting her trust in the wrong people. Jules never wanted to see her best friend head down that path again.

"No, okay!" Rose hissed and crossed her arms. "I'm clean. I... there's just a lot going on with me right now, alright? I need to lay low. Stay off the radar for a while."

"Okay..." Jules began, trying to keep impatience from her tone. "But what does that have to do with me? Are you safe? Fuck, is Ghost back? Is there something I can do?" Ghost, Rose's boyfriend and dealer, had somehow spent less time in prison than Rose, which was something Jules was still trying to figure out. She'd counted it as a small favor that he disappeared after getting off light on his own criminal charges. But if he was back, Rose could be in danger.

Rose looked up and shook her head slightly. "You don't get it, do you? This isn't about Ghost. You think you can save everyone, Jules, but you just can't. Alright? Sometimes, people let you down. Sometimes they don't even deserve it. And-and you just have to deal with it, okay?"

"Rose, what the fuck are you talking about?" Jules was having trouble tracking the conversation. It was as if Rose was grasping at whatever idea came into her head, just to get Jules to go away. "Rose, please. Just talk to me. Tell me what's really going on. I can help."

"You know what? Fine, here's the truth." Rose's hands moved up and down to indicate Jules. "It's you. I can't be around you anymore. No, scratch that. I don't *want* to be around you anymore, alright? I can't *stand* you."

"What?" Jules's heart felt like it was being ripped from her chest, and she clutched at it to make sure it was still there.

"Every time I look at you. I see the old me. I see Rose the Fuck Up, Rose the Addict, Rose the Helpless. I just... I can't. It hurts too much, you understand? That's why I never let you visit while I was... gone."

"No, I don't—I mean I guess I understand. But damn, Rose. We were best friends. We can get back to that. You don't need to be ashamed of anything, especially not around me. You know that." Jules reached for her again, but Rose shook her head and evaded her touch by turning to leave.

"Look, if you came to check up on me, you can leave now. And don't come back on my account." Rose stopped short at Jason's presence in front of the doorway. She turned back to Jules with her hands up in question. "And you're with this asshole again? After what he did to you?" Rose shook her head. "Fucking perfect. Not everyone deserves forgiveness Jules." She scoffed at Jason's wince and bumped his shoulder as she rushed past him. Jules hadn't even realized the door had opened again, let alone that he'd followed them there.

"But Rose—"

"Jules, just stop, okay?" Rose held up her hand again as she stood in the doorway. "Respect this. Respect my decision. There's so much I want to forget, Jules. So much I *need* to forget." She paused before looking Jules straight in the eyes. "Until I can move on from my past, you're at the top of the list." Without a second glance, Rose turned into the crowd, her worn black wings all Jules could see as she walked out the door of the Confessional.

Jules felt her lip tremble and she gritted her teeth at the emotion burning in her eyes. She blinked rapidly to clear them. There was no fucking way she was crying in a strip club, for everyone to see. A shadow entered her vision, making Jules lose eye contact with Rose's black wings, and a large familiar hand cupped her shoulder. She tried not to think about how her body relaxed under Jason's touch.

"Are you alright? That looked... intense."

She raised her eyes to face him. To tell him to leave her alone, question why he'd followed her to the Confessional, yell, scream, do anything to get the ache from inside, out of her body. But his brow was furrowed above his stormy gray eyes, crinkled around the edges with worry. For her. Damn, it'd been a while since she'd felt someone care enough to worry about her. Whatever he saw in her own gaze prompted him to fully step into the Confessional with her and shut the door behind him. He put his hands on her shoulders, his thumbs tracing her neck. The caresses felt too good to push away and she allowed a breath of tension to release.

"I-I tried everything I could with her. We didn't end on good terms. She had a bad time of it for a while, after I got out of law school. Her drug problem had gotten so, so much worse. I hadn't been paying enough attention..."

With Jason's gentle caresses against her neck, Jules let go of some of the stress over Rose she'd accumulated over the years. Jules told him when she got out of law school, Rose was in jail, held without bail, awaiting trial on charges that could send her away for life. Prosecutors claimed she was the leader of a poly-drug conspiracy and trafficking ring. According to police reports, Rose caused a tragic wreck, killing three people in a family of four, with only their seven year old boy left alive. While investigating the wreck, officers found Rose passed out in the driver's seat and a shit-ton of drugs in the trunk.

Jules was fresh from passing the state bar exam, but after some intense investigation of her own, she was able to convince prosecutors that Rose wasn't the culprit. Not only had Rose been so strung up on heroin at the time of the crash that she couldn't possibly have been conscious, let alone the driver, the child also said that he saw a man move "a sleepy woman" to the driver's seat after the collision. Considering Rose's boyfriend at the time was also her dealer, it wasn't hard to put two and two together.

But by that time, Ghost was in the wind, and there were three deaths and over fifty kilos of cocaine, heroin, and—God help us all—fentanyl in the trunk of the car. Someone had to answer for it. In the end, Rose decided to take a plea deal so that if she testified against Ghost, she would only get the minimum prison sentence. Jules hadn't liked it. Rose could've gotten off entirely, but it'd ultimately been Rose's decision.

At the end, Jules took a breath and choked back a sob.

"Shit," Jason whispered. "Come here." He wrapped her in his arms and she let him hold her. His hard chest was comforting with his tight embrace and she rested her head against his pecs, fitting her head perfectly under his chin. One of his hands massaged her nape and his warmth was a balm on the blistering chill she felt from Rose's words.

"She didn't want to make that poor little boy testify," Jules continued, her cheek up against his heartbeat. "And she got sent to prison for a crime she didn't commit. It was all so wrong, Jay. Her being locked up like that." She shuddered.

Jason raised her chin with his thumbs so she could look at him. "You know none of that is your fault, right?" Jules meant to nod her head yes, but hesitated. Couldn't she have done more? "Listen, I'm sure you told her the consequences, right?"

"Yes, but—"

"And, knowing those consequences, she made her decision of her own free will?" Jason asked, his face relaxed but his brow arched.

"You don't understand, Jay. She shouldn't have gone to jail—"

"You did everything you could to help her?"

"Yes, but—"

"Then that's all you can do, baby girl."

The endearment rolled off his tongue and barreled into her. She became hyper-aware of how they'd naturally become entwined. His rough, calloused hands were cradling her head. Their bodies were flush against the other's. Their lips, a breath from touching. She slinked her arms from behind his back and splayed her hands against his chest. His fingers pulsed on her neck, seemingly itching to possess her. She pressed her palms against his pecs and pushed firmly enough for him to back away.

"So, um, I guess we can leave." Jules cleared her throat and rubbed her arms. She cautiously stepped past Jason to get to the door. "We've asked everyone if they know anything and I don't know where the hell Cyn is. I'm sorry it was such a waste of damn time."

Jason's sudden grip on her arm made her pause. "Jules, it wasn't a waste. We don't have any leads on Ellie right now and we weren't getting anywhere but frustrated trying to brainstorm ways to find her. We came here and did what we could. We'll go home, regroup, and try again tomorrow." Jules winced at the word 'home,' but apparently Jason didn't notice as he continued. "Hopefully we'll think of something or, hell, maybe Ellie will prove me right to Aunt Rachel and she'll show up tomorrow, all sorry for acting like a careless teenager." He laughed, obviously trying to make himself hope for the unlikely, before sobering and facing Jules straight on. "And as for Rose, you did what you needed to do and you tried to help a friend." He pulled her closer and she allowed herself just one step into his embrace. "One thing Rose got right is you do try to save everyone. Never change that about yourself, okay? We need more of you in the world. Your drive to forgive everyone is one of the things I love about you."

On the last sentence, Jules couldn't handle his platitudes anymore and she ripped her arm from his grip, as if his hand burned just as much as his words. "Yeah, we need to fucking go. I'll just, um, pay our tab." She collected herself before turning for the door. When she pulled it open, the musky scent of sex, sweat, and overworked air conditioning blasted against her, and her hearing was once again accosted by the intense bass of the house music.

"Jules!" Jason called for her, but she pretended like she couldn't hear. It was loud enough that she hoped he'd buy it. He was hot on her heels as she headed back through the curtains to the Eden bar to pay their tab. The hair on the back of her neck stood on end at his nearness and her skin had goose bumps from where the warmth of his touch had cooled. She upped her speed. She had to get the hell out of there and away from him.

"Hey Jezebel, can we get our check?" She waved her hand for the bartender to see and signed the check as soon as she got it. As Original Sin's attorney, she'd normally just put the check on her tab, but she needed to calm down and do something with her hands before she lost control and rubbed them down Jason's firm body.

"Fuck, why's it gotta be so goddamn loud in here. It's gonna make me go insane," Jason complained before placing his hand against Jules's on the bar. He leaned in to speak with her, his lips almost touching the shell of her ear. She tried not to react, but it was all she could do not to give in and relax against him. "Jules, what's going on? Talk to me baby."

She bristled again and took a deep breath to keep from whirling around to give him a piece of her mind. Her head swam with anger as she tried to formulate into words exactly how fucked-up it was that he thought he could waltz back into her life and be concerned for her. That he could just hold her and make her feel better. That he could say all the right things and set her at ease. How fucking dare he make her feel anything at all for him.

"Jason, you can't just—"

"Hey handsome. Been a long time since I've seen you around here." The husky feminine voice made Jules's spine snap ramrod straight up from her position leaning against the bar.

"Goddamnit," Jules whispered. Inch by slow inch, she turned to see Charity's hand stroke down Jason's chest with familiarity. Somehow, Charity had already gotten so close, he might as well have been inside her.

It was exactly what Jules had tried to avoid from her first step back into Original Sin. She hated to admit it, but having Jason around sparked feelings inside her she didn't want to confront, the most embarrassing being jealousy. And that was before she felt the comfort of his touch again. Jules had been worried what she'd do if she had to watch Jason be seduced right in front of her. Hence, their position in Eden, far away from the stages and closest proximity to where she could get drunk fastest if necessary.

She'd thought the Sinners would respect their code and leave them be once they realized Jason was with her. It'd worked so far. But she should've known one particular she-devil would take advantage that the "sinfully" hot former bouncer was back.

"You look a little stressed, Jason. You wanna take me somewhere private? Just like old times?"

"Fuck off, Charity." Jason stepped away, but Charity's hand cupped the front of his pants. Even in the dark Jules could tell he was already excited about the prospect.

Typical.

"Oh, I'm trying but it feels like we might not make it to a room. Why don't I take you to the back... alone—" He snatched her wrist, stopping her from continuing her pursuit.

"No." The force behind the growl caught both Jules and the angel in the blonde wig by surprise. "I came with Jules." He threw her wrist back at her exquisitely perky breasts. "And I'm staying with Jules..." He sneered before looking intently in Jules's eyes and using Charity's words against her, "Just like old times."

"Really? After all these years you still choose *Delilah*?"

Jules felt a cold sweat on the nape of her neck and narrowed her eyes. Normally, she didn't have this type of animosity toward other women, especially not as a former Sinner herself. She knew the score, it was all about getting the bills paid. Still, there was a special place in lady hell for little miss silver-eyed *Charity*. It'd probably look like a convent.

Jason crossed his arms and stepped toward Jules. The hellcat gave Jules a once-over and smirked.

"Suit yourself. But you know where to find me, big guy." Charity sashayed away, presumably to find her next prey. Her tiny ass swayed with every step.

Jason chuckled and leaned on the bar. "Damn. Didn't she see I was with you? Bold move."

Jules scoffed. "Like that's ever stopped either of you before."

"What the fuck's that supposed to mean?" he asked, his brow furrowed.

"Are you kidding me right now? Don't make me say it." The anger she'd tried to control frothed over.

"Jules, what are you—"

"You! Fucking a Sinner! Obviously, it's not anything new for you."

Jason had the nerve to laugh. "But that was you." He stalked toward her, the heat in his eyes causing her to shiver. "I'd fuck you right now if you'd let me." Seven years ago, that cocky grin would have made her soaked faster than he could say "come." But after seeing him let Charity maul him, Jules felt her stomach heave.

"First of all," she yelled over the bass beat. "You're a client. I don't fuck *clients*. Second, I'm not the only Sinner you've ever fucked." She flicked her head in Charity's direction before turning her glare back to Jason. "And I won't be the next."

Jules was unprepared for the confusion, followed by utter

devastation that flooded Jason's entire demeanor. He looked so dejected, she almost lost all of her nerve and felt the urge to comfort him.

"You would think that... wouldn't you?" He tilted his head up and closed his eyes. She couldn't help but inch toward him and slowly close the distance.

"Is there a reason I shouldn't?" Her hand on his cheek gently pulled his gray eyes back to hers. The icy pain inside them pierced her heart. Could she have been wrong? Could this all have been a fucked-up misunderstanding?

But then he shook his head slightly and the hot acidity of betrayal sank deep in her stomach. She tore her hand from the burn and backed away, not caring that she was bumping into passersby. His eyes widened with alarm.

"No, Jules, I—"

"Juliet!" A male's nasal yell rose above the music. She turned to see a blond whirlwind rush through the cloud curtains from The Fall. "Juliet, I'm so glad I found you. We need to talk." Once he was close enough, he hunched over and grabbed her arm for stability, trying to catch his breath.

"Andy, what're you doing here?"

CHAPTER NINE

"She doesn't want to talk to you," Jason interrupted behind her. She looked around and was glad to find no one was paying any attention to them, even though they were clearly making a scene. Thank God for drunk hedonists.

Andy blanched at Jason's towering form. Jason pulled her away and stepped in front of her, his fists clenched at his sides.

"Excuse you." Jules pushed Jason to the side and glared at him to back up. She knew the silent chastising worked more than any shove she could deliver. *He's half the size of a freaking bear.* Jason lazily stretched against the bar countertop, but his still clenched fist belied his relaxed pose.

"You don't speak for me," she chided.

His stern eyes bore into her, everything in them saying, *if you need me, I'm here.*

She nodded once at his silent communication before turning to face Andy.

Honestly, she was a little shocked, not just that he had the audacity to be at OS of all places, or that he knew where she was to begin with. No, it was the first time she'd ever seen him so... frazzled.

His perfectly moussed hair was standing on end. His tie was

askew and his pressed white shirt was wrinkled and untucked. She watched as his hands fidgeted in that methodical way of his. Strangely enough, Jules thought he'd never looked better... if it weren't for his sweaty pallor and wild glances toward the exit.

"What're you doing here, Andy?"

"What is *he* doing here? Does he just follow you around now?" Andy raised his voice over the constant thrum of the house music.

"Look who's talking, stalker."

"Watch it, you two. Jason, go take a walk. You damn well know I don't need you to fight my battles." He harrumphed and crossed his arms. When he still hadn't moved, Jules shooed him away until he backed up into the shadowed corner at the end of the bar. It was only a few feet difference, but she could tell that was as much privacy as he was willing to give. She turned back to the problem at hand and tried to gather as much patience as she could muster. It was growing thin with all the exercise it'd had in one night.

"Andy, why are you here?"

He took a gulp of air and darted a glance into the darkness where Jason was hiding. Andy then stood up straight, cleared his throat, and attempted to fix his tie.

"Seriously, *are* you following me?"

"No, I-I-I came here for other reasons. Do you think we could go somewhere else? I really need to speak with y-you," he sputtered. He glanced around and his eyes grew wide before he muttered under his breath. Of course, Charity took that moment to walk by, again. Andy noticed and grabbed her close, his grip awkward and tight on her waist.

"Ah, here she is. Just who I was looking for." Startled, Charity looked up to see who had her and smiled stiffly. When she saw Jules tapping her foot across from them, she cuddled into Andy's embrace.

"Oh, Andrew," she purred. "I was wondering when you were going to come back. It's been a while now. Couldn't stay away?"

Andy barked a laugh, but Jules could've sworn he looked nervous. He worked his hand underneath the back of Charity's skintight white top, making her wings flutter. When walking the floor, the girls could choose what type of angel they wanted to be for the night, heavenly or fallen. Charity insisted her name required her to always be a heavenly angel. It was the role she was born to play as "God's gift to men."

"Just making sure you miss me. What do you say you get us a room?" He lifted her chin up with a finger and watched Jules out of the corner of his eye. "I think I need to make a confession."

Obviously able to see Jules in her periphery, Charity giggled. "I'll meet you in Confessional 3." She strutted through the cloud curtains to Heaven, no doubt to make good on her word.

Once she was gone, Andy's fidgeting became more pronounced and he ran his hand through his hair. He abruptly took a few steps toward Jules, getting in her space, but oddly not looking directly at her. She backed into a wall and put her hands up to stop him from getting any closer.

"I don't have time for this. Jason and I were just leaving," she insisted.

Andy had been distraught over Jules refusing to see him the past few months, but he'd been acting even more strangely recently. It was creeping her out. When she felt a gentle push behind her and strong hands on her hips, she quickly realized the "wall" was Jason. She leaned back against him and allowed his presence to support her.

"You heard her. Say what you came to say or leave," Jason demanded.

Andy's eyes flitted to the curtained entry again and he leaned in to whisper to her.

"Juliet, please. I can't talk to you with him around. I need to speak with you privately." His eyes glistened with unshed tears. Jules almost felt sorry for him. Almost. She'd heard his crap for months and it was time it came to a stop, once and for all. He needed to move on.

He wasn't looking at her anymore and he stumbled back quickly. When she followed his stare, there were only people seemingly preoccupied by their respective Sinner. She turned back to Andy and watched as he adopted an arrogant stance once more and combed through his hair. His demeanor flipped with the passing of his hand over his face, like a Greek theater mask with two faces. This was a different side of Andy than she'd ever seen before and a shock of unease passed through her.

"It's funny I ran into you here—"

"What the—"

"—But I have some *business* to take care of in one of the private rooms, if you know what I mean. Father wants me to get more involved with pro bono work. Good for the firm." His white teeth glinted in the strobe light.

"Andy, what the hell? You stopped to talk to me. What are you talking about?"

He laughed harshly and looked around, as if to ensure he had an audience. "I've always given freely to Charity." When his eyes found Jules again, they were manic with an emotion she couldn't identify. "You would know, since you were my first case."

He rushed past her and bumped her shoulder, earning a growl from Jason. She grabbed her huge bodyguard by his biceps before he hurt someone.

"That fucker! How dare he talk to you that way?" Jason breathed heavily, like a bull as it kicked back its hooves. Jules knew it was only a matter of time before he charged past her. Even though she was tall, she still fit just below his chin, and she burrowed herself into that position against his chest. Wrapping her arms around him tightly, Jules tried not to relish the touch in the tense moment. He hesitated, only briefly, but then surrounded her with his arms like she'd float away if he wasn't holding on. His breathing calmed until they were in sync. She found herself stroking his back and barely kept from moaning when he massaged her neck again.

They stayed that way for a while, ignoring everyone else. It felt so good to lose herself in his embrace. He was bringing back the security and feeling of home she'd had for only a brief moment in her life. She'd made herself forget he'd been her safe space all those years ago. Before he left her and everything went to shit. That last thought, and the sound of a throat clearing behind her, brought her back to the present. She turned to see the owner and namesake of Original Sin, her former boss and practically a second mother.

Cynthia Turner stood in front of them with her hands on her wide hips. She'd reminded Jules of Reba McEntire as a kid. That is, if Reba overly lined her eyes and only wore tight black leather. Her signature red hair changed colors with the strobe lights and Jules felt Jason tense as he looked up and promptly let go of her.

"Tell me what I'm lookin' at here, Jules, 'cause I know it ain't Jason Stone that just walked up into my club. I know he wouldn'tna had the balls to show his face here again."

Cyn may have been half Jason's size, but she was mean as a hornet if someone messed with one of her girls. Jules felt Jason gulp against the back of her head before he spoke.

"I-uh, I..."

"Cyn, we came to see if anyone knew anything about Jason's sister, Ellie. She's missing. We haven't gotten anywhere here. Do you know anything?"

Cyn's glare faltered, replaced by concern as she frowned. "Sorry, hon. Don't know nothin' 'bout that."

At Cyn's slow shake of her head, what little hope Jules had for a lead, plummeted into her stomach. They were losing time they didn't have and the whole night had been a total waste. Jules closed her eyes and sighed through her disappointment.

"Alright, well... if you hear anything, will you let me know?"

Cyn nodded. "Sure, of course. But she's just a kid right? How long she been gone?"

"We found out she was missing when she didn't turn up at school this morning," Jason offered.

Cyn frowned. "Well, howdya know she ain't just foolin' 'round?"

Jason's lips tightened and Jules brushed her hand on his forearm. "We don't, but Ellie's a really good kid, and we're getting worried. Keep me posted, okay? If you hear something?"

Cyn nodded and Jules turned to leave before the image of Rose storming off flashed in her mind. Jules turned back to Cyn.

"Hey, Cyn. I just saw Rose... I tried to talk to her, but she blew me off. Do you know what that's about?"

Cyn shot a glance around the room before taking Jules's arm and hauling her through the club into the back halls. They stopped in front of a familiar closet. Jules's hand inadvertently stroked the faded stencil, *CRYSTAL*, written directly above the less faded *DELILAH*. She'd spent most of her life behind that door, one way or another.

With the beat of the music dampened, Jules turned to Cyn for answers. "The truth, Cyn. What's going on with Rose? She said she wasn't. But is she... is she using again?" Jules gulped after the question, afraid to hear the answer.

"No, no. Nothin' like that. It's worse." She took a deep breath and continued. "Her ex has been harassin' her again."

"Fuck. That asshole is still around?" Jason's gruff voice reminded her that he'd followed them back there.

"But Rose said Ghost wasn't the problem."

Cyn shook her head. "Nah, she ain't tellin' you the truth. He's been comin' 'round here, actin' a fool. He sneaks in somehow. We've had to kick him out several times and I've had to fire a few pansy-assed bouncers. I've got her comin' in under the radar. Eden and Confessionals only. No dancin', but still gettin' somethin' to pay bills. She ain't goin' on stage until he loses interest again. I have a sneakin' suspicion he's got some of my people in his pocket. There ain't no excuse for him showin' up outta nowhere like he has been. That's why I wanted somewhere more private to talk. Never know where his ears are."

"Has she called the cops?" Jules asked.

"No, nothin' to tell yet. Besides, them cops ain't what they used to be. We're keepin' an eye out. You should keep your head up, too."

"Why would he give a shit about me?"

"No tellin' what that maniac will do or who he'd get to do it. You're the one who convinced her to testify against him, so I figure you might have a target on you, too."

"She knew it was the right thing to do. She didn't need me to convince her of anything."

"Good Lord, for her sake, don't tell him that. I think one of the only reasons why he hasn't actually come after her is 'cause he's afraid of what you could do."

Jules snorted. "Lot of help it did last time."

"Why? What'd Jules do?" Jason asked.

Cyn cocked her head at him and grinned. "She didn't tell ya? That's a story I'll let her share. It's a good one too. The shithead had it comin'."

"Damn," Jules interrupted. "I want to be there for her, but she's not talking to me. I don't know how to get in touch with her anymore. Seeing her tonight was a total coincidence that didn't go well. She never gave me her number or address or anything. Nora can't find anything on her either."

"If she ain't told, I ain't tellin'."

"But Cyn—"

She took Jules's hand and squeezed with the other on top.

"Maybe that's what she needs right now to feel safe, to be untraceable. Rose has been one of my girls for years. Almost as long as you. If she wants to be left alone, I'll make it happen. She'll come out when she's ready, you know that. She's done it before."

Jules felt her eyes get hot and a lump grew in her throat as she tried to bite back the tears that threatened earlier in the night. It was a hard pill for her to swallow that she might not be what her friend needed, and she couldn't help the nagging feeling she was failing her... again. But Cyn was right. Jules had to be patient and let Rose come to her. Although she'd always been shit at waiting around. Jules was used to tackling every problem head-on. It's how she flew through high school and college, finishing law school by twenty-three years old, two years younger than most of her classmates.

"Come on Jules, let's go." Jason tugged her shoulders to follow him.

"You'll tell her, right? Tell her I'm here for her? That I-I miss her?" A lone tear fell down her face before she could stop it. She hoped the darkness hid it, but Cyn frowned as she nodded.

Jules wiped her face and turned on her heel, breaking free from Jason's grasp and bolted out of the back hallway.

"Jules... Jules! Wait," Jason called, trying to catch up with her quick clip.

She stopped abruptly to face him and he almost ran into her. "What, Jason? What? I'm having a shitty night, if you couldn't tell. What the hell do you want?" He started as if to say something, but logic must've gotten the best of him after seeing her death glare.

"Never mind," he answered.

"Good. Don't talk to me again until you have something important to say. Let's get the hell out of here and I'll drop you off at your apartment"

"But I drove to your apartment—"

Jules tightened her fists and bit back a frustrated scream. "Fine! Then I'll take you back to my apartment, where you can then leave to go to your apartment. I need a break from you, alright? I need to be alone for five fucking minutes, do you get that?"

She powered ahead of him to the exit. He followed her out like a shadow, never missing a step, all the way through the curtains into Eden's bar area.

"Jules!"

Oh, for the love of God. What now?

Behind the bar, Jezebel was waving a piece of paper like a white flag.

"What's that?"

"I dunno. One of the girls said they found it in a Confessional. It had your name on it."

Equal parts annoyed and intrigued, she took the paper and unfolded it. She brought it close to her face in the dark and read it. Her head grew light and if it weren't for the strong hands holding her up, she would've collapsed. With one hand holding her close, Jason snatched the paper with the other. His growl vibrated Jules's body until he erupted in a murderous roar that drowned out the pulsing bass.

The girl is up for sale. He can't go home.

CHAPTER TEN

My sister is being sold.

    The irony of his situation wasn't lost on him and Jason wondered if he was being punished for his past failures. At one point in his life, he'd expected to save everyone from a similar fate. After every good intention blew up in smoke, he didn't know how he was supposed to deal with the thought that Ellie might be suffering. If his former special ops unit was still in action, would they have prevented something like this from happening? One thing he knew for sure was that his teeth were going to grind into powder if he didn't stop clenching them.

    He and Jules had searched high and low in the past thirty-six hours, including while they were at Original Sin. When they received the note, they asked every customer and Sinner at OS—whether fully clothed or not—if they knew anything. No one seemed to have a clue, and Cyn refused to let Jason rough anyone up during questioning. He was using all the willpower and focus he'd cultivated in training during his time as a Night Stalker in the Army, and later as a MF7 black ops soldier. But he'd never endured terror like this. Knowing his sister was in immediate and grave danger was harder than jumping out of any helicopter, scarier than staring down any gun barrel. Each word of the note felt like a bomb being dropped over his head, and he'd never felt more powerless.

Despite the late hour, Jason had insisted on immediately reporting the note to Investigator Burgess. When Jules and Jason got to the precinct, they demanded to speak with Burgess even though he was technically off duty. But once he finally arrived, all hope for collaboration was lost.

If Jason never saw that fat, lazy, waste of taxpayer dollars again, it'd be too soon. By the time they were finished screaming at each other, he'd been three inches away from ripping the idiot's pornstache off and shoving it down his throat. It'd pissed him right the fuck off that Burgess didn't even take the note into evidence. He'd insinuated that either Jason or Jules had fabricated the letter. For what? Jason didn't know what shit the investigator told himself. It was too much of a coincidence for the letter to be inauthentic, and his gut told him it was important.

He'd made his indignation known by nearly poking his own finger into Burgess's eye while yelling in his face. He'd been promptly escorted out after that, which then pissed *Jules* off. Not only did she want to find Ellie, but she had to maintain some kind of relationship with these fuckwads and, apparently, they didn't take too kindly to her clients calling them "fuckwads" to their faces. So, both of them were pissed off, even hours later.

Thanks to the note, Jules hadn't wanted Jason to go home, which was fortunate for them both because he hadn't planned on leaving her alone. It was a fight he'd prepared for, but he was glad she'd put up no argument. Once they'd gotten to her swanky apartment she'd immediately gone to her room and shut the door. He'd posted up on the couch and tried to sleep the best he could. He knew he needed to be somewhat rested to find Ellie, but good shuteye eluded him with intermittent visions of Ellie as a child and nightmares of the present.

He'd tried to focus on the good. Ellie's and Sasha's playful shrieks as he pushed their swings in the park, getting the tar beat out of him in monopoly, her infectious belly laughs when he chased her around at Aunt Rachel's. But it hurt to realize he had so few memories of Ellie after her tenth birthday. He'd been an MF7 operative ever since then and when he got back into the States a few months ago, his anxiety had gotten the best of him, making it nearly impossible for him to go out and enjoy anything, let alone time with his sister. She'd grown up and he'd missed most of it. He vowed to change that as soon as they found her. He wouldn't let another day go by without getting to know his baby sister as the smart young woman she was becoming.

As soon as the sun came up, alert as ever, Jason had woken Jules up to go out searching. Jason didn't dare to say out loud that—because of the note—he now suspected the worst, and he could tell by the tenseness in Jules's movements that she felt the same. Without any other leads, searching aimlessly was their only recourse as they hoped to stumble on some sign that pointed them to Ellie.

They'd checked the hospitals again where there'd been a mix of relief and frustration to find neither she nor Sasha were being treated. They'd had no set destination, but instead scoped out Ellie's favorite haunts as soon as either of them thought of one. Jules, knowing teenaged Ellie way more than Jason, was able to think of places they hadn't tried yet, but all of them came up empty.

Every moment they took without finding her was another minute against the odds. They had a lead now—sort of—but no idea what to do with it. He'd hoped the police could help, but that had been an utter disaster. Jules kept reminding him not to get discouraged about the seconds of the forty-eight hours dwindling away. He understood what she was saying, that all the easy answers were found within the first forty-eight, and that Ellie could still be found after that. But it was only a small consolation when his imagination was running wild.

After a frustrating day with nothing to show for it, they were back at Jules's swanky apartment. It was posh as hell and he couldn't be prouder. It was a long way from a fucking closet in the back of a strip club. Jules was pacing and he was laying on her surprisingly comfortable pristine white couch, staring up at the ceiling and trying not to feel as defeated as they were.

He'd hated having to call Aunt Rachel and coming up with some bizarre excuse as to why Ellie hadn't come home yet. He still didn't want Aunt Rachel to freak-out and have a heart attack, but he didn't know how much longer he could put off telling her the truth. He turned to watch Jules as she paced. He wasn't sure how optimistic he could pretend to be if Jules wasn't helping him. No, that wasn't true. He knew. He'd be a fucking wreck. She was the only thing getting him through this nightmare.

Honestly, he felt lucky Jules was even still talking to him. Besides the fact that he'd been an insecure, selfish idiot seven years ago, his record lately hadn't been too shiny either. Since she'd walked back into his life, he'd been in handcuffs yesterday morning, been a perv last night, and gotten them kicked out of a police station in the early morning hours. God, his plan to woo her back was fucked.

He was encouraged, though, that she'd been the one to invite him to her apartment after searching all day. Granted, it was to come up with a game plan to find his sister and clear his name as a suspect... and if he were being *really* honest, she probably only suggested her apartment because she didn't trust him in public anymore. They'd been racking their brains and going in circles trying to figure out ways to find Ellie, but coming up empty.

"Is it five yet?" Jules asked, interrupting Jason's thoughts. She bit her lip and brushed her honey hair back as she checked her phone. "Five-oh-three. Finally. I need a fucking drink." Her bare feet sank into the plush carpet as she glided to the liquor cabinet. When she reached for glasses in the cabinet, Jason couldn't help watching her tight dress ride up her long legs. She'd insisted on looking ready for court even though all they did was search the town. At first, he'd been annoyed at having to wait. But he no longer minded when he saw her dressed in fabric that clung to her curves in a way that made his fingers tingle to do the same.

"You want one?"

He shook his head. "What?" he asked as he rubbed his hand over his face and sat up, trying not to think about pushing her up against the liquor cabinet.

She wiggled a whiskey glass in her hand. "I asked if you wanted a drink."

I want you.

He dismissed the idea as soon as he thought it. "Um, yeah. Sure. I could use one." Jules said it best. He was her client now, and he had to respect that. Still…

Being around her at OS the night before brought back vivid memories. Since coming home from his last mission as an MF7 operative, he'd noticed newfound hatred for a few things he used to love. Crowds and loud noises were at the top of the list and he'd about lost it at the club. Dulling his senses with alcohol and sticking close to Jules had been both a necessity and a comfort. They'd helped keep at bay the overwhelming urge to accidentally-on-purpose tear the closest speaker off the wall, drop kick it outside, and then never step foot back in again. Instead, he concentrated on all of the times he'd seen her up on the stage, grinding on a pole. It'd immediately made him harder than the steel she danced around the first time he saw her.

His friend, Hawk, a fellow ex-Night Stalker, got him the interview as a bouncer at Original Sin seven years ago. Jason was aimless at the time, having been honorably discharged for a few months. Even though he hadn't even wanted the damn job, he'd still been a ball of nerves at the interview. Stick him in the middle of a firefight any day, but put him in front of Cyn Turner? She's no southern belle and she suffers no fools.

The interview was held during off-hours while the women practiced. She'd asked him pointed questions and he'd answered to the best of his ability, staying focused on her the entire time out of fear that he'd say something stupid to piss her off. Turns out that was the trick. He'd gotten the job on the spot. Apparently, all a guy had to do to be hired as a bouncer at OS is pay attention to the task at hand. In other words: don't drool over the women.

Carefree teenaged Jason would've had a half chub every second of being a bouncer. But after Jason's parents passed and he became a soldier, he understood the weight of responsibility that came from having people depend on him. Knowing the dancers needed the money even more than he did, and that they were working their asses off for it, garnered the respect he needed to maintain a professional distance. There was mild flirtation, but nothing more. Not until...

Delilah.

The first time he ever saw her, she was performing something he'd learn was called a low flow dance—a combination of pole work, fluid dance, and floorwork. She was writhing on the floor in a sensual rhythm, her scantily clad breasts the highest point of her nearly naked body, her knees splayed, and her arms stretched out. Her face had been toward the crowd and he could swear she'd been looking right at him as he walked in. Their gazes locked and as she undulated on the floor, he imagined himself pistoning above her, her legs wrapped around him, his hands on her ass moving her body in time with his.

After that, he'd been obsessed.

He tried desperately to get her to flirt with him. She gave in a little, but mostly she was focused on doing her job well, getting her college degree, and getting into law school. It wasn't until after an extra "friendly" customer got too handsy that they'd finally gotten together.

Cyn ran a tight ship and hired men like Jason to keep perverts and violence away from the club. But thanks to Jules's feistiness, Jason hadn't even had to lift a finger. Though that certainly hadn't stopped him from doing it anyway. His heart was hers after that, and she'd seemed grateful he was there, even though he hadn't actually done a damn thing. Not only did she give him her *real* name—the ultimate sign of trust from a stripper—they became inseparable.

Except for when she practiced her performances, and for good reason—some of her moves scared him half to death. Before OS, Jason thought what everyone else did about stripping—a woman twirling around in ungodly high heels, shaking her ass, and taking her clothes off. What he found out was, yes, it's definitely that, but when done correctly, it's also a hell of a workout. If a pole dancer looks toned and fit, it's because she's been training her body to defy gravity.

Jules always insisted on challenging herself, and she took her craft seriously. He remembered the day she conquered the aptly named "Death Drop." Unbeknownst to him, she was working on one of the most dangerous moves in pole dancing, but because she'd refused to practice it in front of him, the first time he witnessed her do it was along with the rest of the customers during a performance.

With her black glossy fallen angel wings attached to her back, she'd climbed all the way up to the top of the fourteen-foot pole, in time with the throbbing music. Next, she'd flipped upside down, only hanging on by her legs as they wrapped tightly around the pole, eight inch high heeled black Pleasers poking the ceiling, and held her arms outstretched. Then she fucking dropped.

Jason had just about shit his pants.

Thankfully, she'd stopped with her nose mere *inches* away from the floor, hence the name, but other bouncers had to hold him back to prevent him from going on stage and death dropping her himself. After that, he'd demanded to see her dances before she performed them. Of course, she'd laughed in his face and he'd had to settle with having a heart attack watching them for the first time with everyone else.

He hadn't loved that she danced nearly naked in front of strangers every other night, but she'd refused any money he offered. At twenty-six, he hadn't yet come into his trust inheritance, but he wanted to help. Not just to get her off that damn stage, but also because he cared for her and wanted to see her achieve her dreams. Jules insisted on paying her own way and he respected the fuck out of her for it.

That isn't to say he didn't fantasize about her barely-there lingerie outfits and those long, tan, muscular legs wrapping around something much thicker than a fifty-millimeter chrome pole.

It was one of those wet dreams that nearly got him castrated last night when that bitch, Charity, came on to him. Being distracted as he was—from the loud noises, strobe lights, and the enticing nostalgia going through his head—he hadn't been able to extract himself from Charity's claws quickly enough before Jules saw the effect of his daydreams, *not* the effect Charity had on him.

It still pained him that Jules must've mistakenly thought his hard-on was for that fucking whore. Way back, he'd tried for months not to think the worst of that woman. Eventually, the fact that she'd throw herself at him every night, despite knowing that he and Jules were together, made him realize how manipulative she was.

"Jay!"

He jerked back to the present. "God, what?" A glass of amber was in his face and he automatically took it.

"Don't snap at me. I've been saying your name. Here's your drink."

Now with a glass of wine in her hand, she rolled the lip of the glass against her own and took a swig before continuing her thoughtful circles. She'd been pacing for a while, and Jason had made sure not to disturb her. He knew if he interfered with her process, she'd lose her train of thought and her shit along with it. She was an impatient thinker, prone to near lethal flashes of rage when interrupted. He took a swig of the old scotch and wondered why she had his favorite label in her cabinet.

With nothing to do but think, he meandered around her immaculate living room, waiting for her to come to a stopping point. He ran his hands along her full and dustless bookshelves and caressed the soft pillows covering the couch. Even though his sleep was restless, he knew for a fact they were comfy as hell despite looking brand new and unused. He reverently brushed his fingertips over various items around the room, wishing he could soak up the touches she'd freely given them.

But from looking at the perfectly staged apartment, he doubted she ever used the place. He stopped at a picture of an unbelievably happy couple and passively wondered who they were to her. He took another sip. They were obviously important since they earned a position in her meticulously decorated home, but the couple looked *too* perfect. Nice wooden frame though.

Finally, she came to a halt again on the rug.

"I think you should call your old team."

The scotch may have been expensive as hell but no liquor tastes good during a spit-take.

"Ugh, gross, that was about a hundred dollars you just spit out, ya big oaf." She unrolled a wad of paper towels and came to his rescue, all the while trying to stifle her one-glass-of-wine giggles. "I thought that only happened in movies." Her southern accent lightly coated each word. Apparently, wine was enough to make it come back out.

Her smile caught him off guard and Jason felt his chest rumble as her chuckles became infectious. Even though what they were talking about was damn serious, it felt good to enjoy the moment. It felt like before.

She eventually pulled herself together and continued to blot his shirt, carefully wiping the remnants of his surprise. Her hands pressing into his chest sparked his desire and by the time she patted down near the bottom of his tee, the effect her ministrations had on him was apparently too obvious for her not to notice.

She abruptly dropped the paper towel. "Good enough!" She turned around to refill her wine glass to the brim. When she tipped it back, Jason chuckled. The woman could dance naked in front of a hundred horny strangers, but confronting her own desires? It seemed as though she still hadn't conquered that fear. Jason decided he'd steer clear of that conversation, for now. From the way she gulped down her full glass and her frantic turns of the corkscrew on the new bottle, he could guess she wasn't open to any tough personal talks just yet.

"Another paycheck?" he asked, pivoting the conversation.

"What?"

"The scotch... was it a payment for another case? You know, like Larry?"

"Oh, uh, sure." She took another gulp. "But never mind that, don't change the subject. What do you think about calling them?"

What'd he think about calling the Crew? He thought it was the worst best idea she'd had. Getting in contact with them wouldn't be as easy as it would've been months ago. He hadn't spoken to anyone since they parted ways at the airport after their last MF7 mission failed horribly. They were supposed to be a specialized black ops team that extracted victims of human trafficking from their captors. It was too painful to think of what should've been their final rescue. The hard truth was, although they'd saved some lives, they'd made others' worse. Or they were lost altogether.

Both he and Hawk were recruited for the team of seven. Hawk tried to get Jason to go out for a beer with everyone since they'd gotten back, to hash things out with the rest of the Crew. He said it was important that they stick together for their sanity, to respect the lives that were lost. Jason made sure to ignore every call and text message. The nightmares were reminder enough.

"No."

"Jason, you heard Investigator Burgess, the cops aren't going to help us without more evidence and we can't do this alone. Your team has the skills to find people—"

"I can find people, too. I'm a goddamn bounty hunter, for Christ's sake!" He avoided admitting that he hadn't had a job since before he left, and that he'd lost all those contacts.

"But other than a ripped piece of paper, we have *no* leads and no resources. We have no choice—"

"We're not there yet, okay? I can do this," he growled.

Coward.

He shook his head, trying to get the voice out. He wasn't afraid, was he? He'd been doing fine without them. They didn't need the Crew.

"How do you even know about them anyway?"

She paused, turning away from him. She placed her empty glass on the table and poured more wine.

"Nora, my assistant. She looked for any mention of you in the news after the call from Andy. Strangely enough, she scoured the web and didn't find anything about Ellie. But she did find something... about you," she said, hesitating before she turned around. "I don't know much, except that you were in some military group in the Middle East and you and five others on your team were medically discharged... for psych reasons. After that women's shelter in the Middle East blew up? And the seventh..."

"Fuck." Her words triggered something in his brain. He breathed deeply through his nose, laced his fingers over the top of his head and abruptly turned away. But the memory stabbed at his brain like an ice pick threatening to paralyze him.

He held the trigger. He had the shot.

"Stand down! You could get Masuma!"

But he had the shot.

A sharp cry pierced the night, and the enemy laughed as he gripped the woman by her hair and threw her in front of him.

"I said, stand down!"

But he had the shot.

"Jason, it's okay, you can talk to me. All you have to do is get

in touch with one of your old team..." Her voice became distorted and he was having trouble understanding her muffled words.

"It wasn't a women's shel-Fuck..." *Fire. Screams.* He closed his eyes against the dark images and the moans of death that loudly filled his head every night. Except this time, the faces he'd only had a glimpse of became too familiar, as the women's hair grew long and bleached by the sun. Their faces were younger and lighter, with soft freckles over their noses. His sister's caramel eyes blinked wide everywhere he looked, red with tears as she cried out for him.

The girl is up for sale...

He swallowed against the thickness forming in his throat as he came to the shameful realization he was putting his own fears ahead of his sister's life. He couldn't allow any of it to happen again, and he tried to say as much, but he couldn't breathe. Relying on the Crew again... confronting his past... it could break him, but could he trade one nightmare for another?

Jules came up behind him and gently placed her hand on his back. He jolted away from the shock of her touch. He didn't deserve to be comforted.

"NO!" he yelled at her and his memories, the decision still on the tip of his tongue. He spun around and threw his hands down before trying another attempt at stabilizing his breath. "No-I can't, I just can't... I can't-I can't, Jules—"

Is this what hyperventilating feels like...

She closed the small space between them and rubbed her hands up and down his arms, soothing him. "Shh, shh, shh. It's okay. It's alright. We won't call them. Not yet."

"No..." The air he expelled came out in a whoosh. "You're right. We-we'll call them."

"Are you sure?" Her gaze searched his face.

He wrapped his arms around her and held on, anchoring his body to hers, his cheek rested on top of her soft, honey-brown hair.

"No. But it's the best chance Ellie's got."

Jules nodded and tried to break away again. "Let me get my phone."

He squeezed tighter. "Not just yet... can we... I'll call them, I promise." He breathed deeply until the air entered and exited his body at more normal intervals. "I need... let me just do this for a moment." Many of those deep breaths later, he felt, more than heard, her sigh and he tensed at what she would say next.

"Jay, I get you need time, but if at some point I have to do it for you, I will. The odds are already working against us. If we can't find her soon, it could be too late."

He nodded jerkily, knowing she was right. But dealing with the Crew *and* Ellie? It was all too much. Jules pressed against his chest lightly, but he refused to let her go. She slowly moved her hands from his chest and resumed rubbing his back.

"It'll be okay, Jay." The calming pressure she applied along his spine made his muscles relax and tense, simultaneously. He and Jules stayed that way for a while, holding and taking comfort from one another. Now that he had her in his arms, he didn't want to let her go.

He kissed the top of her head and, keeping one hand on her hip, pulled her closer. He loosened his grip so he could look into her eyes and see if she wanted him with the same intensity that he needed her. She brought her hands to his chest and continued kneading with her fingertips. She lifted her gaze to his and her cyan eyes burned as he tilted his face closer to hers. Closer and closer, he felt her warm breath caress his lips—

"Stop." The firm push against his pecs was an unwelcome surprise, but he immediately let go. "Jay, we can't do this. You're upset and vulnerable—"

"Hell, Jules, don't blame me. You know I want this, and I think you want it as bad as I do." He took a step toward her but she backed away and kept her defensive stance. He stutter-stepped to a stop as he realized the truth. "And that scares you, doesn't it?"

"We can't do this. You're my *client*. I have a code of ethics I follow as an attorney..." She babbled, but Jason stopped listening and went straight to the entry table. He grabbed what he wanted and riffled through it.

"What the hell are you doing? That's my purse!"

"And *this*"—he waved his prize in front of her— "is my five dollar bill!" He snapped it straight before he made a show of putting the bill in his pocket.

"Okay..." she said, her eyes narrowed.

"It was *my* five dollars and now it's in *my* pocket. I took it back." He pulled it out of his pocket and put it back in, as if in slow motion. At Jules's bewildered expression, he sighed. "I'm not your client anymore."

A look of understanding washed over her face and she shook her head hesitantly. "Let me rephrase... I won't do this."

"Why not, Jules? I *know* you want me. I *feel* you wanting me. I'm not acting on my own here. So, what the hell's stopping—"

"YOU!" Jules threw her hands up and started to pace again. "Us. There aren't many logical reasons *to* explore it. There are so many more reasons not to."

He scoffed. "Oh, yeah? Like what?"

She halted mid-turn. He stepped toward her but paused at her anguished groan.

"You... You... cheated on me, Jay. You left. And then..." She clutched her stomach and tried to collect herself before continuing. "How can I ever forget that? How can I ever... *forgive* that?" Her cry that escaped tore through his heart. "God, we were together for that one year... and it's been seven years since. You still make me a fucking mess."

His heart ached as he realized the problem. All those years ago, when Jules had talked about having a life together, a house with kids running all over the place, he'd been ecstatic but petrified. He wasn't sure how a fuckup like him could ever be father material. He wasn't even worth the spit to shine his stepfather's shoes. Greg Stone had been the greatest dad a kid could have.

He'd taken on a surly kid and treated him as his own. It's why Jason took his last name when his mother changed hers. He never knew his biological dad, and when they added Greg into the mix, their family felt complete. But Jason had been a troublemaker and his family had paid dearly for his mistakes.

Being afraid of fucking up a perfect family—again—caused nightmares back then. But he'd also been worried for Jules. The more she talked about being with him, the less she talked about her true passions. He'd been terrified that his life as a drifter would stop her from pursuing her dreams.

So, he'd told her the one lie he thought she'd never get over, that he'd fucked one of the Original Sinners behind her back. She'd been distraught. Heartbroken, he'd thought. He still remembered her crumpling to the ground as she asked, "Lies?" and he'd had to swallow all of his honor when he croaked out, "No lies." He'd waited for her to berate him, to scream or yell at him. But she'd just laid there and, with shame poisoning his soul, he'd left. Little did he know then that shame would continue to kill him slowly until she allowed him back into her life.

He'd signed on to a covert military unit that required complete and utter secrecy while they were cut off from everything back home. At the time, it seemed like a small price to pay to be a hero and save the world. MF7 had the lofty goal of ridding every nation of human trafficking and bringing the fuckers to justice, preferably in court, but by bullet if necessary. It was a noble cause, one that he felt if he completed, he would finally be worthy of the love Ellie and Jules freely gave.

He hadn't told Ellie exactly where he was going, just that he was "reupping" a tour. He'd hoped that Jules wouldn't care by the time he had to leave. He knew he didn't deserve for her to wait around for him, and he'd known if he gave her any hope, that's exactly what she'd do. She would've put her whole life on pause just to support him. But he didn't even know if he'd come back, and she needed to focus on bigger dreams than a life with him.

Choosing not to say goodbye was one of his biggest regrets.

But Jules didn't know that. Jules didn't know all of the guilt and shame he felt over his decision over the years. And Jason had no idea until last night that Charity apparently cast herself in the role of homewrecker. He'd had no intention of anyone ever corroborating his lie. How could she even think that he would slum it when he'd had the best?

Of course, she would think that. I never gave her any reason not to...

"Jules..."

"No, it's okay. I worked at a strip club, I understand... it's h-h-hard to keep away from temp-temptation sometimes—"

"Fuck that. That's not what this is about."

"Then explain it to me, *please!*" She wrapped her arms around herself and hugged tightly. Her bottom lip trembled as she valiantly kept tears from falling. "Please... tell me. I don't understand... I guess I never did."

He felt the weight of his body down to his toes. He hadn't fully realized it until that moment, but his burden had been so incredibly heavy, and he couldn't fucking stand it anymore. There was no reason to keep up the lie. The damage he'd done to himself? To Jules? He hoped it wasn't irreparable. He knew he didn't deserve it, but he desperately hoped she'd come back to him. With his next words, an unexpected relief poured from his bones.

"It wasn't true."

CHAPTER ELEVEN

"What?" Jules must've had too much wine.

"It wasn't true. I-I made it up. I never cheated on you."

She tried to quell her sudden wave of anger by grasping on to logic. She couldn't believe he had the nerve to fuck with her at that moment. "Who the hell lies when they're admitting to cheating? That makes no—"

"—no sense. I know. It's a long story, but I guess the short of it is… I was worried about you."

Jules's face scrunched. "What're you talking about?!" Her hands flew up in exasperation as she growled, "Worried about what?"

"A lot of things, okay?" He stepped toward her and held her arms down. His image wavered in her watery eyes, but she refused to blink in fear that a flood gate would open. "Look, I was a fucking idiot. I never should've said it. I had my reasons, but not one of them has seemed worth a damn since I left for that godforsaken desert. I've regretted it every moment I've been away from you."

Jules's chest tightened as she tried to process the information. She was going to pass out from the informational whiplash. "So, no Charity?"

"Oh *fuck* no. I'd never touch that woman."

"But... you just... left us?" She faltered and choked, she was giving too much away and she tried to reign the words back in. "Me and Ellie, I mean. You have no idea what I've been through. What that did to me. You... leaving."

"I know." He stood up tall and put her hands on his chest and cupped her face. She gripped his shirt tightly, her nails scratching his pecs. Agony flowed from him in waves, and Jules clung to him for dear life as she searched for the truth in his storm gray eyes.

"I'm sorry, Jules. I've made so many bad choices in my life. Lying to you? Leaving you? Hell, like you said, leaving *both* you and Ellie—those are by far the choices I regret most."

The tears she'd been holding fell silently down her cheeks. His thumbs gently wiped them away and he kissed her forehead, cupping her nape with one hand and holding tight around her lower back with the other. She couldn't believe they were having this conversation. His confession had caught her off guard. His emotions were eroding her walls, making them crumble and exposing the pain she'd hidden for years from him and the rest of the world.

Hell, could she forgive him? Maybe for some things, but not all of it. Never all of it. He could never know the depth of her heartache. But maybe, in this moment, they both needed each other.

She had to be a stubborn fool for even entertaining these thoughts. The *former* love of her life just told her that most of the terrible things she'd thought about him over the years weren't true. After so much time of thinking the worst about him, she didn't know if she could believe anything good. And even if she did, Jules didn't know if she could go where she knew they both wanted to go.

What does it matter if it doesn't go anywhere? It won't happen again... I just need... relief. We both do.

He wasn't a client anymore. It was due to a technicality of

course, but that'd always been enough for her. Who said you needed to be in love to have sex? She'd been exploiting that particular loophole since her last year of law school, and it hadn't stopped her since. Why should it now? They were two consenting adults in need of a stress reliever. Why not knock boots? But if it was casual, why did she need to know whether he lied or not?

I just need to know the truth.

She didn't know why it mattered so much. She just knew they had to get past this part. Past this pain. But just the thought of being with Jason again made her heated skin sensitive to the tight fabric of her dress. Awareness coursed through her body and her nipples hardened against her satin bra. After a steadying breath, she tried to regain her focus.

Jules lifted her head up and saw the deep hunger reciprocated in his eyes as he waited for her to make a decision—and immediately lost concentration again.

Just a yes or no. Casual. No big deal.

The warmth she felt sank and merged with the hunger in her core. Pulling his shirt taught, Jules brought him closer to her and his eyes flared in response. Her pride was holding her back. She usually met life head-on, but when Jason was involved? He always made her run off the tracks.

Damnit, it's just sex. Who cares?!

Still, she wanted to believe him. Something had always seemed off about how their relationship ended. But, with no evidence to the contrary, she'd eventually chalked the feeling up to pathetic hope.

Now that she allowed herself to think about it, Charity bragged for *years* but never gave specifics. There was one *huge* detail in particular that, if Charity had referenced it in her torture, would've been devastating corroboration. Even more than that, though, a little whisper of a memory floated to the surface.

"Lies?" Jules asked. She watched him and... he looked away.

"You weren't telling the truth, when I asked you."

"I know, I'm sorry—" He didn't get it and she was glad she hadn't revealed her smoking gun. It'd always bothered her that he'd refused to look her in the eyes when she'd thought she'd forced him to tell the truth. It was her experience that honest people kept eye contact and he'd never lost it before. Ever. The exchange was something they'd done for the entirety of their relationship. He'd known how important honesty was for her. Having an addict for a mother made Jules realize early on that telling the truth could literally be a life or death situation. He'd always respected that and made a point to meet her eyes when he responded. He couldn't face her that day, out of shame, she'd thought.

But, what if?

"When I asked you to tell me the truth..." Her heart pounded and she was so close to him she wondered if he could feel it pounding in her chest. She closed her eyes and gathered up her courage, still debating with herself what the smartest move should be. Without her sense of sight, the campfire scent of his body wash overwhelmed her with its heady pull. Opening up, she licked her lips and stared into the gray, making her decision, all the while looking for any sign of weakness.

"Lies?" She held her breath.

He moved a stray hair out of her face and held her close again, his thumbs grazing her throat as she swallowed. He met her gaze, straight on.

"No lies."

Jules gave in and tugged on Jason's shirt to crush his mouth to hers, causing a stitch to rip somewhere. They didn't give a shit. She felt soft pressure against her throat from his thumbs as they stroked her. His tongue swept into her mouth and she bit his bottom lip when it retreated back. He grunted and palmed her ass, lifting and carrying her to the dining table.

It's casual. No big deal.

Was this a bad idea? Definitely.

Had she forgiven him yet? Absolutely not.

Would she ever forgive him? Debatable.

She was hoping the answer would come to her after she came herself.

We'll cross that bridge when we come to it.

Sitting on the table, Jules shut her brain off and instinctively opened her legs for him to enter into her space. She was at a perfect height to feel the hard length of him pressed against her heated core. She grabbed the back of his neck and continued to kiss him, moaning when he sucked her lip. She reveled in the feel of his coarse fingertips as they stroked her outer thighs underneath her black bodycon dress, thankful for the easy access it provided him. His fingers slid to her thong and tugged, ripping in one swift pull.

With her dress around her waist and her sex completely bare to his thirsty eyes, he paused to trace the faint red line on her hip caused by the ripped lace. She quickly unbuckled and unbuttoned his pants, revealing his long, thick cock, still bound by his boxer briefs. While she was mesmerized, he grabbed the back of his shirt with one hand and slid it over his head, giving her a view of his hard abs and obliques.

She scratched her nails down the blue jay tattooed over his heart and his defined pecs to the top of his boxer briefs, pulling them down. She stopped and reverently wrapped her fingers around his length, sliding down the round head and relishing the velvet firmness. He hissed and his fingertips clung to the valley of her hips.

With one hand Jason gathered her hair and lifted her chin to face him. Still holding his cock, she swirled her thumb around the glistening tip and she tasted her cherry lip balm as she licked her lips in anticipation. When she finally met his gaze, his eyes were stern, his grip strong, and there was no doubt he would leave fingerprints.

"Jules, if we do this—"

Precum slowly seeped over her fingers from his swollen tip, but Jason jerked her hair back, forcing her to look at him.

"When we do this, it changes everything. You hear me? I'm not letting you go after this."

His eyes were dark with intensity and she found she couldn't hold his stare. She giggled nervously and tried to hide behind a careless smirk.

"Shut up, Jay." She bent down to get a taste and her tongue swiped up the salty liquid coating the head until she was roughly brought to sit up straight.

"No." He growled. With his fingers still tangled in her hair, the pain sparked a twisted pleasure. He grabbed one of her ass cheeks and brought her to the edge of the hardwood. He lined his thick cock up to her core, and squeezing her close to create pressure, he slid up and down her folds, hitting her clit just right as he soaked his cock with her readiness.

"Fuck, baby," he gritted between clenched teeth, clearly having trouble holding on to his restraint.

He held on to her neck and his other hand took her own and placed it on the table to keep her steady. When he massaged his tip on her clit, she moaned and closed her eyes, but he tugged her hair to look at him again. She bit her lip hard enough to draw blood. The pain spiking at various points on her body tasted delicious. He lined up the tip of his cock and entered just slightly as he filled her vision.

"This"—he pierced her with one swift stroke— "changes everything."

He held her head, making her confront the heated yearning in his cool gray eyes, until she nodded, overcome with so much desire and anticipation that she'd agree to, or do... anything. To. Get. Him. To. Move.

"Oh my God, please Jay." She was going to hyperventilate if he didn't give her some relief. She wanted to feel every inch of him deep inside.

"You feel me, baby? You feel what you do to me?" He carefully withdrew, only to reenter at an agonizingly slow pace. "I've been hard for you since you walked into that police station."

"Yes, I feel you, Jay. Please…"

He continued the slow assault against her pussy, and she couldn't stand it. She looked down to see him and groaned as she watched every ridge disappear, right before feeling them inside her.

"Please… Jay… please, I need—"

"Tell me what you need." He chuckled darkly, no doubt feeling full of himself, too. She glared at him and lifted slightly off the table. She grinned mischievously and purposely dug her nails into the back of his neck until he took a sharp breath.

"Fucking… MOVE." She squeezed her inner muscles around him and was satisfied by his strangled gasp. He grabbed her ass roughly with both hands and pulled out enough to slam back into her, forcing both of them to moan. Barely on the edge of the table, it was easy for him to piston into her back and forth without pause. She held on to his trap muscles as his neck tensed and he gritted his teeth.

"Need to taste you," she breathed. Wrapping her knees around him, she lifted herself up completely off the table to kiss him. He moved his hands to get a better grip and held her close as he stumbled back. His pants were still halfway up so her landing against the sheetrock was hardly soft as he barreled her into the nearby wall. The stock photo beside her crashed to the ground. She didn't care though, she'd only bought it for the pretty frame. She hadn't had the time, nor a cutesy photo to fill it anyway.

Their tongues fought and their teeth clashed together. With her back against the wall she was able to get more leverage so Jason didn't have to do all the work. She got a better grip with her legs and wrapped around him like a fireman spin on a pole. He moaned when she rolled her hips with him inside. Letting go of her altogether, he leaned his forearms against the wall, on either side of her head, and met her stroke for stroke.

"Fuck, baby. I don't know how I lasted so long without you. Never again, Jules. Never. Again."

Her eyes filled and burned so she shut them against his words. She didn't want to hear it, but her body felt differently as her core tightened around him. He growled into her ear, nipping the lobe, making her cry out at the sharp pain. Higher and higher, she climbed that invisible peak, but she couldn't catch her breath. In tune just like he'd always been, Jason took over. He lifted her again with one forearm and pounded into her, surely leaving a dent in the wall. Her moans became more frequent and grew to a higher pitch.

"Yeah, that's it, baby. I can feel you tighten around me. Come for me."

Damn, but was he right. He could bring her right to the edge just by talking to her like that. She was so, *so* close. She gripped her nails into his back, taking advantage of the rhythmic grind of the rough skin and hair above his cock against her swollen clit. He paused for a second to resituate his arm—

"No, no, no, no, no, Jaybaby *please*—" The plea ended on a desperate moan as his right thumb found her clit and he pushed himself back in, to the hilt.

"Don't worry. I got you. I've always got you." He lifted her face and brushed her hair back so he could look into her eyes as she nodded. He picked up the pace again. She dug her hands into his short hair and hung on as he plunged his cock into her at a punishing speed. "I *said*, come for me."

The pleasure was so intense as she climbed that peak, until finally...

Finally...

She crested and moaned loud and long, her breaths punctuated by his rhythm. He kept up the pace even though her tightening contractions gripped his cock like a vice. It felt endless. Nirvana.

As she came down from her high, his thrusts grew uncontrolled and he shoved his face into her neck, biting hard enough to sting. Her inner muscles squeezed in response and he gave one last stroke until he was flush up against the bottom of her thighs. He pulled her impossibly closer and rumbled a loud groan through his gritted teeth as he released warm jets of cum deep inside her.

Their ragged breaths filled the silence, neither one knowing what to say in the moment. As Jason's tense, muscled body relaxed, one of his hands massaged the nape of her neck, releasing any leftover tension enough that she began to slide down his body. Luckily, his forearm still holding her caught her and he lifted her up to meet his stormy eyes.

I could get lost in those eyes, forever.

Shit.

Her pulse began to beat frantically as she realized where her heart—*no brain, keep that stupid heart out of it*—was going. She could *not* go there again with him. This had to be casual. She'd nearly ruined her whole damn life over mourning a breakup caused—apparently—by one fucked-up lie. She was in a good place. She couldn't let trivial hormones take over and let it all come crashing down again.

I have to create some distance. She cleared her throat slightly and Jason sucked in a harsh breath.

Her lips mumbled nonsense and Jules wiggled until he let her go and she slid down. They both groaned again as he slipped out of her, still mostly hard. She backed away on limp legs, trying to straighten her dress and tug it down further than it was made to go. Jason stood up, pulling his pants up partially, and put his hands on his hips, eyebrow raised, obviously waiting for her to say something.

Hell, I'd like to know what to say right now, too. She took a deep breath.

"So, um, thanks."

"*Thanks?*" The look of bewilderment on his face, with that damn eyebrow raised to the ceiling and his mouth hanging open, would've been funny if she hadn't been mortified.

Thanks? Who the hell thanks someone after the best sex they've had in years?

She wanted to say something profound. Something that would downplay how irrevocably lifechanging sex with Jason was. Still. She couldn't believe she'd forgotten how good it had been. He'd been her first, and over time, she'd tried to convince herself that was the reason her body had always been so responsive to his. Damn, was she wrong. She stood up straight and let out a cleansing breath.

Despite the fact that their bodies seemed made for one another, that his touch lit a fire on her skin, and that he intuitively knew just what she needed... Nope, it most definitely could not happen again. He was a distraction, and pole dancing had taught her the hard way that distractions could hurt a girl if she couldn't get a grip. Plus, he'd left her once, over some vague-as-hell bullshit. Who was to say he wouldn't do it again?

"Um, yeah. Thanks. It was great, but..." She cleared her throat more roughly and squeezed her legs together, trying not to think about his cum dripping down the inside of her thigh as she unceremoniously kicked him out of her apartment. "You should probably leave. Like now. There's nothing we can really do right now. Nothing that requires us being together, at least. I've got clients to call and bills to pay and since I'm not even getting five dollars from you..." She laughed and picked up his shirt, handing it to him as she became mesmerized by his strong hands buckling his belt.

"Jules, what the hell? We need to talk about th—"

She tore her gaze from his hands. "I'm clean!" she blurted out, her cheeks immediately reddening at her outburst.

The confusion stuck in his narrowed eyes as he pulled his shirt back over his head. "What?"

Don't look at his abs. Don't look at his abs. Don't... look at his abs...

"I said, 'I'm clean.'" She cleared her throat. "I was tested. After Andy. He'd cheated on me—sort of, I guess—so... yeah... there hasn't been anyone since. And that was a while ago."

At his silent stare, she filled the empty air with babbling.

"I mean it was stupid not to be safe. We should've used a condom, obviously. I always use a condom and God knows where you've been, right?" Her laugh drifted into the air and landed like a brick. She cleared her throat again. "So, yeah, anyway. I'm clean."

He nodded slowly and his lips tightened. "Yeah. Me too."

"You're clean, or... it's been a while... or?"

"Yeah." He was looking around the room as if to find something, but he hadn't come with anything else.

"Okay. Well good, um. You need to probably go home, right?"

"I'm not leaving you, Jules. We need to talk about this, and there's Ellie..."

Pain pricked her heart. How could they have gotten so carried away when Ellie was missing? Granted, there wasn't much that could be done at the time, and emotions made people do crazy things.... Still, it was unacceptable.

Jules blew out another breath, but it was doing nothing to calm her heart rate or assuage the guilt that was creeping in. "Okay, yeah. You're right. But I need at least a little break, Jay. I-I'm sorry, but this is all too much. Can't you at least go get some clothes or something?"

He kept that stormy gaze on her until she met his eyes. Whatever he saw in them, must've convinced him she needed the space. "Then come right back?" he hedged.

Her eyes clenched shut and she answered, "Yes, fine. Then you can come back. Although I don't know for what purpose. I guess you can sleep on the couch again. In case the cops find something or we figure something out."

He nodded and seemed like he was going to finally leave, until he paused and turned back to her. "What about—"

"What about what?" she interrupted.

"What about birth control?"

She flinched but waved her hand away at his question. She

couldn't fault him for not knowing. It needed to be asked. "That... that's taken care of."

His mouth opened and closed, as if to say more. Then he shook his head and grabbed his keys from the entry table.

Watching him reach for the door handle to leave, the sudden pang in her chest surprised her. She wondered what he was thinking. But since she was incredibly relieved he hadn't pressured her with any "so what does this mean" conversational bullshit, she let her curiosity slide.

She rushed around him to open the door and, before he left, he bent down and kissed her. It wasn't overtly sexual, but neither was it chaste. It was a promise. Of what, she wasn't sure, but she'd be lying to herself if she said she wasn't excited. She could've ripped herself away from it, but one kiss wasn't going to hurt. Not after the skin-tingling sex they'd just had. They parted, and she resisted slipping her tongue between her lips to taste what was left of him.

"I'll be right back. I'm giving you what you need now, but you're gonna face this with me. This isn't the end of this conversation... or us." He smirked and winked at her before he waltzed down the hallway of her apartment building.

"No Jay, it's over. That was the last time!" she yelled without thinking.

He turned around, going backward and smiled wide.

"Sure it was, Jules. Whatever you say." He laughed and pressed the elevator button.

"When you come back, you better act like nothing happened, you hear me? I mean it, Jay! No more!"

He kept his eyes on hers as the steel doors chimed open. "Lies?" he asked loudly.

Her eyes narrowed and she crossed her arms.

I can say it. If he can lie, I can too, she thought.

The elevator chimed again.

He gave her another infuriatingly smug wink and stepped inside.

Letting out a deep growl of frustration, she stomped her foot like a child before slamming her apartment door.

As she leaned against it, she closed her eyes.

It's casual. No big deal.

She repeated the mantra even though she could've sworn she heard his cocky ass laughing all the way down to the lobby.

CHAPTER TWELVE

"What the fuck did they know?" A man growled. Ellie tried her best to listen through the haze to the other side of the phone call. Strangely, she felt she had to have her eyes open as she listened or she couldn't keep track of the conversation. Her body was having a hard time doing even one thing, let alone two. Some senses were more vivid than others at times, but whatever she'd been drugged with prevented sight, smell, and touch from working together to paint a complete picture.

"Alright. It's not good, but not a game changer. I think it will be resolved when you find the girl. That should be imminent, right? Even if the DA sorts that shit out, everything should be in place by then and we won't have need of you for a while." He paused, listening.

"*What*?!"

Ellie blinked slowly. Time was passing at odd intervals when her eyes closed. Her lids cracked for as long as she could hold them up. She needed information—desperate to escape.

"No, I can't tell you when the next shipment will come in. That's not the priority. You're going to just have to wait. Besides, I need you sharp until the auction. If this goes bad, it goes bad for *all* of us." He listened and then held the phone's speaker close to his mouth. "What does that mean? I'll tell you what it means. Not only will you lose your score, you pathetic piece of shit, you can kiss your pretty pension goodbye, you fucking hear me?" The man sneered, his faint Russian accent laced with anger.

He threw the phone across the hotel room and Ellie faintly registered that if she had all her faculties, she would've jumped at the explosive reaction. Instead, her barely open eyes wandered of their own accord. She and all the other girls were spread out in the hotel room. Since Ellie had been there, they'd been moved from either the bathroom or the bedroom at random intervals. From what she could tell, their movement depended on ease of access for the revolving door of men. It seemed that the number of women had stayed the same. Ellie wasn't sure because she'd been in and out of lucidity, but she thought at least two more had been *handled*. Like Sasha.

There were less hazy times than others. But even those moments felt like she was watching from the ceiling, screaming at herself to escape, to help, to do something. But she never did. Instead, that was when she used the toilet or passed around the cup of water they shared in the bathroom. She couldn't remember if she'd eaten. Hopelessness drifted in on waves of nausea. Or maybe that was a side effect of the drugs. She thought she remembered someone saying there was something... special about the rest of them.

Lucky us...

She blinked and could tell from their voices that the two Russian henchmen and Fancy were there with the angry man. Her brain latched on to the familiarity in Fancy's voice every time he spoke, but her head was too heavy to lift and her eyes weren't cooperating enough to confirm her suspicions. He was still emotional, but trying his darndest to keep it together. She probably wouldn't have noticed how high-strung he was if his fingers weren't so perfectly square in her fading vision.

Thumb to pointer, thumb to middle, thumb to ring, thumb to pinky. Thumb to pinky, thumb to ring, thumb to middle, thumb to pointer.

Thumb to pointer... The jittery energy was oddly mesmerizing to her heavy eyes.

Angry's yelling wasn't helping Fancy's nerves. How long had he been there? Was he there the whole time? She didn't even know how long *she'd* been there. She tried to count the days but couldn't get her numbers straight. They kept getting jumbled up with music in her head.

Happy birthday to me...happy birthday to me...happy birthday dear Ellie—

"GODDAMNIT! They know too much. *How* do they know about the auction? WHAT... THE... FUCK?" Angry's arm flashed out and grabbed Sidekick. His accent became more pronounced and turned into a guttural roar as he used his strength and fury to choke the Russian henchman. The other two men watched and stared, Fancy's whimpers a dead giveaway he wasn't used to violence. When Ellie blinked her eyes open again, Sidekick was curled on the ground, coughing.

"We have a spy." Angry paced, his steps muted in the hotel carpet. "I need to call Nikolai. Tell him to lay low."

Someone's throat cleared before Fancy spoke in a cautious voice. "Dmitri, uh, sir, do you think we should abandon the operation?"

"What? Fuck no! Are you out of your goddamn mind?"

"It's just, a girl has already died—"

"You're right, and maybe if *someone* could have helped control the fucked-up idiot who can't keep his pecker in his pants—"

"I know, I couldn't stop him! Believe me, I wanted to. But if we're going to be found out, shouldn't we minimize the damage and our liability? Maybe it's best if we just... return the rest?"

Ellie's heart couldn't help but skip a beat at the proposition, even though she knew on some level that would never happen. She'd been praying Jason would come save her. In her imagination, he'd bust down the door, guns blazing, and snatch her up. She could almost feel his strong arms enveloping her in one of his huge bear hugs. The ones he freely gave when she was a child. If she ever saw him again, she'd bulldoze down the wall he'd erected since coming back from his last military stint. She could tell he was ashamed of the way he'd just up and left them without a trace. Ellie had been so excited when he finally came back, but he'd been distant and obviously hurt deeply by whatever happened to him. Some sister she was. Instead of helping him, she'd capitalized on his pain by using him. Now look where it'd gotten her.

She vowed to herself that after he came to save her—and she had to believe that he would—she'd do everything in her power to save him back. Ellie would try her darndest, but if she couldn't do it alone, she'd make Jules get on board. By herself, Jules was a force to be reckoned with, so together, there was no way his walls could stay intact. Maybe then they could get their Jason back.

"Um, Dmitri? Sir? What do you think of my idea?"

Ellie could feel the heat from Angry's glare and wondered why Fancy didn't just shut up. It obviously wasn't going to do any good.

"You listen to me, boy. You're not much better than that prick. His stupid code names and shit makes him think he's playing a fucking game. I'm not playing a fucking game. Are you playing a fucking game?

"N-n-no, sir."

"Good. Now, I'm allowing you to get in on this as a favor to your father. If you can't handle it—"

"I can *handle* it. I'm just wondering how wise it would be to continue."

Angry resumed his pacing and muttering while Sidekick regained his breath and slowly stood up.

"We think we know spy. Spy is just a rat." He spat at the end of the sentence, as if he was so disgusted by a spy, he had to get the idea out of his mouth. "Rat is easy to catch. We find rat, *ser*. We do this thing. They find girl soon and heat off us, *da*? If that not work, we have plan for woman, too, *da*? If she is gone, no more trouble." His voice was rougher than before, but his words made Angry stop and tap his chin.

"You know who the spy is? W-what if there is no spy? How do we even know there's a spy?" Fancy blabbered on, but none of the men were listening.

"Yes. Do that. Good plan Gor, we need to take care of that bitch if the original plan doesn't work. Without her, there's no way he's going free. I'm trusting you men to finish this job." He made his way toward the door, closer to Ellie.

"Is everything ready for the next location?"

"*Da, ser.*"

"Next location? What location?"

"Well you can't stay here the whole time, idiot. These things require constant movement. Someone's bound to have noticed the... *noises*. A different holding area would lessen the probability of someone trying to stick their noses where they don't belong."

"B-but, if we leave, won't that cause more attention too?"

"No." Angry's curt answer hissed through his teeth, brooking no further response except for someone's audible gulp. Probably Fancy's.

"I don't want to be called again for another goddamn body. We can't lose any more. Vlad, Gor, you're paid *handsomely* to figure this type of shit out yourselves. This is a fucking waste of my time. Am I clear?"

He seemed satisfied by their mumbled, "*Da, ser.*"

"Good. I have a client meeting. You stay here until further instructions." More nods. "Vlad, walk with me."

Angry and Honcho stepped over Ellie and stopped at the door. Their words decreased to a hushed whisper.

"You watch him. The idiot looks like he's about to crack."

"*Da, ser.* I keep eye out for him *and* rat." The two stared at one another until Ellie's eyes closed again. When they opened, everything was black.

CHAPTER THIRTEEN

There's no way I'm gonna let this be a one-off, Jason thought as he drove to his apartment. Jules was crazy if she actually believed he'd leave her after what they'd just shared. Although, if he was being honest with himself, he knew he didn't have a good track record.

I'll just have to show her.

He still couldn't believe he'd finally gotten to taste her kiss again. Her lips were softer than he remembered but his own still felt raw from her plush assault. How had he forgotten the delicious sting of her scratches down his neck and back? And as for the rest of her... Damn. The tangible memory of her velvet grip on his bare cock was making him hard all over again. Jules was the only woman he'd ever gone bare with, and it was intoxicating. He couldn't wait to get drunk off her again. Shit, he couldn't wait to do more than that.

He shook his head slightly and he covered his wide grin with his hand as his elbow rested on the door of his truck. All it took was one taste and the dam broke. Everything he'd never let himself have with Jules flooded back in and filled his heart to the brim with hope for their future. A brief vision of her, round with their baby, flashed in his mind and he grinned at the possibility.

The thought had terrified him seven years ago. The fear of chaining her to him forever and letting her down rode him hard into making stupid decisions for the both of them. But now? Now the thought thrilled him.

He didn't know which switch had flipped to kick his ass in gear but damn was he thankful for the motivation. The first couple of months he'd been back, he'd been too chicken to contact her. After that, he started watching her, listening for news about her. It was creepy as hell, but he'd never had the courage for anything more. He'd tried to get answers from anyone and everything.

He'd even enlisted Ellie. She desperately wanted them to get back together and even told him she constantly talked him up to Jules. He didn't want to get the poor girl's hopes up, so he'd only questioned her occasionally and covertly. He'd asked about Asshat and, at first, her noncommittal answers tortured him. They got him thinking either Ellie was being a good friend and keeping Jules's relationship a secret. Or worse, being a good sister and trying to protect him from the harsh truth.

But the more he asked, the more he realized that, although Jules and Ellie were as close as sisters, there were still some things Jules kept close to the vest. Ellie was giving him the same vague answers that Jules was no doubt giving her. He'd only known about the prick from the inevitable small town gossip and local newspapers at Drop, the only decent coffee shop in town. But he hadn't known the truth of the rumors until the phone call in the McLaren.

Hearing Jules confirm the end of her non-relationship with Asshat was a balm to a wound he didn't deserve to have healed. Realizing this could be his do-over with Jules gave him new life. He couldn't fuck it up again.

There'll be no end this time.

He moved his hand from his mouth and grinned like a fool, allowing himself to be happy in the moment. Thank God for Ellie, his sweet little enabler—always ready for recon and to put a good word in for her big bro. He couldn't wait to tell her he was going to go for it. Try again. Ellie would be so—

He swerved on the road as he realized what he'd just done.

Ellie...

He cursed and slammed his hand against the steering wheel. How the fuck could he forget her for even one second? The girl was an angel and he didn't want to begin to imagine the hell she was being put through by whatever bastards had her. He'd seen enough to know the knowledge would drive him insane.

And what was he doing while she suffered? Having a great fucking time. Literally. Trying to get back together with his ex, dreaming about his bright future. Meanwhile, his baby sister may not have a future at all.

What is wrong with me?

His chest tightened with guilt as he berated himself, because really, who does that kind of shit while their sister's life is on the line? He could rationalize with himself that both he and Jules had lived lives where compartmentalization was survival. In her childhood, if she'd dwelled on all the things that were wrong, she would've never made it out sane. She most likely still experienced it as a criminal defense attorney, that need for separation. Same went for his life with the military and MF7. He knew, from personal and professional experience, the ocean of pain and heartbreak people with constant stress in their lives could set aside to experience a drop of normalcy or relief.

He had plenty of reasons and excuses, but none of them mattered. None of them would get Ellie home. The rubber steering wheel cracked under his grip's damaging squeeze, and the soft pop brought him back to his senses.

Guilt wouldn't do anyone any kind of good. His shaky hand massaged his forehead to the point of pain as he tried to focus. He and Jules had at least made some kind of plan. He was getting his clothes and they were going to call the Crew.

He'd tried for months to forget about them, everything they'd done, but as the hours passed by with no Ellie and no other clues, it was looking more and more like Jules was right. He'd been thinking about involving them himself, but he wanted to try literally everything else before that. Confronting those demons might kill him. At the least drive him insane. He spun his phone around in his right hand. He needed to call Hawk—

"I said, stand down!"

He hesitated until the percussive bomb blew him back against the wall. Fire blistered his skin. Screams tortured his ear drums. He spat out the taste of metal on his tongue and choked as he inhaled the stench of burned flesh—

He rubbed his nose and shook his head violently against the flashback. "I'll call when I get home," he told himself aloud. His promise settled on the air until it felt just as suffocating as his memories.

He forced his concentration on getting lost in strategizing any unanswered questions. And it worked—for the most part. Who the fuck was selling women? Why did they want Ellie? Was this about him? About what happened on their last mission? Was it about Jules since she was the one who got the note? Who of his bounty hunter contacts could be helpful? Were there any that would still give him the time of day? He hadn't been active since before he left for MF7. He'd come into his trust money and the inheritance was enough that most went to Ellie and Aunt Rachel. The rest was either saved or used to sustain his Spartan lifestyle—just enough to get by. Maybe Jules could ask around with her clients? He didn't know how that worked.

He made the final turn into his section of the apartment complex when a barrage of flashing lights blinded his vision.

"What the... hell?" he murmured.

The back of his apartment building was cordoned off and flooded with the black and blue uniforms of law enforcement and EMS personnel, along with the bright red of the fire department. He would've noticed them if he hadn't been so preoccupied.

What the fuck happened?

He hoped everyone inside was okay. He didn't care about any of his stuff. His apartment consisted of the necessities—bed, fridge, TV. Nothing to miss there. He slowed when an officer flagged him down.

"What's going on? Is everyone okay?" he asked, panic creeping in for the other residents of the building.

"Do you live here, sir? This area is under police investigation."

"Yeah, I live here. What's going on? Are the other residents alright?"

"Name?" The officer looked down at some papers on a clipboard and made some notes.

"Jason Stone," he huffed, growing frustrated at her lack of answers.

The pen in the officer's hand stilled and she raised her head. She spoke some gibberish over the radio on her shoulder and waited. Nonsense was repeated back and she nodded, apparently hearing what she needed.

"Mr. Stone, why don't you park right over there?"

Her tight smile made him uneasy. "No. Why don't you tell me what's going on?"

Too casually, she slid her free hand to the side of her hip, near her Glock 22. "Sir, go ahead and park or get on out the truck. Alright? We've just got some questions for you and I'm sure you know why we're here. This can be easy or hard."

A furtive glance confirmed the other officers in the vicinity were also on edge, their steps toward his truck seemed nonchalant, but every single one of them had a hand resting on the butt of their firearm.

What the actual fuck?

"Over there?" He mimicked her finger point and she gave a small nod, her hand tentatively falling away from her belt. He pasted on his false smile and put the car in drive.

"Thanks officer, headin' that way." A sweat broke out on his brow and his palms stuck to the steering wheel. He didn't know what was going on, but as he slowly rolled his truck where the officer had indicated, he felt in his bones that he needed to leave.

At the last second, he did an about-face and booked it to escape the parking lot. Immediately, two police vehicles converged across the exit, effectively blocking him. His beat-up pickup wasn't gonna make it out in one piece if he tried to go through.

In the blink of an eye, he was surrounded by yelling deputies and pointed guns. It'd been a long-ass time since he'd had that many bullets aimed at him. He knew all too well the manic happiness of a trigger finger and held up his hands.

"I'm coming out!" he yelled. He made all the necessary movements to turn the truck off while one hand remained raised. His entire body vibrated with the need to run. He was a cornered mouse in a snake hole, but he didn't know how he'd gotten trapped inside.

He opened the door and stepped out. Dozens of commands blasted against his ears as his hands were ripped from their surrendering position and handcuffed behind his back. His feet were kicked out from beneath and his knees and cheek landed roughly on the grated asphalt parking lot. He wanted to fight back. MF7 had taught him some nasty tricks on how to get out of a jam, but he knew if he pulled those out on tens of officers, he was as good as gone.

Eventually, an officer announced that the cuffs were double-locked for tightness and Jason was hauled to a police car. A small crowd was forming behind the caution tape.

"Can someone tell me what the *fuck* is going on? Why am I handcuffed? I want to talk to my attorney!" he demanded in a last ditch effort to get them to respond. It was the third goddamn time in less than thirty-six hours that cops were giving him the runaround and treating him like a criminal.

"Calling your attorney already, Stone? Only the guilty know when they're that fucked." The rough smoker's voice was all too familiar and Stone whipped his head around to the speaker.

Investigator Burgess wasn't looking so good with his hair sticking straight out and bloodshot eyes.

Knowing Burgess would twist anything else Jason said, he slammed his mouth shut, locking his jaw until his teeth were on the brink of grinding to dust. The escorting officer put his hand on the crown of Jason's head to force him into the back of the cop car. Before he could step forward to get in, he noticed movement in the corner of his eye.

Several EMTs were solemnly rolling a gurney from the alley behind his building. The chatter around him quieted as everyone watched the silent parade of paramedics. The push on his head lessened and he halted on the foothold of the police SUV. After a few seconds, the only sound was that of one of the wheels squeaking as it turned uselessly on its leg. At first, the procession was so unexpected, all he could do was follow it to the ambulance.

Holy shit. His body stilled and his stomach leadened. The small black body bag on the gurney cracked any self-control he had left. Burgess stepped into his field of vision and Jason tried to search behind him.

"Who—"

"Don't act like you don't know who that is, you sick fuck. With what you did to her—" Burgess spat. "You thought you could play the worried brother card, but I saw right through you."

Ellie.

"No, no, no, no, no, no. NO! *ELLIE!*" He started fighting the officer, refusing to get into the car and trying to get to the ambulance before it drove away. The siren wasn't even on. Why wasn't the siren on? What did that mean? He knew a body bag meant too late, but his brain wasn't functioning past the horrible reality. A wave of nausea crippled him as the worst fear of his life gripped him in its truth.

"It was a pretty stupid fucking move to dump her body behind your own damn apartment."

"NO!" he roared, thrashing about blindly until he felt a sharp tingling sensation and the immediate loss of control of his limbs. He vaguely felt the abrasive pavement on his cheek as he crashed to the ground again.

Rage and scuffed boots filled his vision.

"Aguilar didn't listen but I knew it was you all along, boy."

Jason was picked up roughly by his arms and his weight was barely supported by uncooperative legs. Much shorter than Jason, Burgess was eye level with him now that Jason was temporarily paralyzed.

"You know, in prison? They don't much like men who fuck and kill young girls. You'll get yours." Burgess took a drag of his cigarette and flicked the ashes in Jason's face.

Jason couldn't feel the rest of his dazed body, but the acute pain of failure stabbed his heart. An anguished roar escaped from deep within his chest. He hadn't saved them. *Again.*

"Jason Stone, you are being arrested for the kidnap, rape, and murder…"

He'd joined MF7 for many reasons, one of which was to stop women from being sold, used, and discarded. He'd seen how they were treated all over the world.

"You have the right to remain silent…"

The screams intermingled with the rasps of the barely living and the stench of the burning flesh of the dead.

He'd tried desperately to save them. All of them.

He'd failed.

CHAPTER FOURTEEN

Clickclackclickclackclickclack.

The staccato of her heels on the godforsaken government tile work was faster than a firing squad at an execution. Jules was finally allowed to see Jason after he'd been arrested late last night. The station where he was being held before his bond hearing didn't allow visitors until morning, so she'd had to wait. That, plus the fact she'd had to park on the street made her skin crawl with frustration over potentially being late for his bond hearing in eighteen minutes.

The new parking attendant at the judicial center complex told her it was closed to non-court personnel for the day, so she'd been forced to park in the only spot left on the street. Now, there was almost no time to speak with her client prior to his arraignment and the threat of being unprepared for one of the most important arguments of her life was driving her insane. Never slowing down, she took a meditative breath to compartmentalize her feelings from the job she had to do. She focused on resisting the urge to gnaw at her fingers. She was already going to have to make a nail appointment as soon as this nightmare was over.

Jason was officially charged with rape, murder, and two

counts of kidnapping. Sasha had been found brutally murdered and callously tossed into a dumpster behind Jason's apartment. The cops had come to the most convenient conclusion that since Sasha was found there, there'd been probable cause Jason had taken Ellie, too. He was facing life without parole, if they were lucky. If politics got involved, however, he could be looking at the death penalty.

A somber sense of déjà vu crept into her mindless ramblings as she entered the station. Whispers she usually reveled in were distorted to a judgmental din. The heated glares of hatred were new and uncomfortably stifling, but she held her head high. That was the job. Defense attorneys are the last line of defense for the innocent, and normally she'd stomp right up to one of the self-righteous officers gossiping... *if* that were the only reason for their scorn.

Unfortunately, they were no doubt thinking of the last time she and Jason were at the station and he'd shown his ass. She probably had some friendships to mend and more enemies to watch for. Combine that animosity with the tragic death allegedly involving her client... she knew there would be no pleasantries.

Everyone hates a murderer.

Especially if he took the life of a pretty, innocent, young woman.

Jules's calves were on fire as she finished her power walk to the all too familiar interrogation room. She didn't hesitate and barged in to find officers hovering over a man in a faded orange jumpsuit.

"Thank you, gentlemen. That'll be all. I'll let you know when we're finished. You can uncuff him while you're at it," she said calmly. The officers stood ramrod straight and one of them coughed.

"Ma'am, he needs to be cuffed and you need someone to supervise the visit, for your safety."

"Actually, he doesn't and I don't. He's the client, I'm the

attorney, which means cuffs off and you—" She pointed at them and then the door. "Out."

Since they'd thought he was dangerous before he'd even been charged, asking for the cuffs to come off was a stretch. But if she didn't ask for it, it wouldn't happen, and Jules hoped her forcefulness would scare them into obedience.

But no one budged, and one of them had the audacity to cross his arms at her. She rolled her shoulders back and stalked to within inches of them as she spoke.

"Let me make this very clear for you. My client has a court hearing in fifteen minutes and I have to speak to the judge *before* that in five. Which means you are wasting my time. If I don't get a chance to talk to my client prior to his bond hearing, I'll have no problem telling the press afterward that the police prevented this man from speaking to his attorney. Sheriff Motts is up for reelection this year, isn't he? I don't think he'd take too kindly to having reporters question him about denying American citizens their fundamental Constitutional rights. Bottom line? Heads. Will. Roll."

She stared at them straight on, but the officers averted their eyes. With furtive glances at one another while one of them fiddled with his handcuff key, Jules could tell they were uneasy as to whether to listen to the pretty little lady or follow orders. She felt they could successfully comply with both.

"Uncuff him. Now. And get. The *fuck*. Out." She never raised her voice, but her steely scowl fractured their resolve. Officer Brown snapped to it and quickly uncuffed Jason before they hustled out.

With all the restraint she could muster, she softly shut the door behind them and sagged against the warped glass. She closed her eyes and exhaled all the rage and sadness that accumulated the past few hours.

"I gotta tell ya, Jay. Representing you is a freakin' roller coaster—" She was abruptly picked up by her waist and shoved against the hard cement wall of the corner of the room.

"God, Jay, what the hell are you doing? Cameras! If they come in here right now, you'll never get a freaking bond," she hissed. The station wasn't "allowed" to have their audio/visual equipment going when attorneys were meeting with their clients, but she knew all too well that some officers conveniently forgot to turn the system off.

He jerked his head to the only camera in the room, above their heads, to indicate that they were out of view. His closeness made it possible for them to whisper, their position protecting them from being seen or heard.

He'd plastered them against the wall. His hands and arms caged her inside and he sunk his face into her hair. Her heart raced from the anxiety of getting caught and—even as inappropriate as it was—the enticing firmness of his body against hers. She breathed deeply to calm herself down, but was filled with more of his scent, pine and woodsmoke.

"It wasn't me. I didn't kill Sasha. I sure as hell didn't kill my sister. You have to believe me. You have to... I-I thought..." Warm air puffed against her neck, causing her to shiver. "I thought it was El in that body bag. I fucking lost it, Jules," he breathed, his lips brushing the shell of her ear. She turned to whisper back.

"I know." The two words were simple, but she felt the tension in his body loosen in relief at the sincerity behind them. "That means she's alive."

"But what if—"

She gripped the back of his neck and tugged him even closer. "No. That means she's out there. Waiting for you to rescue her."

He shook, trying to choke back a sob before it escaped.

"It has to mean that you understand?"

After a few breaths he nodded and rested his forehead on her collarbone.

"You have to be smart, Jaybaby. Keep your cool. I can get you out of this, I swear."

"I don't give a fuck what happens to me. You have to find her. It's been forty-eight hours, Jules. She can't be gone. She... can't..."

She felt him shudder against her, and confronted with his vulnerability, she finally succumbed to her own. She blinked back tears as her heart broke into a thousand pieces at the fear that time might be up. She knew what the timeline technically meant, but it was hard to separate it logically when she was flooded with emotional memories of Ellie.

At one point, Ellie had been the only thing that glued together the tattered remnants of Jason and Jules's relationship. When Jason left, Ellie was all Jules had and she leaned on the young girl more than she should've. That's how Ellie became so much more than just a tie to her ex. Jules finally lowered her walls enough to admit that the past few days without her felt like she was missing her own sister. Even without his plea, she would have used every resource in her power to find her. She knew the only thing keeping Jason afloat was the fact that Ellie's body hadn't been found. They had to choose to think that meant she was still alive.

She wrapped her arms around him and kissed his neck, trying to provide any comfort she could. "I'm so sorry. I'll find her. I'll get you out and I'll find her. I promise you." She went to kiss his neck again but he turned at just the right angle and captured her lips with his. His hands traveled to the small of her back, and pulled her in, aiming to soothe them both. The pose under different circumstances would've made her ache with desire, and she knew he felt the same when his hardness pressed against her soft belly.

It was wrong. It was insane. It was insensitive. But their bodies were responding to what had become a constant barrage of highly stressful and emotional crises. The mind, body, and soul, could only withstand so much for so long. Any relief was welcome, so giving in, even just a little, was like stepping on carpet after wearing heels all day. Her knees buckled and Jason caught her with his thigh between her legs, scooting up her skirt and holding her in place.

The sudden intimate contact brought her back to the moment and she gently pushed him away. There would be a time and place they could explore this further. *If* they should explore it further. In an interrogation room with him in the county's finest orange uniform was not it.

His stormy eyes met hers and she nearly caved at the hurt behind them. She would do anything to keep the pain away.

Even ruin my career? Endanger his case? Probably his life?

The questions struck a nerve and the severity of the situation shocked her back to reality. She shuddered as she mentally stripped herself of the emotions she'd allowed in, and suited the armor of responsibility and learned detachment back into place. No matter what was happening, she couldn't lose sight of how hard she worked, especially if her rash behavior could somehow jeopardize Jason's case. Ellie's *life*. If the media found out she and Jason were together... Jules grew lightheaded at the thought. She didn't have the capacity for the morbid creativity for which the media was known, so she couldn't possibly imagine the ramifications. She knew if she didn't keep it in her skirt, multiple lives could be destroyed.

Sasha's parents had already come out and demanded whoever was responsible be prosecuted to the fullest extent of the law. Jules didn't blame them. Not one bit. In fact, she would demand it too, only for the right defendant. She feared what a vindictive jury and judge could mean for Jason.

Juries were fickle, and twelve "peers" could easily turn into mob mentality when they saw the evil involved in the case. She'd witnessed firsthand how juries can forget the facts entirely and search to blame any man called "defendant." Without a shadow of a doubt Jason was innocent, but whoever was behind this was trying hard to make him look otherwise.

Jason stepped back but moved his hands to hold tight to her upper arms.

"I promise. I'll do everything I can, okay?" She put as much conviction in her voice as she could muster. "Can you tell me anything? Anything at all that could help me get you out of this? I know DNA will absolve you, but that analysis takes time we don't have."

He shook his head as he stepped away, his hands scrubbing back and forth against his short hair. Jules immediately missed his warmth. She nodded and smoothed her suit, the black and chevron Armani jacket was slightly off her shoulder where his lips had brushed her skin. Her black dress had ridden up to reveal the lacy tops of her thigh-highs and she tugged the hem of her skirt back down. When she felt composed enough, she looked back to her client only to find an incorrigible grin on his face.

"Really, Jay? You're gonna be a smug bastard at a time like this?" She chastised and waved her hand around, indicating the four cement walls surrounding them. He scowled and plopped himself back into the chair behind the table to which he was supposed to have been handcuffed. She immediately felt guilty and nearly reached out to console him before the door swung open.

"Miss Bellerose, ma'am... Mr. Stone has to go back to his cell now. His arraignment is gonna start soon."

"Thanks, Henry. I was just about to leave." The rookie blushed when she called him by his first name and quickly moved out of her way as she made for the door. Just before she left, she turned to find Jason's gaze singularly on her.

"Trust me, Jay." He nodded once and she walked resolutely all the way out of the station to the austere government building across the street.

She had a job to do.

CHAPTER FIFTEEN

"Counselor? The judge will see you shortly."

Jules nodded at Judge Powell's dowdy, but pleasant, administrative assistant and took the opportunity to mentally prepare her argument for the judge. She had to be convincing enough to get Jason out on a bond he had no business being granted. Crimes as serious as Jason's usually meant the person stayed in jail until their trial date, which could take months. Years. Not only did he not deserve that, they didn't have time for it. The best chance they had at finding Ellie was together, and they couldn't do that if Jason was rotting away for a crime he never committed.

For the first time in her career, Jules was worried. Nerves about court were a given, but she'd never truly been afraid for her clients. She typically approached each case methodically, rarely allowing her feelings to play a part.

Sometimes her clients were obviously innocent. Most of the time they were guilty as the devil himself. All she could do in those instances was her best to make sure their prosecution was just and fair. Contrary to recent public opinion and screwed up media narratives, not everyone is wrongfully accused. If she had to put a number to it, at least seventy percent of her clients had done exactly what they were accused of, twenty had done something equally bad or even worse, nine percent were probably overcharged, and a whole whopping one percent were honest to God in the wrong place at the wrong time, trusting the wrong people. She worked equally hard for all of them because everyone deserves proper justice and their day in court. Everyone deserves a second chance, and she'd argue to the death for that belief, but it was up to juries and judges to grant them.

However, this case was personal for Jules and she was having trouble maintaining her trained impartiality. She was terrified Jason wouldn't be able to get out of jail. Finding the body of the defendant's missing sister's best friend, in the dumpster behind the defendant's apartment no less, is a dead ringer for a guilty verdict. Pardon the pun. Of course, she could—and would—argue how stupid it was for a trained military operative to dispose of a body in such a careless way, but it was hard to say whether a jury would care about logic. They tended to vote on the side of whatever answers were easiest, even if they didn't always make the most common sense. And the thought of someone she cared about being locked up, and wrongfully at that, twisted her stomach to the point of pain.

No. She berated herself. She couldn't let her thoughts go there. Instead, she let her mind wander until she paused on her memory of Jason in his orange jumpsuit. Which brought her back to the moments he had her against the wall in the interrogation room. And inevitably her train of thought derailed into the gutter as she remembered another time he had her up against the wall.

Was that really less than twenty-four hours ago? She still couldn't believe she'd slept with a client. *Well, not a client anymore, per se,* reminding herself of his cheeky five dollar stunt. Still, it went against every oath she'd taken. 'Never mix business with pleasure' was an adage older than her professors who preached it, yet she'd brazenly ignored the warning.

And what a fucking pleasure it was.

She shook her head. *God what is wrong with me? Not the time.* She was off her game and realized that if she didn't analyze her situation with Jason soon, she was in danger of being incapable of the separation she needed to perform at her best. Later... that'd have to come later.

Later? Later when? When your friend is found dead? Or when the only man you ever loved is convicted for her murder? She put her fingers to her temples to will away the negative inner monologue. It was so not helpful at the moment, and Judge Powell's administrative assistant looked at her with a curious expression more than once.

I don't blame you, Suze. I'm sure I look like a loon.

Jules took a deep breath and held it, attempting to keep a hold on at least one thought. She was never so distracted, and it couldn't have been at a worse time. There were too many lives on the line.

Moral of the story? Don't fuck clients. Especially not ones you've wanted to have babies with... The thought was too full of pain and loss, but did the trick as it stabbed at her heart enough to clear her head for the task at hand. She needed to convince Judge Powell to grant Jason bail.

Depending on who I'm up against, it could be a—

Her opponent strode into the small waiting area.

—piece of cake.

CHAPTER SIXTEEN

Jules sat back with her arms crossed and a cocky smile she couldn't hide as Assistant District Attorney Marco Aguilar shook Susanna's hand. The admin's plump cheeks blushed and she beamed at one of his compliments. Jules knew from experience the warmth of his attention would linger for the rest of the day.

Jules smiled when he turned to her. "Marco. As I live and breathe."

He gave a poor attempt at looking disappointed as he turned, but the brightness in his dark eyes and the grin he couldn't contain said differently. Before Jules could stop him, he gripped her arms and kissed her on the cheek. She breathed through the heat attempting to rise up her neck and into her face, conscious of what his familiarity might imply to nosy Susanna.

The administrative assistant tsked and shuffled paperwork loudly. Jules refrained from rolling her eyes, but she had no doubt that by lunchtime, the entire courthouse would be gossiping about how flirtatious *Jules* was. To his credit, Marco winced at Susanna's passive aggressive display and mouthed an apology.

Jules waved her hand at it and shrugged. It was a nuisance,

but nothing she hadn't heard before, especially considering the job she held prior to becoming a lawyer. Being a stripper before and during law school wasn't something she'd advertised, but the Ashland County Bar Association was a relatively small group of lawyers. Many of them were her classmates at the time, and many of the rest liked to pretend they hadn't seen her perform live. It was better to keep her head high than bow low in the face of judgment by small-minded people. Besides, petty gossip was certainly nothing a box of breakroom Hot-N-Ready donuts couldn't fix.

"Juliet Bellerose, what did I do to deserve to see you again so soon?" Marco joked. His wide smile sparkled against his darker skin and she remembered why she'd fallen into his bed more than once in law school.

"I don't know, but you might wanna beg for forgiveness."

He tipped his head back and laughed. He stepped closer, but Jules smoothly went back to her chair and lounged, well out of the way of his charismatic pull. As a dancer, she'd perfected the art of polite distancing from unwanted advances and had since used the skill a disheartening amount as a female attorney.

Thankfully, Susanna called them into Judge Powell's chambers before Marco could continue his pursuit.

The statuesque dark-skinned woman stood behind her desk, thumbing through the written motions and orders blanketing its mahogany surface. Seemingly finding the file she was searching for, Judge Powell gracefully took her seat, her regal poise rivaling any queen's.

"Counselors, what can I help you with today? I understand you'd like to speak to me about a—" she glanced over the case file "—Mr. Jason Stone and his imminent bond arraignment?" Her practiced dry tone made unfamiliar and inexperienced attorneys uncomfortable. They thought she was either bored, uninterested, or uninformed about their case when, in actuality, she knew more about the facts than the lawyers did.

Judge Powell was one of the toughest and fairest judges in

the entire southeast, if not the nation. Jules practiced all over and had the honor of being in front of her a number of times. She was intimidating as hell, but if there was ever someone she idolized, it was B.A.B. Judge Powell. Not that Jules would *ever* tell her idol that she mentally called her a Boss Ass Bitch, although knowing the judge she'd probably get a damn kick out of it.

"Yes, Your Honor, my client—Mr. Stone—has recently been arrested for several charges for which we would ask you to consider a bail—"

"*Murder*, being just one of the many violent offenses, Your Honor. I would like to clarify that," Marco interrupted and Jules stopped herself from glaring at him. He was doing his job, just like she was.

"Yes. That is one of the *allegations*," Jules contended. "But I can assure you he is being wrongfully accused. There's no way he could have done what the State claims. If you'll allow me, I'd like to take this opportunity to explain the extraordinary circumstances..." Judge Powell assessed them both as she settled into her high-backed leather chair, eventually nodding her head for Jules to make her case.

She explained how Ellie texted Jason and asked him to dinner but Jason had backed out and never saw his sister. She drew attention to the fact that the cell phones had been conspicuously planted in front of Jason's apartment door, and how he, being a law-abiding veteran and all, turned them in, thinking they would help find Ellie. She hit hard that Jason's history included saving women from tragic fates such as Sasha's. More difficult was trying to simultaneously gloss over and emphasize the fact that Jules had been around him nearly twenty-four seven in the past forty-eight hours, and it would've been impossible for him to hold hostage, rape, murder, and dump Sasha's body, let alone keep Ellie hostage as well.

"You see, Your Honor, Mr. Stone should be granted a bond, and the defense would welcome *any* amount, at the court's discretion. I can assure you he isn't a flight risk and will appear in court, and, as I've laid out, he is absolutely no danger to anyone in the community, especially not his sister."

Judge Powell dipped her chin at Jules before she gave her regard to Marco.

He stepped forward and cleared his throat, eyeing Jules curiously as he spoke. "Your Honor, Jason Stone is charged with heinous violent crimes, with one of the victim's whereabouts still unknown. He can't be let out onto the streets. He's a danger to the community and must stay in jail until his court date. At the very least, the State would ask Your Honor to consider that the defendant injured officers before he was finally subdued by a taser. It's going to be hard to convince—"

"Of course, he fought the police!" Jules interrupted. "He believed he'd just seen his sister in a body bag and he was rightfully emotional and terrified at what could have possibly happened—"

"That may be the case, Judge," Marco continued over Jules's objections. "But it would be the position of the State that you deny bond. We... we respectfully disagree with the defense." He dipped his head and stepped back.

Jules's brows raised involuntarily at Marco's abrupt conclusion, and she quickly schooled her face to hide her surprise at his half-assed argument. If the judge thought the same, she was better at hiding it than Jules. She and Marco patiently awaited the judge's decision.

After a few brief moments, Judge Powell, sat up and templed long manicured fingers together as she spoke.

"Assistant District Attorney Aguilar, based on the defense counsel's presentation, do *you* believe Mr. Stone committed this crime? This is off the record, of course, but I'm intrigued." She bore her dark eyes into his. A lesser man would've caved under her stare, but Marco kept his cool. Although in her periphery, Jules saw Marco's fidgeting fingers behind his back. The only indication he was uncomfortable at the directness of the judge's question. Jules avoided his eyes boring into her profile as he spoke.

"Judge, to be frank, I recognize that Ms. Bellerose's assessment of the case is compelling. She and I went to law school together, and I have to admit, I ask her opinion in unaffiliated cases from time to time. I respect her judgment..." The two women waited for him to finish. He'd obviously hoped he was done, but under the judge's heavy scrutiny he realized he had to come completely clean. His feet shifted their weight as he continued.

"The facts before the State are tenuous and circumstantial at best. We would leave the decision of granting Jason Stone a bond amount and allowing him out of jail before his court date at the court's discretion." He bowed slightly and retreated, having conceded as far as his government position would allow.

Judge Powell turned away from them both as she thought over their arguments. Marco's eyes flicked toward Jules's and she silently mouthed, *Thank you*. He quickly averted his gaze forward.

Jules knew how much Marco was jeopardizing for her. His noncommittal answers were prosecutor-speak for siding with defense counsel. It was a decision a state attorney could potentially lose his job over. She didn't know why he was taking such a risk, but her heart stuttered over the anxiety of yet another person depending on her. Trusting her. Despite everything she knew in her bones, that Jason was innocent, anything could happen. If something went terribly wrong, even some unknown and unforeseeable anomaly, Marco could now lose his job, too. Even though it'd been Marco's choice to say his piece, she couldn't help but feel like that debt would be hers to pay.

They waited patiently for Judge Powell's decision as she sat, looking out the window, contemplating all the possible outcomes, no doubt. Basically, it was up to her whether a purported murderer should be free to roam the streets before he was given his day in court. America was the land of the free and home to "innocent until proven guilty," but rarely did someone go back out into the world with allegations as severe as Jason's.

Minutes passed and Jules barely resisted flooding the silence with irrelevant rambling. After an eternity, Judge Powell finally made her decision.

"I'll grant the defense's motion. Mr. Stone will be able to get out of jail if he is able to pay bond. I will see you both at the hearing where you will once again argue and I will make the decision public record, at which point in time, this preliminary ruling shall be final."

Jules closed her eyes briefly as cleansing relief washed over her. She allowed herself that one moment, no longer than a blink, before opening her eyes again.

"Thank you, Judge. You won't regret this."

Judge Powell's brow nearly rose to the hairline of her shortly cropped natural hair as she crossed her arms. "You see that I don't, Ms. Bellerose. I don't make a habit of being wrong."

Jules laughed nervously and shook hands before exiting. Even though Marco essentially lost, he customarily thanked the Judge and followed closely behind. They waited until they were well out of earshot before speaking. Reporters crowded the bottom steps of the courthouse, wanting an exclusive soundbite from the ADA or defense attorney on the recent murder case.

"Jason's clothes... I have to get them from Larry so he can look semi-respectable for when he gets out. I'll meet you at the hearing, okay?"

Although Jules wasn't able to visit Jason earlier than that morning, she was able to get his apartment key from the jail inventory. She'd been optimistic and hoped Jason would be released after the hearing, so she'd stopped by his place to retrieve his clothes before meeting with him. When she'd walked inside, the bare walls, plain bed, and empty kitchen clutched at her heart. She'd reluctantly reminded herself that, although her apartment was chicly decorated, it was no more lived in. She barely had enough time to sleep, let alone enjoy it. She'd dreamed of a *home* since she was toddling around, dodging dingy carpet stains in the government housing she'd shared with her mother. She'd like to say she wanted to be infinitely busy, but lately Jules felt like she was missing... something.

"You know bail's gonna be millions of dollars. You think he really has the money to pay for that?" Marco scoffed, then halted at the top of the stairs. "Oh shit, why are you smiling like that?"

"I'm disappointed, Marco," Jules tsked, lacing her tone with false concern as she shook her head. "I would've thought you'd be more familiar with your case."

"Spit it out, Bellerose."

"Jason Stone? Son of Kathy Pinckney of the Carolina Pinckneys, and stepson to Greg Stone? Both of whom made millions independently, then pooled their resources together, and split them into trusts that Jason had access to when he turned thirty?"

"No!" Marco gasped and brought the side of his hand up to his mouth in a fist before sliding it over his hair. "Damn... why didn't I know that?"

Jules shrugged. "You were always slack at doing your homework."

He made a frustrated noise and gently tugged Jules by the elbow, leading her away from the reporters and toward her car. She'd anticipated the thirsty mob, so although she'd been forced to park near the street, she'd chosen one of the few spots inconspicuously on the opposite side of the main entrance so as to avoid the vultures snapping for scraps. When she and Marco were nearly to her car, he stopped.

"You really think he didn't do it, Jules?" He spoke in a quick whisper so the group rushing toward them couldn't hear their conversation. As she searched his face, blessedly devoid of any inner turmoil, she knew that, for whatever reason, he believed Jason was innocent, too. He just needed reassurance. Jules made a point to look square into his eyes as she answered.

"He didn't do it, Marco. I swear." She held his hand and squeezed as she spoke. "We've worked together. You know me and you know I wouldn't back a monster who did *any* of what Investigator Burgess is claiming."

Marco squeezed her hand back and nodded as he ran his other hand through his soft moussed black hair.

"I thought so. Damn, Burgess really fucked this one up. He's got a hard-on for your boy for some reason. You got any idea who could be behind that girl's murder?"

Jules purposely ignored the part of his assessment where Jason was "her boy" and firmly shook her head, wishing she had any name to give him. She could tell that he, too, was frustrated that someone so dangerous was still on the loose, and most likely with his next victim, Ellie, as the judicial system wasted energy on the wrong suspect.

"I don't. But I'm going to find out. All we have as a lead is that note, and that's a damn mystery."

"What note?" Marco's brow furrowed and Jules's mouth opened and closed several times as she searched for what to say.

"Did Burgess not tell you?" At Marco's shaking head, she told him about finding the note and Investigator Burgess's insistence that they'd fabricated it.

Marco cursed. "Burgess, *tu hijo de puta*. That motherfucker. I had no idea. Something's going on with him lately. I'll try and get him to look in a different direction. It won't be easy, but I'll see what I can do. We gotta put the right asshole in a cell for good."

Jules relaxed at his words. "Thank you. I'll tell Jason that you so-called good guys are gonna start actually looking for the right bad one."

Marco pursed his lips and cocked his head.

"Is he the one?"

Caught off guard, Jules sidestepped from what she feared he was asking. "No, of course he's not the one who did this. I just told you that."

Marco chuckled and groaned. "Don't be an ass. You know what I mean. Is he the one who kept you from staying the night?"

Jules blushed. She and Marco had their one-night stands periodically beginning in their third year of law school. She'd thought she'd finally gotten over Jason and needed to blow off steam. It'd only ever been casual, but every time Marco tried to persuade her to make it more, she'd politely shot him down.

His fingertips brushed against her rosy cheek and he sighed. "Damn. He is, isn't he? What a lucky bastard."

She shifted away from his touch and his hands found his pockets.

"Did I ever have a chance at all?" His dark chocolate eyes penetrated her heart and her voice cracked as she spoke.

"N-no. I'm sorry. I tried to be up front—"

"I know, I know. But a man can dream, right?" Marco shrugged and backed away to a distance more appropriate for a conversation between two colleagues than lovers. He laughed good-naturedly and the ache in Jules's chest loosened. She cherished Marco's friendship and was thankful it would remain intact. Yes, she'd had great sex with him from time to time. But she'd always been honest that their friends-with-benefits situation could never go further. It hurt to know that a dear friend of hers had held out hope for something she'd never had the capacity to give. Whether she'd wanted to admit it or not at the time, her heart had been full for someone else. She was still afraid that was the case.

Marco cleared his throat. "Hey, park good 'ol Larry in the personnel parking lot. It's safer back there. Some crazies are coming out of the woodwork on this one."

"Psh... Larry's fine." Jules chuckled, thankful for the segue. "Don't be so dramatic. Besides, it's closed to non-court personnel today."

"Closed?" His face scrunched in confusion. "That's weird. They must've changed their minds because plenty of non-courts were parked there when I got in this morning. Anyways, just move Larry before the hearing. You'll be able to avoid the press on the way back in, yeah? Plus, it's away from the street.

Wouldn't want the handsome man to get injured." He laughed at his own joke. He'd thought it was hilarious when she named her prized possession Larry and refused to leave her alone about it.

She rolled her eyes and grinned. "*Fine*. But if that attendant kicks me out again and I lose this spot, too, I'm gonna be pissed. Especially if I'm late for the hearing because I've been driving all over the damn complex."

The crowd was closing in, their boom mics raised like swords ready to charge. They were slowed thanks to a couple of officers trying to keep Jules and Marco from being bombarded.

"Mr. Aguilar—"

"Ms. Bellerose—"

"—Is it true a war veteran raped and murdered his own sister?"

"Will he plead guilty—"

"Can you comment on—"

The wake of vultures positioning over their kill was oppressive until Jules felt Marco's hand lightly touch her elbow.

"Sounds like my cue. See you back at the hearing, *sirenita*." He winked, straightened his tie, and turned on that killer politician smile. John F. Kennedy, Jr., himself, would've been jealous of that handsome mug. The prosecutor always knew how to schmooze his way out of a situation.

Jules made a break for it and dug into her purse for her keys. The yelling behind her grew louder and she tried not to let it spike her nerves. There was no use for anxiety right before court. She found her key fob, but in her haste to get away from the mob, she dropped it and watched it skitter under a nearby public trash can.

"Shit..."

She bent behind the trash can to retrieve the fob and pressed the button right before she got up, unlocking her car with a *bleep-bleep*—

BOOM!

Her body was blown back from the percussive explosion, and

heat enveloped her. She tried to get up, but the pain in her head and waist kept her still. Dust and shards of metal pricked at her skin like tiny fiberglass splinters. The sharp tang of ozone stung her nose and filled her lungs until they were too full to breathe. Sharp cries drowned out all thought as she tried to close her eyes against the shrill.

It took an agonizing moment to realize the screams were her own.

CHAPTER SEVENTEEN

"Holy shit! That hot lawyer bitch just got blown the fuck up!"
Fucking action movies. They never get the real thing right.
Jason rolled his eyes and refused to devote his attention to trash television when, instead, he could spend his abundant free time moping in his seat in the rec room of the county jail. He couldn't believe he was locked up. Not while his own sister was out there. Hopefully alive.
NO. Definitely alive.
Jules was right, they couldn't think any other way or he'd go certifiably insane and blow *these* assholes up himself. They wouldn't have to watch some shitty movie to get their kicks.
The jail tried so hard to make sure everyone was docile toward one another, or at the very least separated from dangerous people and materials. Little did they know they had a MF7 Weapons Sergeant in their midst. Jason prided himself on being the MacGyver of the Crew. Just from one cursory sweep, he found five objects that would make for a mighty fine weapon, and if he tried harder, maybe even a bomb.
Good thing he was an actual law-abiding citizen and not the piece of shit rapist murderer Investigator Burgess claimed he was. Or else the place could already be up in flames.

Can't think like that. Jules will get me out of this.

They'd find Ellie together, with a little help. Recent events scared him into finally deciding calling the Crew as soon as possible would be a smart move. He had to face his fears some time, and yeah, being confronted with the people who witnessed and suffered from the worst mistakes of his life would be hard... but now that he'd faced the harsh possibility that his sister could die if he didn't suck up his grief and pride? That shit would be on him, and he'd literally never recover. Seeing Sasha's body bag taught him that.

He sat making a game plan, until the *whooping* and *oh shits* of the peanut gallery near the TV became too distracting. Against his better judgment, he got up and joined the crowd. Hell, maybe getting his mind off reality and on trashy bullshit would do him some good.

"Yo, man! They're startin' the vid over. Dude, it's sick, yo! Watch!"

He took the skinny drug dealer for his word and watched the screen. To his surprise, he saw Jules... with that ADA motherfucker. He felt heat rise up on the back of his neck and his fists clenched and unclenched. They had a history, no doubt. He didn't know what it was, but the idea that *any* man had a taste of what was his? Of his Jules? It made his blood burn and he wanted to rip the guy apart. Not that the ADA was small. The suit might even be a good fight. But Jason sure as shit wouldn't let the guy think he had a chance with her again.

Don't tell Jules that. He chuckled to himself wryly. Jules wouldn't even want him after knowing he thought "possessive male BS" like that. *Whatever.* He could say what he wanted inside his own head... so long as it never got to Jules. The woman was a damn mind reader.

Jason couldn't draw his eyes away as the ADA touched *his* woman's elbow and pulled her in to speak to her. Touching *his* woman's cheek. The fist around his heart squeezed to the point of pain, but he couldn't look away from the display.

Was she happy to speak with him? Did she wish he held her closer? The uncertainty was killing him and he didn't know what to do with his excess energy. He wished he had time to do some burpees, push-ups, or go to the basketball court and shoot some hoops. But the hearing that could decide the rest of his life was starting soon. He'd find out if he was allowed out into the world before his trial, able to look for his sister, or whether he would be made to rot, leaving his sister alone in this scary world. He shuddered at the thought and submitted himself to the emotional torture on the screen.

Whoever had the shot was running and the camera was bouncing up and down, liable to make queasy anyone who'd never flown and jumped out of helicopters for a living. He continued to watch as Jules smiled and turned toward her car. All of a sudden, a deep, sickeningly familiar rumble vibrated the video feed. Fire filled the screen and the camera was blown back and landed on the ground. To his horror, Jules was still in view, lying down on the ground... not moving.

"What the fuck?!" His heart beat sped up and the sharp breath he sucked in had nowhere to go in his tight chest.

"Yeah, dude, crazy right? That bomb straight up *merc'ed* that chick, yo!"

Jason, unable to take the pressure inside, grabbed the skinny drug addict and pulled him up close.

"What are you talking about?"

The drug addict gulped and looked around frantically, probably hoping whatever gang he ran with would come to his rescue. But Jason knew that as big as he was, no one was coming to help the little meth head.

"The l-l-lawyer lady. They said someone planted a c-c-car bomb and she's p-probably d-dead—"

"Is it true?"

"H-how should I know, man? You saw the TV dude! She looked fuckin' blown up to me!"

Jason went numb and dropped the addict, ignoring the tears

as they fell down the pathetic fuck's face. What did that shithead have to be scared of? He wasn't the one who'd just witnessed one of his worst fears come to life.

Jules couldn't be dead. There's no way. Jason continued to watch the news report, but the camera on Jules was abruptly kicked away and no one got a good visual afterward. The pundits then speculated on who would've tried to murder Jules and how her health status was still up in the air. The uncertainty seeped deep into Jason's bones and he was cemented to his spot, fated to watch the love of his life die over and over again on a jailhouse TV.

Men laughed and joked around him, but Jason stood still, a confused mess over the contradictions warring in his body. His heart stopped beating, but his pulse clawed at his throat. He couldn't breathe, but he was hyperventilating. His skin was slick with sweat, but he shivered at the chill in his veins. The juxtaposition of feeling too little and too much, ached through him.

Was this it? *Really* it? He tried to envision Jules laughing, talking, making love. Anything. Memories of her carried him through the worst times of his life, but all he could see now was her body lying lifeless on the ground. He expected everything they'd been through together to play in his mind, but nothing came. Wasn't that the saying? Life is supposed to flash before your eyes right before you die. But what happens if it's someone else's death that ends your life?

He wanted to run to wherever she was, but he was plastered to the floor, turning to stone from the inside out. The newscasters had moved on, but he hadn't. He never would.

By the time he was called to his bond arraignment, a black cloud of depression had seeped into his bones and he had to be physically moved to the courtroom. His feet didn't work. His brain didn't work. In his fog, all reason escaped him and he let irrationality swallow him whole. His parents were gone. His rescue targets in the Middle East were gone. His sister was gone.

The love of his life was gone. What else did he have to live for? Nothing was worth it. He'd just fuck it up in the end.

But in the bond hearing, Jason came alive when he saw the ADA and nearly attacked the prosecutor as he strolled into the small courtroom, unscathed.

"Assistant District Attorney Aguilar, where is Attorney Bellerose?"

Aguilar gave Jason a furtive glance before he spoke. "Your Honor, may I approach?"

"Certainly."

Jason couldn't hear what was being said, but from the gasp and small frown accompanied by the pitying look toward Jason on Judge Powell's face, his heart sank to his stomach.

She cleared her throat. "We'll move forward based on the prior agreed upon in-chamber communications even though Attorney Bellerose is-uh-unable to make it..."

Nausea took over and Jason had to swallow back bile to keep from getting sick. What did the judge mean? Was Jules actually gone?

The rest of the hearing was white noise. The million-dollar bond issued by the judge barely registered. He paid it, no problem, thanks to his parents, whose only fault was believing in him. They would've loved to know the first time he'd dipped that deep into his trust for himself was for a chunk of their endowment to go to bail money.

Hours later, after finally being set free from being behind bars and under paperwork, he aimlessly walked out of the jail in a daze, not knowing what to do or where to go next. He could've called Hawk, but why? What was the point? His emotions were torturing him, and he wasn't sure he'd survive the agony. All he wanted to do was go back to his apartment and hope his favorite whiskey would take the edge off of—

"Stone!"

In his daze, Jason couldn't tell if his head whipped around to the voice, or if he turned in slow motion. But when he saw the man who could've saved Jules, rage brought him back to crystal clear clarity. The ADA had been *right there*. There must've been something he could've done. Before he could stop himself, Jason lunged for Aguilar and held him up by the lapels of his hoity toity jacket, nearly shaking the man to death. If the prosecutor wasn't so big, he probably would have.

"What the fuck were you thinking? How could you let that happen to her?! I oughta end you right now, you fucker. How—" he gasped for breath as his chest constricted. "How could you let her..." The last words were wrenched from his body and he couldn't go on. He dropped Aguilar back to his feet and nearly doubled over at the ache in his heart.

Aguilar gave him a funny look as he fixed his blazer and stood up straight. "Real nice, Stone, threatening a public official, you know that's a felony—"

"I couldn't give a fuck, asshole," Jason spat, watching Aguilar before collapsing on the nearby bus bench. The prosecutor brushed back his hair and sighed.

"Look man, she says you're innocent and I believe her. But you gotta cut it out with the harming police officers and other government agents crap, alright? Even if you're innocent of your current charges, I'll have no choice but to add to them if it's appropriate. Understand?"

Jason shook his head and shoved his head into his hands, his elbows digging into his knees. "She's gone. Ellie's gone. I don't give a fuck anymore what happens to me. Go ahead and walk my ass back in there if you gotta." He shook his head and his hands scrubbed his face.

"What do you mean 'gone?'"

Jason stopped and peered from between his fingers to glare at Aguilar. The nerve of the fucker to make him actually say it out loud.

"The bomb... it killed—"

Aguilar's single laugh hitched and he cleared his throat at

Jason's look. Even without a mirror, he knew his face was murderous.

"No, man. No. She got hurt, yes. But she's alive. An ambulance came to pick her up. She's in the hospital, but she's definitely alive, *amigo*."

Jason's mouth dropped as he stared at the messenger he'd been tempted to shoot seconds before. "Really?" he croaked. His mouth was dry and it was all he could muster out. In his depressive mental state, he'd jumped to the worst conclusion, certain it was true. The heavy fog lifted and he felt lightheaded with its absence. If she was okay—

"Yeah. I-I actually came to take you home, *cabron*. Didn't think you'd want to chance the ever-reliable government transport. You've had a shitty enough day." He paused before continuing. "I can take you to her instead, if you want?" Aguilar didn't seem excited about his offer, but Jason didn't care. He also didn't know what *cabron* meant, but by the guy's tone every time he said it, Jason was starting to believe it wasn't nice.

"Isn't that a conflict of interest?"

"Yeah, a hell of a conflict," he scoffed. "But I need to do this."

"Why?" He couldn't believe he just asked that. The why didn't matter. He just needed to go to Jules. *Great move asshole, now you're gonna have to wait for a damn bus.*

"Because... because she's *good*. She sure as hell deserves way better than you, and me, for that matter. But it's you she wants." He indicated Jason with a wave of a hand before sighing. "I'm doing this for her. Not you. She's a damn good attorney, alright. But... she's an even better woman... and friend. You? I think you should rot in jail a little while for what you've done to some good officers. But... no, she wants you, so... I'm giving her"—he gestured again with both hands that time—"you."

"Why?" Jason couldn't help himself, but he couldn't ever imagine delivering another man up on a silver platter to Jules.

"Fuck, I don't know, man. Obviously, I'm an idiot." He laughed harshly. "You wanna see her or not?"

"Hell yeah, let's go." Then, as if someone smacked the knowledge onto his forehead, the full reality of the situation hit him, "Oh, God... she's *alive*." His fingers wove into his short hair and pulled as much as they could from its length.

The ADA chuckled and stepped off the sidewalk into the parking lot. "Okay, come on then."

Jason followed him to a modest Volvo in the visitor's parking lot still in total shock Jules was alive. She was the only woman he'd ever loved. He knew then more than ever what it would feel like without her in his life, and he wanted no part of that shit.

He wanted a home with her. He wanted kids with her. He wanted it all. He wanted *forever*.

"Fuck..." Jason whispered under his breath as he slid into the car that was going to take him to the rest of his life. He knew it was a gamble. Jules may not want him. He was messed up to the extreme. There was absolutely nothing worth a second glance, let alone a second chance, but she continually gave it to him. He had to convince her he was a good bet. There was no way he could go on without her, not after knowing what it felt like to have her in his arms again.

As they drove, Jason retrieved his cell phone from the plastic jail inventory bag and dialed.

"Who are you calling?"

Jason gave Aguilar a side-eye. It wasn't his business, but he answered anyway.

"Hawk."

The ADA nodded absentmindedly, as if he knew one of the members of Jason's former clandestine special forces unit. It didn't matter though. The call was important, and he was beginning to believe Aguilar had Jules's best interest at heart. He could at least trust the guy with her... to a certain extent, of course.

"Hawk." The voice on the other end was deep and... eager?

"Hawk… it's Jason."

"I know asshole, I have caller ID. You ready to come back or are you gonna keep yankin' my balls?"

Jason hated to ask for help. Since they left the Middle East, he hadn't done a single damn thing for the men of his Crew, but he needed them now. He only hoped they would be open to it.

"Hawk… I need your help." He waited only a breath before he heard his answer.

"Anything."

CHAPTER EIGHTEEN

The dim light weighed down Jules's eyelids, the heaviness making it difficult for her to open them. That, plus the soothing smell of the outdoors, gave her no incentive to wake up. With her eyes closed, she lazily took stock of where she was. The scent was intoxicating, warm smoke and pine filled her nostrils. She cuddled up closer to the big tree she was latched on to.

No... not a tree. That'd be weird.

Her hands lightly grazed where they'd landed and she felt firm skin over divots and valleys. She peeked an eye open. A tan male body was wrapped in her arms.

Jason.

I don't think this is a dream. Without memory of how her cheek ended up on Jason's bare chest, the thought to panic flitted across her mind, but her exhausted body didn't see the point. Besides, two big, warm familiar hands were cuddling her closer. She decided to revel in it and molded to her captor. He made her feel safe and secure and, dream or not, she'd roll with it. It'd been, what, seven years, since she'd felt that measure of peace? After having nineteen years of independence, that one year of security was enough to remember and crave for a lifetime.

A phone vibration startled her and Jason patted her arm

before shifting to retrieve it from the bedside table. She lifted herself up slightly and hissed at the pain in her side.

Definitely not a dream.

"Shit Jules, lie back." Jason helped situate her against strategically placed pillows before answering the phone on the last ring.

"Stone here." He glanced at her to make sure she was okay before turning to look out the window.

"Yeah. Yeah, she just woke up..." His voice dropped low and Jules took the opportunity to take in her surroundings.

The hardwood floors, exposed beam ceiling, and wood-paneled walls were all the same natural pine. She was lying on a thick apple red quilt with sewn-in black bears lumbering across the bottom. The bed frame looked like it'd been carved from a tree. On either side, there were two Aspen log nightstands with rustic branch lamps. There too, black bears traveled across the bottom of the lampshades. The only light came from one of the dim lamps and the crackling stone fireplace in front of the bed, making the small room feel cozy and warm. Jason was peeking out the matching red plaid curtains with—Jules squinted in the dim light to confirm—yep, more black bears stitched across the bottom.

"What's with the bears?" she croaked, wondering why her voice was hoarse. The pain in her head was so sharp, she winced as she spoke.

"Hold on Snake, let me call you back." Jason turned and only had to take a short step to reach the bed. He knelt on the comfy quilt and his hand brushed her cheek. Tentative fingers brought her awareness to the bandages and fresh bruises crisscrossing her body. She couldn't help thinking she resembled the patchwork quilt loosely covering her lower half.

"What happened to me?"

He shushed her when the pain in her throat made her wince.

"There was a bomb. Someone must have planted it in your

car. It went off as soon as you pressed the key fob to unlock it. Thank God you weren't too close. Do you remember anything?"

Jules closed her eyes. She only saw flashes, but there was enough to connect the images. She brushed her fingertips against her ribs, where a wrap covered the upper half of her torso.

"You're banged up all over. The doctor said you bruised your ribs bad and you have a nasty bump on your head. It wasn't bad enough to cause a concussion, but it'll hurt like hell. All in all, you got out pretty good for a girl with a hit on her."

For a girl with a hit on her... Her eyes widened and jerked to his, making her so-called "bump" pound. It hurt a hell of a lot more than a "bump." Her eyes stung and she wanted to ask more but her burning throat was a powerful deterrent. Thankfully, Jason must've understood because he kept talking as if she'd questioned him.

"I don't know who did it. I don't know why. But I think it has something to do with all this shit with Ellie." He lightly squeezed her thigh and bore his gaze intently into hers. "I've called the Crew. They've agreed to help us find out who did this to you... and help us find Ellie. One of them even helped grab a bag from your apartment before we left the hospital." At the slight tilt of her head he explained, "Your keys were found on scene and cops dropped them off at the hospital. One of the guys used your keys to get into your apartment and grab things you might need for... an extended vacation."

Jules nodded delicately then paused, her brain slow to catch up. "Wait, car bomb? Is Larry okay?"

A small twitch in the corner of Jason's lips would've made her scowl, if she'd had the energy.

"I'm sorry, baby. Larry didn't make it. But damn am I glad *you* did."

She resumed slow nods and tried not to cry. The corner of Jason's lips lifted and he leaned to kiss her forehead. She gripped his arm and held him close. His lips whispered across her skin and they breathed deeply together for a moment.

"Hold on." He squeezed her shoulder, thankfully one of the few parts of her that didn't ache, and got up to leave the room. Before she was finished situating the pillows behind her to sit up further, Jason was already back and handing her a glass of ice water.

"Where are we?" The words were barely a whisper, but the low volume made them tolerable. He winced at her sigh of relief after her first sip of water.

"Your throat might hurt from all the smoke inhalation" —his jaw ticced as he continued— "and screaming."

Jules trembled and hugged herself to soothe away the sudden memory of intense heat and pain. But her shrieks echoed across her mind.

"I thought I was going to die…" she whispered.

"Oh, baby girl." Jason kissed her forehead again and wiped her lone tear away with his thumb. "I'm so, so sorry." He brushed his lips against her damp cheek before he tilted her head up to look into his stormy eyes. "But hey, look at you. Here with me, still sexy as hell." She could tell he was trying to cheer her up and she decided to let him. "How you came out with that beautiful body of yours so intact is a fucking miracle." He winked.

Her laugh sounded and felt like gravel was stuck in her throat. She sipped more of the cool water, allowing it to cool her aching vocal cords, and shivered as the chill flowed under her skin.

"We're in the cabin the Crew bought," he said, answering her earlier question. He looked around with a glimmer of… pride? It was so rare to see an emotion like that on him, Jules second-guessed herself, but hearing him speak about the house confirmed her suspicions. "The Crew and I bought it while we were overseas. We thought it'd be a great place for us to get together and fish, hunt, shoot the shit." He smoothed a fluffy white Sherpa blanket over her, tucking it around her waist. "Maybe someday take our families."

Jules cringed and pushed his hands away, fluffing the blanket where she needed it.

"I brought you here because I didn't know where else to take you." One of his hands ran through his hair and he took her hand in his free one. "Hawk and I agreed staying in town was too risky, so I signed you out of the hospital and took you here. I guess you could call it a safe house. We're about an hour outside of town but way back in the woods on Mount Ash. It's completely untraceable to either of us or any of the Crew."

"I'm supposed to be in the hospital right now?" Jules faintly remembered someone talking with her and the harsh scent of antiseptic, but everything else was blurry in her mind.

"No... no. You were cleared, but you were exhausted. The doctor said we could wait, but I wanted you out of there. As soon as you woke up, you were in so much pain, he dosed you again with some meds. You were awake, but apparently so out of it you don't even remember?" He lifted his brow in question and Jules shook her head. He shrugged. "Well, I took you anyway."

"Why would they let you do that?"

"The hospital didn't like it, but they couldn't say no to your 'husband'—" Jules's eyes widened at his finger quotes and Jason winked. "Hey, I did what I had to do to get you outta there ASAP. I was too nervous to keep you there any longer than you had to be. And in my defense, even though the drugs made you loopy, you still signed yourself out. I'm a little surprised you don't remember anything." An image of her signing a document and giving it to a frowning man in a white coat crossed her mind and Jules nodded at the jogged memory. Jason shook his head and his calloused thumb stroked the top of her hand. "You've basically been drugged ever since. This is the first time you've been entirely lucid since I saw you this morning."

Jules couldn't stand the brokenness behind his eyes and squeezed his hand. His face crumpled before he covered it completely with one of his large hands, swiping down his scruff as he spoke. He looked off as he spoke, but obviously wasn't seeing anything.

"You have no idea h-how... shattered I was." He cleared his throat before continuing. "When I saw you in that hospital bed. Jules, I about fucking lost it. It was good Aguilar and Hawk were there."

At his confession, Jules's brow furrowed. "Marco was there? Why?"

"Because... he was the one who picked me up from the jail and took me to see you." He patted her hand and let it go. Jules was still confused. The working part of her brain understood his explanation was as good as any, but the rest of her head was far behind all of the information getting to it.

Jules watched Jason as he milled around the room. Her gaze caught on the beautiful blue jay inked in black on his chest. It was tattooed in such a way that it looked as if it was trying to pull his heart free from a loosely stitched wound. An homage to his mother, she'd always been his little blue jay, he'd told Jules. When she died in a car crash along with his stepfather—a crash Jason had survived—the losses had ripped his heart out.

Jules rubbed at the ache in her chest and distracted herself by taking in the rest of his hard pecs and abs. She felt a twinge of disappointment when Jason pulled a gray Henley over his head, and a soft groan escaped her lips. He chuckled and her face grew hot. She pretended like she hadn't been ogling the hell out of him, and her inspection drifted around the room. Without warning, soft cotton draped her face. She held the fabric away, and blinked at him.

"Put that on."

For the first time, Jules looked down and realized that while she was covered in hardened bandaging, she was still only clad in a sports bra. As quick as her arm would move in her pained state, she covered her belly and turned her body slightly away from

Jason. She felt his hot gaze on her and hoped he hadn't seen her stomach. She wasn't ready to talk about the scars just yet.

Concern flashed across his face, but whatever he saw on her own made him keep his thoughts to himself. "Put the shirt on, baby girl."

Robotically obeying—and glad he was letting it go—she gingerly dressed in the overly large T-shirt. His signature outdoorsy scent flowed over her as the cotton caressed her face.

"I thought you said I had stuff here."

"You do."

She waited for him to explain why he'd given her one of his shirts instead of her own. He didn't. She had a sneaking suspicion the jerk wanted her to flat out *ask him* to explain. She didn't.

"I called Aunt Rachel while you were sleeping. She's worried, as you can imagine. Luckily enough the police only talked to her once, and since then I've convinced her Ellie's just hanging out with friends and being a teenager. If they'd hounded her, I think she'd have had a heart attack. She doesn't know anything anyway." He scrubbed his stubble with his hand. "And thank God she doesn't watch that 'Devil box' or she'd have seen Sasha, me, and even you, all over the news. Hopefully she stays in the dark until we find El."

Jules nodded gingerly, only half listening. Jason seemed to be talking for his own benefit rather than for hers. She'd learned that talking out his thoughts calmed him when he was stressed. And no doubt they were both very stressed.

"I need to call the Crew back. If we share intel, we have a better chance of figuring out who this bastard is." He grabbed a remote from the bedside table and sat next to her before turning to the auxiliary channel on the big screen TV hanging in the corner of the room. How she hadn't seen it, she had no idea, but her expression must have shown how out of place she thought the monstrosity was. Jason's low laugh shook the bed.

"Yeah, Snake was in charge of the electronics and got a little carried away. He was our Intelligence Sergeant in"—he paused before nodding once to himself and seemingly making a decision — "MF7."

At the cautious tilt of her head, he continued.

"That was the Special Operations unit I was a part of. I didn't just reup a tour. My team was an elite military operation that worked outside of the government, specializing in extracting people from slave labor. Mostly women and... children." Jules's eyes widened at the explanation and the gears in her brain tried to unclog. She took another sip of water to gather her thoughts before speaking.

"So that's what y'all were called. Nora wasn't able to find the name of your team in her research. If you were doing that, then all those women on your last mission—"

Jason's cell phone rang and the previously blank TV screen came to life. An attractive, clean-shaven Clark Kent look-alike with glasses and navy blue hair filled the screen. His smile broadened and he gave a small wave.

"Oh, hello Juliet."

CHAPTER NINETEEN

The man stepped back to reveal four others behind him, and Jason turned away from her to acknowledge them.

She cleared her throat. "Jules is fine."

He smiled good-naturedly and, despite his young appearance, his kind eyes wrinkled at the edges behind his black rectangular glasses. "Jules it is, then. It's good to see you alive and well. And to finally meet you after all these years. Jason wouldn't shut up about you, you know." He winked before continuing, "Allow me to introduce us. I'm Wesley—"

"—Snake," one of the men interrupted with a laugh. He fidgeted with his backward ballcap while balancing his chair on only two of its four seemingly perfectly functioning wooden legs.

Wesley shook his head and grumbled. "We talked about this, *Felix*. We agreed we'd use our *real* names."

"Um... did I miss something?"

Wesley let loose a defeated sigh. "We're BlackStone Securities, a private security firm. We all used to be an inaugural unit in the military... Paramilitary—if you will—up until a few months back. We nicknamed our unit the 'Crew' and strictly used call signs. We got used to them to the point that, around each other, we only go by those now. Although, I *thought*" —he turned and eyed the man in the baseball cap— "we could introduce ourselves like the civilians we are now…"

"Come on, man. It'll just confuse her. If she really wants to call us by our civvy names she'll ask." The baseball-capped man smiled wide and began to point around the room. "Like I said, that's Snake… the angry blond giant in the back's Draco. Our beautiful strawberry blond asshole here is Devil Ray. Hawk's our fearless leader. And I'm Phoenix," he finished, pointing his thumb against his chest. "There's no use using our real names. We hardly even respond to them anymore." He pointed toward the screen at Jason beside her. "You've got yourself a pretty little Jaybird." He laughed and Jason rolled his eyes.

"You know, he's right, actually," Jason agreed. "I don't even think of them with their real names anymore."

Jules lifted a shoulder before responding, "That's alright. I get it. Hell, I was Delilah at the strip club until I got my first paycheck as an attorney."

"Hot damn, that's right! I forgot you were a stripper!" Phoenix clapped his hands and sat back down in his chair.

"Watch it," Jason growled.

The jokester put his hands up and smiled, resuming his balancing act in his chair. "S'alright Jaybird… just saying, she's used to codenames already." His toothy grin got wider and he winked at her.

The one in charge, Hawk, a tall dark-skinned man with a buzz cut, scowled at Phoenix. The rest of the men straightened a fraction as Hawk crossed his arms and cleared his throat. "Let's move on, Snake."

Snake pushed his glasses up on his nose and faced them. His actions grew more animated as he talked and he had to push his hair back when a dark blue curl fell and got in the way. "Jaybird, we weren't able to get any info on the mechanism behind the car bomb…" He was talking a mile a second and Jules's foggy brain couldn't keep up. She watched numbly as Jason spoke with the men about the attack, but tried her best to tune back in when they began speaking about Ellie.

"I've uploaded her photo into our facial recognition software and searched all the hotels in the area." A social media post Ellie uploaded a few weeks ago filled the corner of the screen and Jules's heart fractured at seeing her friend's smile, so happy and carefree. "We haven't been able to find her, but we all know these scumbags have ways to hide in plain sight."

"We'll have to get creative again," Jason spoke, scrubbing his five o'clock shadow. Snake nodded and pushed up his glasses.

Jules's brow scrunched. "How do you know she's in a hotel?"

The men on the screen shifted their eyes toward one another and waited until Jason spoke.

"Finding women like Ellie is what we used to do." Jason's face darkened and though his eyes were still on the screen, Jules knew his mind was elsewhere. Without thinking, she laid her hand on his back. His muscles bunched up beneath her touch and she tried to snatch her hand back. Before she could, his hand reached behind and covered her own. The men on the screen were silent, and Jules noticed they were all staring at her and Jason. All except the one with gorgeous hair seated next to Phoenix. Devil Ray's wild strawberry blond hair and beard surrounded a face solely focused on the computer on the Crew's side of the screen.

"That's her? *That's* your little sister? Goddamn, when'd she grow up?"

She felt Jason's growl vibrate his back. "Shut the fuck up, Dev, that's my sister you're drooling over. My *baby* sister. She's not even eighteen until—" Jason's voice cut off abruptly as he choked on the words and Jules rubbed his back, cold understanding washing over her instantly. She checked the date on her smartwatch to confirm.

"Tomorrow," she whispered and released a deep breath. "Her eighteenth birthday is in just a few hours."

The men on the other side of the screen cursed. The situation was already a nightmare, but somehow, the fact that Ellie was spending her first day as an adult woman kidnapped, or worse, put everything in stark relief.

"Fuck, sorry, man. I-I didn't mean anything by it. I guess the last time I saw her was that picture you had on base of her as a gap-toothed kid." Devil Ray's low voice rumbled over the silence and his hand ruffled the back of his thick hair.

Hawk shook his head as he looked at the picture. He carried himself differently than the others, his shoulders were large and slightly hunched. And he was tense, as if he was afraid to drop the heavy burden he carried.

"We'll find her. We've got feelers out all over Ashland and the surrounding counties. We'll cast a wider net if we have to. As soon as we get a lead, we'll load up and load out." Hawk then turned his gaze to Jules as he spoke to her directly, "Jason said you received a note?"

Jules cleared her throat to speak loudly enough for them to hear her but only a pained noise came out.

Jason reached for the water she'd placed on the bedside table and handed it to her.

"Yeah, she got a note at Original Sin, the club she used to dance at. They're still a client of hers and we were asking around the day after Ellie went missing. Before we left, the bartender handed us a ripped piece of paper that said, 'The girl is up for sale. He can't go home.'" He shuddered.

Hawk tapped his lips as he thought. "We gotta get back in there."

Jason's head whipped to the screen. "Jules isn't stepping foot back inside that city until the threat has been neutralized."

"What are we going to do then? What if there's another note? Do you have a better idea?" Hawk's voice lowered as he peppered Jason with questions.

"I said no."

"Nora can go," Jules tried to interject, but the males were on the verge of yelling.

"She's obviously connected somehow. We need to get her back in there—"

"—Nora can go," Jules rasped.

"—The fuck we do! We'll figure something out. One of us can go check it out, or—"

"—*Nora* can go!" She put as much volume behind the words as she could, which wasn't much, but it was enough to get the men to stop. Everyone stared and she squirmed under the attention.

"Who?" Hawk asked.

"Honora French... Nora. My assistant." Jules took another sip of water. "She goes there all the time to check in with Cyn, the owner. She can see if there are any more notes." She paused again to swallow. "Shoot... Jay, where's my phone?" Jason hopped up and hurried to the corner to rifle through his bag. Once he found her phone, he handed it to her.

The rapid tapping of Jason's foot against the hardwood worked her nerves as she waited for the damned iPhone to turn on. Once it did, the room filled with shrill tones and vibrations.

"Shit, that's a lot of messages," Snake commented.

"That's saying something coming from Super Geek over there," Phoenix joked.

"It's probably just Asshat," Jason grumbled.

"Who's Asshat?" one of the men asked, but she ignored it. She wasn't in the mood to explain her ex-non-boyfriend to strangers. Especially since she could hardly make sense of it herself.

Jules thumbed through past messages and notifications to get to her contacts list and chose Nora's name. She heard Snake asking Jason for her number and saying he was going to do some kind of techno voodoo. Not his words, but she'd already tuned him out as she listened to the short dial tone on the other end.

"For the love of the *goddesses*, Jules, do you think you could answer your damn phone sometime? I know I'm screening your calls for you but, come *on*. You get blown up and still don't think

I should know what's—Oh... who the Hades are you people?" Nora's singsong voice echoing from above drew Jules's attention to the TV, where the Crew shared one side of the screen with Nora on the other. Her perfectly shaped periwinkle eyebrows were slightly raised in question against her smooth alabaster skin.

So that's her color of the week. Nora changed her hair—even her eyebrows—to fit her mood. At this point, Jules had no idea what Nora's natural hair color was. Just a few days prior, Nora's current silver-purple long bob was stark white ringlets long enough for her to sit on.

"I projected Jules's screen to ours so we could all see each other."

Jules nodded slowly at Snake's explanation, still not fully understanding exactly how he did it, but he seemed pretty proud of himself. She wondered if Nora and the navy blue-silver streaked Snake would get along. They both seemed to love technology and color coordination. Without Nora, Jules would still be using the crappy laptop she had throughout college and law school. The woman was a savant at all things techie.

"Well, no duh. I asked who you were, not what you did. *Obviously*, I know how to use the screen to screen function remotely."

Jules slipped her hand over her mouth and tried not to giggle. Guess they wouldn't be getting along after all.

Snake's cheeks pinked and he fiddled with his glasses. Jules cleared her throat to try to save him.

"Nora, these are Jason's military buddies..."

"The guys you researched and no doubt know exactly who we all are." Jason narrowed his eyes at her.

Nora only shrugged at the borderline accusation and gave a cheeky grin, causing Jason to chuckle back. All the while, she never looked up from her typing. She was like that—all business with a side of sass that everyone adored.

"So maybe I did... hey, Babs?" At hearing Nora's nickname for her, Jason's brow raised toward Jules. She shook her head slightly, indicating she'd explain later. "First off, love the new husky voice thing. Hate you almost had to die to get it. But most importantly, what're you doing on top of a mountain?"

Before Jules could answer, Hawk interjected.

"It seems like you're more in-the-know than we are. I'm sure you heard about the explosion?" He continued at Nora's nod. "BlackStone Securities is trying to help figure out who's behind all this. We think everything is connected, the bomb, Ellie, Sasha. Jules mentioned she received a note from Original Sin. We want you to go—"

"Oh, Babs! Cyn gave me another note when I went to check on OS, last night. I haven't opened it yet but I can take a pic and share it to your albums. Turns out while you like to get blown to pieces and take vacation, I get stuck doing the dirty work." She lowered her sky blue butterfly glasses to reveal her bottle green irises in mock judgment. Jason scoffed but Jules laughed softly.

Nora always made Jules feel better, apparently even after being "blown to pieces." It was one of the main reasons why she still worked for her. Before Nora, Jules never kept an assistant longer than two months. There was always something wrong with the relationship, and Jules wound up planning for the inevitable.

At the regularly scheduled bimonthly termination meeting, Jules tried to find a reason to let her go, but Nora had refused. The gutsy little pixie literally stood up from their one-on-one meeting and said, "Okay, see you tomorrow," like she hadn't just been fired. Initially, Jules was more confused than anything, and she didn't know what to do when Nora did, indeed, show up the next day. After the shock wore off, Jules was impressed, so she'd allowed it. Now, Jules couldn't think of a life without her. She'd become so much more than an assistant. She was one of Jules's few chosen friends.

"What'd the note say?"

Nora's eyes narrowed at Hawk's question, unintimidated by

the ex-special forces team lead, and she turned her questioning glance to Jules.

"It's okay. We can trust them."

Nora bit one of the two rose gold snakebite studs under her lip before she decided to continue. Jules thought she heard a soft groan on the other side of the screen. Nora must have heard it too because she stayed silent until the blond giant on the other side cleared his throat.

"Got somethin' to say, handsome?"

The suspect cleared his throat again and crossed his muscular arms against his chest, his tight black shirt barely containing his biceps. The toothpick in his mouth rolled around and he resumed his severe scowl.

"What's your name?"

"Draco."

Nora's giggle bubbled over the speakers. "No way... Draco... as in *Malfoy*? That can't be your real name..."

Phoenix laughed so hard his chair slammed back to all four legs. The bearded Viking growled and settled into his seat. Phoenix tried to gain his composure, as if he wanted to harass Draco more, but Snake cut in before he could stop laughing.

Snake reintroduced everyone again, ending with an explanation for Draco's call sign, "It's not related to Harry Potter. He's named after the Draco lizard."

"Hm... see, yeah, I can't—with a straight face—call someone as delicious as *you* the same name as a villain from my childhood. What's your real name, handsome?"

"Drake. You can call me Drake."

"Well that's not so far off." Nora smiled and mouthed his name like she was tasting it on her tongue. She winked before furrowing her brow at a thought. The Viking blushed and he tried to cover it up with his hand as it brushed his thick, short blond beard. If Jules didn't know any better, she would've sworn he was hiding a smile, too.

"Wait..." Nora mumbled to herself about blue jays,

phoenixes, flying snakes, lizards, and stingrays. "You're all named after flying things? Because some of you were Night Stalkers—those big bad helicopter trained soldiers? Before you were part of your little, super-secret military group! Am I right? I'm totally right, aren't I?" The men shifted on their feet and Hawk and Snake demanded to know how Nora knew anything about their special ops team.

Nora ignored their indignation. "Oh, my goddesses, that's effing adorable." They grumbled at her giggles and made half-hearted objections. Phoenix seemed to think it was hilarious. Jules was beginning to wonder if he ever took anything seriously. The bearded Draco was grinning like a madman, his toothpick shaking with silent laughter.

"This is a waste of damn time. Cut out the flirting shit, there's a girl missing here." Hawk waited, probably checking to make sure everyone felt sufficiently chastised before addressing Nora. "How do you know about MF7? How did you know where Jules was, and what did the note say?" His crossed arms were so tight, it looked like his biceps were going to split his shirt sleeves open.

"Touchy about our names, are we? *Hawk*, was it?" She smirked before getting down to business. "First, I didn't know what you were called, but I know about MF7 because I'm good at *my* MFing job. See what I did there?" She rolled her wrists as if to say, *voila*.

Deep laughs rolled out of Draco, and one by one the men on the other side stopped, mouths agape, and turned to stare at the big man. He quickly sobered up and coughed.

"What? That shit's funny." He leaned back in his chair again and his toothpick worked overtime.

"Who knew the big guy liked puns so fucking much?" Phoenix asked no one in particular.

"I don't think I've ever heard him laugh before..." Jason mumbled under his breath so only Jules could hear.

"Second," Nora continued without missing a beat. "I use the

GPS Find My Friends function to know where Jules is. She knows where I am, too. And before you get your boxers all up in a twist, it's Jules approved, and useful when she needs to get an out from a meeting. Or... when I need to get out of a crappy date. Nothing like an impromptu work emerge to free you from a creep. Third, I've sent the note to Jules's phone. She can pull it up on the screen."

Jules and Jason hopelessly tried to navigate through the call while Nora and Snake argued over each other to explain how to pull up the photo. Finally, the picture opened up to the large screen. The words were hard to read and possibly hastily written. All they had was an address and a single word.

Hurry.

Jason bristled. Hawk and Snake asked Nora an endless amount of questions. She was given the note the night before, but since Jules shut her phone off thanks to Andy's incessant ringing, Nora hadn't been able to get in touch with her. She'd gotten it from Cyn, and neither she, nor Cyn, knew who wrote it. The note had been left in a Confessional again, and a Sinner gave it to the bartender to pass along to Cyn. With some searching, they realized the address was to a hotel in the middle of Ashland.

"You think Ellie could be there?" Jason asked, the hopefulness in his tone made Jules's heart ache.

"I don't know what else the second note could be about," Jules answered. "What should we do? Call Investigator Burgess about the note?"

"Fuck no! Are you crazy? We can't tell the police!"

"'Scuse you, Mr. Devil. Don't be an ass to my boss." Nora wagged her finger at the camera.

"Why can't we tell the police? It's literally their job," Jules argued.

"Because, their job was 'literally' locking Jaybird up less than twenty-four hours ago. You think they'll trust anything you give them? The fuckers will probably turn it against him," Hawk reasoned.

"They've got a point, baby. Remember when we tried to tell Burgess about the first note. That sure as hell didn't go well."

Jules threw her hands up. "What do we do then? How do we get Ellie out of there?"

"*We* do it."

Jules stared blank-faced at Hawk's declaration. "Say what now?"

"We're a security firm. It's our job to recon, protect, search, and rescue. You name it, we do it. This is exactly what Black-Stone Securities was made for," Hawk explained. "It's exactly what we were *trained* for."

"Um... isn't all that illegal?" Her head was starting to hurt again and she was having a hard time following. "What if you get caught? You can't just go into a hotel, guns blazing!"

"We don't have another choice at this point," Hawk argued. "We're running on borrowed time as it is. Nora found that note twenty-four hours ago."

"Besides, it's only technically illegal if we get caught. We won't let that happen." Phoenix winked.

"Hear that, Babs? A technicality! Your fave!"

"What if it's a trap?" Snake asked.

"We gotta at least try!" Devil Ray's shout silenced everyone.

To Jules's addled brain, things happened rather quickly after that. Snake was able to look online and find the layout of the hotel through its fire escape plans, but it was taking him a little longer to hack into their surveillance system. They agreed that while he did that, Jason could use the time for a much-needed power nap before meeting the rest of the team at BlackStone. By the time they wanted to leave Snake would hopefully have the run of hotel security and be able to find out who booked the room.

Still, they wanted to get to Ellie as soon as possible, so there wasn't time to have everything perfectly laid out. Some things they'd have to go in blind. They hoped having Jules, Nora, and Snake using the same three-way calling to connect with the Crew's headsets and cameras would help with any holes in their plan. They'd support the Crew with live updates of any security measures, organized electrical shutdowns, and any other relevant information they might need on the spot.

With a game plan in place, they were about to hang up their calls when Snake paused, his eyes narrowed behind his frames. "Nora, you said you follow Jules's location... does anyone else follow it?"

A shock of worry made Jules break into a cold sweat as she waited for Nora to respond.

Nora worried over her lip studs again and made a fervent glance toward Jules.

"Well..."

"What? Can someone else track me?" Her breath came out in a short pant and Jason gently massaged her nape. She was grateful for the gesture, but his grim expression didn't do much to soothe her.

"Andy could be tracking you. I've suspected it for a while, but I didn't want to say anything without proof." Nora made her decision and sighed, her scarf rippled with her breath. "If he is tracking you, it's some way I don't know about. You know how I make those routine checks for viruses on your phone?" Jules nodded. "There were a few times early in your 'relationship' that I found he'd enabled the Find My Friend function between your phones and your location was available to him. I didn't tell you because I just thought, 'Oh, typical crazy Andy,' and I didn't want to bother you with it. I took care of it every time, but just in case, I included stalkerware sweeps in my checks. A lot of abusers use them, and he's definitely crazy enough to try to install one, but at last check he's never used any that I know of. Still... it's possible. The guy's loaded and desperate... a pretty scary combination."

Although Jason vibrated with energy, he stood up slowly from the bed, leaving Jules's neck cool from the absence of his touch. His fists clenched and unclenched as he paced.

Although Jules was just as rattled, she tried to calm him down. "Jaybaby, it's just Andy... So, he used to follow me. It's no big deal. He's harmless."

He shook his head roughly and dug his fingers into his short hair as he paced. "Fuck. How do we fix that?"

"Without having her phone with me, I can't check it myself," Snake explained. "The best bet is for you to upload Nora's contact info to your phone, Jason. You've still got the same phone, yeah?" Jason nodded. "Okay, then yours is safe. I installed a sweeper program on all of our phones once we got back into the States to prevent anyone outside of the Crew from tracking us. Shutting off Jules's phone should do the trick for the time being, though. It's nearly untraceable to civilian programs if it's completely shut off. As for the men we're dealing with, they're usually not sophisticated enough to know how to remotely install stalkerware and track her, but it's better to be safe with it shut off."

"Babs has had her phone off since last night, too, so it's been live, what, fifteen minutes? And she's had it on her this whole time, so I doubt anyone has had the opportunity to install anything directly."

Jason nodded and huffed out a deep breath. "Okay. Yeah, let's go ahead and do that. We have a plan of action. I'll leave for BlackStone as soon as you text me you're ready. You all talk to me from now on. Jules is off the grid." Heads nodded on the Crew's side and Snake began to type on his keyboard.

Nora blew a kiss to Jules, "Love ya, Babs. Stay safe... in every way." Her giggle was accompanied by a deep male laugh on the other side of the screen before both the screen and sound shut off abruptly.

CHAPTER TWENTY

He leaned his head back against the leather seat of the Confessional and allowed the muffled bass to lull him into a trance. The honey-brown hair in front of him bobbed up and down on his cock in time with the beat. The whore occasionally looked up, no doubt trying to give that porn star stare she thought every man craved, but she only reminded him of who she wasn't. She did it again and he shoved his hand into the thick wig he'd requested, causing her to gag.

"Ah, Juliet..." he moaned. She shook her head but he forced her to take him to the base, choking her, and hopefully making her realize he didn't give a fuck about what she had to say. She couldn't possibly understand the amount of stress he was under and he needed to take a load off, so to speak.

Figuring out what to do about the fucked-up shit he'd found himself in had led him to Original Sin—again—and he'd hoped a nice blow job could relieve two problems at once. Unfortunately, he should've remembered second rate sluts were nowhere close to the real thing. Shit, the current one was barely keeping him hard.

He shoved her off in frustration and disgust and her back hit the opposing wall in the small room. Her dull brown eyes looked up at him tearfully and he faltered as he shoved his flaccid penis back into his Versace trousers.

What the fuck am I doing?

He'd aimed to go into the Confessional with the look-alike under the pretense he was there for a quick fuck and his usual kink. Old habits die hard.

The real Juliet wasn't answering the damn phone, even though he didn't know what good it would do him at this point since he was certain they were bugging his calls. To make matters worse, the imbeciles had been following him around all day so he couldn't change up his routine. Going to OS was his only option. He had a task to complete and, disappointingly, his weak resolve had made him forget his purpose for being there in the first place. OS didn't usually allow "hands-on" activities, but he'd seen the track marks on the inside of her arm and knew he could convince her to do whatever he wanted.

Juliet had been so high and mighty about how clean and perfect and wholesome OS was, but it was still a fucking strip club, and she obviously didn't know how deeply seated the problems were again. She'd alluded, here and there, about how there was a drug use problem back when she... *danced*. She was convinced she and her friends fixed it. But here he was getting a lousy blow job from a 'rock star.'

He grimaced at the street name. Whatever the euphemism— a whore like the one in front of him was always looking for an easy payout to get her next high. It's why he hadn't felt the slightest bit guilty asking her for her services. It was a mutually beneficial relationship. The knockoff Juliet had taken one look at his designer suit and offered him sextasy, no doubt hoping to get him good and wasted before she stole every penny he had. Seeing as how she was nearly naked on the floor and his dick was wet but still uninterested, maybe he should've taken her up on it.

It was this form of trade he'd bought into. Willing whores and the plethora of drugs were what he'd expected. Rape, slavery, *murder*... was not. Father said he was naïve, that he'd never been intelligent enough to "see the big picture." All he knew was he'd been sold on participating in the firm's newest pursuits. He'd been under the impression that the firm liked to sweeten contracts with promises of off-the-record, no-strings-attached deals on the side. It worked multiple ways in that clients were more inclined to work with them—thanks to the added bonus of women at their beck and call. And the added blackmail made sure the clients never left for other firms.

He was told it was the firm's wish to cut out the middleman and would be doing the recruitment themselves rather than leaving it up to the unsavory pimps that normally came with the escort business. Without dealing with the criminals, it would actually be safer for the sluts, who were usually careless with whom they trusted, only eager to make a quick buck for a quick bang. He was even fine with supporting the other side of the firm's exploits and encouraging a little drug use here and there, in both the clients and the whores. Rich men loved playing with fire, especially the kind that got them high. He'd thought it was a win for everyone. It was distressing how much Father's firm had been led astray.

Although he hadn't realized it at the time, recruitment was partially the reason for the firm's participation in the party two days prior. The party's purpose was for all the influential bigwigs in town to honor some lucky idiot money for college. Apparently, the young women who didn't make the cut were still persuaded to join the firm's "internship" program. Several had jumped at the offer and were now escorts for hire on the firm's dime. That business relationship was what he'd signed on for when his father spoke to him the morning after the party and essentially promoted him.

But that had nothing to do with the fate of the drugged women in that god-awful hotel room. That horrible night was when he realized how the less than willing women were being "chosen," and that those particular women wouldn't be escorts at all. He was still in the dark as to where the other captives came from, since they'd only found two that were suitable enough from the party. He shivered at the memory of the women lying mostly naked and unconscious on the hotel bathroom floor. The fact that he knew one of them was something he couldn't think on too much. This had to stop, and unfortunately, it seemed as though he was the only voice of reason at the moment.

"Hey, get up. Go look out the door." He grabbed the whore by the arm to get her up. She stumbled there and cracked it open.

"Wh-what am I looking for?"

"Those two men who accompanied me... are they still out there?"

"Um... they're by the stage."

"Keep your eye on them."

"Why—"

"Just do it," he hissed and slithered to the corner of the small room where all the equipment was kept. "Tell me what they're doing."

"Hmph," she grunted as she maintained her post. "Just watching Charity."

He chuckled to himself, *that little minx has helped me more than she even knows.* Making sure the crackwhore was preoccupied as a lookout, he stuffed a small envelope near the Confessional's sound system. He knew the druggie wouldn't notice, but hopefully whoever turned off the equipment for the night would see it and turn it in. He was disappointed that he'd had to resort to cloak and dagger bullshit, but he'd had no other choice since Jules refused to answer the damn phone.

He straightened his tie and inspected his garments for any untoward stains. He huffed out a breath and walked out—

A small hand grabbed his arm before he exited.

"Hey wait! What about my tip?" She crossed her arms and waited. The fake, stringy honey-brown hair lay crooked against her glittery temples. She was much skinnier than Juliet and, frankly, if he hadn't been so desperate, he would never have debased himself with this type of filth. It disgusted him how many women stooped so low and he was baffled at what could possibly lead a woman to decide to whore herself out. He dug into his pocket and tossed her a small baggie of whatever the fuck the Russians were selling these days. She lunged for the small respite from her miserable life, and he was all but forgotten.

He was hoping what was inside the envelope would cover his ass in case the predicament went to court one day. Yes, what he'd signed up for was wrong, but he'd been told that all of the recruits were not only volunteers, but eager participants in the escort program. He'd figured if the girl was willing to sell her body, who was he to stop her?

Willing. That was the operative word. He ignored the faint niggling in his mind that told him the line he'd drawn in the sand was faint, and he stood behind it firmly. He didn't know how much further the firm was willing to go, but at some point, he needed to make sure his legacy was still intact and his culpability was at a minimum.

He needed to reestablish the status quo ante, what the partners originally intended. Even a pedigree as refined as his own couldn't deny that sex sells, especially in this type of economy. A business opportunity such as the firm's escort service had some potential, and apparently even some government backing from on high. He had to ensure certain greedy idiots kept their short-sighted pricks out of it. He'd do what he could, but he could tell there were bigger dogs in this fight, and there was no way he'd let himself be the small yappy chihuahua getting nipped in the corner. Or if shit hit the fan, confined to a cage.

He'd been promised a fast-track to partnership, and he was certain Father couldn't know the extent of the wayward leadership. He definitely couldn't have known the extent to which the partners were willing to go to blackmail his own son into keeping his mouth shut.

He hadn't realized he was being watched early on and had

nearly ruined everything by blurting it all out at OS the last time he saw Jules. Thankfully he'd seen the Russians enter the club before it was too late and he'd been able to divert attention to sexual exploits with Charity.

Now he needed to lie low for a while. In the meantime, he'd glean information while phasing himself out of the most unsavory side of the business. Best case scenario would be that once freed, the women would have been too out of it to indict him as a major player. They could go on with their lives, and no one would be able to pin anyone at the firm with the blame. Worst case scenario?

He shuddered.

Best not to entertain that.

He made his way to the exit of the club, knowing the Russians would be following closely behind. He hoped they saw his trip to the Confessional as only a necessary release of built-up tension, but his paranoia grew as Vlad picked up his cell phone and rapidly spoke in those infernal consonants. The men were advertised as his bodyguards, but they were beginning to behave more like the prison variety.

He swallowed back the sour taste in his mouth and chuckled wryly. Vlad gave him an odd look, stopping his laughter as soon as it began.

Jules would come through. She had to. With her expertise and discretion as a defense attorney and professional relationships at the DA's office, she was his only hope of saving everyone. The grim irony wasn't lost on him that the one person he'd constantly fucked over, was the only one who could keep him from getting fucked.

He only hoped it wasn't too late.

CHAPTER TWENTY-ONE

"Babs?" Jason asked, chuckling to himself.

"What can I say? My staff thinks I'm a Boss Ass Bitch." Jules grinned and sank into the many pillows Jason built up to support her, allowing herself to release all the tension she'd collected since—well, since she found out Ellie was missing.

"That Nora's something. And how big is she? She looked small even on a screen."

Jules shrugged, her eyes still closed. "Not sure. She is tiny, though. Can't be more than a buck ten soppin' wet."

"Small woman, big personality." Jason laughed and Jules heard his footfalls as he got up and walked into the en suite bathroom. Although she couldn't have been awake for more than an hour, she was already exhausted. As she turned over to cautiously fluff the pillow underneath her, Jason walked back into the room and stood stock still by the bed.

Still trying not to speak too much, she exaggerated her furrowed brow to ask what he was doing.

"I can sleep in the living room. Or one of the other guest rooms," he offered, his eyes following his fingertips as they traced the grooves in the wooden bedframe.

Oh. Jules hadn't even thought he'd sleep anywhere but with her. "Why would you sleep somewhere else? I woke up on you, didn't I?"

Jules was certain the firelight was playing tricks on her. There was no way Jason Stone was blushing.

He cleared his throat. "Uh, yeah... that was different."

She waited for him to explain, but he didn't. "Different... how?"

He continued to follow a wooden groove even as he spoke, "I just needed to hold you... before. I'd been worried, and... well, now you're awake and—"

"Oh, so now that I'm awake, I get a choice of whether you sleep with me or not?" Just as she hoped, Jason whipped his head up at her accusation, but gave a slow smile when he saw her teasing grin. The idea of being away from him made her stomach roll but she didn't want to come off as needy. Giving him a hard time was always the better option.

You did just survive a bomb this morning, she thought, deciding to give herself a break.

She fingered over the threading in the quilt. "You know, you could..."

The inhalation of breath a few feet away fueled her as she tried to voice her desires without seeming too weak. She knew he wanted to stay with her too, but the sting of rejection and betrayal by him hurt enough the one time. To subject herself to a similar fate twice? She didn't know if she would be able to come back from it. Still, the temptation of having him so near overrode her fears. She could give in—just this once—again. "You could stay here. It'd, um, be silly to have to clean more sheets."

She dared to look at him and was pleased to find him trying to stifle a grin himself.

"Yeah... that'd be silly." He chuckled, emphasizing the last word as he came around the bed and pulled the quilt down low. "Plus, it'd be safer for me to be as close as possible. Just in case there's another attack on you."

It was Jules's turn to grin, but her upturned lips flattened as soon as she attempted to try to maneuver herself under the cool, cream-colored cotton sheets. Jason's hands worried over her until she was finally situated comfortably. Her muscles melted with the relief brought on by not having to hold herself up anymore, and she was already fighting sleep.

"You never know when a bomb could go off in the mountains," she said matter-of-factly. Jason waggled his eyebrows as he pulled his shirt off with one hand by grabbing the back collar. Every other time she'd seen him strip that way had made her hot, but at his unexpected goofiness she couldn't keep a straight face and burst into laughter. Just as soon as she started, a groan escaped her at the immediate spike of pain in her bruised ribs.

"Shit, Jules. I'm sorry." His brow furrowed before he flipped the lamp off and slid under the quilt. He positioned himself so they were flush together face-to-face. Her hands brushed down his chest and abs, absentmindedly tracing each divot before she felt his heated gaze and she realized what she was doing. She cleared her throat and carefully rolled onto her back, staring up at the ceiling. Jason did the same.

"Goodnight, Jay."

"Night, Jules."

Jules closed her eyes, fully expecting sleep to overwhelm her after an exhausting last few days.

Unfortunately, that didn't happen.

"You still up?" Jason's deep voice rumbled.

For either of them, it seemed.

"Yeah," Jules croaked. She carefully turned to face him, finding that he'd done the same. "What's up?"

He breathed deeply before he answered, "I'm worried."

She nodded before whispering back, "Me too. Wanna talk about it?"

He nodded.

Jules listened intently as the strong soldier in front of her opened up about all of his fears about the last sixty-odd hours and the anxiety he felt over the next twenty-four. It felt like the first time they were able to actually talk with one another. They'd been nonstop for so long, or awkward as hell for one reason or another. It felt good to just *be* with him for a few quiet moments. Before long, she couldn't help but lightly trace his face with her fingertips, releasing calming energy for both of them. He sighed deeply, his bare chest rising to only a breath away from her. Her skin tingled with the anticipation of him returning the soft touches she was giving him.

"I should've gone to dinner with her, Jules."

"Why didn't you?"

A momentary deep crease formed on his forehead, and she trailed it by feel more than by the fading dim firelight.

His hand slid to her back and stroked over the T-shirt's soft fabric.

"Ever since our last mission... I haven't been the same. Crowds, loud noises... I can't keep a promise or a plan to save my life. It's all too much." He blew a big breath against her hair.

She weighed her next question before asking it. "Do, um... do you have PTSD?"

He shook his head. "No."

Even in the dark of the waning fire, he must've seen her skeptical look. "I promise. I was checked out *extensively* after the Army declared me medically compromised. I'd wondered myself whether their allegations had any teeth. But no. It's not quite PTSD. At least not clinically. It's not debilitating and it doesn't even really affect my life, but there are these... quirks I've got now. Things that I'd just rather not be around anymore if I can help it, ya know? It makes me stress, almost to a panic, but I don't ever have an actual panic *attack*."

Jules was having trouble following the difference between what he was describing and Post Traumatic Stress Disorder, but she decided to trust him. It sounded like he'd attempted to address his mental health after all the things he'd seen.

"So yeah, when she texted and asked me to dinner, I said yes. But eventually I said no, like I always do. The idea of going out and having a one-on-one conversation with her just built up inside me until I couldn't follow through with it. Then I canceled." He barked out a derisive laugh. "What kind of big brother can't even keep a dinner date with his baby sister?" He sighed again. "Maybe if I'd kept my word, she'd still be safe and sound at Aunt Rachel's."

Jules stopped tracing and held his cheek in her hand, making sure he was paying attention before she spoke.

"Jaybaby, you gotta stop, okay? Beating yourself up right now isn't gonna help anyone." His mouth opened and she moved her thumb over it, trying not to think about how soft his lips were. Heat flared in his eyes, but she kept going.

"One thing I know? People are damn unpredictable. You can't count on them, and in the end, they're liable to surprise you, one way or another," she continued past his wince. Her words weren't meant for their history, but if he took them that way, she couldn't stop him. "From what I gather from this case, it seems like calculated evil. Someone is out there, hell-bent on doing vile things and sticking you with the blame. Maybe you're a convenient scapegoat, maybe it's intentional. I don't know why, but we're gonna solve this together. Just know that whatever you did—or didn't—do couldn't have affected what ultimately happened here. Someone had Ellie in their sights, and they would've struck one way or another, with or without you saying no to a dinner date.

"Besides, it sounds like this was something you'd gotten in the habit of doing?" She waited for his agreement, the tightening of his lips accompanied by a slow nod. She brought his winter gray eyes back to hers. "Odds are Ellie might've even known you were going to cancel. Who are we to say what could've happened if something had been different? We don't even know what *did* happen. Let's nail that down before you hammer yourself to that cross, okay?" He nodded and she resumed tracing the fine lines that had formed near his eyes since the last time they'd been in bed together.

"Even if you don't wanna believe my esteemed advice"—her hand left his face and pressed against her chest as she mocked herself— "there's no use playing the 'what if' game." The corner of her mouth rose up slightly. "It's a game designed for losing. So, let's just focus on what we can and can't change and play to win, okay?"

He returned her half-smile and she resumed tracing his face while he searched hers. She focused on the new scar over his ear. It almost looked like the result of some odd sunglass arm injury, but she knew that didn't make any sense. Her fingers caressed the smooth mark.

"That was from our last mission." His voice was barely a whisper and she continued her caress, moving her fingertips to trace the shell of his ear until he shivered.

"What happened?" she asked quietly, hoping it wasn't too invasive of a question. She knew from experience with him that she shouldn't ask him about his time deployed. But he'd mentioned the last mission enough, so she held her breath, hoping he wanted to share. He stared intently at her until her gaze met his. Breathing deeply, he held her like a life raft, her cheek against his warm chest, before the weight of his sorrow dragged to the depths of whatever trauma he'd suffered.

"We were sent to the outskirts of a Yemeni village to save a group of women we'd heard were being kept there against their will. We got a lead on a target, and Eagle set everything up after the commander's go ahead. Phoenix was the pilot. You know Hawk and me were trained as pilots in the Night Stalkers—" Jules nodded, remembering him mentioning it when they first met, during that brief period of time between his stint in the Army and his recruitment into MF7. "But we went through a rigorous training program to perfect the skills we'd learned prior to entering the Night Stalkers, so instead of flying the Bird, MF7 had me as one of the men who would jump out of it." He stroked her back as she shivered at a vision of him jumping out of, as they say, a perfectly good helicopter.

"Everything went off without a hitch. Hawk, Eagle, and me, we found the room where the target was holed up. Hawk kicked down the door, like we planned, and I went in and immediately locked onto the target. Only... he wasn't alone." Jules felt the light movement of his throat as he swallowed.

"What we saw—" Her heart stuttered at the eerie monotone cadence he'd adopted as he valiantly kept going through his story, as if he was reading it aloud from a script hidden somewhere deep in the recesses of his mind. "There were so many women. All of them were sick, or drugged, or... I don't know... suffering. There weren't supposed to be any victims. It was the bastard's home. He never kept them there. But the target had a woman, Hawk had known Masuma had helped us with intel. But the target used her against us. He was wearing a vest. It took me half a second to realize it was a bomb. A fucking *bomb* strapped to his chest. My finger was on the trigger. I had the shot... Hawk and Eagle were yelling at me, but I had the shot..." Although she didn't see it, she imagined him clenching his eyes closed against the memories. "But they were yelling at me, and I hesitated. Just long enough for him to pull the trigger himself."

Jules stopped rubbing his back but kept holding him, sensing he wasn't finished. "The place was up in flames before we knew it. Fucking Hawk jumped in front of me like a goddamn hero. Who knows? Maybe I would've died without him. It all happened so fast. The women were screaming. I know they were in pain. The ones that were still alive anyway..." He swallowed again. "But we left them there. Eagle was our team lead, basically our commanding officer when we were out on the field. He grabbed both me and Hawk and we were running away from it all. We fucking *ran*, Jules. What kind of man runs away from dying women? From slaves?"

The anguish in his voice made her close her eyes against the burning emotion threatening to spill out. She'd been angry at him for leaving all those years ago and she'd never given one thought about the hell he'd endured while he was away. Whatever she'd thought about him over the years, he'd gone halfway around the world to save it, only to have everything blow up in his face. Her hands trembled against his back as she realized how close he'd been to never coming home. Jason squeezed her and rubbed her arm, apparently thinking she was cold.

Jules cleared her throat. "But it was only your team, right? What on earth could you have done to help them? You'd have ended up lying next to them." She tried to focus on Jason's pain instead of dwelling on her fear, her relief, or how good his touch felt against her skin.

He shook his head, obviously not wanting to hear her reasoning. She waited a minute for him to continue. The fact that he was pushing through this emotional turmoil proved to her that he desperately needed to get the chains off his chest.

"We got out of there, that hell. We were high-tailin' it back to the Bird and all of a sudden, we were taking on friendly fire. Well... we *thought* they were friendlies. Apparently, that wasn't the case. They were locals I'd vetted, given them weapons... and they turned on us." He lightly grazed the scar above his ear. "This was from someone who wasn't MF7, but I thought of him as a fellow soldier. I'd thought we were on the same side at least." A bitter laugh broke free. "Shit, was I wrong. I'm tellin' ya, Jules, when he fired that shot, straight at my face, I thought for sure I was done. Honestly, I didn't care in that moment. I think I was still in shock at seeing all those women"—he swallowed hard—"dead. Because of me."

Her scowl brought her eyebrows so low, she felt her eyelashes brush against them. "How the hell do you figure that?"

"If I had just taken that shot. If I'd gotten that piece of shit between the eyes. They would've all been saved. He wouldn't have been able to set off that bomb." He shook his head violently, his chin brushing against the top of her head. "If I'd just trusted my gut. Trusted my training. None of it would've ever happened. Goddamnit, hesitating in that moment... it's the worst thing I've ever done.

"And if Hawk hadn't tugged me the rest of the way to that Bird, I would've never made it out alive. And shit... Eagle—" He shook his head. His silence brought to mind what Nora had told her about his team. That not all of them had made it.

"We found out later, while us cowards ran for our lives, the women who *had* survived, were smuggled away. To reenter the market."

Jules's chest tightened from the waves of despair barreling into her with his every word. Her job depended on always knowing the right thing to say, but, for once, she was at a loss. Jason had convinced himself that every wrong that happened that awful night in the desert was his. And he'd been punishing himself ever since.

Jules hadn't been there, so she didn't feel qualified to disagree with him. That would have to come from someone who was there. Hawk, it sounded like. She'd deal with that later. All she had then was her gut and it told her this man was good. Instead of relying on words that wouldn't resonate, she held him close, hoping he knew that no matter what happened, she was there for him.

It sounded to her like the mission was doomed from the start. There were a few things that would royally fuck up a case: bad intel, bad facts, and a lying client. She knew that if she had to rely on any of those as she stood in front of a judge at the pivotal moment of her client's reckoning, there was no hope. It seemed to her that one of those was the case for the MF7 Crew on their last mission, but that was the last thing he needed to hear at that moment, that all of MF7's hard work had been in vain. They were silent as she searched for what to say, but she took comfort in the strong beat of his heart, and hoped she could somehow keep him from drowning in his memories.

At a loss for words, Jules knew she could still provide some measure of comfort in a different way. Despite the pain she felt in her ribs, she lifted her body to kiss him. Their lips latched, their tongues rolled, and before Jules knew what was happening, the kiss became passionate and intense. Until he moved his hand to cradle the back of her head and she hissed in pain.

His hand shot off her head, as if he felt the throbbing beat in her skull. "Shit, Jules, I'm sorry. I can't believe I did that." In response, she pressed a soft kiss on his wet lips and massaged his back with her fingertips, trying to alleviate yet another moment of misplaced guilt.

He slid his hand up the inside of her T-shirt and lightly grazed the skin of her lower back, below the bandages. "Damn, baby. You have no idea how bad I want to make you feel good right now."

"Then why don't you?" she asked, trying her best for a sexy husky voice, instead of an injured one. "Let's make both of us feel good."

His chest vibrated against hers as he chuckled.

"Not the 'hell yes' I was lookin' for there, Jay," she huffed.

"I appreciate the enthusiasm, baby, but you're hurt." He smiled with contrition, she hoped. He gently massaged her nape, staying clear of the back of her head. She moaned softly as she succumbed to the comfort of his touch.

"Not that hurt," she whispered, before trailing her lips up his neck. She grinned when she felt him harden against her belly.

She could tell when she had him by the hitch in his breathing and the slow undulation of his body flush against hers. Her hand trailed down the bare skin of his abs, so lightly that she felt the tiny hairs stand on end underneath the gentleness of her touch. Her fingertips traced the top of his boxer briefs until she dipped in and took hold of his thickness, being sure to use the amount of pressure he'd always unraveled for.

"*Fuck*," he cursed as he inhaled sharply. He began to lose control and ground against her torso, making her suck in a stinging breath of her own. She tried to hide the hiss that escaped, hoping it could somehow be mistaken for sexual pleasure rather than the actual discomfort pulsing in her ribs.

His grinding came to an immediate halt and he huffed out a

groan that turned into a soft laugh. The tension in his muscles released as he moved her hand from his length. In one fluid motion, Jason settled to his back with her head comfortably at rest against his firm pecs. He cradled her hand in his own against his chest.

"What in the world—"

"Shh-shhush, just rest, baby girl. There will be time for all that later." He kissed the top of her head. For multiple reasons, she felt a bolt of frustration strike through her.

"Don't you dare shush—"

"Shh-shhush. Come on, baby. Aren't you tired? Just rest your head for a minute, okay? If you do that for me and still feel ready to go, I promise to make you feel so good."

Jules grumbled at his patronizing tone and almost insisted on sleeping in a guest room all by her own damn self, *especially* when his chest rumbled in amusement at her curses. But then his hand resumed its soothing massage against her neck.

Would it be so bad to take advantage of this and close my eyes for a few seconds before he takes advantage of me? She reluctantly agreed with her inner vixen and closed her eyes.

I'll rest. Just for a minute.

CHAPTER TWENTY-TWO

Jason wafted the mug underneath Jules's nose, half hidden under her arm. He was already dressed and ready to rescue Ellie, but he'd held off waking Jules until the last minute. They'd only slept for around two hours and while the power nap gave him enough charge to run, she needed way more than that after what she'd been through.

But no matter how tired she was, if he let her sleep through the mission, she'd kill him. He also knew if he didn't wake her in *just* the right way, as in, with her liquid addiction ready, she'd still kill him. Despite the danger, he was hoping getting Jules out of bed was the scariest thing he did all day.

Jules's elbow shifted and her nostrils flared a fraction at the bitter aroma. She brought her hands, eyes still closed, toward the mug. He helped her hold it as she blindly sipped just a drop. The relaxed sigh that followed went straight to his black fatigues, but he tamped that down. He needed to keep his head in the game.

"Baby girl, go ahead and open those beautiful eyes for me so I can get this show on the road."

She cracked an eye in response and peeked at his gear. Every inch of him was strapped in black, with Kevlar under his civvie style shirt, and strategically hidden weaponry. Not particularly stealthy if they'd planned to spend time in the city in broad daylight, but plain enough that they could blend in with early morning shadows. At the very least, they hoped no one would fuck with them. He felt his chest puff up at her inspection, and he even enjoyed her scowl at his peacocking. Still, he preened for a second more before she took another loud slurp, bringing him back to the moment. He cleared his throat as he left the mug in her hands.

"I gotta go, baby. Hawk and Snake said they were able to figure out the layout of the hotel's security. Everything's ready. We gotta hit 'em quick, before something changes and we've already lost a lot of time. Especially since we don't know when this auction is actually gonna be." He brushed his lips lightly across her cheek and backed away.

Her honeyed locks were still in the haphazard bun she'd gathered sometime in the night and his shirt was so big, it nearly fell off her shoulder. He could practically see the gears in her mind flicking switches and turning on lights, readying her for the day. She was cute as hell in the morning. Unable to help himself, he kissed her once more on the forehead, reveling in how normal the gesture could become if she got on board. He straightened and turned to leave. Now that she was awake, he needed to meet the Crew ASAP.

"Jay—" Her voice cracked from her injuries and he stopped in his tracks. She worried her bottom lip as it rested on the mouth of the mug. "Come back... 'kay?" His heart clenched and he nodded without saying a word.

He'd never make her another promise he couldn't keep.

∽

Phoenix parked the dark van in the shadows of a forgotten alley near the hotel, with Jason, Draco, Hawk, and Devil in the back.

"Remember, I'll loop the camera feeds for the security," Snake explained in their earbuds for the umpteenth time on their ride there. Jason didn't mind the repetition, though. Snake's tendency to talk fast and frantically as he recounted mission directives had a strange calming effect. "Phoenix, you remain in the alley unless I give you the sign you need to drive around a bit to throw off attention—"

"Ten-four," Phoenix affirmed, his wisecracking subdued for now.

"Jaybird and Hawk, enter through the west alley entrance. Draco and Devil, you enter through the east. Both teams will be able to navigate their nearby stairwells. I've got the security feed on the lobby, so with Phoenix in the alley, all exits are secure. For the next forty-five minutes, I've removed the necessary guest card swipes on the exits and the room where our targets are being held. You'll each enter the third floor and head to Room 318. I'm doing a quick recon on video surveillance as we speak, but it's taking more time than I'd like to get to real time. If the vid time stamps are correct, surveillance goes back to around a week ago, but I haven't gotten to the last twenty-four hours yet. I did see a couple of men bringing in several large duffel bags over the course of a few days. That's most likely how they're transporting the women. The last two bags carried in was approximately eighty-four hours ago—"

"You think that could've been Ellie and Sasha?" Devil asked.

"Shit," Jason grunted. "If it was them, then our forty-eight hour clock was off by twelve fucking hours. We never had a chance."

"Jay, remember we talked about this. It's just a timeline. It doesn't mean anything other than we've found all the easy answers already. We're getting to the real answers right now."

Jason tried to be as positive as Jules, but until they actually found Ellie, it didn't matter what hour they were supposedly on. They all felt like an eternity.

Snake cleared his throat. "Since those last two... bags, um, entered the room... a number of different men have entered and exited. Pixilation is grainy, so it's going to take some time for me to cross-reference the videos with facial recognition software. Might not even work, but I'll try it. Okay, here's something... hm... that's odd. The men who enter sometimes have large bags, but they leave without them. But here, around sixty hours ago, one man left with just one duffel bag..."

Jason's breath froze in his lungs. "Sasha," he choked on his realization.

"Oh, fuck, right. Sorry, Jaybird."

Silence filled the van. It burned knowing they'd been too late to save Sasha, and Jason refused to imagine what Ellie and the other women were enduring. On top of all that, if the rest of the Crew were like Jason, then the memory of their last mission festered in their minds and the reminder of more women they hadn't been able to save kept cutting at the wound.

"If there are other victims, why aren't the authorities looking for them, too? Why are the police only looking for Ellie? Hell, why aren't the freaking FBI involved?" Nora demanded in Jason's earpiece.

"From our experience," Hawk began, carefully choosing his words, "these assholes find, lure, or kidnap victims that won't be missed. Plus, sometimes traffickers have their victims for days, weeks, or even months, until either their... *usefulness* is up, or until they're ready to sell. The government has stricter parameters to abide by and if the traffickers are ever caught, they're given a slap on the wrist after years and years of waiting for the judicial system to prosecute. MF7 was created quietly to operate under government direction, while still off the radar, in order to extract women all over the world by any means necessary, and take down trafficking organizations. By capturing and prosecuting, or through other ways that are less... *available* to well-known government agencies. Without intervention, traffickers thrive best when no one misses the victims."

"They've stolen the wrong girl this time." Heads nodded at Jason's statement.

Snake coughed and continued on, "I hate to be a pessimist, but if something unforeseen happens, the plan is to—"

"There's no room for error. We're getting Ellie outta there," Devil growled before Jason could interject. Dev's face was carved stone, but his words were a window to his true emotions. The only outward hint of nerves was the vibration in Dev's right leg. Jason wouldn't overanalyze it. As long as the man's head and heart were in the right place at that moment, he didn't give a fuck what was going on underneath all that strawberry hair.

Jason was trying his best to calm his own anxiety, but when they pulled up and stopped behind the hotel, he had to swallow hard against his dry mouth. A shrill beeping tone made him jump, and he looked down to see that his body-worn camera was on. Snake must've activated the devices remotely since he was watching live from BlackStone's HQ. Jules and Nora were able to access the feed from their individual screens.

"Coast's clear. Godspeed, men."

At Snake's confirmation, they exited the back of the van and hustled to their prospective entries. No one was fully in their battle stance since there was no evidence there would be danger before they got inside the hotel. Still, their Glocks were racked and waiting as they were held covertly against each man's thigh. The teams split and, for once, Hawk let Jason take lead as they approached the west alley entrance. Just as Snake promised, the solid metal side entry opened without a key card. With Hawk holding the door, Jason entered first and at his head twitch, Hawk followed closely behind. They both immediately entered the adjacent stairwell, only an arm's length away. Hustling upstairs, their feet were quick, light, and softly faint against the gray cement stairs.

Seconds later, they went through the same song and dance, and came out to the hallway at Snake's command, perfectly timed with Devil and Draco. The two groups converged on Room 318, and Jason wondered if the men and women inside the silent room could hear his heart slamming its fists against his chest, threatening to break free. He sidled up to the door, Hawk on his right shoulder, and Devil mirroring him across the entrance.

Waiting for Snake's count to open the room door, it seemed both Jason and Devil were trying to steady their breathing. This was the moment. Ellie and the other women were in there and Jason's finger was on the trigger, a breath away from lightin' up anyone who got in the way of saving his sister. They weren't planning on killing anyone. They'd been taught how to use just enough violence in order to subdue and retrieve, and then follow up with an anonymous call to local authorities. Basically, do all the hard work and leave the targets gift wrapped for the "good guys" to take the credit.

But this time, Jason was ready to have Ellie and Jules safe and sound at home, whatever the cost. After this, there was no fuckin' way in hell he let either of them out of his sight. If they'd thought he was overbearing before, they were in for a whole new world of alpha male.

Snake's countdown felt like it took much longer than a classic "three-two-one" should, and when the door was accessed remotely and the key card slot flashed green, Devil pulled the handle down and Jason burst in low, gun raised high enough to shoot the bastards where it'd count.

He blazed into the room, with only cool air to meet his entrance. The other men checked the bathroom and the rest of their surroundings.

"Clear." Hawk cursed out. Hawk and Draco relaxed while Jason and Devil maintained battle posture. It'd been a long time since Jason had held his fighting stance for an extended period of time, and that, combined with his adrenaline fading, made his shoulders grow tense and his hand developed a slight tremor.

"I said, 'Clear,'" Hawk repeated. The safe word grated against Jason's eardrums.

"But... but they were here. The note said..." He shook his head roughly to try to shake away the truth, hoping to escape it.

The other men were silent as Jason probed under the naked king bed.

"They were here alright. And whoever this is, they know what they're doing," Hawk said after investigating the bathroom. "They stole every towel and sheet here. Trying to hide DNA." Hawk's observation made Jason's empty stomach turn over, and Devil punched the wall over the bed.

"What the fuck happened? They were supposed to be here! Where the fuck are they?" Devil demanded.

Snake was cursing rapidly and the punch of keys on the other end kept pace. "I'm uploading the remainder of the hotel security footage to include the past twenty-four hours, playing it back at decuple the speed and minimizing delay on the audio—"

"English, Snake." Jason silently thanked Jules's quiet reminder over his earbud. Another beat passed before the computer whiz continued.

"Fuck… basically, I compressed all the video into a short time period and skipped most of it up until a few hours ago and it looks like men—who knew their way around hotel security—left with their precious cargo only a few hours ago."

Jason's knees went weak and he depended on the flimsy wall sconce to keep him up. Devil put his weight under Jason's arm and helped situate him back to standing.

"Snake, were you able to find out who booked the room?" Hawk asked.

"No, they used Ivan Ivanovich, so it's a dead-end."

"What do you mean, 'a dead-end?' Let's find this Ivanovich bitch," Devil growled.

"No, that's the problem. Ivan Ivanovich is a dummy name. It's basically the 'John Doe' of Russia. It's no good."

"So, does that mean… they're gone?" Nora's lyrical voice struck the wrong chord, and Jason felt like he was going to throw up. He probably would've if Devil hadn't fuckin' punched him in the arm.

"Dude, what the hell?"

A curl of the large man's strawberry blond hair escaped free from his black headband as he shrugged. "Pain helps you not think about it." Devil's deep timbre cracked through his forced stoicism, and the approaching morning brought his abnormally green pallor to light. If his coloring was any indication, it seemed Devil might've needed a punch himself.

"Guys, we've got a problem."

Hawk swore. "Fuck, Snake, we've talked about this. You need to work on the clichés—"

"SWAT is closing in on the hotel. You've got approximately three, no—two minutes until they reach 318. Commence SERE maneuvers."

The silent room filled with curses as they bugged out. Each team relied on their survival, evasion, resistance, and escape training they'd perfected for MF7 and exited the way they entered in order to minimize the possibility of capture. Jason and Hawk opened up the stairwell door to their escape when Snake cursed over their headsets.

"They're heading up the stairs... shit *and* the elevators..."

"Both?" Hawk asked.

"What?"

"Both sets of stairs and both elevators? There's two of each—" Their leader clarified.

"Yes... No... Wait..."

Hawk growled in warning, "Fuck man—"

"No! Both elevators, and the west stairs."

Good, Draco and Devil won't get caught—the relief only lasted a millisecond before he realized what that meant for him and Hawk. Jason sucked in a fortifying breath as he stared down the long hall past the elevator doors, wondering if they had enough time to try to escape to the other stairwell. The ominous *ding* of the elevator answered his question.

Hawk cursed but with no other option, they spilled into the stairwell. Only, he made the game-time decision to ascend rather than meet the beating drum of footsteps. It sounded like they were still in the hotel hallway, but there must have been a lot of them because Jason could hear them approaching the stairwell door from three floors above. On silent and agonizingly slow tiptoes, Hawk and Jason reached the top floor of the stairs where the landing bore the sign "ROOF ACCESS ONLY," displaying prominently beside the door.

At each second, Hawk exaggerated a nod to indicate his count and it made Jason nearly explode with impatience. Finally, Hawk twisted the handle and leaned against the door. The SWAT team, a cacophony of footsteps below, effectively masked Hawk's movements. Once they were both on the roof, Hawk guided the door as he allowed it to *snick* shut.

"Thank God for amateurs," Jason breathed out. Hawk agreed with a single nod.

"Turn off non-guest access to all doors, Snake."

"On it, boss. Dev and Draco are already in the van with Phoenix. They're just waiting for you."

Even though they'd only had a floor to rise up, Jason felt the exhaustion from matching each quiet step with a SWAT member's stomp. He leaned against the wall and Hawk paced toward the corner of the roof and peered over.

"What're you doing?" Jason's whisper-yell carried.

"Math."

Jason felt his eyes squint and his mouth opened to question until he realized what the crazy fuck meant.

"No! NO!" He put as much force as he could while in a lower decibel, but Hawk kept his head over the edge.

"It's actually not that far down. We've jumped out of worse."

"Yeah... with a fucking parachute!"

Hawk ignored him and shook the gutter with both hands. He nodded to himself when the metal attachment barely moved. "Seems sound."

"That's fucking suicide, man!" Jason knew his logic fell on deaf ears when Hawk's leg disappeared over the side.

"*Hawk!*" But once again, Hawk ignored his feverish whisper.

"Come on! We'll climb as far as we can and jump off the rest of the way." Hawk had just about lost his damn mind, but nearby sirens clanged in Jason's head and he pulled away from the wall, reluctantly joining his insane comrade.

He, too, checked the stability of the gutter, and smirked at Hawk's scowl from below since the man was already well and truly down the pipe when Jason insisted on shaking it. One fucked-up thing the Army, Night Stalkers, and MF7 had all taught him? How to find humor in literally the most inopportune and inappropriate times.

He hoisted a leg over the corner and noted Phoenix had driven the van directly underneath Hawk as they shimmied down. Jason looked up to the calm, blue morning sky and briefly thought about praying, until he heard the rattling of the upstairs roof access door. Instead, he put one hand below the other and relied mostly on his upper back to take him to safety. A loud *bang* from both above and below made him pause until he realized Hawk had landed on the roof of the van. When he heard the shouting from above, it registered the SWAT had finally made it on the roof.

The sweat in his grip increased, and he slipped partially down the metal gutter. Only his calloused palms catching on pipe connectors slowed his descent until he was able to tighten his legs around metal. He was about ten feet from the top of the van when the first SWAT member aimed a MP5 right at his head. At the first shot, a raspy feminine gasp filled his earbuds. He slid five more feet down before landing in a roll, on top of the van.

His hands quickly found purchase on the metal ski rack, and he hung on by the tips of his fingers as Phoenix hit the gas. Shots increased in frequency, but thankfully not in accuracy, as Jason crawled inch by inch, rung by rung to the open sunroof. He'd never seen a sunroof on a utility van, but he didn't give two shits about that when he had to grip the hole for dear life just as Phoenix took a hairpin turn around the corner.

His knuckles whitened at the sudden presence of air under

his free-flying legs and he realized he was eight fingers away from a nasty fall. His forearms were ropes of fire as he pulled against the momentum of the van. Suddenly, he felt a tightness around his wrists and found himself launching into the dark, hoping for a gentle landing.

"OOF." Jason felt the grunt of the man below him and heard the screech of tires as Phoenix peeled around another corner. Jason inadvertently gripped the chestnut hair underneath him, crinkling its perfect coiffe.

"*Fuck*. You're welcome, asshole. Now get the hell off me."

Hawk rolled his back until Jason landed on his own. With each right-angled turn, he, Hawk, Devil, and Draco pinballed against one another until, *finally*, Phoenix must've hit the highway. He expected Phoenix to make some joke about taking extra turns to keep them suffering, but when Jason was situated, he noted Phoenix's grim expression. Now that they'd had even a second to breathe, there was no doubt they all carried the same look.

"What happened?" Phoenix asked in the rearview mirror, questioning anyone who would answer. A sharp pain stabbed Jason's stomach at the hopelessness filling his gut.

"They weren't there," Hawk answered simply. Phoenix cursed.

"Bad tip, then?"

They all shook their heads and Jason grew annoyed as he realized that under Phoenix's ball cap, both of his ears were naked of any audio.

"You asshole, what're you doing without your fucking headphones—"

"No, not a bad tip. They'd been there. Either we were late, or they were clued in on our op somehow," Hawk breathed out his explanation before leaning back to rest.

His ear tickled and Jason realized that Jules had been running hot on the other end.

"—what kind of motherfucking SWAT team shoots a fleeing

subject when there's no danger?! Who were they sent to find? Wait... is that Investigator Burgess on the screen?"

"Burgess is there?" Jason asked.

"Affirmative," Snake answered. "The security cam feed I've channeled has finally caught up to real-time. It looks like he's beside the SWAT commander. Audio confirms he's called in ID to Room 318."

"If he's calling in the investigation division, then he must've gotten a tip for that room," Jules huffed.

"Same as us." Jason felt his lips tighten as he met Hawk's gaze. Hawk gave a curt nod in agreement.

"This doesn't make any sense. I mean, it fucking sucks ass that we were too late. But why would someone send us in, only to send the cops in there too?" Devil asked, his strawberry brow peaked.

Jason could practically feel Jules pacing on the other end. "Why send Jules a note specifically?" he asked. "Especially if the goal was to rat me out somehow to the cops? What's the end goal here? Something's not adding up."

"Someone's playing us," Draco growled.

"Or..." Jason paused to form his response. "Someone's getting played."

"Whatcha mean Jaybird?" Hawk asked, leaning up from his perch against the back of the passenger seat.

"What if someone's trying to point Jules in the right direction... but someone *else* is a step ahead?" His hypothesis was met with blank stares.

"Look, I know it sounds crazy. But Jules got that first note from Original Sin. It said"—he swallowed— "'The girl is up for sale.' But it also said, 'He can't go home.' I go home, and next thing I know, I'm arrested for Sasha's murder." He could see ideas percolating, but no solidity yet.

"Then, the next note we get is the hotel address. We act on it, but the cops somehow know our move. It makes no sense to both help me not get arrested, and then try to have us get caught. Seems to me, we've got someone on the inside, who doesn't know he's on the outs."

"You think we've got a double agent who's about to be double-crossed?"

"Exactly." Jason snapped his fingers at Phoenix's assessment.

"Shit, man, what do we do with that?" Phoenix asked.

The men shook with the van as it plowed down the highway. Phoenix took random exits and turns periodically so that no one could follow, but their silent brainstorming and lack of ideas made the ride seem exponentially longer.

Like every other mission he'd been on, he walked through a mental version of an after-action report to analyze all of the mistakes he'd made. He'd been *so* close to Ellie. He knew it was all in his head, but he could've sworn he could smell the memory of her, a sunny spring morning. Every brotherly sense he had told him that Ellie had been in that room. And they'd just missed her.

Jules's letter had to have been telling the truth. Because the alternative, that their only clue to finding El had been a trap, caused the pit of hopelessness slowly settling in his stomach to roil and burn like lava. He thought back to the mission and retraced his steps, all the way back to the strip club, wondering if he could piece it all together, until he was interrupted by Jules's new husky voice.

"I need to go back to Original Sin."

"Abso-fucking-lutely not." He growled back at her. He knew outright refusing her would ignite her stubbornness, but he'd rather her lose her cool than lose her altogether.

"OS is the only place we've gotten answers, Jay. We'd be shootin' ourselves in the foot if we didn't use the leads we have," she argued, her accent breaking through. He missed her twang, but he hated it came back out when she was emotional.

"I said, *no*. There's gotta be something we missed—"

"There isn't, okay? Don't you think we would've acted on any other tip besides 'storm the fucking hotel?'"

Jason felt a rumble come from deep within—

"Don't you dare growl at me again, Jason Stone, you hear me?"

The Crew sniggered at him and he flipped them two birds.

"Jay, listen." He focused on her lowered voice, pretending like it was only the two of them on the radio. Even her injured vocal cords provided some measure of comfort to his soul, and would've soothed him entirely if she hadn't been talking about putting herself in harms' way. Again. "I didn't go with y'all to try to save Ellie. I wanted to, believe me. You know I wanted to—"

"Yeah, 'cuz you're a fighter."

"Sure, but I'm also not an idiot. I don't have a trained assassin bone in my body so I'll leave it up to the professionals every time. There's no place for me on a battlefield or rescue mission, but, at one point, Original Sin was literally my home." He heard her sigh and his heart clenched. "I feel useless here, Jay. Ellie's out there... let me do what I can to save her. *Please.*"

He was doused with a splash of panic and he swallowed at her last word. The lump in his throat had a hard time traveling down. He didn't want to deny her this, her chance to try to help Ellie any way she could, but it was too dangerous. If he lost Ellie *and* Jules? He didn't think he'd be able to recover. Especially when he was so close to getting Jules back for good. A soft thump against his shoulder drew his attention to his side. In the darkness of the back of the van, Hawk sat back again and his eyes bored into Jason's as he spoke.

"Jules, it's too much of a liability."

Jason tilted his head, eyes closed, and mouthed *thank you*, grateful that he didn't have to be the one to shut her down.

"You're obviously a target at this point," Hawk argued. "You've been the victim of a *bomb*, Jules. We don't need to risk you when we can send someone else who doesn't face the same danger."

"But—"

"I can go again!" Nora piped up. "They won't expect me to be a part of any of this. It'll be business as usz' if I go when OS opens tonight and chat up Cyn on a routine client check-in."

Jason's head rested against his knees, nodding slowly and silently praying to any deity listening, thanking them for the fact that someone was speaking reason to his girl. He used to be the one who could do that for her. Somewhere along the way—fuck that, he knew exactly when—he'd lost her trust.

"No way, Nora, it's way too dangerous—"

"Pssh, yeah right, Babs. No more than any other time I deal with one of our clients. Why would they think I'm a threat? I'm basically unaffiliated and adorable, so there."

The breath that had stalled in his lungs seeped out with Jules's sigh over the earbuds. He'd have to figure out how to thank that little pixie.

"That could work. Draco can go into town to make sure Nora's safe," Hawk suggested. Draco grunted in agreement from his corner. At least that's what Jason assumed. If Draco didn't want to do something, he usually wasn't shy about it.

"Fine," Jules forced out.

"Great! 'Kay, so this was actually a pretty terrible and disappointing time and it's gods-awful early, so I'm going to take a nap before I have to do my job today. I may even show up late. Don't tell my boss, though. She can be a real bitch. Byeeee!"

The stolid blond Viking in the corner chuckled for the second time in the past twelve hours.

"Who *are* you, man?" Phoenix asked, eyeing him from the rearview mirror. Draco scowled, pulled out a small cylinder from his pocket and deposited a toothpick in his hand.

"Fuck you."

CHAPTER TWENTY-THREE

"Juliet, please. Call me back. I can't talk much right now, but it's really important. I-I've messed up, alright? I need you..." Andy's voice on the other end of the message lowered. "Please. Just... call me."

Jules's sigh fogged up the window. She rubbed her hand against her chest, massaging the ache that formed after listening to all of Andy's messages. They were the same as all the ones she'd been hearing for months, and she didn't know if it was because of the stress she was under or the near-death experience, but she was starting to feel bad for the man. Yeah, he'd been an ass, but at one point he'd been her friend. A good friend, actually. Once they found Ellie, she'd agree to a long overdue heart-to-heart with the poor guy. After all, maybe his personality change wasn't entirely his fault? It hadn't been until he started working for his father's firm that he began to act like a total douchebag.

The firm might have a philanthropic public persona, but Jules knew the men who worked there were nothing but sleaze-bags. She tried not to judge others. After all, her job was to make sure people got a fair shake in life. But facts were facts, and the truth was the men of Ascot, Rusnak, and Strickland, LLC were by far the most frequent, and least desired, guests at Original

Sin. They would come in, demand a good show, berate and belittle the Sinners, then complain that the women weren't good enough for one reason or another. To top it all off, they'd inevitably end the night by refusing to tip. Cyn tried to figure out a way to ban them from the club, but the women the firm chose never stayed long enough to really make a fuss.

The shower in the en suite bathroom squeaked off and drew her out of her head. She and Jason hadn't talked since he got back but she'd been so relieved to see him come through the front door. Per BlackStone Securities instructions, her phone had been off since their first talk up until now. She'd used Jason's cell to join the video feed with Snake and Nora. So, when she'd heard clomping footsteps on the porch, she'd armed herself by snagging the closest lamp by its faux branch base and held it high. Thank God, it'd been Jason.

She'd seen his stormy gray eyes first, and let her makeshift weapon fall from her fingers to the floor. During the mission, when Jason was being *shot* at while trying to flee—by those poor excuses for law enforcement, no less—she'd been sick with worry and rage. When he finally entered the cabin, she'd leaped onto him without thinking twice, only sliding off when she noticed he still had his gear in his hands. Then, she'd realized what she was doing and quickly let go before taking a healthy step back.

His posture had been weighted by more than just the equipment on his back and Jules realized the depth of how distraught he was at the outcome. She'd been incredibly disappointed that they hadn't found Ellie, but to be honest? Jason coming back to the cabin, even empty-handed, was still a relief she hadn't expected once those first shots were fired. She didn't know how to feel about that, but got sidetracked from her thoughts as he'd dropped his heavy bag by the door and stood, his haunted eyes watching her. She'd taken a tentative step closer again, as if approaching a wounded animal she was sure would flee. When she saw the creased lines even deeper than the ones she'd traced just hours earlier, the heavy bags under his eyes, the tired brow, she'd instinctively known it was the first time he'd let his guard down since he'd left that morning. That intuition told her what they both needed. She'd rushed to him again, wordlessly giving him another hug. She only barely caught her groan when the breath was knocked out of her by his tightly returned embrace.

Once they'd let go, he'd trudged to the bathroom and had been in the shower ever since. The man was hanging on by a thread. After the last note, they had next to nothing to go by to find Ellie. It was that feeling of desperation that had caused her to turn her phone back on, just for a minute, in order to check to see if she'd received even just a hint of a clue to finding Ellie. So far, her phone had only provided countless irrelevant messages from a desperate man clinging to the dying gasps of a relationship that never was.

She only hoped Nora could come through with another letter from OS. Jules was nervous about the potential danger her friend could get herself into, but as much as she hated to admit it, Nora and Hawk had been right. For some reason, Jules had a target on her back. As far as they knew, Nora didn't. She was also one of the smartest and most capable women she'd ever met. Whatever Nora found out, if anything, she'd know what to do.

Jules jumped as her phone, almost forgotten in her hand, vibrated and she glanced back to the closed bathroom door, hoping it didn't open before she turned the phone back off. Just before she pressed the right buttons, she realized who was calling.

"Marco? What's going—"

"Jules, are you okay? *Dios mio*, I'm so glad you answered." His frantic voice on the other line had a rare hint of his Spanish accent and she was immediately put on alert.

"Yeah, yeah. I'm okay—"

"*Joder, bien. Sirenita, yo estaba muy preocupado*—"

"English, Marco. The only words I understood just then, were 'fuck' and 'little siren'. I'm sure the two were unrelated, but knowing you, there's no way to be certain."

"Jules, this is not a joke. I was worried, alright? Investigator Burgess just came by the courthouse, claiming he almost busted Jason Stone in a trafficking ring."

"*WHAT?*"

"I know. He said that he got an anonymous tip from someone at the hotel that men were smuggling large bags from a hotel room. Apparently one of the bags had… had blonde hair hanging out of an opening before whoever had the bag repositioned the zipper and stuffed it back in." Jules gulped at the implication and felt sick to her stomach. Could that have been Ellie's sunny blonde hair? She was so preoccupied by the thought and her churning tummy, she almost missed what he said next.

"Excuse me, what the fuck was that, now?"

"Investigator Burgess said he looked through the video feed and observed at least two men hustling from the hotel room in question. Jules, I hate to tell you this, but he recognized Jason from one of the cameras…"

Jules went numb and she had to hold the phone with both hands. She knew for a fact that was impossible. But what could she say to convince Marco that Jason wasn't the bad guy in the situation? How could she tell the prosecutor that it was impossible for Investigator Burgess to have seen Jason on video, when Snake had cut the feed?

At least… he'd said he cut off the hotel security feed. But law enforcement was called… Did Snake tell the truth? Was Burgess the inside man they'd been worried about? What if…

She shook her head at the seriously worrying detour her mind was taking. Surely, they could trust BlackStone Securities. But although Jason had faith in them, the fact of the matter was that Jules didn't know them enough for that. All she knew was that they and Jason had been part of some clandestine paramilitary group. And that they were medically discharged for psychological reasons.

Marco was still talking, but Jason emerged into the bedroom clothed in only a cloud of campfire steam from his delicious body wash and a towel barely large enough to cover his best bits. He gave her a half-smile until he realized she was on the phone. *Her* phone. He scowled and marched over to her but she quickly stood up and put her hand up to stop him.

"You could be being tracked!" he hissed on a whisper. Jules covered his mouth with her hand and tried to focus on what Marco was saying.

"He's wanted to bring in the feds and is planning on asking the judge for a human trafficking warrant. I've been trying to call you all morning, but your phone was off. Goddamnit Jules, why don't you ever answer your phone?" Jules's fingers vibrated against Jason's mouth as she felt him express his displeasure on yet another growl.

"I'm sorry, Marco—" She ignored Jason's narrowed eyes and turned away from him to the corner of the room. He was entirely too distracting. "I've been busy, but I'm okay. I know I've asked a lot of you lately, but please. You have to trust me. There are bigger things at play right now and Jason's not the one you're looking for."

Her friend cursed in Spanish on the other line but fell quiet for a long time.

"You have to give me more than that, Jules. There's shit on my side that you don't know, that I can't tell you, yet."

"Like what?"

"I just told you I can't tell you! Let's just say that Burgess has more than enough to get a warrant right now."

She felt her brow scrunch. "He has more than enough evidence against Jason?"

"Well, no. Not Jason, specifically, but they've got enough evidence to put *someone* away for several lifetimes, and Burgess is itching for Stone to be that someone."

"Please, Marco..." Her mouth opened to say more, but Jason shook his head. He was right. She'd just questioned his own team's loyalty. Marco could be obligated to share their information, as meager as it was, with his own bosses.

"Trust me. I've never let you down before, have I?" She refused to look at Jason, but she counted his deep breaths as they waited. *One... Two... Three—*

"Fine, I'll tell Burgess he needs more evidence. That we can't take Stone in on just a hunch."

"Make him show you the video."

"But won't that show—"

"Just make him produce the video. Trust me." She could almost hear him nodding as he made his decision.

"Okay, okay. I'll see what I can do. But I'm telling you, Jules, your man's on thin ice. If you're wrong about this—"

"I'm not wrong, Marco, I swear—"

"—My job is on the line, alright? This is a huge case, and if you're wrong about this, fuck, not only is my job on the line, but we could be wasting valuable time we could be using to save the girl."

"I know, I know..." She rubbed her fingers against her brow and Jason pulled her against him, cupping the back of her neck. His warm skin was still slightly damp, but she nuzzled into his chest.

"Please, Marco. Just trust me. We're trying to figure all this out on our end, too. We need to be working together and Jason needs to be finding his sister, not worried about getting arrested on trumped-up charges."

"You have twenty-four hours, Jules. I don't think I can hold Burgess off much longer than that. Then he'll be coming for Stone. And you, if you're harboring a fugitive... I can't protect you then. No matter how good of friends we are."

"Got it. Thank you, Marco. For everything."

He grunted and hung up as big hands grabbed the phone away from her ear.

"Hey!"

Jason made an exaggerated show of turning off her phone before tossing it into his open bag on the floor. "Don't 'hey' me. What do you think you're doing? You know you're not supposed to be on your phone. If Asshat is following you, God knows who else could be. What were you thinking?"

He was right and she knew it. But she couldn't help bristling at his rough tone. "We don't know if Andy is tracking me!" His eyebrow raise infuriated her even more. "What does it matter if he is?" she growled. "You want to know why I checked my phone? You want to know what I'm thinking? I'm thinking that I feel useless right now and I need to be doing something! Marco said that Investigator Burgess is trying to pin all this on you. Again. He's trying to say you're the one that's trafficking women! And from the sounds of it, he's got a lot of evidence to charge someone with, but he wants it to be you. You know where I got all that extremely valuable and important information? From. My. *Phone.*"

Jason jerked back, as if burned from her words, and ran his hand through his hair, causing small droplets of water to land on her cheek before he turned.

"This is all such a fucking mess. We need to find Ellie. Has Nora said anything yet?"

"No, but she'll probably go right when the club opens up tonight. That's when she usually checks up on things for me. It's not an open practice day, so there's no one there now and Cyn would've told us if someone left a message for me last night."

He nodded and sat on the bed, his head in his hands. "That's good," he said through his fingers, muffling his words. "That way Nora won't tip anyone off by changing up her routine."

She sat beside him, their thighs almost touching. She didn't know what to say. It *was* a fucking mess. All of it. But all they could do at this point was sit and wait, hoping to God that Nora would find another note. And then hoping that note wasn't a trap. Ellie was out there and they were no closer to finding her than from the start. Slowly, she let herself lie back on the bed and covered her eyes with her forearm, suddenly exhausted.

"Is that all Aguilar wanted?"

She lifted her arm just enough to peek one eye at Jason. His attempt at nonchalance made his question sound more like an accusation.

"He wanted to tell me that. Make sure I was okay—"

"Why does he care if you're okay?"

Jules sat up on her elbows and noted only minor discomfort in her ribs thanks to the ibuprofen. She cocked her head at the crazy man beside her.

"Hmm, let's see. We have a few things to pick from. Let's try, 'I just survived a car bomb recently and he's a decent person?' Or maybe, 'My client is a wanted man and was almost apprehended.' Or how about, 'He's been my friend since 1L year—'"

"1L year?"

"It means first year of law school."

He nodded before waiting a beat to ask the question he'd really been hinting at since the conversation started. "Is that all he was?" His stormy gray eyes pierced hers.

She twisted her mouth around, biting her tongue before she felt patient enough not to bite his head off. "Seriously? Is this really happening right now? With everything going on?" His expression didn't change but he stood up from the bed and faced her with his arms crossed.

She swallowed at the view. "First of all, if we're gonna do this, I'm gonna need you to put on some damn clothes." He scowled, but dug around his bag to put on shorts. He dropped the towel and she saw a brief glimpse of firm muscular ass before she shut her eyes.

"Okay, done. You had a first of all... what's your second?"

She cleared her throat and dared to resume her glare, thankful to find that he was indeed clothed. "Well, second, I don't see how any of my life is your goddamn business."

"Just answer the question."

His trained calm demeanor lit a fuse she didn't know was so short. She sat up on her knees on the bed in order to be eye level with him. Despite her tall stature, without her stilettos on, he would be too tall to yell at properly from the ground.

"You know what? I don't owe you anything. But I'll tell you anyway. Yes, Marco was my friend in law school. Yes, we slept together." She ignored the pang in her stomach at the sight of his wince. "But you know where you were when all that happened?" She was surprised he wasn't looking away and tried her best to keep her anger in the face of his hurt.

"I was gone."

"You're damn right you were gone. You *left* me, Jason. I thought you were it. I thought we were going to have a life together. I thought—" She choked back emotion, her throat reminding her that she was still in physical pain. "I thought I *loved* you. But that was when you were here. Then you weren't. You didn't leave a number, an address, you even left Ellie." His eyes shuttered. *Good*, but even in her mind, the word didn't hold satisfaction.

"It was just me and Ellie, for seven years. I grew up without you. I owe you nothing. Did I sleep with other people? Yes. I'm not a fucking nun. I was a stripper for God's sake. But it took me years to get to the point where I could even look at someone else." It was her turn not to meet his heated gaze, but she felt it blaze on her skin. She took several breaths to cool down, but she knew she needed to keep going. She had to free what she'd kept locked up.

"You cheated—"

"It wasn't true. I told you that—"

"How was I supposed to know that seven years ago? Was I supposed to just hold out? Hoping you would come back and grace me with your presence again? Pray you would tell me that everything you said was a lie? You don't know what I went through. What Ellie and I both went through." She couldn't handle being on her knees in front of him anymore and, as gracefully as she could with the breath of pain she still felt in her ribs, she unfolded off the bed. She wielded her manicured finger as she approached him, but even with all the anger she held pent up, the force behind her weapon as she stabbed into his shirtless chest only made him grimace.

"Why did you lie?" she demanded, the question as pointed as her nail. "You know, if you were any other client, I'd fire you on the spot for not telling the truth."

"Because..." He tapered off. But she waited. "Because I thought I was doing the right thing, okay?"

"What's that supposed to mean?"

"It means... Jules, my parents died on their way home from picking me up in high school."

"Jay, I know, but—"

"Just listen. They were arguing, I know you know this. But they were arguing over me. I was a total fuck up and I didn't care. Mom was incredible. Understanding. Greg was a great dad, but he was still a hard-ass after being in the Army, and I rebelled at every turn." He swallowed and reached for her hand and held it. "They were arguing... and then that truck hit us—"

"Jay, I'm not trying to be insensitive, but we've been over this. It wasn't your fault."

"I know that now. Really, I do. But back then. Damnit Jules, you know how fucked-up I was. I carried that shit with me for years. Living up to the expectations of a ghost was why I went into the military in the first place. I didn't need to have the guilt over you too."

Jules tugged her hand away. "What's *that* supposed to mean? I *never* gave you a guilt trip, Jason."

"Damn, I'm saying this all wrong." He tugged at his hair and she could practically see him searching for the right words to say. "It means you weren't going to go to law school. Because of me. You were ready to have a family. With me." Jules instinctively clutched her stomach at the phantom pain. "I'd gotten the call from Hawk about MF7 and without a single doubt... even if it took years for me to come back... even if I never came back, I knew I had to go. For you. You were willing to wait. For me. Move.

For me. You were willing to give up everything you'd worked so hard for, all that you'd earned to get out of that fucking closet at Original Sin. You were ready to give everything up for me—"

"Don't put this on me, Jason—"

"And I'm not fucking worth it."

Jules stopped. His pain was etched around his eyes, the weight on his shoulders made them sag. He was begging her to understand. It almost broke her heart. She wanted to reach out to him, but it didn't feel right. She held his gaze and studied him. He was grieving over his words, over what he thought was the truth. He wasn't lying necessarily but there was... *something* off. Her gut was telling her his truth wasn't the whole truth, and it was high time they faced whatever he was hiding from.

"Bullshit."

His brow scrunched and he huffed out a breath on a groan. "I don't know what you want from me, Jules! It's the truth. I've told you everything." He shook his head and paced.

"Nope. I don't buy it. There's more. There's got to be more."

"There isn't, Jules. I didn't want you to abandon everything for me and I needed to leave."

"But why? Why, Jason? Why did you need to leave? I don't understand—"

"I just did okay? And when you still invited me to your graduation... even after I ghosted you and stopped calling you. Fuck, I really thought it was for the best. I wanted you to go to school and achieve your dreams. But when you invited me to your graduation, I realized that it still hadn't been enough." He gulped. "I went, you know... but I couldn't go in. I waited in the parking lot. I even turned off my truck and waited until the heat was too much. I'd hoped it would smoke me out. But in the end, I couldn't do that to you. I couldn't give you hope I'd be back. I don't know what more to tell you... I just..." He turned away from her. Shutting her out.

She held her breath hoping for the rest, but once she realized that was all she was going to get, all the fight left her and she was dizzy from its absence.

"Not good enough. I'm gonna need more than that. It's like I don't even know you anymore," she spat. "And to what started all this. Marco's my friend. He was trying to help. You didn't used to be jealous. I don't even know where this is coming from, or why now?" She stepped past him to leave. "Besides, we have bigger lies to expose."

"But, Jules—"

She stopped to face him briefly, searching for words to cut him deep. "Let's focus on our actual problems and just forget about the ones that don't matter, alright?"

She left the room, knowing she'd hit her mark. But every step further was a twist of the knife in her own heart.

CHAPTER TWENTY-FOUR

He realized how dangerously distracted he'd become when one of the Russians—the psychotic gold-toothed one—smacked his arm and made a vulgar gesture, reminding him he was supposed to be ogling the half-naked woman on stage. He resumed pretending like he was watching, but couldn't help his grimace. There was a peculiar pit in his stomach at the thought that only a few weeks ago, hell only a few *days* ago, he'd sat in the exact same seat, but with a completely different view.

Everything had changed with one news story. Becoming partner at his father's firm had always been his sole purpose in life, but he hadn't signed up for this. For having someone he cared about getting hurt. His father knew how important Jules was to him, knew that he was desperately trying to get back in her good graces. When he saw the firm's handiwork all over the news, Jules nearly dying—he swallowed back bile at the image of her lifeless on the ground. He'd wanted to visit her, but his stupid watchdogs barely gave him room to piss by himself.

He'd hoped he would make a difference at the firm, at least become a major player. That was obviously not the plan anytime soon, if ever. He wasn't even sure he still wanted it. The attempt on Jules's life, despite his blatant feelings and intentions for her, was a betrayal. His father had blown him off when he'd tried to confront him. The man had been too busy for his own son and had complained about him being a nuisance without ambition. Of course, his father's contempt for him was nothing new. He'd ignored it for years, foolishly believing the best in dear ol' dad. Honestly, if his father was so casually involved with murder and human trafficking... what the fuck else should he expect?

He tipped back his drink as he tried to focus.

With all of his revelations, he couldn't help but wonder why the woman in front of them chose to be up there. *Was* it her choice? Like he'd always assumed? The women always seemed so eager to cater to him and the firm. Was it all an act? Were her circumstances so bad that she couldn't think of a better option? Was he even more of an ass for thinking this was a 'bad' option? He shook his head at the endless ramblings that had taken up shop there lately.

Never had he thought he'd be this conflicted. He'd had a plan. Get the job. Get the girl. Get the promotion. He'd gotten the first, lost the second, and wondered now if he even cared about the last. Another image of Jules lying on the ground invaded his thoughts, punctuating his realization that he wasn't sure what he wanted anymore.

Absentmindedly, he realized Vlad had been using his mother language for some time and was now using it to seemingly berate his voyeuristic counterpart. After a long string of what he assumed were curse words, Vlad's gesticulating settled down, although he continued to speak to whatever the guy's name was. He couldn't be bothered to actually remember the minion's name.

"English."

Vlad gave him a side-eye, but he spoke anyway. "You heard boss. We have spy." He jutted his chin to his counterpart. "Spy is just rat problem. Best way to catch rat? With trap." The glint of a gold molar accentuating the crazy in the other Russian minion's eyes was unsettling.

"A trap? What're you—we going to do?"

Vlad frowned across the table. "We have plan. You find out soon enough," he stated, fixing his eyes on the dancer in front of them and not so much as giving him a second look. "Some things may be too much for you, *da*? We take care of it."

What the fuck does that mean?

He leaned back, hoping his guards didn't notice his bouncing leg or fidgeting hands as he tapped each finger to his thumb, one at a time. He gave the bar a quick glance but decided against it. There was only so much liquor a man could drink to quell nervous energy. After that, the alcohol itself became a liability. They were all lucky he wasn't vomiting on the cheap carpet as it was. His phone vibrated and he quickly pulled it from his pocket... only to see a standard Original Sin notification. He didn't know why he still held out hope for anything else.

Can your angel forgive your sins? Or is she a Sinner herself? Meet her in Confessional 2 to find out.

He glanced up to find the burnt honey locks he'd pre-paid good money for. The winged petite woman waved by the Confessional door. He sighed.

Guess she'll have to do, for now.

The angel midget was a poor substitute, but he had other things on his mind. He stood, pulling at the lapels of his Brioni suit, briefly wondering why he insisted on always wearing designer suits to a fucking strip club.

"Well, boys. You have your fun. I've got a date with a Sinner." The dumb one fist pumped him without removing his stare from the stage. Vlad just eyed him from his peripherals. The big man always watched. It was fucking intimidating.

As he made his way across the room to the Confessional, he noticed a glimpse of vibrant hair make its way to the bar. He knew looking back at his guards would only bring more attention, so he tried to surreptitiously scan the club, hoping like hell his brief pause over the bar seemed bored and disinterested. He strained his hearing over the thump of the bass, and the lyrical voice he'd hoped for rose above the beat.

"Hey girl, just a vodka soda, minus the vodka if you catch my drift. I'm technically on the clock," the little pixie, Jules's right-hand woman, asked the bartender. Maybe he wouldn't have to go through the song and dance this time. The whole facade was growing trite. He felt in his breast pocket for the folded note, but as soon as Nora glanced around the club, he ducked his head and redirected to the Confessional and the bewigged angel.

"Hey handsome. Andy, right?" He immediately bristled at her familiarity. Her lip gloss was heavily applied, as if she was unused to wearing it. It made her lip stick to one of her teeth, turning her smile into, at best, a deformed wince.

"No. Don't call me that." He scowled hard enough to make her avert her glance.

"Oh okay... well, I'm waiting for—"

"I know. Just get in."

Her eyes widened at his command, not daring to ask any more questions.

Once they entered the small room, the little angel flitted to the sound system in the corner, but he grabbed her arm just above her elbow, causing her to squeak.

"Do you have a phone?"

"Um... no, angels have a direct line to God, we don't need phones—"

"Cut the shit. Do you have a phone or not? I'm not going to fucking tell your boss."

She nodded quickly and continued to the system, reaching behind it to pull out a furry pink phone with ridiculous bunny ears. Without hesitation, she unlocked it and tried to hand it to him. He hissed away, making sure not to touch it.

"I don't fucking want it. Do you have the bartender's number?"

"Uh, Je-Jezebel? Yeah..."

"Text her. Tell her not to let the purple-haired woman leave before she gets an envelope."

Her dull, questioning eyes were a mockery of the bright green-blue he craved, but he returned her stare until her small fingers flew over the screen. Once she was finished, she looked to him expectantly, waiting to know what to do next.

Honestly, he had no idea. For the first time, he allowed himself to peruse her body, briefly contemplating whether he should let her suck his cock. She didn't *look* like she was forced to be there. No track marks indicative of a drug addict doing anything for her next fix. He had no way to be sure. With Jules not accepting his calls and this whole conscience thing kicking in, he was going to have to actually go on dates now to get his dick wet. *Pathetic*.

Her phone lit up, highlighting where her drab wig met a dark black hairline. "She said okay, but it sounds like the lady might leave soon. She only came to talk to Cyn but she's not here."

"Fuck." He pulled out the envelope and stuck it into her hands before she successfully shied away from it. "Okay, take this to her—"

"Jezebel?"

"No, you idiot. The purple-haired freak." She blanched and he swallowed back more curse words, realizing that none of this was her fault. He needed to reign in the toxic persona he'd adopted to emulate the partners. It'd developed and grown over a short period of time, but the stress of everything pushed the boundary further still.

"Sorry," he ground. "Please give this to the woman with purple hair. She's at the bar. Make sure no one sees you... please." He tacked on for good measure. She stayed silent and panic shot through him at the thought that Nora could leave before she got the envelope. It might be too late after that. "I'll give you a tip!" he blurted out, hoping that would work.

But the angel seemed unimpressed and he began to feel unnerved by her stare. Her dark eyes narrowed as she gave him a perusal of her own. He stiffened and wondered what she saw. Did he seem confident? In charge? Worthy? Or did he look as desperate as he was beginning to feel?

He nearly caved, unsure of how to sweeten the deal if a tip wasn't enough, when she waved the envelope before hiding it in her bustier. "Got it. I'll be right back."

Before he could berate her for treating this like she was on some kind of James Bond mission, she slipped out of the room.

He cracked the door and watched as the little angel doppelganger weaved through the crowd and approached Nora's chair. She tapped on her shoulder and handed her the envelope. Nora looked like she was asking questions, but thank God, the angel just shrugged and pointed all around the club. The purple-haired pixie nodded and turned with the envelope in hand, digging into an impossibly small bag hanging from her side.

He hoped this would be enough, this time. He still didn't know nearly enough to get the whole truth in this situation, but maybe Juliet could fill in the blanks where he lacked. Meanwhile, he'd keep his questioning up, just in case.

The angel turned and her bright white wings flitted through the club as she made her way to him. Her eagerness was so innocent, causing a more acute prickle of the unfamiliar and strange emotion that settled deep in his chest. Was it guilt? Was that what he'd been feeling all this time? He shook his head. No way was he allowing himself to believe he'd stooped so low as to have any ounce of emotion for these whores. They'd gotten themselves into this lifestyle, after all. The pang echoed against the hollowness of his former convictions.

The little angel continued to beam at him as he fully realized the extent to which his worldview had been so completely upended. As she grew closer, the flashing lights of the club brightened her face. Her eyes weren't dull, like he'd originally thought, but deep, delicious chocolate brown. She hopped to him, obviously pleased with herself, and her pleasure was infectious until a huge black shadow blotted her out. Vlad's ugly mug accosted his vision and he schooled his face to meet the Russian's.

"We must go."

"Yes, of course, I just want to check on—"

"No... we must go. Now."

He gulped and nodded once before he followed his guards out without another thought to his Jane Bond. Slowly, too, too slowly, he realized who was in front of them.

Dread filled every pore in his body and he frantically searched around to see if there was anyone, anything around to stop the inevitable. But as the four of them exited the club and navigated the crowd, anxiety bore into his bones. From the corner of his eye, he noticed a shadow in his peripheral, but its stealth was no match for the speed of the predator in front of him.

They were all helpless as Vlad closed in on his prey.

CHAPTER TWENTY-FIVE

Oh, Aphrodite, he is fine.

Nora swirled her vodka soda, minus the vodka, as she forced herself to look around Heaven. All three pole stages lining the back of the club room had a woman performing in varying degrees of undress. She knew some of the Sinners by their faces, but she couldn't tell who was who in the dark and strategic lighting. She could've tried harder if her mind wasn't so preoccupied.

She kept her gaze anywhere but the hulking giant lording over a corner high top table. BlackStone Securities placed Drake as her bodyguard, and the blond Viking was taking it fucking seriously. He'd staked out the club before she'd arrived and had been brooding from his shadowed stoop ever since. He eyed the crowd, casually sipping on his clear drink, nonalcoholic like hers, most likely.

Even though they'd gotten to OS almost as soon as the doors opened, a fair number of clientele were already enjoying the Sinners walking around. Despite there being plenty of OS women to choose from, some of the men still had wandering eyes. She tried not to let their skeevy perusal bother her, but she couldn't help feeling coated in their stares like oil pouring over her skin.

There was only one set of eyes she wanted on her. A few times, she would've sworn her skin tightened and warmed as she got her wish. Her woman's intuition told her that Drake was keeping watch over more than just his surroundings.

Slowly, hoping he wasn't looking, she found him again and followed his delicious body from bottom to top.

He looks even better in person.

She couldn't see his feet, but from his hands' casual placement over the table, she could tell they were huge. Nora couldn't help but fantasize about the truth of the whole big hands, big feet, big you-know-what myth.

Exploring with her gaze, his thick forearms and biceps were corded muscle. Even in his relaxed pose, his black shirt was straining against his sculpted chest. His throat was thick and she wondered what he would taste like if she climbed over his rock hard body and licked all the way up to his lips. She'd bite the bottom one and run her hands through that beautiful blond hair as she stared into his gorgeous eyes—

Said eyes met hers and matched the heat she felt in her core. She quickly turned away, like the chicken she truly was. She feigned nonchalance with her back against the bar, a cat on the sill watching for prey, and waited. She wouldn't look at him again. If she could help it. She'd just remind herself of her reason for being at OS in the first place.

Being tasked with finding out if there was another note made her feel like one of Charlie's Angels. She softly sang the lyrics to Destiny's Child "Independent Woman," hoping the Almighty Bey would give her the strength to focus on her mission. Not on Drake.

Hawk from BlackStone Securities insisted they share their contact information, so if she *needed him*-needed him, she could just call him. But she wouldn't cave until then.

Shaking her head against the positively lustful thoughts pervading it, she decided to go over the facts of the "case" as they knew them. She'd pored through Jules's files and analyzed every bit of data they had on OS's Sinners and clientele. Despite all the information, she was still unable to puzzle out the connection between Ellie's kidnapping, the attempt on Jules's life, and what the hell they all had to do with a strip club. It was way too coincidental to be anything but planned. Lawyers would deny it to their graves, but most things in their profession boiled down to the math of it all. What was the common denominator, the common thread? For the life of her—or Ellie's or Jules's—Nora couldn't add it up. All they had were the letters Jules received from Original Sin.

So, Nora sat, her blush blistering from Drake's heated gaze. All she had was hope that their plan, that wasn't really a plan at all, would work.

She'd texted Cyn as soon as she got there, to make sure her cover was intact. There was real work to be done, so Nora'd brought some paperwork. Even though it wasn't due to be filed in court for some time, the Trojan Horse would still roll as a good excuse to drop in.

The long thin strap from her mini hatbox purse vibrated, and she opened it to check her phone inside. Jules gave her the Harry Potter novelty bag after she'd finally realized Nora refused to be fired. It was wholly impractical, barely fit anything inside, and made in Hedwig's image with a little owl post in her beak. It was single-handedly the best gift she'd ever received and she fucking loved it. No... she *floved* it.

Client/Cyn Turner: Not there 2nite sry. Catch u l8r g8r.

Nora frowned. Abbrevs were fine, but she hated when people bastardized words in text messages in a way that it was obvi' so much harder than spelling the damn thing out. Though, at the moment, she was concerned enough to let it slide. It was extremely rare for Cyn not to be holding down the fort at her own business.

Everything ok?
Client/Cyn Turner: Rose = havin sum trble.

Client/Cyn Turner: But dont tell Jules. Rose sd I wasnt supposed 2 tell u.

Ok... Well, I'm leaving the paperwork at the bar w/Jezebel. Can you trust her to get it to the safe?

Client/Cyn Turner: Y

Nora's fingers hovered over the screen and she felt her scowl deepen as she tried to discern what the enigmatic letter meant.

Are you asking why? Or...?

Client/Cyn Turner: Yes. Jezebel + safe.

Were there any messages for Jules?

Song after song played and women in their wings chatted with men and their cash. She went to OS often in the name of business and it never ceased to amaze her how much power the Sinners held. Of course, the men thought they were in control, but the honest truth was these women had them in the palms of their hands. Not for the first time, she wondered what it was like to be lusted over that way. She wondered what it would feel like if *Drake* felt that way. She shook her head, disappointed in her hormones. She watched passively until she felt her eyes glaze over.

An eternity passed and Nora huffed, growing tired of checking her phone every five minutes, irritated beyond reason. She probably wouldn't receive a reply until *after* she'd left the club. That was the way of it. Cyn was a freaking troglodyte and if Nora thought she could hear her over the thumping house music of the club, she would've bitten the bullet and called her instead. Nora *j'adored* video calls, but Cyn was even more infuriating with that mode of communication. They'd tried and failed spectacularly numerous times, and Nora vowed never to attempt it again. Actually talking on the phone sans video chat may be a millennial nightmare, but an old person trying to navigate video was the *worst*.

The assignment was quickly proving to be a dead-end, so Nora decided to look at the positive. Now she had a good excuse to talk to *him*, thus ensuring he had her phone number just in case he'd somehow forgotten to add her as a contact. A flash of feminist guilt made her wonder if she should feel some type of way about being the first one to reach out to the man, even under the auspices of professional circumstance.

Whatever, feminism is what I say it is damnit.

Despite her newfound personal freedom, she refused to turn around as she typed, afraid to meet his gaze. That would be too needy.

Cyn's not here. No word on any new notes. Looks like we're out of luck. :(

Nora didn't dare glance behind her, worried that Drake would see the sad attempt at conversation for what it was... a sad attempt at conversation. Dots formed across her screen and she refused to feel bad about the giddiness that overcame her.

Honora French, get a hold of yourself girl. It's just a damn man... a damn fine man but—

Draco (not Malfoy): K

"Seriously?" she complained out loud. Eye roll. The man was not the best conversationalist.

What should we do? Should we leave?

Draco (not Malfoy): Bartender know anything?

Nora felt her brow squinch. Jezebel was new so she wasn't sure if Cyn would trust her with a letter to Jules, but she might. According to Cyn's texting symbols, the girl was in charge of the safe, after all. At least that's what she thought "Jezebel + Safe" meant. Nora turned and lifted her hand until the girl hurried down the bar, passing by the waved cash of waiting customers. Even if Jezebel was new, most of the employees at OS knew that she and Jules were VIP.

"Hey Jez, can you get these to the safe for me? They're for Cyn." She slid the paperwork over the bar, thankful that OS was cleaner than most clubs and she didn't have to worry about dirtying the envelope. "Do you have any messages for me. Or Jules?"

Jezebel nodded once and shook her head twice, tucking the

envelope under one arm and leaving to pour several drinks simultaneously. The poor girl was a wee bit stressed, and Nora could empathize. She'd spent many a night herself as a frazzled bartender... among other things. She went back to her cell phone.

Barkeep's got nothing.

Dots...

Draco (not Malfoy): Damn. K let's haul out.

Nora sighed and nodded, even though Drake likely didn't see. She packed her phone up in Hedwig's snow-white feathers, ready to call the night a dud.

"Excuse me?"

Nora turned at the light tap on her shoulder. The owner of the husky voice smiled wide. She was a cute little thing, petite, with hair oddly similar to Jules's—

"This is for you," she said, stepping closer to hand her an envelope as if it held state secrets. Nora's heart skipped a beat and, without thinking, she snatched the letter and dug into her purse for her phone again.

"Who's it from?"

"It just came to me, as if on high." The girl gestured all around grinning. She closed her eyes solemnly and held her hands up in a prayer stance.

What the eff?

Nora couldn't help it but give the little weirdo a funny look. The girl then peeked one eye open and burst into laughter, giggling herself away. Obvi the girl was having way too much fun playing Iris, the messenger goddess, but who was she to rag on a good time? Or a nerd, like herself?

She found her phone just as it vibrated again.

Babs via (OMG it's THE) Jason's phone: Find anything?

Even though she was all nerves over holding another piece of the puzzle, she snorted at the name she'd given Jason Stone's phone number. Poor Babs was off the grid, so Jules had to communicate through his phone.

Over the course of working for Jules, she'd heard of the man. Nora had gathered from tidbits of information that he was the one that got away. Seeing him over video chat was the first time she'd seen him in the flesh, so to speak. She could see the appeal, but he wasn't as drool-worthy as Drake.

Nora put the phone in her mouth as she tore through the envelope. Vague one-liner with no identifying information? Check. She released the phone from her jaw's hold and took a picture of the letter as her response to Jules. From what she could tell, it was exactly what they'd been waiting for.

She nodded to Drake before folding the note impossibly small and sliding her phone into her Hedwig purse. From the corner of her eye, she watched as Drake set his drink down and meandered through the curtain to Eden, scouting the premises to make sure the coast was clear. She counted to lucky number thirteen and hopped off the barstool to follow.

Her skin vibrated with the hopefulness of their new clue. From what she saw, it could've been an address of some sort, although it didn't look like any she was familiar with. She probably should've waited longer to see if she could have identified where the note came from, but it wasn't like the adorably hot messenger had any clue. The girl might've been given it from a stranger who got it from a stranger, for all Nora knew.

Maybe Drake saw something. She'd ask him when they met back up, and if she was lucky, maybe she'd get more out of him than just business. *That* was a man she'd like to get to know. She wanted him to stick around at OS before she left. He may even turn stalker and follow her home. Perhaps she could convince him to take a more hands-on approach and insist he sleep on her couch. She shook her head slightly. The couch was way too uncomfortable, she reasoned as she planned her future argument. Obvi the only place he could be relaxed while maintaining his broody bodyguarding ways was in bed.

And who better to help him relax than herself? It was the only solution. Plus, they both deserved a stress-free night after playing spy. Who was to say they shouldn't spend it with each other?

She couldn't contain her smirk at her devious plan. The bouncer at the door grinned from covert earpiece to earpiece. Of course she grinned back. She certainly hadn't meant to suggest anything to him, but she didn't want to be rude.

On her way to her Chevy Spark, her phone chirped again from inside Hedwig. Now that she was outside, the infernal ring jarred her out of her daydreaming. She scrambled to silence it, but Mary Poppins physics prevented her from finding it despite Hedwig's purse-head being so small. Just as she felt her sleek iPhone, she heard crunching on the gravel. She grinned and adopted her best sexy damsel voice.

"Thank goddess you're here, Drake... I was getting so scared —Oh, wha-Ow, you're hurting me! Let go of me, asshole!"

The strong hands gripping her arms from behind bit into her skin despite her faux leather jacket.

"Drake, that hurts. Let go, dickhead!" She tried to pull away, but a bodybuilding giant stepped in front of her. Cold chills shivered up her spine and she looked behind her to find a very *unsexy* non-Drake with a glinting tooth in his mouth.

"Who the fuck are you?" she yelled, causing the man behind her to adjust his grip so his sweaty palm covered her—gross —*open* mouth. She quickly clamped her lips closed but gagged from the salty grime that coated her tongue. The combination of the man's large hand over half her face and her attempt to flee, caused her butterfly glasses to fall to the ground.

Where the Hades is Drake?

"You come with us." The giant's accent reminded her of someone speaking English back home, but she couldn't place the accent out of its natural language. Trying to understand him took her a second, but once she did, she shook her head violently, causing the hand gripping her mouth to tug against her snake bite studs.

"No! Let me go!" she screamed until the large mass behind her squeezed the breath out of her. The giant grabbed poor Hedwig and riffled through her. He found Nora's phone and threw it to the ground, stomping on it. Once again, she tried to scream. The man holding her captive, now hard in places she couldn't think about, punched her in her side before rapidly returning to cover her mouth.

"Stop!"

Nora stopped struggling immediately at the familiar voice. She winced at the pain in her jaw but tried to turn around to see if she was right. The rapid fist to her side quickly changed her mind.

"I said stop! Fuck. Do you fools ever listen?"

"*Andy?*" she wheezed, now held by both of the gold-toothed man's arms. Nora felt like she was about to pass out, from either the pain to her side, or the lack of air, she wasn't sure. But Andrew freaking Ascot stepping into her vision was the hit of smelling salts she needed to wake up. She growled at the traitor. After all he'd done to Jules? Then after all he'd done to try to get Jules back? He flinched at the fury she knew raged from her eyes.

"What're you doing? Are you out of your mind? You can't just steal someone from a fucking parking lot!"

"We take care of problem. Lawyer, Stone, this girl—" The giant threw his large hand in her direction. "They are problem. Every time we are here. She is here. They use this girl to spy. We take care of it." He nodded to the gold-tooth guy behind her and before she could stop it, a grimy hand clamped back over her mouth. "She will spy no more. No more rat."

Despite her best muffled curses, gold-tooth guy easily picked her up and began to carry her.

"But we play, first." Her captor's accent was even thicker than the giant's. She grew nauseous with each bump against his perverted hardness, and the hot pants against her ear tunneled her senses to a different nightmare...

"Don't tell me you don't like it, vadleany" —a tongue slithered up the shell of her ear— *"my little wild girl."*

Possessed by muscle memory, she fought against her captor, kicking the chunky heel of her boot into his vulnerable shin. Even though he had to be the size of a horse, her tactic worked like a charm. He dropped her like the writhing snake she'd become and she fell on her hands and knees hard onto the gravel.

The air cracked as if it had been whipped. A heavy weight dropped onto her back and she lost her breath as it knocked her flat to the ground.

"Holy shit." She could hear Andy's whisper as he appeared to lose his footing and fell somewhere near her on the ground. Quick steps crushed the gravel and moved the earth around her. Grunts and thumps against fabric and flesh were interrupted by harsh consonants from the giant way above her.

"Nora, fuckin'—" More rustling and cursing. "Run!"

At Drake's voice, her tense muscles relaxed a fraction. Nora cried out in relief knowing he'd come to save her. With his encouragement, she tried to lift herself from under the heavy weight on top of her, but it barely moved. A warm liquid slid down her neck and fell to her fingers as she pushed. Dark and thick, she almost vomited when she realized what it implied. She struggled against the ground as hard as she could with rocks digging into her palms and knees. The pain barely registered but a groan escaped her when hundreds of pounds of dead weight made it impossible for her to save herself.

She trembled and opened her eyes wide in the dark, searching for a clue as to what was happening around her. But she was unable to see anything with her face mere inches from the ground. A particularly loud crack against something soft led to a sharp hiss, different from the other clamor of combat. She froze in another attempt at a pathetic half push-up.

"Nora... please... run..." Drake growled low. Another thump.

She dug deep from within and shoved every ounce of her

ninety-nine pounds against the ground and the man on top of her. Her shriek from the burn in her arms and legs and the fear clutching her heart, was certainly loud enough to alert someone that shit was going down. But no one came. She pushed and pushed, hoping the new dampness she felt on her brow was her own sweat... not the blood of her captor. It could have been two seconds, or two minutes, but all the while she heard Drake fighting. *For her.* If he would put his life on the line for her, the least she could do was try to run away.

But it wasn't working.

Racking her rattled brain for a different solution, she shifted her shoulders and strained to roll away from the sounds of the argument on her right and the crunching gravel on her left. Her fingers on the loose rock provided no purchase, but still she mentally counted.

One. Two. Three—

She was just about to give up when the weight on top of her suddenly disappeared. Her momentum caused her to pop up from the ground and stagger. She caught herself on a nearby car hood and shouted with relief. There was no way that should've worked, but obvi the goddesses were on her side.

Nora leaned against the car and turned to the fight behind her.

The big blond Viking was on his knees, one hand holding his side, the other migrating to his hip. The giant in front of him held his arm outstretched, a black object in his hand pointed at her kneeling savior. She wasn't stupid enough to run to him, but everything inside her wanted to reach out for the man who'd saved her.

"Nora... go, run." Drake's voice was hoarse and his chest heaved. She desperately wanted to help him and her feet took a step closer. She knew she should be running away. Far, far away. But seeing him there made her hesitate. She scanned his body and caught his eyes. Pain and something else etched around them. Was it fear? She doubted the man had been afraid in his entire life. She couldn't see their color in the dark, but the urgency clouding them was crystal clear.

Without registering anything else but Drake hurting, she bent to help him.

"Drake—"

"Nora, no!" He shoved her away from him and she fell to the side.

Another crack whipped the air. A thud met the ground.

Nora looked over her shoulder from her spot on the ground to find Drake.

The giant lifted the object—the gun, she realized—in his hand away from its target. Feet away from her, Drake lays lifeless on the ground. His knees were still bent and his face was covered partially by his arms as they reached out. To Nora.

She felt the burn of a scream come up from her stomach and throat and choked on it. A strong, rough grip on her arm hoisted her in the air, and the scream she'd expected turned to vomit and she threw up on the gravel. The giant dropped her and gave her a wide berth as she doubled over.

When there was nothing left inside her, she stayed down and vaguely overheard the conversation beside her.

"Ohgodohgodohgodohgod, are they dead? What do we do with them? What do we do now? Oh God. What the fuck just happened?"

"Yes. They are dead. Only one more. Then we go. We teach lesson to rat."

"Go? Go where? Don't we need to call an ambulance? What if they're still alive?"

Two consecutive thumps, as if the giant was kicking the men on the ground, brought a new wave of sickness.

"See? Dead."

"Don't you care about your partner, you sick fuck? We can't just leave dead bodies lying around. We have to do something!"

"No. We do this thing. Then we leave."

"No... no... I can't keep doing this. I can't be a part of this.

Kidnapping women. Selling them? Not to mention we're now leaving a fucking *trail* of bodies wherever we go. This has to end, now."

"We leave now"—the giant's low voice was punctuated by an ominous click— "or you stay. With them."

Nora lifted her head, carefully making sure not to look at Drake again. She watched as Andy visibly gulped at the gun pointed at his face. He looked haggard, and much older than the pompous playboy she was used to. His head nodded slightly.

"Good."

Her focus on Andy's increasingly alarmed features, she didn't see the giant face her, but she could feel the weight of his stare. He hadn't uncocked the gun.

"What the fuck are you doing?"

"We must go. Boss would not like witnesses. This the lesson for rat." Nora closed her eyes and blinked back the moisture filling them. A sting in her lower lip and the taste of metal made her realize she'd been biting back her sobs so hard she was bleeding somewhere in her mouth. She didn't know why she was doing that. She was likely about to be shot. Murdered in a parking lot. Just like Drake. She wanted to scream. Her head told her to. But her head didn't feel so in charge anymore.

"Wait! Listen. We-we can just... let her go. Or do *something* other than kill her. That can't keep being our solution. Maybe she could be of use some other way? We can brainstorm, or we could go back to the 'leaving her' idea."

Silence. Numbness washed over her. Could this really be happening? Jules's ex-fling was arguing over her 'usefulness' so she wouldn't be murdered. She'd just seen two men die—shit, one man bled out *on* her—the other died *for* her. But, if her lack of reaction at Andy's words were any indication, she was never going to recover from this.

"Think about it and think fast. Let's just let her go. Or we could even take her and just drop her off somewhere. Anywhere. Fucking Alaska, for all I care. It couldn't hurt, right? I mean, what's she really going to say? Plus, there're no more dead bodies that way."

After a few moments, the giant expelled a grunt and uncocked the gun.

"Get her in car." The giant's large steps scattered rocks everywhere as he walked away.

"Thank you," Andy whispered. He bent and tugged Nora off the ground. The adrenaline pumping in her veins was completely tapped out, and she tripped as soon as she got upright. Her eyes fell over Drake's body again and refused to look away. She begged silently to anyone who would listen, that he would somehow get up. She couldn't see where he'd been shot, but it had been twice if the cracks in the air had been any indication. With the way the giant was confidently leaving him behind like trash, they had to have been killing blows.

"Hold on." Andy picked her up and cradled her like an injured child, holding her close. His hand raised to her cheek and she let him press her face into his chest since it blocked everything else out. The only thing she could see was the lapel of his suit. She clung to the fabric as she swayed in Andy's tight grip. The crunch of the gravel under his steps alternated with her heavy breaths. Their staccato cadence grew louder and louder until they were the only sounds, the only thoughts she had.

"Nora, stay with me. You're hyperventilating."

Is that what this is?

But realizing what was happening didn't make it stop. She succumbed to her body and hoped that meant she was going to pass out. Quiet was welcome, but her mind only got louder.

She hadn't known Drake, but there had been something that stuck with her from the moment they'd met, despite that it was only through video. Her attraction to him had been instant and instinctual. His quiet chuckles at her quirkiness, and the Crew's surprised reactions, told her that every time she'd made him laugh, he'd given her something precious.

Drake died trying to save her. Why? Because it was his job?

Was it for honor? Where she came from, it was every man for himself. When she first saw him, she wanted to get to know him. She still wanted to learn more about the man who would die to save a stranger. Now she wouldn't get the chance.

The already dark night grew dimmer around the edges. As if a passenger in her own body, she vaguely understood that she was going to get her wish and she was finally going to pass out. As soon as she felt the truth in that resignation, a panic rushed through her body.

Drake-can't-die-he-can't-die-because-of-me-someone-needs-to-know-he-tried-to-save-me-must-call-Jules-Jason-someone-anyone-they-must-know-phone-someone-save-Drake-where-phone—need-to-save-Drake-phone-they-have-need-phone-phone-phone-phone-need—

"Phone?" she asked dumbly, unsure if she'd actually spoken anything aloud. One part of her knew it was supremely stupid to ask her murdering captors for her phone. But the other part of her was only ruminations and confusion.

"What? Fuck, she's practically dead weight. I think she's in shock," Andy grunted.

"Phone is broken."

She heard a curse that might have come from her or maybe it came from the traitor kidnapping her. Her hand fell to the side and she let it hang there.

"So, uh, I guess that means no one can track her through her phone?"

"*Da*. If someone follows, they will find broken phone in bushes over there. They cannot track her."

Andy scrunched up his face and looked down at her as he tried to pull her hand back up from hanging down. He probably hoped she would grab on to him again.

"What about her..." His words trailed off as he slowed down. He maneuvered to lift her hand up to his chest again and held on to her wrist at a weird angle. The light from her watch lit his scowling face and he kept hold of it in that odd twist long enough for her wrist to start hurting. When he finally let go, her hand dropped back down. "So, are we just going to drop her off somewhere, or what? I think we should drop her by a hospital. She's in pretty bad shape."

The sound of a trunk popping open vaguely registered. Far away she heard screams and shouts. Far, far away she thought she heard sirens.

"Finally..." Andy muttered. The conversation echoed around her as she was placed inside the back seat of a car.

"What about what?"

"Hm?"

"You say 'what about her' then you stop. What about her what?"

"Oh, right, um. Well, what about her? I mean, she's freaking out. What're we going to do? Like I said, I was thinking we should drop her off at a hospital."

She heard the giant rifle through a bag in response.

"What? No, we can't drug her."

"She will be like the rest and ready for the sale. Good idea."

"What the fuck are you talking about?"

"She small. Looks young like the rest. She will be good replacement for one already used up. Good job, *durak*."

If they kept talking, she didn't know. She felt a slight pinch in her arm and welcomed oblivion.

CHAPTER TWENTY-SIX

Jason glanced over the fridge door into the living room at the infuriating, stubborn woman of his dreams, dressed in short shorts and a simple T-shirt. Her own, this time. Reality stars on TV were yelling in the background while Jules was curled up on the couch, speed typing on his phone. She'd been checking it every few minutes for Nora's update. He knew Jules texted only a second ago to see if there was any word yet.

"Want anything to eat? Or—" The fridge was fucking empty. There goes that idea. "Something to drink?" He studied their surroundings, waiting for her answer as she alternated between checking the phone and changing the channel on the big state-of-the-art TV. Aside from the more inconspicuous speakers in the corner of the room, it was completely out of place in the rustic cabin.

Except for the unique stonework framing the person-sized fireplace, everything was made of gorgeous varieties of wood. The monstrous TV lorded over the corner of the room, away from the fireplace, so that people in any given part of the open concept living area could choose whether to zone out watching a show or zone out from the peaceful crackling of burning wood. The TV seemed out of place, which was a shame, but he was glad Snake hadn't installed it above the fireplace because it would've covered a good bit of the craftsmanship in the stone chimney. The open room had timber walls and wall-length picture windows, all angled to accommodate a stunning view of the small lake at the bottom of the low valley.

The cabin was placed at a very strategic point on the mountain and difficult to find. It was off any normal route and only accessible with a vehicle capable of driving over purposely felled and inconvenient trees. Jason's truck worked like a champ. A car like poor ol' Larry—may he rest in peace—wouldn't have made it.

Coming back to the moment, he watched Jules as she sat in one of the brown leather couches, a faux fur blanket draped over her bottom half. Lamps similar to the ones in "his" room were on the side tables. His favorite decoration was the huge-ass chandelier made to resemble a crown of antlers. Fucking badass.

Jules called it "rustic chic" earlier. Before she'd gotten pissed.

She finally lifted a shoulder and grunted at the question he was sure he'd asked ages ago. He let out a steadying breath. It'd been like this since their fight that morning. He tried to start a conversation. She shut it the fuck down. He tried to say something nice. She looked at him like he was a crazy person. Their day started early and had already been a major disappointment full of stress, so they'd both taken a nap since their fight. He'd hoped she would've cooled off, but nope. She might've even gotten worse, if that was possible.

Eventually, he'd decided to let it go. She was mad. He got it. Deserved it. He just couldn't wait until they got past it. They had bigger things to worry about than the status of their relationship. She'd said it earlier, meaning to hurt him. And it had. But damn if it wasn't also true. He didn't want to dwell on, or think of anything other than how to save Ellie. But honestly? There wasn't a whole bunch else they could do while they were effectively "off the grid" on a mountain. All they could do was wait and reflect.

"FUCK YES!" Jules hopped off the couch and ran to him, her grin wide across her cheeks. He instinctively opened his arms and braced for impact as she jumped and wrapped her legs around his waist. He caught her with his hands on her butt, but her momentum rocked him back into the kitchen counter.

"Jaybaby, oh my God, Nora came through! Here, look!" She whooped, waving his phone screen way too close, and he blinked and widened to try to take it in. He felt her laughter bubble up against his chest and it warmed him down to his soul.

He chuckled softly. "I can't see it, baby girl. You gotta calm down."

She frowned and turned the phone to her, manipulating it with her fingers. She showed him again, still smiling. He had to concentrate on the dim photo in front of him, instead of the brightness glowing behind it.

1000 Commerce Interstate Port, SE Lot 3 CTIU 148729 7, 3pm tomorrow, bring backup

"It's an address?"

"Yeah, it must be where they're doing the drop... off." Jules's excitement deflated as the reality of what they were celebrating sank in. Nora sent a picture of the note from OS. They were looking at the address where his baby sister would be sold and exchanged like a *thing*. Apparently at three the next afternoon. He swallowed back bile and let Jules slide down his body and step away.

"Send that to Snake."

She nodded and typed on his phone. The phone lit up with Snake's face and Jules answered the video call. Jason moved so Jules's back was flush up against his chest so they could both be on the call.

"I just mapped the address. It looks like it's for the Inland Port," Snake explained. "The rest of it indicates the lot number where the" —he gulped— "shipping container... fuck, let's just assume all they're doing is meeting there."

Jason swore as he shook his head, but agreed. He wouldn't

think of it any other way, either. The more likely alternative made him want to throw up.

"I'm gonna do a little security recon and then we're gonna come up with a plan. Phoenix and Hawk have stepped out for a brief meeting with one of our clients."

"Who could be more important than Ellie?" Jason demanded.

"Chill, Jay. It makes sense they wouldn't sit around hoping a letter might show up. How could they have known there'd even be one? I'm sure other people have their own Ellies they need BlackStone Securities to save." Jules looked up as she spoke, and her lips nearly brushed his as she turned. Her cheeks pinked and she quickly focused back on Snake.

"Yeah, sorry, man. We had no idea how successful Nora and Draco would be. But everyone, including Draco, should be back here within the hour. I'll call you back when they get here and we'll come up with a plan. I'll contact Draco in the meantime and see if he has any other information on who could've left the note." He continued to type before speaking again, "Oh look, okay I found it. Damn, it's way out in the middle of nowhere, but not too far from the city. The drive can be done in a couple of hours, max. If we leave around thirteen hundred hours in a Bird, we'll make it with plenty of time to spare. I'll call you within the hour. Over and out." Snake hung up abruptly and the screen went black.

"Thirteen hundred hours?" Jules questioned. "That means... damn, I hate military time. Officers use it constantly, and I'm like, hello? What time is it for the rest of us—"

"Jules, focus. And after twelve p.m., just subtract twelve from the military time and that's the time in the afternoon. Snake's initial guidance meant we'll be leaving BlackStone around one p.m."

"Right, sorry. God, I'm shaking, Jay. This is it. I can feel it." Jules fluttered her hands over her heart and bit her lip.

"Yeah, we're close, right? I feel it too. Maybe that's wishful thinking—"

"No, we can't think that way. This has to be it—"

"But what if it's not?"

"It is."

"But—"

She slammed her hand over his mouth. "Shhh. This is what's happening. This is the information we have. We have to act on it with the best possible outcome in our minds. Prepare for the worst, hope for the best. We're hoping for the fucking best, Jaybaby."

Jason nodded once and she retracted her hand. He immediately enveloped her in the embrace he sensed they both needed. This was it. She was right. It had to be. He didn't know what would happen to him or anyone around him if it was another fucking dead end.

Jules massaged the muscles along his spine with her fingertips and he melted. The groan that escaped him might've been too much for her because she stopped abruptly and before he knew it, his back was up against the counter behind him again. Granted, it was only a few inches away from the starting point, but her shove set him well and apart from her.

"Jules, what the hell?"

"I can't, Jason. I'm happy and so freaking relieved about Ellie. But I can't just leap into your arms because of that. I can't keep using you that way."

"Yes, you can. Do it! Leap away. I'm right here."

She shook her head, but he could tell she was trying not to smile. "No, I can't. That's not fair to either of us. We should keep this professional. After we find Ellie, it'll only be a matter of a few conversations with Marco and Investigator Burgess and your name will be cleared. Then we won't have to deal with each other anymore. It'll be like before."

Jason felt a cold rush of sweat sheen his skin. "What're you talking about, Jules?"

The pain shrouding her eyes made him jerk toward her, but as she hugged herself and walked slowly backward into the cozy living area, he realized that he might not be wanted. She was shutting down right in front of him. Was that how she felt all those years? He'd pushed her away. Rejected her. At least in her eyes, he'd given her no reason to think otherwise. Had she suffered with this feeling the entire time?

Fuck.

If she felt half the way he felt right then, it was no wonder she was keeping her distance. His throat grew thick with emotion, and he tried to swallow it back. The idea that he'd made her feel this way literally made him feel sick and he eyed the closest repository, the sink.

"You're my client and—"

He growled.

Goddamn, we're back to that shit again?

"I think we both know that's not all I am, baby girl."

Jules gulped and nodded quickly. But when she turned away, he followed, gripping her arm and tugging her back to him.

"No, we're talking about this." He brushed her honey-brown hair behind her ear. "So, talk."

She shook her head and pressed her lips together. Jason was about to prompt her again before she finally spoke.

"Lies?" Her bright sea blue-green eyes captured his.

"No lies," he answered confidently.

She gave a curt nod and stepped away from him again, crossing her arms. "I don't believe what you said before."

"About..."

"About how you were afraid I was going to throw away everything for you... so you took yourself out of the equation."

His heart began to pound and his brow furrowed. "Okay..."

She walked further into the living room and sat down on the couch. He stepped back and leaned against the island counter separating the kitchen and living room space. Her hands picked at her nails absentmindedly as she continued.

"I think you used me as an excuse. I think the answer is much simpler than that. I think... you were afraid."

Jason bristled, but he physically shook away his discomfort at the accusation. Moments passed by before she continued on a sigh, seeming to have finally ordered her thoughts together.

"I believe you, that you think you weren't good enough." She stood up, seemingly unable to maintain one position, and stalked toward him. Her voice increased in volume with each statement. "I believe you, that you think your parents' death screwed you up beyond hope. Trust me, I know." She shivered, no doubt from her own memories of the shitty things her drug-addicted mother put her through. "And I even believe that you were afraid I would put you above law school."

He felt his eyebrows scrunch together. If she was in agreement then...

"But fuck you for making that decision for me."

There it is.

"I think you were afraid."

Her words were deliberate and her logic flowed as she slowly paced a short distance around the room. Although he was ashamed of everything she said, he was in awe as he witnessed The Juliet Bellerose give her closing argument.

"Maybe all of that played a part. I won't discredit or discount that. Or take it away from you. But if you were really concerned about how I would act, you could've just *talked* to me. Have I ever reacted in a way that made you feel like you couldn't talk to me?"

A pit of shame hit the bottom of his stomach and he shook his head in the negative.

"You didn't have to make the decision to completely remove yourself from my life. You took that decision from me. What made you believe you could make better decisions for me than I could? I'd been making decisions on my own for *years* before you, and had been doing just fine without you." She cleared her throat. "And I would do fine without you in the future."

The stone in his stomach turned to molten lava and he was sure it'd burn a hole through him.

"But... I don't know if I want to do that anymore," she whispered.

His breath hitched and he dared a glance at her. Her eyes glistened, but he could tell she had so much more to say. He ached to go to her, but she was clutching herself so tightly, almost holding herself away from him.

"And that's scary on its own. I don't think I could handle it if you left me again. If it didn't work out. Last time—"

"It won't be like that. I promise. I was fucked-up back then. And no lies, I'm still fucked-up. But not about you, not about us. I want you. I want to be here with you—"

"When you left—"

"I know. It won't happen again—"

"No, listen! When you left me." She laughed sharply and shook her head, choosing to no longer look at him. "Jay, you think you're broken? When you left, I *broke*." The emphasis on the last word into two syllables made each a punch in his gut. "When you left me..."

"Jules—"

"...I was pregnant."

CHAPTER TWENTY-SEVEN

Jason stopped in his tracks. "What?" he breathed. He took more notice of her posture and realized she wasn't just holding herself tightly. Her hands were clutching at her lower stomach.

Those three words tugged the pin holding back faint memories. Thoughts that hadn't felt important enough to register at the time of their creation. A *pinging* resounded inside his skull as he realized he'd been missing something vitally important every time they'd talked. His pulse raced while sweat pricked at his brow, and he tried to get a clearer visual of the images in his mind. A random thought from grenade training told him he had maybe four seconds before whatever she said next detonated.

"I..." Jules met his eyes, confronting him head-on. The pain there made keeping her gaze so much worse. She took a steadying breath. "I was pregnant. I tried to tell you. But I didn't find out until you were gone. And by then... it was too late."

One second.

Her scoff cut his insides. "You didn't answer my texts. My calls. You even left Ellie in the dark. We didn't know where you went, or what you were doing. We just assumed you'd joined that military group you'd told us about."

He was so confused, and had so many questions, but he was

terrified of every conceivable answer. Instead of asking, he braced for impact.

"Even though you were afraid—and I stand by that. You can try to feel better by telling yourself some bullshit that you were 'making sure I wouldn't let myself down'. But, for the record, I think what sent you to that fucking desert was fear of *you* letting down someone else you loved. It was easier for you to leave again, to go and save random strangers, than to disappoint the relationships you already had." He tasted the truth in her words, and his swallow burned as it went down.

Two seconds.

"So even though you were afraid of us, and you were gone, I got excited on my own. I hoped until the end that you would answer and respond to some form of communication Ellie or I sent you—"

"We weren't allowed to talk to anyone. We had to disappear..." The excuse felt flimsy as it fell from his lips.

"Maybe so. But you didn't have to disappear without saying goodbye." He didn't respond. But he didn't have to. She was right.

Three seconds.

"I didn't tell El. I wanted to tell you first. I took the test, made the appointment, decided she was a 'she' because to hell with callin' my baby an 'it.' But I only had two weeks to be afraid, anxious, excited, hopeful.

"Two weeks... God it still feels like it was so much longer and so much shorter at the same time. But in those two weeks, I made plans, looked for apartments to get the heck outta that closet at OS," she huffed a laugh, but immediately sobered, "fantasized about becoming the family I'd always wanted. I was scared, sure. But I thought, 'Even if I don't have Jay, maybe I could have a piece of him.'" She shuddered a sigh.

"But I couldn't even have that. I-I lost her."

Boom.

The bomb she'd just dropped shattered him from within.

Little tells he'd missed the entire time they'd spent together since the police station, exploded into the forefront of his mind. Every time her blue-green eyes clouded with an unfamiliar darkness. Every time she cringed or winced when he mentioned having a family. Every time she'd held her stomach when she spoke about him leaving her... *them.*

She choked out a sob and Jason stopped breathing entirely. He grew lightheaded with her confession and couldn't stop staring at her slender fingers as they became white-knuckled fists against the bottom of her stomach.

"That last day she was mine... I felt a cramp in my left side. It was different from anything I'd ever felt and the pain became a constant that got worse and worse as the day went on. I didn't know what was happening, so I went to the ER. I hadn't even had a proper appointment yet. That was supposed to be the next day. They did an ultrasound to find out I was ten weeks along. I'd known that already, of course. We had a pretty definitive ending to our relationship, so it was easy to know when she could've been conceived."

Jules's words were ripping Jason's heart from his chest, one vein at a time. The island counter kept him vertical. He could only guess that Jules was still standing because she'd lived with it for so long. By herself. And he'd been too much of a coward to even fucking *text* her back. He shook his head and allowed the crippling tension in his muscles to rise to the point of pain as she continued. The least he could do now was listen.

"She was an ectopic pregnancy. Basically, she was growing in the wrong place. My left fallopian tube instead of my uterus. They rushed me into surgery. I was in so much pain and they were talking so fast and getting me to sign all these damn papers and make these decisions. Whether I wanted to" —she swallowed— "*terminate* her with a fucking shot of some medication or have her cut away from me in surgery..."

She sighed and closed her eyes. The droplet slowly sliding down her cheek did it for him. He couldn't take it anymore. He grabbed her to hold her close and cherished the moment she wrapped her arms around his waist. As if he was finally holding her up, like he should've been all along.

"That's where the scars on my stomach came from," she spoke into his shirt. "They said the fallopian tube she was in could rupture at any moment and that would've been very, very bad for me. No matter what, there was no way to save her. She'd never even had a chance." He rubbed her back slowly as she trembled with emotion. "I was a mess and wholly incapable of making my own decisions, so the doctor chose surgery and they removed it. They removed *her*." He squeezed her close and felt cool air over his own damp cheeks.

He couldn't bear the thought of what she'd gone through. All without him. Without anyone. Leaving her had been the most cowardly thing he'd ever done. She was right. He'd been scared. Scared to let down another person he loved. He'd told himself joining MF7 would finally get him that redemption he craved. Then he would be good enough for her and El. But there were ways to heal and get rid of wounds without giving them to someone else. He'd chosen not to do that and these wounds he'd caused were unforgivable.

"You asked about birth control before. Well, like I said, I haven't been with anyone in a while and even when I was, I always used protection... but as far as pregnancy goes, it doesn't matter anymore. There were complications in the surgery. I can't give you many more details. I honestly don't know them myself. When I heard them say having a family naturally someday would be 'difficult to the point of near impossibility' I zoned out. I haven't let myself think about it since."

He remembered back to the beginning of their relationship and the look of awe she'd get when she dreamed aloud about being a mom someday. Back then, her cheeks were rounder with youth, but they'd glow with anticipation. Her blue-green eyes would shimmer with hope, and her back always straightened with a spark of determination. Her mother had been a nightmare like her mother before her, and Jules planned to break the cycle. He'd never thought about kids before her and when she spoke about being a better mother than hers ever was, it scared the shit out of him. Of course she'd be a good mother. A great mother, no question. It was all him. His insecurities. He hadn't known his biological father, but the man he chose to think of as his *dad*, Greg Stone, wore some big shoes to fill. Shoes he'd felt he didn't even deserve to shine.

Coming back to Jules this time around, the idea didn't scare him, anymore. He knew at this point it was crazy to think Jules would grant him that honor. After everything he'd just heard, he was surprised she hadn't let him rot in jail that first day. He deserved nothing less.

Jason stepped back and lifted her face in his hands. He silently thanked her when her arms she'd slid around his waist stayed there, and though her beautiful cerulean eyes were filled with tears, there was no hate or anger in them. Only sorrow. A new, unyielding heartache that would forever float on the surface of twin blue-green seas. He cursed inwardly, mad at himself further that he hadn't noticed. His thumbs brushed away the sheen on her cheeks and her hands clutched his wrists.

"What will I do if you run away again?"

His heart broke from the rare vulnerability she was allowing him to see, trusting him. He leaned in and brushed his lips over her soft, burnt honeyed hair. Bending to rest his forehead against hers, he demanded her gaze. From the pain etched in her face, a stranger would think she was ready to crack and fall apart. But he knew she was too damn strong for that. He just had to remind her.

"Baby... Jules. What I'm going to say will never make up for what you went through. Nothing said can do that. But I promise, from this moment forward, I'll do everything in my power to heal you, to comfort you, to love you."

Her eyes flashed on the last phrase. He raised his head from hers but kept cradling her face in his hands. He swallowed and prepared to give away the rags from his shredded heart to help wrap hers.

"Leaving you..." He sighed. "Leaving you was the worst mistake of my life. You're right. I was afraid, and I'll never get those years back. I thought about you, every day. Coming home to you was my ultimate goal. That last mission, it's the one that gave me more scars than just the one on my head. I was ready to come home to you. But what happened... happened. I came home and I was a mess." He closed his eyes against his shame, but he knew he had to continue.

"The night Ellie was kidnapped... I told you I bailed on her because the thought of going made me too anxious." He spoke low and moved his hands down her throat, his thumbs skimming over her soft skin. "That's the last time I'm letting myself give in to that feeling. Anxiety is one thing, but giving in to fear? No. Being scared has taken my sister from me, it took you away from me for seven years, I'm not letting it have another minute with you. I've felt braver over the last few days with you, than I have in a long time. I know there will be moments I'll struggle... but I know what I want. I know what you need. I'm prepared to deliver on both.

"What happened when I left..." He felt her thin fingers squeeze his wrists harder and he gently massaged his fingertips against the back of her neck. He made sure she was listening and he hoped his words would resonate.

"I am so sorry," he whispered to keep his voice from breaking, but cleared his throat before continuing. "I'm sorry it happened at all. I'm sorry you had to lose her all alone—" She squeezed tears from her eyes but kept them closed. "No baby, look at me. You need to know this and remember it. My heart is broken for you. But *you* are not broken. I don't care what the doctors think they know. What happened doesn't make you any less to me. And once we find Ellie, I won't need anything else but you. I can be what you need, too. If you let me. We don't have to figure everything out right now. We've got forever. I love you, Jules."

Jules shook her head slightly and tapped his wrists. He let go, instinctively knowing the signal, and dreaded what she was about to say. If she rejected him, well that was going to fucking suck. But she had every right to, and if she did... he stood stock still, waiting for her. Hoping he would never have to solve the answer to that question.

"You can't love me. You don't even know me anymore. We've been apart for seven *years*. I'm not the same nineteen-year-old girl you fell in love with way back then. We've practically met each other again for the first time."

Jason laughed softly, but tried to regain his composure as she narrowed her eyes at him. He relaxed a fraction at the pivot their conversation had taken. Each moment before had been thick with tension and pain, but he couldn't stop smiling after her ludicrous statement.

"You really think I don't know you, Juliet Bellerose?" She put her hands on her hips and scowled at him. He stepped into her space and smirked when he saw the moment she convinced herself to stay put. "You're right, I may not know everything that happened in your life while I was gone. I may not know what your daily schedule is anymore. I may not know your immediate plans in the future. But I. Know. You."

He grabbed her hand and held on before she could take it back. He played with her fingertips. "I know everything in your life is controlled as much as possible. Your apartment is flawlessly decorated and clean, and absolutely unlived in. I bet you're always working, always caring about your clients, and never there. The only real flaw that I can see, besides that damn sexy temper, is this." He held her hands up in front of her and her eyebrows scrunched. "You get fake nails because—if your bad habit had its way—you'd bite them to the quick."

She tugged her hand free and crossed her arms. "So, what, Jason. Big deal, I'm a workaholic who bites her nails. Oh, I feel *seen.* That proves nothing." He almost lost it again at her overexaggerated eye roll.

"No? Okay then." He stalked slowly toward her, but this time she retreated two small steps back. "I may have met you when you were only nineteen, but you'd been acting like an adult for much longer than anyone had noticed. I've seen you dedicated and determined to get what you wanted. I've seen you take down men twice your size with words alone. And a little something extra that one time." He winked and she rolled her eyes again. "I've seen that none of that has changed."

She scoffed as she crossed her arms, but it was only fuel to his fire.

"You took care of my baby sister when I checked out. You did such a good job raising her, Jules. She's beautiful, and God, so good. Way too good for this world. I know I sure as hell didn't do that. Aunt Rachel's great, but she didn't do that either. You've been the mother she needed because our parents are gone... you've been the sister she needed when her brother was gone." She jumped a fraction as she realized she'd backed herself up against one of the timber walls near his bedroom.

"Okay."

"What's that?" He held his hand to his ear. "Still don't believe me?" he joked, knowing at the uncertainty in her eyes that he was getting to her. "How 'bout another quirk? Hm... let's see. Your accent comes out when you've been drinking, which is rare, or when you're mad, which, unfortunately is not rare. Especially not around me." He slid his hands up her arms until he gripped her shoulders, hoping the pressure there would make her realize how serious he was with what he said next.

"You are going to be a great mother to our child one day." Her breath hitched and she closed her eyes. He moved one hand to cup her nape and the other to lift her chin. "No matter how that happens. Know that it will. I'll give you everything you want, maybe not exactly how you've dreamed it, but it will still be the life of your dreams. And one of my favorite things about you? You're brave. You'll let yourself fall, even knowing no one is going to catch you. And that? That's fucking fearless, Juliet Bellerose."

She melted in his hands and he bent close, only a breath away as he whispered. "I've seen you argue for second chances, baby. I'm just over here, hoping you're willing to give me one, too." His lips brushed hers.

"I love you, Jules. I've always loved you. I never stopped. Please. Let me love you again."

Her hooded eyes met his, the emotion in them bore into his soul as she spoke.

"Lies?"

He choked on the hope bubbling in his chest.

"No lies."

It was all up to her. The rest of his life hinged on this decision. Her decision. He held his breath. He'd laid his tattered heart in her hands, her forgiveness was the needle and thread, and he hoped they could stitch them both back together. Still holding his breath, Jason nearly gave in before he heard the sweetest sound.

"*Yes.*"

CHAPTER TWENTY-EIGHT

Before Jason could exhale in relief, Jules threw her arms around his neck and smashed her mouth against his. Her hands threaded through his hair and tugged, demanding he come closer. From her frantic movements, he could tell she was trying to take charge. And when the nerve endings in his scalp fired off a pleasurable sting from her nails, he almost gave in.

A flash of them fucking rough and uncontrollably on her dining table shot straight to his cock and it twitched in anticipation. But that wasn't happening this time. This time he would savor every inch, every moment, as he made love to her inside and out.

He stroked the back of his hands up the satin skin of her arms until he reached her needy fingers clutching his hair. Interlacing their fingers, he withdrew their hands and brought their arms down together, wrapping around her back. Her breath caught when she realized he wasn't letting her out of the position and he paused to see the look of uncertainty in her eyes. He knew the angle of her hands captured behind her lower back wasn't physically painful, but any time Jules gave up control was a threat to the walls she put up emotionally. Her letting go in his arms, leaving their pleasure in his hands, would be a humbling show of trust.

The gentle brush of his lips against her brow smoothed away the worry there and the muscles in her hands and face relaxed. With her melting into his embrace he bent to tease his tongue in past the seam of her lips. She opened deliciously and drew his tongue to hers, rolling them together in a motion he hoped to mimic against her body soon. He pulled her closer until her breasts were flush against his chest. Withdrawing his hands from hers, he smoothed them over her short shorts until he could palm her ass. He dipped his tongue into her mouth and lifted her slightly so he could grind his hard cock against the apex of her thighs.

His rhythm started slowly at first and everything he did with his lips and tongue flowed down his body to be mirrored by his insistent cadence against her mound. Her breasts pressed against his chest and her thin T-shirt made it possible for him to feel her nipples peak with arousal against his pecs. By the hitch in her breathing, he could tell each curl of his spine ended with his length hitting where she was most sensitive just right. He reveled in her breaths against his lips as they grew into moans the deeper he rolled.

Her hands were free and grabbing his biceps but when he dug his fingers into her bottom cheeks, she followed his encouragement and hopped onto him, squeezing her arms and legs around him like she couldn't let him go. That she still remembered the subtle signal made him smile wide enough to break the connection of their kiss and he nipped her bottom lip.

He wanted to savor the taste of cherries from her lip balm as the familiar ambrosia took him back to a time when this was all they ever were. Passionate need, ready to combust under just one caress. With her straddling him in the air, he carried her into their bedroom. On their way, she let go of him completely and pulled her shirt over her head and threw it. His hand gravitated to her nape, and brought her back to his eager lips. They met in a clash, clinging to the other, and he growled when she dug her nails into his traps.

Still carrying her, he was mindful of any pain from the attack she'd suffered. While one hand stabilized them as he crawled on the unmade bed, the other pulled double duty by unsnapping her bra with his fingers and ensuring her body was flush against his. Making sure she was safe as he laid her out on the creamy cotton sheets. Kneeling over her as she relaxed onto the bed, he unwrapped her arms to release her hold from his neck.

After they both took the moment to catch their breath, he slid down her body, trailing his fingertips along the outline of her hourglass figure until he settled on the elastic of her shorts. She sat up on her elbows and he watched her follow his movements hungrily as he dipped his fingers inside her shorts and pulled them down her legs, leaving her only in a simple black cotton thong.

He returned her heated gaze, stepped up to the edge of the bed, and took her in. Having lost her before, he knew now more than ever how important it was to take his time. Memories of her had given him hope in his darkest times, and he never wanted to forget this moment when she let him back in.

It was then he allowed himself to drift his gaze over the marks on her stomach. A thin line, about an inch long, from her belly button. A darkened spot, no bigger than a pencil eraser, on the inside of each hip bone. Even though they were only slightly darkened against her creamy skin, he'd still noticed them when she was bandaged up. He'd wanted to ask her about them then, but when she'd covered herself so quickly, he'd understood the need for privacy. Wounds aren't meant to be cut back open.

"Jason, don't—" She tried to cover her battle scars, the ones she'd had to suffer for all by herself, and he grabbed both her hands and held them over her head with one of his. With his free hand, he gently brushed his fingertips over the silk of her skin down to her marks.

He shook his head and focused his eyes on hers, willing her

to see the raw emotion that was threatening to break him apart. "Please, Jules. I've wanted to do this with you for so long, baby."

She watched him intently, searching his expression, and he hoped she felt the strength of his love for her. "Wanted to do what, Jay?"

"Worship you..."

He squeezed her hands into the bed and covered her body with his, kissing her deeply, catching her bottom lip in his teeth as he separated from her. When he lifted up, she tried to follow but he kept her pinned. She frowned as she lies back down, but he laughed and caressed every inch of her arms down to her waist. He open-mouth kissed and sucked down her jaw, her neck, her chest.

Her body rolled under him, reminding him of the first time he ever saw her, urging him to bestow attention to the skin she raised to his lips. When he got to her breasts, he was pleased to find her warm and blushing from his ministrations. He swirled a pink peak around with his tongue and waited for her tell as he laved. A soft breath hitched and he sucked roughly until he heard the moan he'd been silently begging for. Then switched to the other rosy crest, not wanting it to feel neglected.

He continued his perusal down, leaving his hands to knead her breasts while he trailed his tongue down her torso. When he reached the scars, she raised her head to look at him, but kept her hands away like he'd wanted. He watched her bite her lip, and her eyes glisten as he laid soft reverent kisses on each scar. He slid up her body to lay a final kiss on those plump lips. He returned to brushing his hands down her trim torso, stopping halfway there to tug and roll her nipples in his fingers, spreading the wetness he'd left there. He sat up and grinned at her frustrated growl.

"Easy, easy. I promise I'll get back to those perfect lips. But you'll like what I'll do with mine in the meantime." He traveled his hands to hook the thin material of her thong and enjoyed watching eager understanding take over on her face. He dragged the material down her long legs and he imagined her steadying breaths were to ease her anticipation. His cock, hard and impatient by how much time he was taking, was excited enough for the both of them.

She closed her eyes and let out a deep breath, and he backed off the bed to shed his clothes faster than it took to load and cock his Glock. She peeked open one of her eyes and groaned.

"Oh God, Jason. Do you have to look like that?"

"Glad you like what you see." He winked.

A blush took over her cheeks and she quickly threw her hands over her face to hide it from his view. To him, for a long time, his survival depended on the amount of time and effort he put into working out and staying fit. Since he became a civilian, the need hadn't been so great, but damn, the maintenance was worth it if he got that type of reaction from his Jules.

His hands skimmed her hips and the outside of her thighs until he slipped his hands under her knees and pulled her swiftly to the edge of the bed.

"Jay!" She stopped covering her face and gripped the sheets underneath her, only to tug them along with her.

"Hands up, baby," he tsked. He didn't much care at that point. It was more about teasing her into relaxing. Although with what he was about to do to her, he'd actually take deep satisfaction in any wounds she couldn't help but claw into him. She rolled her eyes, but the brightness inside eased something in his heart.

He knelt at her feet and positioned her legs over his wide shoulders, and cupped her ass, bringing her closer for his feast.

"Damn, I love that you're bare." He blew a cool breath over her and she shivered. "Better to eat you." She lifted her head and groaned at his waggling eyebrows.

"God, Jay, that was terrible—"

He swiped his tongue along her outer lips, finding them already soaked. Her moan made his cock pulse against his shorts.

"Fuck, you're already wet for me." With another glide of his tongue in and out of her core, he spread her sweetness all around, knowing he was driving her crazy.

"Yes, Jay..." Long fingernails pulled on his short hair and her hips thrust her heat into his mouth. But he refused to let her have control.

"Like I said, baby. I've waited a long time to do this to you again. I'm gonna take my time."

"No, Jay, I need-I need..." Another moan as he licked her from top to bottom and back again, swirling around her hardened little nub before stopping.

"Shh, shh, shh... I know what you need. Let me love you." He said the last on a breath and blew against her most sensitive spot until she trembled. Coating a finger in her wetness, he slid it into her and stroked, curling it just inside her entrance and feathering against that place inside her that always made her scream his name. She tried to squirm away from him, but he slid his other arm across her torso, his fingers brushing against the curve of her breast. The hold allowed him to keep her pressed to the bed and still enough to torment her. She'd completely abandoned his "hands up" command, and at the sight of her stroking her fevered skin, particularly her pert nipples, he found that his cock couldn't take much more.

He squeezed in another finger inside her tight channel and sped up his light touches. Knowing her groans of frustration were for him, he still continued to tongue her into a heated frenzy as he massaged all around her clit, just barely fluttering where she wanted him most.

The hand he was using to stroke her soft torso left its post to grab tightly to his cock as it wept from the tip. He was almost at his limit, but he also couldn't help but play a little longer. He wanted to hear her give in. He wanted her to—

"*Please Jay. Pleasepleasepleasepleaseplease...*"

Fuck. Yes.

His tongue became a pointed digit while his fingers fixated on that bundle of nerves just inside her. Her clit hardened even more at the attention and Jules's moans were now loud and constant. Her thick thighs squeezed against his head and he tried not to smile, afraid it would interfere with his tongue pulsing against her. Jules was almost at her pinnacle, and he'd be surprised if he had any hair left by the end of it. Pants and moans above him were now higher pitched. It was time. He went in for the kill, sucking on her clit.

"*Jason!*" His name on her breathy cry was almost as delicious as her pussy, and he had to grip himself hard to keep from coming. Even still, he continued to lap until the tensed muscles in her torso and legs relaxed and her breathing became more measured.

He kissed her clit, relishing the shudder vibrating her body. He moved his lips up her thighs, the small dark scars on her belly, her pert breasts, her rosy peaks. On his way to cover her body with his own, he gave her wet kisses and nips until he reached her plush lips. His hand dug into her hair just above her nape and he raised her to his kiss. His other hand tucked underneath her so that he was cradling her as he settled in between her welcoming thighs. Even though she was slick against his cock, he still ground against her wetness, drenching the outside of his heavy shaft.

With her hands kneading his back and her lips so soft, so perfect, it was hard to stop even for a second, but this was important. He lifted up and his stormy grays caught her cerulean eyes. She wouldn't say it yet, he knew that, but he could see the love in that deep sea and he had to choke back emotion as he spoke.

"Baby, we're not strangers, I don't think we were ever strangers. Tell me you know that."

Her eyes were glazed with pleasure, but she nodded. "I'm sorry, I shouldn't have said that. You know me, Jay," she whispered the last and her legs tightened around him. His cock was at her opening, and a part of him wanted to shove inside on one hard thrust, and fuck her until she forgot every other man she'd ever been with. Forgot any time in her life where they didn't love each other.

But that's not what they *needed*. He needed to show her with his body how much he'd missed her, how much he realized he fucked-up, and how much he loved her wholly and completely. Those years apart were torture, for both of them, at times. Remembering their hurt would only make the healing that much stronger. He knew to do that she needed him to hold her, cherish her, and never let her go again. Jason wasn't sure how much he could conceivably convey all that in one night, but dammit he was gonna try. He'd just have to remind her of everything left unsaid. Every day. For the rest of their lives.

Still looking into her eyes, he positioned himself exactly where they needed him to be and spoke, punctuating every word by slowly and barely entering her with the head of his cock. In and out. In and out.

"You know what else I know?"

She tried to close her feverish gaze and shake her head, but he tugged her hair enough for her to know they needed for her to keep them open.

"I know I was your first." He kissed her lightly on the lips. Then he waited until her eyes locked on his and he knew she would understand the promise he was about to give. "And I'm sure as hell gonna be your last." On the final word, he fully sheathed himself inside her and they moaned together.

He began an intentionally slow pace and dove into her deep, dragging his cock against her warm walls until just the head was held in her heat.

"Damn, baby. How are you this tight? Fuck."

Her nails dug into his ass. "Faster, Jay."

"When're you gonna learn?" He shook his head and laughed darkly. "You're not always in charge." One arm continued to cradle her and positioned her so his eyes were all she could see. His other hand trailed down her side until he palmed her ass, holding her flush to him. "Give in to me, Jules."

Then they *moved*.

His body flowed against hers in the dance he'd imagined the very first time he saw her. One they were meant to perform together. He held her close and her nails dug into his back as he slowly curved his cock into her, while she rolled her body in time with his. She moaned when he sank deep inside her, going as far into her as her body would allow. Her whimper as he pulled out, almost all the way each time, made him nearly come with pride. But he kept going, working hard past her toned thighs pressed against his sides, trying to cage him in.

She had nothing to worry about though. There was no way in hell he wanted to be free from her. He would keep that methodical pace forever until he felt her walls pulse against him, tightening and releasing.

"Fuck, Jules."

She whispered unintelligible chants back and closed her eyes as her body seized up in a quickening beat. She cried out his name in increasingly higher pitches and her nails deep in his skin made him grunt in male satisfaction that she couldn't contain herself. But then again, neither could he.

"That's it," he whispered. She caught his eyes and they both refused to look anywhere else. "Come for me, Jules. Show me how good we feel."

"*Yes*," she breathed on a moan. Her body tightened inside and out on the word, and she cried his name one last time on her release. His fingers of his right hand dug into her cheeks and his left arm pulled her closer to his chest as she squeezed around his cock like a fist, triggering his release.

"*Jules.*" He stuttered out her name, ending with a moan. His thrusts increased in speed and power in an uncoordinated rhythm until he was finally spent. He dug his face into her neck, nipped her there lightly, and allowed her soft honey hair to flow around his face. She massaged her fingers down the sides of his spine and he groaned, wondering how he ever fucking left her.

He lifted up and brushed her hair back from her face. Her

smile was soft, warm, and full of love. Any last worry he had about their relationship prior to their reunion was cured.

"Jason..." she breathed. "I..."

He watched her struggle for words, but understood when she slightly shook her head. If she felt the way he did, there weren't any. He didn't need them anyway. Everything he needed was in her smile. He kissed her forehead, his thumbs brushing over her cheekbones. Her body underneath him melted, and her eyes were calm but exhausted.

"I love you, baby girl," he whispered against her lips. He kissed her lightly on the tip of her nose, eyelids, cheeks, and tugged her earlobe with his teeth.

"Lies?"

"No lies," he answered back, returning back to stare deep into her sleepy, satisfied eyes.

"I'm your last, Jules."

"My last?" she whispered, her eyelids were heavy, nearly closed.

Jason brushed his lips against hers as he nodded and held her so, so close and silently promised himself to never make the same mistakes again.

"Your first. Your last. Your only, baby."

CHAPTER TWENTY-NINE

"Ready?"

Andy took a ragged breath before gathering his strength to lift the last bag in order to include it with all the others in the back of the stereotypical kidnapping van Vlad procured for them. Except, if the crazy Russian's bragging over the last half hour of broken English was any indication, it wasn't stereotypical at all. Vlad claimed he'd ordered heavy-duty upgrades, he'd demanded for the van to be "strong and smart." Whatever that meant. As far as he could gather from the Russian's hand gestures and what Andy was sure was Russian cursing, the van may or may not have been bulletproof, but the cargo doors were definitely impossible to open from the inside.

Andy heaved the last burden onto his back and attempted to lay it down as gently as his tired body allowed. He was tired of loading and unloading into various hotel rooms and frustrated that they couldn't just stay the final night in the one they were in. They'd only just gotten there that morning, after he was told they'd leave the other hotel before the crack of dawn.

If they'd been able to stay, he would've shared that hotel address with Juliet and saved him and the women from having to wait for rescue. She could fix it. She would fix it all. But no, they had to move on every whim of a psychotic Russian and prolong this nightmare.

"Almost," he grunted out.

"Good, we must hurry. Boss says we meet tonight."

"Tonight?!" He faltered and the bag slipped from his grip. He cursed as a weak groan escaped from within.

Vlad also cursed in Russian and bent to roughly toss the bag into the van. Another whimper went straight to Andy's gut and he began to feel nauseous.

"I thought we were meeting... whoever we're meeting... tomorrow?"

Vlad unzipped the bag and Nora's wincing violet eyes and lavender hair stood out against her pale skin.

"Get my case."

Andy grumbled but still acquiesced, following Vlad's orders. Now that the gold-toothed Russian was gone, he had the distinct feeling he was the whipping boy rather than the master. Although, he'd realized early on he'd never been the master either. But maybe that wasn't so bad. That way, when the entire operation is inevitably exposed, his culpability will be minor. He hoped.

Maybe he could even convince Juliet to be his attorney, and they could rekindle what was lost. Although, she might never forgive him for this if she realized how deeply he'd let the quicksand bury him.

He'd known he was in over his head when he saw all the drugged girls in the bathroom that first time. That it was all his own damn naïve fault for believing the firm's partners. His father. He'd tried to rationalize it in his mind, separate himself from their agenda. All the while trying to glean information from them, to ensure said information got into the right hands, and hope that it would all work out in the end.

But his forced impassivity punched him in the gut when he witnessed a partner nearly choke one of their own to death with his bare hands. Over a phone call for Christ's sake. And he'd further understood just how little the firm respected him, despite him being a founding son, when they'd tried to have Juliet killed. They'd known what she meant to him and they did it anyway.

He snapped out of his trance. He'd said all this before, in his mind of course, but he was starting to realize just complaining about his situation wasn't helping anyone, least of all him. He gave Vlad his case, only to have Vlad shove the pack he'd retrieved back into him. Andy tried to hand it to him again.

"What're you doing, you imbecile? You asked me for this. I went and retrieved it like a fucking dog. What do you want?"

"No more. You will not blame mirror for ugly face."

"Excuse me?"

"I see you, *durak*. You try to make me bad guy. But you just as bad. You must do it."

"Do what?" he asked, confused by the entire conversation, let alone the command.

Vlad huffed at him and snatched the case, opening it to pull out a syringe and bottle. He filled the syringe and shoved it into Andy's bewildered open palms.

"Girl is awake. She must sleep through sale. Here."

Andy stared at the syringe as the Russian went to start the van.

Vlad had seen right through him. Wasn't he *just* thinking about ways he could minimize his responsibility in the scheme? And blaming everyone else for his involvement?

Nora's eyes were glazed as she watched him, unseeing. Perspiration pricked his brow and sickness burned his esophagus. If she woke up during the trip and exchange, she could maybe try to save herself. Or get herself killed. But if he left her even more vulnerable than she was, she may as well be dead already. He'd thought he'd seen Nora on her phone after she received the letter. But now that point was moot. Since the exchange was on for a mere matter of hours instead of tomorrow, there was no hope for anyone saving any of them.

When he'd shoved the gold-tooth's dead body off of Nora during the fight earlier, he'd thought he was finished with heroic deeds and decisions. But here he was again, at a precipice. The pit that had slowly grown ever since he realized exactly what Ascot, Rusnak, and Strickland, LLC was up to, was starting to eat away at his stomach. He had an idea of what the unfamiliar sensation was.

Guilt. And he was fucking sick of it.

The revving of the van startled him.

"We must go now."

Making his decision, he jumped off the fence and decided to go all in. He gave her the syringe and fiddled with Nora's watch before zipping her halfway.

"Ready." He opened the passenger door and Vlad sped out of the alley before he could get fully in his seat.

"Hey! I don't even have my seatbelt on, yet!" He glared at Vlad from his peripherals, but the Russian was focused as he drove out of yet another hotel back alley. The GPS system notified them in a calm voice that they would reach the Inland Port in a matter of hours. He peeked at the dim light of his phone, but knew Juliet hadn't responded.

Nora was techno-savvy and Juliet considered her another appendage. With as many times as Nora had found and removed an app he'd secretly installed on Juliet's phone, he hoped she'd carried that technological paranoia over to other aspects of her and Juliet's tabs on one another. He'd done everything he could. For all he knew, it'd been for nothing.

But it would have to be enough.

CHAPTER THIRTY

"What do you mean they haven't checked in?" Jason jacked up from the bed.

Jules scooted under the covers to caress her fingers down his naked back and over the tattoo that was the completed image of the bird from his chest. It was the back of the blue jay, but a beautifully detailed and realistic heart was present on this side. The bird's claws sank into it as it tried to pull his heart out of the stitched seam. She watched as the muscles under the tattoo hardened. Even after what they'd just done, he was already tense with worry.

"So, Draco hasn't called? Nora said she was going home, right? She texted us the note..." Jason looked at his phone and winced at Jules. "Less than half an hour ago." He held the phone to his ear but covered it as he whispered to her, "Damn, baby, sorry that was so short—" Listening, his face scrunched into a frown she was sure mirrored her own. "Hold on." He pressed the screen a couple of times and laid the phone—now on speaker—on the nearby bedside table. "Say that again."

"We haven't heard from Draco and he always answers his phone while out on a mission. We have a policy of every fifteen minutes in a stakeout situation, which is sort of what this was.

Phoenix and I came back when Snake told us he'd lost contact," Hawk said, his voice hard.

"I don't know, man." Another male laughed over the speakerphone. "I still say they're out celebrating they found a clue."

"Phoenix, shut up. This is serious," Jason growled. He stood up and riffled through his bag.

"I'm serious too, dude. Did you see the way he lit up like a flare whenever she talked?"

"Ignore him. He started a new romance novel."

"Fuck you, Hawk. This has nothing to do with that. I'm telling you, I don't know if I've heard him laugh so much the entire seven years I've known him."

Hawk continued as if the lovebird hadn't spoken. "His GPS says he's still at Original Sin—"

"Shit, I think I found something. Hold up," Snake interrupted.

During the few seconds of silence, Jason got back from putting on boxer briefs, a sight Jules could hardly appreciate as she anxiously waited for Wesley—or Snake as the Crew called him—to continue. It was hard for her to keep up with them all and she found it easier to adopt their call signs.

Jason sat back on the bed, partially facing her. He tugged the hand she'd used to stroke his back and pulled it over his thigh to hold. His fingers running over her knuckles sent a shiver down her spine.

"Shit, that's bad."

"What?" they both asked.

"Police scanner caught something. Let me turn it up. I'll have to make sure I have the police codes right. It's different for every region. Fuck. There's been a murder at Original Sin."

Jules sat up abruptly, not caring about her nakedness, and grabbed the phone. "Oh, God. Nora..."

"*10-75 vic is a whiskey mike, thirties... no ID. GSW to the head. 10-33. Coroner 10-32.*"

"Shooting victim... unknown white male... gunshot wound...

emergency all units standby... they need the coroner..." Jules robotically whispered the police codes she'd memorized from her cases.

"*Vic's identifiers: Blond, over six feet—*"

"Draco?" Jules felt her numb lips move.

"*—Gold tooth.*"

Jason's grip on her fingers loosened. It wasn't him.

"*Got another vic. Make that two body bags, dispatch.*"

It was Jules's turn to tighten her grip and Jason continued to massage her knuckles with his thumb.

"*10-75 vic two is a whiskey mike, thirties. Again, no ID. Vic's identifiers: Blond, over six feet, tattoo of a... snake... maybe a dragon, in a circle on his neck—*"

Jason tensed as the radio line continued. "*—GSW to the chest. We're gonna need the coroner for this one too.*"

"Fuck!" Jason cursed along with the men on the other side of the line, their voices rising over the rest of the dispatch radio. He kept hold of Jules's hand, just to the point of pain, and covered his face with his other hand. "Draco... fuck, man. Fuck!"

From the police chatter, they were waiting for the coroner and a few moments passed in stunned silence before anyone over the phone said anything.

A throat cleared on the other line. "Well men," Hawk began, his voice hard and cold. "We haven't heard about Nora. We have to assume she's in danger. We need to devote all of our energy in finding out the identity of the other gunshot victim, where Nora is, and how to find those women—"

"*We got a pulse on vic two. He's alive! Unresponsive but he's got a heartbeat! Vic's alive! We need EMS now! Shit-I mean, 10-52! 10-52! 10-31! Fuck it! Dispatch, we need EMS now! Beginning chest compressions and wound pressure until paramedics arrive!*"

"Draco..." Jason's wide-eyed stare at the phone interrupted the radio's chatter.

Hawk immediately began barking on the other line. "Dev,

you and Phoenix get to Original Sin, ASAP. Wait for updates for which hospital to go to."

Jason released the tight grip on her hand she hadn't realized he'd been squeezing to paralysis, and collapsed his head into his hands.

"Men, it's a hell of a coincidence if it's not Draco, but from how surprised that officer was, it sounds like whoever it is, is a lucky bastard. Dev? Phoenix? Keep your phones on."

"Yes sir," was echoed as chairs scraped in the background of the call and the police chatter was lowered to a whisper. There was silence on both ends as they listened to the updates.

"Apparently cops have been there for a while. I can't figure out how long, though yet. But they were clearing the scene because they weren't sure if shots were actually fired, or why the call was made in the first place. It sounds like the incident location is off in a darkened corner of the Original Sin customer parking lot," Jules supplied from her working knowledge of police radio and professional estimation. "They initially only sent one unit to respond because dispatch thought it was a prank call at first. The operator said the call came from a smart product, which is still new technology for this old town. They've been figuring it out since."

"So, no one called it in?" Snake asked.

"They distinctly said it came from a smart tech alert, something besides a phone or they would've referred to it as a 'call' rather than an 'alert.'"

Jason got up and moved about the room, clothing himself before he threw Jules one of his T-shirts. She quickly put it on and grabbed her phone from her purse nearby.

"What're you doing?"

"Calling Nora, what the heck else would I be doing? Draco may be alive, but we don't know anything about Nora yet."

He reached her in two quick strides and grabbed the phone, putting it into his pocket.

"Hey! Jay—"

"No, no, no. Don't 'Hey, Jay' me. We still don't know if you're being tracked through your phone."

"Not even to check on Nora? That's insane!"

"Insane? No, what's insane is if you're being tracked and you lead some psycho here with a push of a button, even after all Nora and Draco did to make sure you were safe! She has my number. If she needed you, she'd call or message me."

Chastised but undeterred, Jules opened her mouth to argue.

"No. I'm serious, Jules. I'm making sense and you know it. For all I know, one of my Crew was just about *murdered*. This is a big fucking deal."

"I know that." She huffed, annoyed at the way he was speaking to her. "I just want to turn my phone on—really quickly—just to see if there's anything from Nora."

He held her stare, like the alpha he was, but she wouldn't back down.

"I think I can remotely jam the outgoing GPS signal for a few minutes. I've been working on it all day, but I'm about eighty-seven percent sure it'll work," Snake offered.

She lifted her brow. Finally, Jason rolled his eyes.

"Fine."

She waited until Snake gave the all clear and grabbed her phone from Jason's pocket and turned it on. Frowning at the screen.

"There's nothing."

"Alright then, turn it off," Jason snapped.

"Our contact with the police department just texted back saying that the victim is a, quote 'big ass white Viking with an impressive blond beard,'" Snake supplied.

"Fucking sounds like our Draco," Hawk muttered.

"At least we know he's alive, Hawk," Jason answered. "For now." His final whisper only loud enough for Jules to hear.

"You're right, you're right. Okay, Phoenix and Dev will be able to give us updates shortly. Draco and Nora went to Original Sin only a few hours ago. We don't know what happened, when, or what happened, generally. Snake and I have almost come up with a plan for the drop-off tomorrow afternoon, but there are still a few kinks. We haven't figured out the layout of the port yet, and it's fucking huge. Let's wait for updates on Draco before we go into all that. In the meantime—shit... I can't believe I didn't think of this before now. Jules, does Original Sin still have security cameras? I thought this was just a recon mission."

"Yeah, I can try to get the codes if I can call Cyn."

"No need," Snake responded. "I thought I remembered this earlier today actually and looked into it, already. A while back I took the liberty of finding backdoors to various cloud servers for multiple security services. Since Hawk installed that camera system back when Jaybird was a bouncer there, I included it. It's taken me nearly all day just to get backlogged video since it's so retro. And from that video, it's taken me half as long just to get the pixilation less granular. It's too bad Cyn terminated services after you left, Jaybird. Your shitty install needs a serious upgrade," Snake responded.

"Shut up, asshole." Hawk fired off a hard look and Snake went back to business. "Keep looking through that system. Maybe then we can get some information on Nora's status."

Jason's phone vibrated and he went to check it. His forehead wrinkled.

"Speak of the devil..."

Jules scrambled up from the bed to reach him, only just stopping herself from grabbing the phone. "Is that Nora? What'd she say?" He scrolled through the screen at a depressingly slow rate. "Jay!"

"She says, '*Could you give me a call?*'"

Jules squealed and stole the phone from him, immediately calling Nora, not caring that it effectively ended the call with BlackStone.

"*Yo betches, obvi I'm not around my phone right now, so I'm either dead*" —Jules gasped— "*or I'm screening your call. So, take a hint. Byeeeeee!*" Her voice caused a pit in Jules's stomach. It didn't help that she'd never heard Nora's voicemail greeting before, so considering the circumstances, the whole reference to death comment made her sick to her stomach.

"Did she send it directly to voicemail? Why would she tell you to call her and not answer? That makes no freaking sense!" she yelled and threw Jason's phone to the bed.

He wrapped her in his arms, purposely squeezing her through her fit. "We'll figure this out, baby girl. Keep your head on straight."

Jules eventually quit fighting and he eased up to hold her face in his hands. "Get it together, Jules. We need you right now." His stormy gray eyes were almost black and she allowed herself to be swallowed in them. She breathed in a cleansing breath and nodded.

As she relaxed, Jason kissed her forehead and let her go, grabbing both phones. He dialed a number on his.

"Jaybird, what happened? Everything alright—"

"Yeah, Hawk, hold on. You still jamming that GPS signal, Snake?"

"Affirmative."

"Okay, I have an idea."

"What're you doing?" Jules asked as Jason turned her phone on.

"Taking your advice," he explained as he typed.

"*Yo betches, obvi I'm not around...*"

Jules felt her shoulders fall as she realized that Nora wasn't taking her calls either. In the history of their work-friend relationship, that had *never* happened. Her eyes burned and she had to turn away before grabbing the phone herself.

"Hm... Jason, you said the message said 'Could you give me a call?'" Snake asked.

Jason reached with one hand to cradle her face again, trying to soothe her, but this time it wasn't working. He checked his phone with the other hand. "Yeah, Snake. That's what it says, exactly."

"Why, does that mean something?" Jules asked.

"It's just strange. That sounds like a smartphone autoreply." His assessment met with silence until he sighed. "Meaning if Nora actually wrote that, there should be more 'betches' and all-around brashness, evident by her voicemail greeting."

Jason's eyes looked far off and he tapped her phone against his chin.

"Snake, with you jamming the GPS signal, will I be able to still use the GPS?"

"Yeah, I just need to work some code really quick. But it should work. What's up?"

"I'm not good at this whole iPhone thing. How do I know if Jules is tracking Nora's phone?"

The techno-wizard walked him through checking her phone until he got to the correct app.

"Okay, what does it say?" Snake asked.

Jason squinted and he and Jules attempted to look at the map on the screen.

"Nora's phone has no location," he said, his voice deadened.

"Wait, hold on..." Jules grabbed the phone and scrolled her finger over the screen. "We still have the location of her Apple watch!" she yelled, ignoring Jason's wince.

"That's great Jules, where does it say she is?" Hawk asked.

She manipulated the map to read it better. "It says, they're on I-57 and they've taken Exit 23. That's weird..."

"What?" Jason asked as Jules heard typing on the other line.

"Well... that area is out in the boonies. There's nothing for miles except—"

"The Inland Port... fuck!" Snake finished for her. "Looks like there's been a change of plans, men. The drop-off's tonight, not tomorrow."

"What? Fuck, *nonononono!*" Jason ripped at his hair with both hands and Jules felt lightheaded as all the blood drained from her face. How were they going to save Ellie? Nora? There was no time.

"Jules, I'm remoting in on your phone so I can see this map in real time."

"You can *remote in* on my phone? You mean, control my phone from where you are? I didn't think that was possible! Can anyone do that? Can the government?"

"Erm... there are private entities that have apps with digital spyware capabilities, which is what Nora checks for you. They'd need certain information, and Nora gave me your phone's specifics so I can do it. I think I can actually make it so Jay can take his phone and leave you with yours. And it's not like the government can't *not* do it—"

"Way to evade the question, Snake. That's a triple negative—"

"Snake. Jules. Focus. We got a status on Phoenix and Dev?" Hawk interrupted.

A few seconds later, Snake responded, "Affirmative, sir. They're at Original Sin. Phoenix is texting me. He says that Draco is still unconscious and unresponsive, but alive. Paramedics are loading him up and out to the nearest hospital. He had gunshot wounds to the chest and side. I'm not able to watch the security system in real time but I'll be able to look at past footage from the night."

"Shit, okay. Tell them to get back to base. We need to move out."

"What about Draco? We shouldn't leave him alone."

"From what they're saying, there's nothing to do for him now. He wouldn't want us to forsake the mission. Tell Phoenix that he and Dev need to come back... and Draco needs to go to the damn hospital and let the professionals do their jobs. That's an *order*."

"Yes sir."

"I've got someone I can ask to watch him, if that's what you want."

"Really? Are you sure, Jules?"

"Henry will love it, don't worry." She queued up the number

on her phone to call as soon as the conversation was over. She'd make a call to Marco, too. Something was about to go down. She could feel it. Having an ADA on their side may prove beneficial.

"Okay, Jaybird? Here's the new plan. There's a private airbase near our facility. We'll take off in our Bird. It'll take us time to get situated, so you drive as fast and as close as you can."

"Will Phoenix be flying?" Jason growled. "He better not pull that same fucking stunt with the headset, Hawk, I swear to God I'll—"

"Yes," Hawk interrupted. "That won't happen again. I've had a major talk with him and he's promised to get his shit together. We'll determine a rendezvous and an equidistant point for pick up before heading to the drop-off. Snake, you got an ETA on Nora to that Inland Port?"

"Whoever she's with, they're definitely heading there. Hopefully she's with the others for the sale and it's not just her going there. Shit, sorry Jaybird, that sounded bad."

Jason was already gearing up to head out and didn't seem to be paying attention to Snake's slipup.

"But it looks like they're still at least over an hour out. Maybe more, depending on driving speed. All that's out there is farmland, forest, and manufacturing buildings, so there'll be plenty of places to land the Bird out of earshot and eyesight."

"10-4," Jason responded, already gearing up to leave. "I'll head out ASAP. Let me know if there's anything else I need to know before I get to the rendezvous. And keep me updated if anything changes." He hung up the phone and tucked it in one of his many pockets in his black-out uniform BlackStone Securities loaned him since Jules could now keep her phone on.

"Gotta go, baby girl."

Her heart squeezed and she could hardly breathe. It felt like this was it. A turning point of some kind, and she hoped that the pivot led them in the right direction to save their family and friends.

"I wish I could go with y'all and help. I feel useless here."

"You have the professional expertise and contacts to help them through the trauma they've gone through. Okay?"

She nodded and took a steadying breath before searching his stormy gray eyes.

"You'll come back?" Her voice was in a slightly higher pitch than she'd intended and she hoped she hadn't let on how afraid she was.

The small smile against his five o'clock shadow sent warmth to her heart. He rounded the bed and cradled her head in both hands, fingers grazing her throat. A hold as vulnerable as the moment.

He leaned his forehead against hers. "One way or another, I'll be back, Jules. I promise. Nothing could keep me from you." She refused to look at him but gentle pressure on the soft skin under her jaw brought her gaze to meet his.

"Nothing. You got that?" She nodded slightly and he kissed her forehead before standing straight.

He looked as if he was about to say something else, but shook his head.

She felt the words they both needed to hear bubble and burn in her throat, but she just couldn't say them. He'd apologized. She wanted to try with him again. But she wasn't ready for that next step. She was paralyzed by the fear of giving herself over to him again. What he did the first time was soul crushing, but would withholding how she really felt make her feel better? She was uncertain as those three words scratched for air on the back of her tongue. Still, she silently twisted on the bed to watch him leave.

"I love you, baby girl."

And then he was gone.

CHAPTER THIRTY-ONE

She'd almost said it.

Down to his very marrow, Jason knew Jules felt the same way he did and that she was on the brink of saying it out loud. Something clicked in him the moment he saw her dance all those years ago, and somehow, he'd known she was his. That feeling never stopped.

Their problems were fear and timing, not what they felt for each other. The first time, he'd been afraid to fully commit. Now she was. Granted, she had a better excuse. The emotions filling him had scared him. The responsibilities that accompanied those emotions had terrified him. The possibility of disappointing Jules had driven him mad until it became a self-fulfilling prophecy. Then, like a coward, he went AWOL on the best thing in his life.

These were the thoughts he tortured himself with as he, Hawk, and Dev made their way from the heavily wooded dirt backroad. Snake found it with his drone and Phoenix landed the Little Bird there, a little over a mile from the drop-off point. The small MH-6 helicopter was known for its stealth and could "sneak" to within a mile of its destination without being heard. Jason was still a little fuzzy as to how the Crew got their hands on a two-million-dollar government model, but he'd tuned out as Phoenix sang the Bird's praises on their way over. From the snippets he gathered, they'd casually stolen it from the United States Army as a dare, and they'd been able to reap the spoils because the government was too embarrassed to admit they'd been duped.

Once they'd landed, his group of three jumped out as they'd been trained. Hawk and him in the Army, and Devil Ray with the Seals. They'd all landed with weapons ready, and eyes alert. MF7 had only perfected their skills. The covert agency took them from their respective military niches and honed them into the paramilitary group the government couldn't acknowledge they needed. It was necessary for the United States to eradicate a pervasive trafficking problem, while also pretending like there was no issue in the first place. After their last mission in Yemen, that secrecy played to the government's advantage. From what the Crew figured, the administration was afraid of the blight on the country that could spawn from their failed mission. They were medically discharged for psychiatric reasons as damage control and for public perception and MF7 was effectively redacted from US history.

He shook his head and kept his weapon low. Despite the adrenaline and nausea coursing through him, muscle memory took over and he eased into a disciplined detachment in times of stress. His practiced stance as they ran through the woods came second nature to him, even as his thoughts were as frantic as a rookie's during his first field training.

They were quickly and quietly covering the mile between the Bird's hiding place and their Inland Port destination. Phoenix stayed behind, just in case they had to high-tail it outta there. Or abort the mission.

There was no way he was letting the last happen.

Come hell or high water, they were going to save Ellie, Nora, and the other victims. He was afraid it'd be yet another dead end, but he couldn't dwell on that fear. Jules was right. They had to prepare for the worst and hope for the best, and they were hoping for the fucking best.

"Can y'all hear me?" Speak of the fallen angel, he smiled to himself as Jules joined their BlackStone communication systems in his earbud.

"Affirmative, Jules," Hawk whispered back. She insisted on being a part of the mission any way she could, and they agreed that because she was connected to this somehow, she may be vital to the mission and should be part of their communications. He honestly hoped it would be an uneventful show and they wouldn't need her. But Nora and Ellie were her best friends. She deserved to be a part of the rescue.

She was hooked up, safe back at the cabin and able to see footage from their body-worn cameras in real-time on the big screen. While Phoenix would only have audio, Snake would have the same access as Jules, and it'd be just like during the hotel mission. Although hopefully with a better outcome. He shook his head at his thoughts. Definitely a better outcome.

"Affirmative," Snake agreed before he continued with the plan. "Crew, you're about a fourth of a mile from where Nora's GPS is signaling. Unfortunately, I didn't have the time to infiltrate the port's surveillance system, but I've pulled up the map online and I'm navigating a drone. I'm not seeing anything yet, although if these guys are smart or really connected, they may have something to jam our systems."

A few minutes of whispering rustles through the tall grass filled the silence before they heard him again.

"Drone's picking up a van moving slowly through the port. I'll maintain visual and radio contact to update you. Over."

"10-4. Roger that," Hawk replied. "We're going silent on our end, since we're so close. Over and out."

Jason saw the towering shadows of their destination. Large shipping containers were stacked on top and beside one another like wall vault graves in a New Orleans cemetery. The long, bent crane arms jutting above the rectangular landscape, were skeletal remains clawing from the cement. The railroad tracks outside the port were interwoven veins for the stationary boxcars and unloaded shipping containers.

They made it to the fenced outskirts of the port in a matter of minutes after talking to Snake. They came upon the heavy-duty chain-link fence they'd prepared to encounter thanks to Snake's recon and Hawk and Dev stood by as Jason knelt to cut it. Once they peeled back the fence, he informed the rest of the team.

"We're in. Where's our target?"

"Lot 76A. Looks like... you're about four lots away right now and you need to head to the southeast corner." Inside the port, they were tucking low in their stances. Hawk, always the team leader on past missions, took the point man position and edged around each container pillar before giving the signal to follow. Aside from the harsh lines of shadows and obvious outlines of containers, it was hard to see any sort of organized 'lots' in the eerie orange light of the lamps interspersed throughout.

"Southeast, got it," Hawk agreed before hesitating. "Will you be able to direct us to Lot 76A? I'm not sure we can figure it out so easily down here in the dark," Hawk asked.

"Who cares?" Dev whispered over their radio from behind Jason. "We don't have time to wait for directions. Ellie's waiting—"

"—and Nora—" Jules interrupted, but Dev continued on.

"—Head southeast. Snake will tell us when we're going the wrong way."

"Erm, affirmative, but I'm having a hard time navigating the drone from a covert distance. Head southeast. Watch your six since I might not be able to be your eyes." Snake recovered from Dev's outburst. Snake was probably just as confused as Jason about Dev's sudden need to take lead. He was never the commanding officer on a mission, but if it got to Ellie quicker, he'd give the guy the reins any damn day.

They continued their methodical pursuit, frustrating Jason

with how long it took to lurk and peer behind each and every haphazardly placed container tower. The height of each one meant it was impossible to see if there was a change in light or sound on the other side, making each movement closer to "Lot 76A" as nerve-wracking as the last.

"Took you long enough."

Jason stilled at the voice nearby, and watched as Hawk and Dev did the same.

"You change the time and expect us to know when and where to be at the drop of a dime? Do you know who I—" At the familiar voice, Jason tightened his grip around the handle of his Glock.

"Yeah, yeah, yeah. You're Andrew Ascot." Jason heard the feminine gasp over the radio, he'd forgotten Jules was even there. "You remember your father works for me, kid. Got it?"

He couldn't place the other voice, but Hawk used a signal from back in the day to tell him and Dev to stop, shut up, and calm down. He tried to focus on Hawk's raised fist and level his own breathing.

"What the fuck, Andrew Ascot's involved?" Jason heard Snake whisper over the headphones, even though they were state-of-the-art and it would be impossible for the other men to hear him. "THE Andrew Ascot? As in, father's firm-owns-all-of-the-southeast Ascot? If they're not in charge, then who the hell is the big dog in this scenario—"

"Well... I'm afraid I'm at a disadvantage." Asshat's voice wavered in the night. If Jason hadn't known the guy was evil scum, he'd have suspected the jerk was nervous.

Laughter grated Jason's focus. "You don't need to know who I am. Do you have the product?"

"*Da*. We have product. You have payment?" A stilted Russian accent entered the conversation.

"Yes, of course. It will be wired to the account we discussed."

"Good. Product in back of van—"

"Is it only you and your driver? Or do you have other peons accompanying you?" Asshat asked in a raised voice.

Beside him, Dev's face scrunched at the odd question. What would it matter to Asshat how many men their contact had?

"Don't worry. I have backup around. Never leave home without it."

Jason immediately glanced around and felt Dev do the same. They hadn't encountered any obstacles or unfriendlies, but maybe they hadn't looked hard enough? Or maybe the guy was bluffing?

Hawk's voice barely a breath over the mic. "Whatever we do. Do *not* kill that guy. He's got the answers we need to bust this thing wide open."

"Yeah, this seems bigger than we thought," Snake agreed.

Jason ignored them and kept sharp, analyzing every dark shadow. It made him an ass, but at this point, he didn't care about the bigger picture. What mattered was saving Ellie, Nora, and the other women.

"Right, well. They're in the van."

Hawk signaled at Asshat's words and Jason and Dev filed out behind him. They stepped through the shadows and watched as a tall, thin man, a short, stout man, a fucking giant, and Asshat crowded around the back of a sketchy van.

"At least two more at the town car..."

"Two on top of the single containers at our nine and three."

"Wait for my signal."

He nodded at Hawk's command. Knowing it could be life or death, Jason dragged his eyes from the van and mentally confirmed the two men with guns at the town car and the two men on containers high in his left and right periphery. His sight went back to the Russian and stout man opening the door, with Asshat and the thin man back a few steps.

"Excellent. Men, get them into the container. It's modified inside to provide the necessities, air conditioning, padding, that sort of thing. All to ensure satisfactory delivery."

The tall, thin man's proud lilt in his voice twisted Jason's stomach.

"We're scheduled to export at dawn, so a few hours. From there, the product will reach the next destination—"

"What the—"

Jason watched, stunned, as a streak of purple fell screaming out of the back of the van and slammed something into the Russian's neck, causing him to step back. Nora jumped out of the van, tackling the giant, and Jason held his gun at shoulder height. It was hard to see, the two bodies were wholly entwined shadows in the dim light. Their outlines switched back and forth, but he aimed down the sights.

"Stand down! You could get Nora," Hawk whispered through gritted teeth. "On my signal."

A sharp cry pierced the night, and the enemy whipped the woman by her hair, laughing.

"I said, stand down!"

He lowered his gun slightly.

But he had the shot.

He raised it back up. At the flash of bright purple passing his vision, he realized he had the shot. He fired. The two of them dropped, but he saw Nora immediately scramble back toward the van, while the Russian stayed down.

"Go, go, go." Hawk's command shattered the stunned silence and Dev broke the line and emerged from the shadows, shooting at three o'clock, making his way to the van.

Jason snapped into gear and slipped into training mode, holding his gun at firing stance and aiming for nine o'clock.

The tat-tat-tat of gunshots and screams of surprise echoed through the metal around them and reverberated through his memory, causing him a life-threatening pause every time he raised his firearm. He blinked past the film over his eyes threatening to inhibit his vision, and swallowed hard against the lump in his throat. His body threatened to go into shock, but he refused to let this be the time he gave way to nightmares. He concentrated on the adrenaline vibrating through his veins, but stilled his nerves. Jason focused on the familiar safety of having Hawk at his back and he shot in front of him, knowing Hawk at his six was doing the same.

The van was in his sights. His sister was in there, he knew it. She had to be okay. She had to be safe. If she wasn't... if he'd failed her... he became single-minded in his pursuit, leaving his teammates in their own capable hands.

We're hoping for the fucking best, Jaybaby.

"Jaybird, get back!" A sharp whistle of a bullet through his cropped hair, a breath away from his scar, brought him back to the present.

He returned fire and a cry died in the night.

The Russian he'd shot to save Nora was laid out by the van, completely harmless. He wasn't sure if the guy was dead, but he at least looked down for the count.

In his peripherals, a short, stocky man charged at him like a deranged bull.

He held up for the shot, but without the practice he'd underestimated the man's trajectory and he quickly found himself on his back and unarmed. The air whooshed from him with the impact of the heavy man bulldozing him. Another, more targeted hit drove into the side of his skull. Dazed, he barely registered another strike to the opposite cheek. In self-defense, he held up one arm and pummeled the man on top of him with his other.

Off in the distance, a scream pierced the night, followed by whimpers that triggered the instincts and training inside him.

He pulled back and wrapped his legs around his opponent's lower half. The smaller man stopped attacking in order to defend himself from the onslaught of Jason's heavy fists. Jason used the opportunity to push off the ground and pull the man to the side, with his legs still wrapped and now the man's head in the crook of his elbow. As he applied pressure behind the sleeper hold, Jason felt the blows striking him get progressively less effective.

He tightened his grip with his elbow and his other hand created more weight to the back of the man's neck.

Around him, screams, gunshots, shouts, the thumps of flesh on pavement, and the slaps of flesh on flesh vaguely registered. Sweat gathered on his brow and stung his eyes, but he squeezed with his arm and hand, preventing his prey from breathing in precious air. It was taking seconds more than he felt he could allow, but finally, the man's own grip against Jason's forearm lessened until he went lax in his hold.

Jason breathed another full, slow breath while the man stayed still with his eyes closed. Confident the man had passed out, Jason extricated himself from underneath. He rolled to his knees and popped up from his stance, ensuring the van was at his back. He sucked in a breath at the sharp pain in his side, but confirmed there was no threat in front or behind him. At that, he turned, dug his toes into the cement, and ran.

Ellie was the only thing on his mind. The back of that van, with its open doors, was all he could see. He didn't know where Hawk or Dev were, but he trusted they could take care of themselves.

He heard more shots around him and he bent low to get to the van. He pulled the doors open just enough to accommodate his large stature, but closed them back against his body, so he and the women inside were mostly protected by the metal doors. It wouldn't allow for much cover if this was a run-of-the-mill kidnapping van, but even a thin layer of metal between them and a bullet was better than nothing. He hoped.

Inside the van was a disturbing amount of large, body-sized, canvas bags. He went to work, unzipping each, not caring that all he was searching for was sunshine blonde hair. If when he opened the bag, anything but that showed through, he left the bag unzipped but continued on.

"Here. She's... here."

He started in surprise at Nora's slow speech. He hadn't even noticed she must've crawled back in the van after the firefight broke out. Something in the back of his brain told him that that amount of preoccupation was dangerous. Nora's haggard appearance was emphasized by her labored breathing. With her last act of bravery and strength she had in her arsenal, she placed her hand against the canvas beside her and patted. She then passed out.

"Thank you," Jason breathed. The bag was already unzipped a quarter of the way and he cursed himself for not checking that one first. Slowly, with trembling fingers, he unzipped the bag much more tenderly than he had any of the others. A sharp bark of emotion broke from him as he saw his sister's golden hair escaped the bag. As soon as he saw her bleary caramel eyes, he melted to his knees on the tailgate of the van. His hands gripped her soft body inside the canvas.

Ellie.

He cried out, and, afraid he would startle her, choked back a sob before frantically tucking his sister into his embrace. She had barely any strength to return, and her weight settled into his embrace. He knew it was his imagination, it had to be with what she'd been through, but as he held her, her innate morning flower scent filled his memories. She had brightened his life since the day she was born, and a fragment of sensory recall was all he needed to alleviate a fraction of the pain that cracked his heart.

"I'm... okay." The whisper against his neck made him squeeze her harder. He only relented when he realized Ellie's heavy breaths could be hindered even more from his hold. By sheer force of will, he gently laid her against Nora as she slept.

"I-I gotta go, El—"

"No, Jason... please. Don't leave. What they-they did to Sash—"

Saliva caught in his throat. "I know. I'm so, so sorry. El. I'm gonna get you outta here."

"Nora?" she breathed, her eyes flitting toward the woman whose hand she was holding.

"Yeah, you, Nora, the rest of y'all. We're gonna get you outta here." The sharp *tink* of a bullet unsuccessfully trying to make its way inside, honed his focus on his sister's safety. He'd eliminate all other threats to her, then get her the hell out.

"Trust me, El." The words hurt to demand, but he knew that this time, he would deliver.

She nodded and closed her eyes. The utter faith in the act of rest clutched at his heart.

He unfolded out of the van and closed both of the doors to protect the treasure inside. He immediately bent to the passed-out Russian and riffled through his pockets for keys, without luck. He would've ripped the wires out of the van, but he wasn't sure if they'd need the vehicle to leave in it.

He assessed around him. Dev was bent on a knee behind the van, quickly sliding out a magazine before reloading. Hawk was incapacitating one of the men held up at the town car. He saw hide nor tail of the tall man or the fucking Asshat. Apparently, there'd been more than six men to watch. From the sheer amount of gunshots he heard, that had to be the case. And he wasn't one-hundred-percent sure they'd incapacitated every target.

He reached for his hip, but cursed when he found his holster empty. His eyes scoured every lit area of the ground. His Glock was on the concrete twenty feet from him, lying beside the short, stocky man he'd had to choke out. Rookie fucking mistake. He hustled across the dark edges of shadows to get to his gun.

When he finally reached it, he inched forward to grab the metal handle, tucking it close to his chest, ready to discharge when necessary. He kept low and inched his way backward to the van, eye ready for immediate confrontation from his left and right.

Once he got in front of the van, he glanced around again.

"Dev, where you at?"

"Checking the perimeter. I thought I saw a guy round the corner."

Jason whipped his head from his nine and three o'clock, but only saw stagnant shadows in the orange light.

"Okay, looks clear, here. I'm gonna check on the girls again."

Still facing out, his non-shooting hand reached for the van door when he heard the vehicle start and rev behind him.

"What the fuck?"

He held his gun at the ready and ducked his head low around the van.

"What the fuck?" he asked again, completely baffled at what he was seeing.

Two figures were pushing and shoving inside the van door. It was dark in the orange glow of the lights high above, but he could've sworn one of them was Andy. He trained his weapon on both of them until he could figure out what the hell was going on.

"You're... not... going... anywhere!" Andy tore the man from the driver's seat to the ground. The man immediately leaned his hips up and drew his gun out from underneath him. But Jason was quicker. Before he could aim his gun at Andy, Jason fired. Once in the man's center of mass and he was out.

"Thank you," Andy wheezed and leaned against the van. "Woo... outta shape..."

Jason focused his gun on him and Andy shot his hands up to the sky despite his obvious exhaustion.

"Whoa, wh-what're you doing?"

"What the fuck is going on here, Andy? What're you a part of? What just happened?" The questions rushed out of him and he waited impatiently as Andy gulped for breath and leaned over, arms still in the universal stance of innocence. Jason grabbed him by the collar with his shooting hand, barrel up against his neck, and he reached inside the van, dragging Andy with him. Once he turned off the van and pocketed the keys, he let the guy loose but kept his gun on his face.

"Answer me! What the fuck just happened?"

"I... couldn't... let... him... take them."

His hoarse, tired whisper, rang out into the night. Jason's brow furrowed and he lowered his gun. He opened his mouth to demand more answers, unsure if he could trust him—

"Watch out!"

Cheek met pavement and two more gunshots in quick succession, followed by a sharp cry, reverberated off the cement ground and metal container walls of the port.

"Got him!" Hawk whooped out, albeit still quietly. "Dev, check the town car."

He heard tires squealing from far off, and Jason felt the vibration against his cheek. Another shot, but the hum of an engine persisted.

"Damnit. They got away," Dev growled.

"What the fuck?" Jason groaned for the umpteenth time, not listening, but instead pushing up from the ground. He sat back and leaned against the van, rubbing his jaw.

"Clear."

"Are you fucking sure?" Dev growled back at Hawk over the radio.

"Affirmative. That douchebag and his driver got away. I think that huge guy got dragged into the town car with them. But I got that last one aiming at Jaybird. Thanks to that—oh, fuck..." Hawk drifted off.

"What?" Since the coast was clear, Jason looked around for whatever the hell knocked him on his ass. His eyes widened to the point of pain when he saw the man lying on the cement. The man who saved his life.

A high-pitched wailing tore through the radio feed before he swore.

"Oh... fuck."

CHAPTER THIRTY-TWO

Body camera footage was nothing new for Jules. She'd watched hundreds, if not thousands. On them, she'd seen victims. Defendants. Some suffered pain. Some caused destruction.

But she'd never seen someone she'd cared for.

Nothing prepared her for that.

Nothing prepared her for seeing Andy.

With sick accuracy, she saw the events unfold on the big screen television. There were scenes of the Inland Port as captured by a drone Snake had somehow dispatched in time to monitor the situation, and video from each body camera worn by Hawk, Dev, and Jason.

Dev's showed him still assessing the perimeter, probably for any stragglers. Even though Hawk said the area was clear, Dev wasn't taking any chances.

Hawk's projected a wider shot of the location as he jogged to the van. Seconds before, it'd shown a man aiming his gun at Jason's back. Her heart stopped the same time he fired. Hawk shot simultaneously and now that shooter was sprawled on the ground.

Jason's bodycam was jostled as he fell to the pavement, so the images were slightly off-kilter. When he turned, Jules was able to see where the shooter's bullet made its deadly impact. But it wasn't Jason who'd been shot.

It was Andy.

Jason must've been on his knees because the view was oddly close to the pavement, where Andy was lying prostrate and unresponsive.

"Oh... fuck," Jason repeated. "Fuckfuckfuck. Snake, cut Jules's feed."

"Wesley James, if you even *think* about cutting my feed I will—"

"I won't, Jules."

She nodded to no one. But kept her stare on the portion of the screen where Jason held Andy's head in his hands. He slapped his cheeks.

"Jason, stop!"

"Ass—Andy, wake the fuck up, man. Wake up!" Jason shook the already pallid face of the man who had once been Jules's lover. Her friend. She shook her head violently and shoved her fist in her mouth. She had no right to call him that. Not after she'd refused to even talk to him during a time when he'd apparently needed her most.

She'd watched everything from the second they'd jumped out of the helicopter. She'd sat in silence as they made their way over the nearby field, through the Inland Port, and waited for their perfect time to strike.

She'd been livid when she first heard Andy's voice. Confused, yes. But she bypassed that real quick and went straight to lava hot mad. Emotion scorched through her veins as she heard him talk to the man running a sex trade right in their hometown. Every word dripped with confirmation that she'd made the right choice in ignoring him, not caring about him, essentially cutting him from her life.

Then all hell broke loose and she'd been caught up in the fight for Ellie and Nora as if she was actually there. Her emotions jerked her heart around in her chest in moments of white-knuckling anxiety for the men, followed by breathtaking gratitude over finding that both Ellie and Nora were alive.

She'd continued to watch the dizzying perspectives of each man. Once the gunshots slowed, she tried to watch Jason's, but he'd been too close to whoever was in front of him, so she'd gone back to Hawk's. It was there she saw one last man as he took aim at Jason's back. Two shots fired in quick succession. Jason's bodycam made the world go off-kilter, as if he'd fallen. And he had. Because Andy pushed him.

Ice had filled her veins. She'd stood helplessly frozen for several seconds, wondering if Jason had been shot. And wondering if Andy had helped kill him. The pain in her heart eased when Jason groaned and got up. But when he turned toward Andy, understanding struck and she'd shattered all over again.

"Andy, for fuck's sake, wake up, man!" Jason choked on the last couple of syllables.

The man she'd once cared for, the man who still loved her madly, was dying in front of her. And she could do nothing about it.

Andy coughed in Jason's arms and a dark substance sputtered out. His teeth appeared as dark, bloody outlines of what had been the most charismatic smile in their law school class.

"Tell Juliet..." More coughing punctuated his words. "Tell Juliet, I loved her."

Jason laughed softly, with what sounded like a thread of hope that Jules clung to. "Tell her yourself, Asshat."

Andy laughed once, only to groan when more dark liquid appeared in droplets on his cheeks.

"I thought you'd be an asshole. Glad to know I was right."

"Get Phoenix here, Snake," Jason mumbled under his breath.

"On it, Jaybird."

"We're gonna get you outta here, man."

"I don't think... that will work." Andy coughed. "I did... love her, you know."

"Nonononononono..." Jules turned away from the television and balled her fists up against her chest, trying to catch her breath against the heavy emotion filling her up inside. She ached for numbness, wanting nothing to do with the burning agony of grief. She'd felt it too much already in her life, what with the death of her mother at sixteen, then losing Jason and their baby in quick succession. So, she shut her eyes and refused to listen.

She tried to convince herself to be indifferent to him again. That would be easier, so much easier.

Andy cheated on her—as much as a man could if he wasn't actually in a relationship, her technical brain reminded her. He'd then harassed her into feeling sorry for him. Now, from what she could see, he'd become a criminal scumbag who sold women.

But thin fissures in her walls of conviction let memories and truth come through, despite her best efforts to ignore them.

She tried to ignore that Andy's harassment was a cry for help.

She tried to ignore her new suspicion that Andy was the man behind the letters.

She tried to ignore the flashbacks of the man she once knew. The friend and solace during difficult times at school. The lover who'd only ever tried to love *her*, albeit in a fucked-up way sometimes. The man who asked for forgiveness, and she'd been too stubborn and proud to grant him even that.

But to ignore the truth was to lie. And she wouldn't lie, not even to herself.

She was immediately infuriated at the cowardice behind her train of thought and forced her eyes open to face the screen. She acknowledged that the fullness in her chest wasn't just grief, but *guilt*, and she fell to her knees at the weight of it.

"Where's that damn Bird, Snake?"

"Fuck, I'm still waiting for Phoenix to get back to me. I'll send the drone to him."

"What? He's just not fucking answering? Christ." He looked down at Andy, as if just remembering he was there. "We're trying to get you outta here ASAP..."

"S'okay. I don't think... it'll be n-necessary." His dark laugh pierced straight past Jules's denial and sent her headlong into anger. It was an emotion she felt comfortable with, and she harnessed it as she spoke.

"I swear to God, Andrew Wilton Ascot, if you die on me, I'm gonna kill you myself. You hear me?"

Andy coughed, and blood spilled out, cracking what little composure Jules had left, plummeting her emotions into yet another direction.

"Help him! For the love of God, help him!" Silence met her over the radio. She stood up and screamed at the TV as if the men on the other side were in the room with her. "Are you just going to sit there while he's d-dy—hurting? What about Phoenix? Where is he?"

Movement rustled against Dev's camera and he left from where he'd apparently been consoling Ellie, to help with Andy. He knelt down over Andy and Jason's camera picked up his grim look. Dev nimbly ran his fingers over Andy's chest. All the while, Andy's breathing grew more labored and his coughs produced more blood. After a lifetime, Dev leaned back and shook his head slightly.

"Jules... it's..." Jason trailed off as he lifted his hand from the darkened fabric above Andy's heart, where Jason had been trying to stop the bleeding.

Snake finished for him. "It's too late, Jules."

"Fuck you!" she screeched in the empty cabin. "It's not too late! It can't be! You just need to get him to the hospital! Where the fuck is Phoenix?"

"Jules, even if he was in the hospital right now, it'd be too late," Dev's detached delivery was too much for her to bear.

"Oh, what the fuck do you know?"

"He's a trained trauma medic, baby. He *knows*."

"Nonononono. *NO!* There's got to be a way around it. Apply pressure! Do that trach thing they do on TV—"

"Jules..."

"Just do it! Do something!"

"I'm sorry," Dev stated flatly.

"No! Oh God. Ohgodohgod. Tell him... tell him I'm sorry," she choked through the mic. "Tell him that I thought he was a good man. That... that he was so much better than his father. So much better than what he was trying to be—"

"Jules!" Jason's voice was sharp, bringing her out of her panic to realize he'd been trying to get her attention. Her breath was on fire in her lungs and she held her hands over her heart.

"Baby, you need to talk to him. He doesn't want to hear us right now. He wants to hear you."

She shook her head back and forth, straining her neck with the fierce movement, as Dev took off his earpiece and unwound the cable connecting it to his communications equipment. He plugged it into Andy's ear. With the mic connected to the piece now closer to Andy, Jules heard his ragged breathing more prominently and she clutched at her chest.

"Juliet..."

"Andy..." she choked out before falling to her knees and crawling over to the TV where Andy's face filled that part of the screen. She could see Andy close his eyes tightly, causing a tear to slide down his pale cheek. She raised her hand up to touch the glass with her fingertips, as if to wipe the dampness away.

"Andy... please. You have to fight. This can't be it for you. You have—"

"Juliet... please. Listen to me... for once." He tried to laugh but only managed a huff and a groan. "I've been trying to tell you this, for a while now..."

Jules stroked Andy's face on the screen and barked out a laugh loud enough for the both of them.

"I'm so sorry, Andy—"

"I-I was so wrong—"

"No, Andy. None of it matters—"

"I was so caught up in impressing my father... the firm... you. I lost sight of everything. I blamed you, but I wanted you to fix it. I said and did such... terrible things to you." His voice ended in barely a whisper, and he took a steadying breath before he continued. "I know you never loved me. You were always cl-clear. But I couldn't st-stand the thought. So, I pretended. It was easier. Until it wasn't." Another breath rattled. "All this... none of it was supposed to be this way. I tried to stop it. I didn't know how. I was too far in. So many excuses. Thinking back... I was a fool. Their fool. They even tried to—tried to kill you"—a painful cough ravaged his broken body, suddenly frail— "But I swear Juliet those letters—"

"You left the letters?" Though she'd suspected it, Jules still gasped at the confirmation. He gave a quick nod. Even with that small of a gesture, he winced in pain.

"Couldn't stop them. Too weak. But you... you were never weak." He rested and Jules took the moment to respond.

"You're no one's fool, Andy. Thank you, oh God, thank you so much for leading us to Ellie, to Nora. You are a good man. So, so much better than what your father was trying to force you to be. I don't know everything, but I know without you, we wouldn't have found them in time. Without you... Jason would be..." Her ability to breathe suffered, but she carried on. "You've been brave. So, so brave. And I'm sorry I couldn't love you the way you wanted me to, Andy—"

"I know... you love him." He closed his eyes and sighed before looking dimmed eyes up at Jason. A tear burned down Jules's cheek as she nodded yes, even though he couldn't see her.

"It's okay. Just know... I'm sorry."

"You did good in the end, man. Jules is right. We wouldn't have found them without your letters. You helped us save them. And you saved me. Why the *fuck* would you jump in front of a bullet for me? I don't deserve that."

Andy's chuckle was quick, "I didn't do it for you. I did it for *her*." His brow furrowed with seriousness. "Take care of her."

Jules watched Jason shaking his head on one of the screens.

"You and I both know that woman doesn't need *anyone* to

take care of her, and I'd probably fuck it up." They both smiled thinly.

"But I'll love her. I can do that pretty damn well."

With what looked like the last of his strength, Andy held up his hand for Jason. "Do it better than last time. Or else she'll end up with a guy like me…" Jason huffed and took the offered hand before shaking for the both of them.

"Deal."

"Andy, please. We just need to get you to a hospital—"

Jules could tell even on the video that Andy's glazed eyes were trying to focus hard on Jason's and seemed to use the last of the energy he had left. He tried to talk, but it only came out as a whisper. Jason bent lower to hear, causing his camera to shove into Andy's torso before lifting back up.

"What? Are you sure?" She heard Jason's deep voice question.

Andy's head nodded slightly. His eyes losing focus completely.

He wheezed out another breath and his grip shook in Jason's hand. "I couldn't… but you have to. Save them… save them all."

And with that, Andrew Wilton Ascot *the Fourth*, was gone.

CHAPTER THIRTY-THREE

"I still can't believe that bastard was the key to everything."

Jason nodded at Hawk on the screen and threaded both hands through his damp hair before glancing at Jules. It'd only been an hour since he got back from rescuing Ellie and Nora and his girl still hadn't talked to him. The only tell in her hardened exterior were her watery eyes. Something the men on the screen wouldn't be able to see.

He rolled his shoulders, trying to loosen the tension he held there, even after saving the women. He and Jules had been under nonstop stress for days, and although he should've been relieved their mission was successful, ending it on nearly no sleep, a gunfight, and covering up a crime scene made him feel exhausted down to his bones.

Figuring out what to do with dead bodies after a mission was a new issue for the Crew. They'd had processing teams in MF7 who did all the dirty work of cleaning up their messes and ensuring the women were rehabilitated. Without that luxury, Jason and Hawk were out of their element and left to figure out what to do, while Dev tended to the women as they woke up.

After a long debate, they'd all come to the difficult conclusion that the police shouldn't be called until after they'd left.

Snake had wondered aloud about who they could trust since they didn't know how big or connected the operation was. All they knew was that the biggest law firm in the southeast was somehow involved. In their MF7 experience, human trafficking supported by the upper echelons of society was covered back up as soon as they were revealed, with only a scapegoat to blame. And Hawk reminded Jason about Investigator Burgess's not so subtle grudge against him.

Everyone agreed when Hawk suggested BlackStone Securities needed to take the traffickers on as a case. Even though there was no client, it was personal for them and without knowing who to trust, they could only depend on themselves to learn the traffickers' true identities, the operation as a whole, and expose whoever was pulling the strings. There was also the added worry that releasing the information on what happened at the port would ruin their chances in finding out who the real masters were behind the curtain.

So that left Jason and Hawk to make sure there was no leftover evidence implicating them in the scene. Even though they hated it, they left everything as it was, including the bodies, and meticulously combed over every detail to make sure any connection with Dev, Hawk, or Jason was eliminated. They hoped they could stage the area into something so that the cops could come up with their own version of what happened.

In the meantime, Dev stayed with El and the other women in the back of the van, helping some of them wake up and calming them down when they became lucid enough to freak-out about being in a bag in the back of a dark van. He didn't know how the giant could be any kind of comforting, but his bedside manner must've contained magic. Ellie seemed to calm with him instantly. Maybe it was all of his strawberry blond hair. It was so pretty it practically neutered his intimidation factor.

Even though Jason had already called Phoenix to come pick up Andy, when Phoenix arrived late, no doubt realizing the shit he'd just pulled, the asshole had silently helped them process the scene. In hushed tones, while Jason gave Phoenix a glare every time he looked over, Hawk explained that, for some inexplicable crazy-ass reason, the man sometimes refused to wear his earpiece now, even on a mission. What good was a helicopter pilot if he never knew where or when to pick up its riders? Hawk had only shrugged and said, "It's complicated, man. Just trust me on this one." Jason would've argued more, but at one point he saw Hawk jerk Phoenix away from the van, and based on the harsh whispers, Jason assumed Hawk was lighting into him like the drill sergeants they'd suffered through back in the Army. It was during that time that he, Dev, and Snake figured out how to tip off the cops to let them come up with their own conclusions as to what happened.

Jules insisted on cluing the ADA in from the jump, arguing that if they needed government backing at any point, he was their best ally to get it. She was right, but Snake suggested calling 911 from a burner they found in one of the dead guy's pockets, to keep them from being implicated directly. If they called Marco first, that put him in a bind because he'd have to disclose how he got the information before dispatch did. Snake assured Jules that they could fill in Aguilar later in the day, after confirming that law enforcement were looking a different way. Then, with Phoenix flying overhead to look for trouble, Hawk drove them all back to BlackStone, Jason in the passenger seat, and Dev in the back of the van using medical supplies from the Bird to help the women.

After getting back to BlackStone, Jason had called Aunt Rachel and let Ellie talk to her. It was the middle of the night, but Aunt Rach had answered on the first ring, blubbering with relief and happiness that their Ellie was safe and sound. Ellie gave her a very tame version of what happened, basically lying through her teeth. It sucked, but Aunt Rachel was having a difficult time lately keeping things straight anyway. Telling her the whole truth would only trigger her paranoia and upset her, and they'd potentially have to go through the tale over and over again.

Once Jason had hung up the phone, Ellie went back with the rest of the women. Dev called one of his hospital contacts and the angel of a nurse came over, no questions asked, to aid the victims and make sure no one needed hospitalization. But thankfully, with what BlackStone Securities had in its medical stash and the supplies the nurse was able to bring, they had everything the victims needed for their physical recovery. Other than grogginess, they were amazingly healthy, all things considered. On the outside, anyway. There was no telling what the women would deal with psychologically.

It was fortunate that the women didn't need hospitalization because without a solid explanation of how they came to be under BlackStone's care, the questions that would stem from their treatment and exposure in the hospital could blow up the future of their investigation.

Of the seven women they saved, Ellie had been the only one declared missing, even though some of the others had been kidnapped for days or even weeks. True to form, the traffickers had chosen women they deemed wouldn't be missed, and unfortunately, for the six other women, they'd been right. The women were safe and sound now, asleep in makeshift beds in a spare bedroom in the BlackStone facility.

"Ellie's memory isn't the best, but according to her, it sounded like Ascot got blackmailed into the scheme. They were threatening to pin it all on him." Dev's voice was even more gruff than usual, surprising Jason back to the present. He knew the importance of an after-action report, but right then, knowing his sister was safe back at BlackStone—with men he trusted—he only wanted to comfort and help Jules.

Jason had been beyond pissed when Ellie refused to leave BlackStone with him. His plan had been for them to go to the cabin with Jules, and meet up with Aunt Rachel when the sun came up. But Ellie had insisted she needed to stay and help the women find their way home. Jason had begged and pleaded with her to go with him back to the cabin, but somewhere in this nightmare, his baby sister developed an admirable—if not infuriating—stubbornness.

"You don't understand, Jason. I have to be here with the other women. They're like me. We went through that... that... we went through it together. I need to stay for them... for myself. And I need to do it for Sasha."

When tears welled up in her eyes, he'd grabbed her into a rough brotherly hug. Deep down, he knew she was finally in good hands. Dev had barely let her out of his sight he'd been so worried for her health. If she felt safe there, he wasn't about to take her choice from her. So, he'd let her go. There was another woman who'd needed him, and he didn't want to leave her alone in her grief.

Right before he left, the Crew questioned Nora about her experience. They didn't want to ask Ellie or the other women just yet. Not until they'd had a restful sleep, time to heal, and they were sure the victims wouldn't be triggered all over again from their interviews. But Nora didn't want to wait. She gave her account of what happened and then promptly demanded to see Draco.

With an ache in his chest, he allowed himself to look to the corner of the screen where Draco should've been working his toothpick again. The seat was empty now. He was still in the hospital, fighting for his life. That's where Nora insisted on Jason taking her after everything had settled.

They'd gotten to the hospital and since the threat was neutralized for the time being, Jason relieved Henry from his post as Draco's guard. The rookie deputy agreed to stand guard, claiming he owed Jules a favor, and damn was Jason glad they'd been able to count on him to keep their man safe.

Seeing his friend in a coma and hooked up to a ventilator, gutted him. The doctors explained Draco had undergone surgery and nearly died on the table. The gunshot to his side was basically a flesh wound, but the gunshot to his chest nearly killed him. An inch to the left. That's all that separated life from death. Although being laid out, unconscious in a hospital bed certainly felt like he was still in limbo. Now they just had to wait and see. He might wake up, he might not. It could be tomorrow, or not at all. Being powerless fucking sucked, but whether he lived or died was only up to Draco now.

After talking to doctors and nurses, expertly dodging questions as to why he was in all black and covered in dark substances that suspiciously looked like damp blood, Jason itched to get back to Jules, but Nora refused to leave. He would've just picked her up and taken her with him, but Draco almost died trying to save her and Jason understood her need to keep vigil.

Hawk tapped his lips as he thought aloud. "Andy also sent the letters. He refused to dose Nora, instead leaving her with the syringe. Because of Andy, Nora was able to incapacitate that big guy with the tranquilizer. He also tried to warn us of how many people were at the port. Hell, Nora says she thinks he sent that smart text from her watch, so we would investigate."

"He most likely used her watch to call 911, too, since the call wasn't a call, but a 'smart alert,'" Snake pointed out.

"Damn, man. I hate to say it, but without him, we'd have all been screwed. Who knows what would've happened to those women?" Phoenix said with a shake of his head. The heavy truth of his statement left silence in its wake.

Hawk sighed and scrubbed his face with his hands before continuing the meeting.

"Right, it looks like Ascot was our double agent, but he might not've been as high up in the organization as we'd hoped. With what he said to Jules, and the meetup changing times on him, it sounds like he only knew the bare minimum, if that. Jaybird, what did he whisper to you in the end?" Hawk asked and Jason cringed, trying not to look at Jules as Hawk referenced Ascot's final words.

When he'd finally gotten back to the cabin, he'd found her on the phone talking to God knows who at that hour. He hadn't questioned it, understanding she needed the space after everything she'd just witnessed. He'd seen her that way before, in times when she felt too full of emotion, and knew instinctively that she needed to push away any vulnerability to desperately regain control.

Instead of interfering with her process, he immediately went to the shower and scrubbed himself clean of the mission. He made sure no drop of Andy's blood remained and threw his wet clothes in the trash before she could see them. Once he dried off, he'd found her on his laptop, sitting awkwardly on the couch, and still talking on her cell. Snake had assured them that he'd remotely encrypted her phone and found no stalkerware on it. Thank God it was only Andy who stalked her, and no one more sinister.

Jason had gently pulled her from the couch, grabbed the laptop, and helped her set up on the bed, all the while she was still making plans and demands. She was already dressed in one of his long-sleeve tees, so he tucked the covers up over her and under the laptop and got in on his side of the bed. He'd wrapped himself around her, mindful of her need to keep working, and positioned them so that she still could.

He hoped his touch would comfort her, like hers did for him, but he wasn't even sure if she noticed him. She was a woman on a mission of her own, and although it stung that she hadn't even so much as acknowledged him, he understood her pain. Hell, after their last mission in Yemen, and watching Eagle die, he'd shut himself off from the world for months. The least he could do was give her a few uninterrupted hours.

He resolved to give her time and fell asleep, the adrenaline rush and subsequent crash of the mission giving him little choice in the matter. He'd known he would only get half an hour of sleep at best, but it was better than nothing. And holding her, knowing she was safe in his arms, relaxed him more than sleep ever would. When he'd woken up, she was gone. He'd padded through the cabin to find her on the couch, working again, if she'd ever stopped.

They'd tiptoed around each other up until Hawk called, and he couldn't figure out how to break her stony facade. Cracking under pressure and emotion was rare for Jules, but it broke his heart that she wouldn't allow herself to break. Not even at the death of a friend. Not even in front of him. He felt his lips tighten in a line.

We'll have to work on that.

In his pause, he noticed Jules sit up straighter and move her knees underneath her on the couch. "Jason, what'd he say?" He caught a glimmer of emotion in those sea blue-green eyes.

"He said, 'It's not just the ones in the van. It's all of them. They're everywhere, especially where you'd never look.' Then he'd said, 'Men at the top. Strickland has a brother.'"

"Sounds like the ramblings of a crazy man to me." Phoenix laughed.

"He wasn't crazy," Jules snapped. "He was *dying*, but he wasn't crazy. Strickland... that's a partner at Andy's firm. He must be involved."

"Right..." Hawk tapped his finger to his lips. "But who is his brother? Sounds like he's the one we need to figure out."

"Also sounds like the women in the van aren't the only victims." Snake's comment rested in the air.

"Well, we have a starting point. You know that guy Nora tranq'd?" Snake asked.

"That Russian fucker I shot? Vlad, I think. Or Nora thinks. He was at the club with Andy and she overheard his name," Jason replied.

"Right!" Snake snapped his fingers. "*He* was important enough to steal away. Either he knew enough to make them afraid he'd talk, or he's vital to the operation. I'm thinking the second one because they could've just shot him dead. But I saw two men on your body cams drag him into that town car."

"Okay, so we have to find this Vlad. Snake, have you checked Original Sin's surveillance system yet?" Jules's voice was hard but Jason felt encouraged at the resolve behind it.

At Jules's question, Phoenix had to catch himself before his chair fell back from its tipped position on its back two legs. "Hold up. They have *cameras* in strip clubs? How did I not know this?"

Jules rolled her eyes. "They do in Original Sin. Hasn't always been that way, but for a while there, some assholes were a problem for Cyn. Jay actually suggested it."

"We were gonna try to see what was happening at Original Sin while you guys were there checking on Drake, but I'm only able to see past footage, not real time," Snake explained. "I'll get on that, Jules. Good idea."

Jules nodded at Snake's affirmation, but only sat back down, resuming her expressionless stare. She reminded Jason of a robot that needed some switch to flip to turn her emotions on and for her speech to kick in.

"Speaking of good ideas," Hawk segued. "Have you been in touch with the women, Jules? Did you get them set up with the organization we've used in the past?"

Jason's head whipped back to her. *So that's what she's been doing.*

"Yes. I talked to them and I looked into where you suggested… but I gotta tell ya, I've never heard of the 'Rahab Foundation.' Since most of them aren't even from here, I've set them up with a reputable shelter service I've used before until we can get the women back to their homes. I refer all my clients in abusive relationships to them. It's a nonprofit specifically for battered women and trafficking victims and it's meticulous about protecting the women's identities. I've never had any issues. The organization should be able to help some of them reenter society, get jobs, get therapy… God, do we all need fucking therapy…"

"Wait, you said you've never heard of the Rahab Foundation?" Hawk asked, his brow furrowed.

"Nope." She shook her head as she answered. "And honestly? It's kind of a fucked-up name if you think about it."

"Why's that?"

She turned her gaze slightly to answer Snake. "Rahab? Like in the bible? I couldn't find anything about the foundation, but I found out enough about her. Rahab's name literally means 'prostitute woman'. Like that's all she was known for. Sure, she was favored in the eyes of God as the story went on, but it's a hell of a name for an organization that saves women and a constant reminder for those who were forced into prostitution."

The men, including Jason, shifted uncomfortably. "Bad name aside, that's impossible," Hawk argued. "MF7 used the Rahab Foundation for years. We saved the women and they went to the foundation where they were helped into a better life for themselves."

"I don't know what to tell you. I've been doing this a while too, and I've never heard of them."

"These places run under the radar though, right?" Snake asked.

"Yes, but—"

"So, it could be as simple as that. Hell, that makes the most sense. With it being backed by the government, it has the capability to act more covertly, like the witness protection program," Snake continued.

Before Jules could respond, Hawk—ever the leader—decided to move on.

"And the prosecutor?"

She cleared her throat. "I notified Marco early once you gave the clear. He's going to subtly suggest looking into the disappearance of these women and try to find a common thread between all of them. It's a long shot, but he said he'd get people he trusts on it. I also *strongly* suggested he consider outside reinforcement. Maybe even the FBI. I don't trust Investigator Burgess. He used to be a good cop. But now?" She shook her head.

Hawk nodded. "Alright men. Sounds like we have a starting

point. Or at least a direction to find a starting point. We'll reconvene at oh-eight-hundred tomorrow, depending on if there are any updates. Jaybird." Hawk looked directly at him through the screen and Jason stood at attention. Old habits die hard.

"You still on for that talk tomorrow?"

Jason glanced toward Jules, but there was no recognition there. She'd shut down again.

"Affirmative."

Hawk nodded once and they said their goodbyes. Jason forced himself not to immediately run to Jules's side. On the screen, Dev high-tailed it out of BlackStone's briefing room. Probably to go check on the women again. Hawk and Phoenix took their time before Snake logged them all off. Then it was just him and Jules.

CHAPTER THIRTY-FOUR

They sat in uncomfortable silence after that. Well, uncomfortable for him. Jason wasn't sure if Jules was even registering anything and seemed like either shock or numbness had taken back over. She stared at a black screen, and he tried not to stare at her. Their reflections in the glass were distorted, with one on each side of the screen. As far apart as they could be while still being on the same plane. He blew out a long, heavy breath and combed his fingers through his hair.

He didn't know how to fix this. Fix *her*. She'd never needed fixing before. She'd been an angry little thing when he'd first met her, but she'd never needed his help. Not really. She needed it now and he didn't even know where to start. She was the one who had all the answers, overcame adversity, could see merit in every argument, and could always sneak out a technicality in her favor.

But Ascot's death wasn't a simple technicality. It was the type of adversity where no answers were adequate, and no argument for, or against, death ever seems wholly valid. Death is unexpected, no matter the circumstances.

And why should she expect the death of a friend? She wasn't like Jason. She was a civilian, who never chose the path that could someday lead to seeing friends die beside her. *For* her. Hell, he'd signed up for it and Jason still couldn't get Eagle's dimming brown eyes out of his nightmares. No, this wasn't something she could have foreseen, nor could she have prepared for it. No one ever can.

He wondered if she felt betrayed. She had to have trusted Ascot on some level, to allow him into her life. He imagined she trusted Ascot to at least not be part of a human trafficking enterprise. Jason couldn't recall the last time someone he trusted blindsided him like that. But Jules had had that happen to her multiple times now.

He welcomed the pain squeezing his chest. He'd deserved that guilt once, and allowed himself to be numb for way too damn long. He would be here for her now. He would be what she needed.

He sucked in a breath and turned to the couch. She continued to stare, unseeing into the black void. Her small body and long, legs were curled up in the corner, seemingly seeking a semblance of warmth in the cool leather. Her teeth absentmindedly ran over her fingers. Not quite giving in to the temptation to bite... but really damn close.

"Jules..."

No answer.

"Juliet..."

Silence.

"Baby girl." He made two long strides to her and knelt down, holding on to her knees. "Look at me, baby," he asked, gently shaking her legs. "Look at me. Can you do that?"

Her head slowly moved toward him, her eyes following behind mechanically. He waited until they were both on him before he spoke. With how spacy she was acting, he hadn't expected to see pain there, and it took everything in him not to look away. She faced everything head-on. So, he would too. No matter how much it hurt, from now on they would tackle life together.

"Fuck, what you saw Jules... was awful. Losing a friend isn't easy." The simplicity of his words felt stupid as soon as they fell out. She wasn't looking at him and he was desperately trying to get through to her. Her pain made his heart ache. He searched his experiences in his mind for any words that had ever comforted him.

"Listen, Jules. I don't know exactly what you're feeling right now, but I *know* how hard it is to lose a friend. Seeing it happen in front of your eyes? It's... devastating. No one should have to see that—"

"I've seen worse," she replied in a monotone as she stared back at the TV screen, her words stilted and emotionless. Robotic. "On body cams, I mean. I've seen bad stuff in real life, too... my mom..."

He shook his head, knowing the disconnect she was trying to mend. "It's different every time. Just because you've suffered before, doesn't mean you have to put on a brave face the next time around. It doesn't mean you're immune to hurting the next time you're in pain. You're allowed to feel."

She nodded slowly, her fingers tracing her bottom lip. Still on his knees, he gently took her hand and held it in his own, rubbing his thumb over her knuckles.

"It's okay to be upset. I know he meant something to you..."

She nodded again. Or maybe she'd never stopped. Her tired eyes never moved from their fixed point on the black screen, so it was hard to say. Her energy seemed endless while she worked. Now, it was as if the after-action report drained her of everything she'd had pent up since before the mission. He'd insist she go to bed if he thought it'd help. But he knew it wouldn't. Sleep only helps the injured, not the dying. And Jules was dying inside.

"It wasn't just about him, ya know." Her head turned quickly, catching him by surprise, but he held her gaze.

"I mean." She sighed and pulled her hands out of his grasp to lean back and away from him. "I mean, it was about him. I can't wrap my brain around the fact that someone else I cared for is gone... first, my mom. And hell, I'm practically dead to Rose at this point—"

"Jules, don't say—"

"Then it was you. Then my bab-*her*. And now Andy." She huffed, "They don't prep you for this in law school. It's all stupid case law and how to read the fine print of what some old white guy didn't have the balls to say outright..." She sighed and looked back at him, the pain had faded infinitesimally, but he couldn't identify the emotion that replaced it.

"They never talk about losing. Not arguments, cases... people. Never talked about the real shit that happens day to day. My life wasn't great growing up, but somewhere along the way, I think I developed this naïve thought that if I got a good education and became a great attorney, my life would only ever be carefree and simple after that. I'd only see the good I could do, and I guess I hoped I'd never have to go through the bad again." She laughed harshly at herself. "Like being a hotshot lawyer made me invincible. And I never thought about what could go wrong. When I told Rose she was going to have to go to prison if she pled guilty, hell, I cried more than she did. I definitely never thought about losing Andy."

She sighed heavily and the wetness in her gaze threatened to spill over. "I'll miss him. The good part of him deserves to be missed. This is bad... but I also think he absolved himself in the end. He died a fucking hero, in my mind. It might sound callous, but that makes it bearable. The decisions he'd been making for the past year weren't good ones and I think he was changing for the worse." Jason felt himself nodding but didn't dare interrupt. "He'd gone down a path I never intended to follow. I don't think anyone could've guessed where it would lead, but I think his desperation to please his father, no matter the cost... I think his sins caught up with him and his conscience. Maybe his choices started to plague that good part still in there. I wonder what he would've been like if he'd gone that direction, instead. It was that goodness in him that I think I did actually love."

Jason felt his breath stall in his lungs, until she continued.

"But it was a different kind of love. I cared for him, yes. But I wasn't *in* love with him." She snorted. "*God*, that sounds like such a trivial distinction when you say it out loud, but I really didn't. I cared for him and I didn't want to see him... leave the way he did. I wasn't prepared for it."

Jason rubbed his hands on the tops of her thighs in comfort.

"But what I was least prepared for? Was losing *you*."

Feeling warmth on his face, he looked up to find her sea blue-green eyes searching for his attention, then holding it.

"Jay... I was watching... and I saw one of those men point his gun at you... and *fire*. My heart stopped. And it was in that moment that I realized I didn't want to live without you. I can't and I won't. I thought, 'that bullet won't hit Jay.' Like I had some kinda power over that shit. But then it didn't. It should've... but it didn't. And it hit Andy instead."

"Jules, that's not your fault. You didn't make that happ—"

"I know that. But there's still some guilt inside for things that *are* my fault. I refused to forgive Andy. Even after I tried so hard for so long to forgive everyone else, you and Andy? I couldn't do it. You? It was damn near impossible for so many reasons. But Andy? We weren't even dating. Still, I lorded his mistakes over him. Did he deserve that? No. But I can't change that now. I meant everything I said while he was... lying there, and I don't regret any of it. He was a good man on a bad path. But he did the right thing in the end. That's all we can ask for.

"But I don't know what I would've done if you were the one lying on that pavement. I don't know if I would've survived it. And that scares the hell out of me."

"Jules, you would've been fine—"

"No, really. I mean, sure I'd be alive. But I wouldn't *live*. I know that because I haven't since you left. I've been a shell of myself ever since. I've done everything right. Got into law school. Made good grades. Passed the bar exam. Won my cases. I went through the motions. But I didn't feel a damn thing. And I don't want to keep being that person. I want to be me, the real me. But I don't want to be a me without you."

Jason felt his heart pound and wondered if she could sense it. He hadn't expected any of this, but it was everything he'd wanted to hear. He started to get up, but she beat him to it and stepped around him. He stood and reached for her, but touch wasn't what she needed at that moment.

"I told you I was coming back. Nothing could keep me from you again."

She nodded, sighed, and then turned away from him. The conversation, too much to face.

"I know you said that. But that's not always the case, ya know? I just..." A guttural shout escaped her as she turned to him, tears finally falling freely. "I hate this so much about myself right now, but I'm so glad it was Andy and not you."

Understanding washed over him. "Oh, Jules..." He approached her slowly, reaching for her and holding her close when he realized she would let him. She trembled against his chest and he swallowed hard. "It's okay, baby," he whispered into her hair. "There's nothing wrong with feeling the way you feel."

She shook her head against him, but he held her tighter.

"No... you listen to me and you listen good, okay? In our final mission, it was me, all me. I made that bad call. It was my finger on the trigger, not theirs. I didn't take the shot and it fucked everyone over. The rest of the Crew has their own story about what happened. Some of them even think it's their fault instead of mine... I know Hawk does. Hawk and Eagle got me outta that hellhole, that friendly fire from the locals that *I* recruited. My Crew helped me dodge bullets left and right. Hawk and I made it... Eagle didn't. And I was *thankful*. I was so fucking thankful it wasn't me that it took me months and months to get over that guilt, along with all the other guilt I already carried. Hell, I'm still not fully over it, and I may never be. For all that time, I shut down. Months I didn't reach out to the Crew. Months I kept Ellie at arm's length. Months I kept myself from *you*. All out of fucking guilt. I convinced myself that everyone was better off."

He held her face close and drank in the emotion in her watery gaze.

"That guilt will take everything you love and twist it into something hateful. More painful than the start. We have to stop this, Jules."

"But Jay, it's not the same—"

"No, baby, it is. All guilt is the same—ugly and useless—no matter where it comes from. We can't keep letting it win." Jason felt a little lightheaded as the words he'd just said reverberated in his mind. He hadn't realized how much he believed them until he used them to comfort someone else.

She nodded slowly. "Okay." Her eyes captured his and he let himself be pulled under. The sadness was still there, but the other emotions had been replaced with resolve. Brushing his thumbs over her cheeks, he couldn't help smiling at her determination.

"I love you, Jules."

Her bright eyes shimmered and her smile brightened, warming him. She coughed past thick emotion and placed her hands around his wrists, squeezing them.

"I love you too, Jason."

"Yeah?" The question lilted with hope.

She nodded and laughed softly. "Never stopped."

He wrapped his arms around her and squeezed, relishing her lithe body against his. Her hands held on, rubbing his back, and he tried not to groan. His muscles were still so tight from stress that her touch, that her simple touch made him want to melt into her. But then those nimble fingers of hers started to massage the muscles down his spine, and he couldn't keep from moaning into her soft honey hair. She lifted up on her tiptoes and kissed his neck slowly, moving up to his jaw and then finally, he bent to meet her plush lips with his.

"You love me?" he asked again, his voice deeper than normal.

He punctuated the question by caressing the seam of her lips with his tongue, begging her to open for him.

Her nod brushed her nose up against his and she pulled him closer, drawing out the heat between them. "Yeah, Jay. I love you."

He swirled his tongue into her mouth and he drank in her moans. He let go only to wrap his arms around the back of her thighs, bringing her up to his height. She returned his embrace and wrapped her long legs around his waist. His fingers dug into the bottom of her thighs and her hands kneaded into his trap muscles, liquefying the tension there until it pooled down to his shaft. She gathered the neck of his T-shirt and broke their kiss to pull it over his head and held the shirt in both hands like a scarf on the back of his neck to drag him in to continue their kiss.

He prodded the bedroom door open with his foot and he turned until the backs of his knees hit the bed. When he let go of her legs, Jules's soft body slid down his hard front, making his cock twitch in anticipation. She pushed against his pecs and he sat back onto the bed. His hands skimmed under her long-sleeve shirt to lift it off her body and found that she wasn't wearing a bra. He growled and dipped his head in to take a peak into his mouth as he divested her of her thong and shorts in one fell swoop.

She tugged on his hair and trailed her hands down his front to encourage him to lie down on the bed. Still letting her fingers travel, they curled around his gym shorts and boxers until his hard length burst from its confines. She bent over him as he vibrated with need and tasted the head. He groaned as her silky tongue licked from the base to the tip of his stiff length, and fought with himself to let her take him in. He was so ready to be inside her pussy, that even though her eyes burned with the desire to suck him, he didn't know if he would last long enough to do both.

Her nails scraped his chest and he shouted at the pleasure-pain just before she widened her lips around his cock, until his sensitive head hit the back of her throat. He dug his fingers into her hair and resisted the urge to fuck her mouth, instead gripping her honey hair so tight that he was certain it was painful. Then she widened her lips and relaxed her throat so the rest of him was caressed by her plush softness and she swallowed his tip into the back of her throat, over and over until he felt he was going to explode.

Reaching his limit, he growled and palmed her neck, giving in to shove his cock deeper than she could take him just once before pulling from between her lips entirely. He sat up and wrapped his arm around her back, still holding her neck and flipped them both until he covered her bare skin with his.

His fingers frantically massaged over her pert breasts, down her torso, her hips, the tops of her thighs, until he met her apex. She gasped when he grazed her clit with a fingertip and easily dipped his finger in.

"You're so ready for me, baby." He pulled his finger out and sucked it into his mouth, moaning at her delicious taste. Lying over her, he spread her legs with his knees and positioned himself at her entrance, reveling in the feeling of his hard shaft gliding against her swollen lips, already drenched for him.

"Say it again."

Her "I love you," came on a single moan as he entered her in one swift thrust. They were moving as one in the next. He held her and hoped she felt how much he cherished those words she'd given him. She responded by tightening around him until he felt every part of her with each deep stroke.

In a matter of moments, the intensity of their lovemaking caught up with them both as she screamed his name and his movements grew uncoordinated when she tightened around him. On the groan of his release, he wrapped his arms around her and, while still inside, he rolled her until she was on top. Her whispers were constant and calmed his racing heart as he held her close. After a few breaths, her words finally registered.

"I love you, Jason Stone."

He wrapped his hand around her nape and pulled her away slightly to see those beautiful sea blue-green eyes, watery and shining brightly back at him.

"Lies?" he asked.

She returned his gaze with a smile.

"No lies."

EPILOGUE

Six months later

"Baby, you ready to go?" Jason asked, his voice higher than normal. He was overcompensating and trying hard not to let his frustration show through while surrounded by suitcases just inside their apartment door.

"Hold your horses, Jay. Don't make my accent come out before I do!"

"Too late for that," he stage-whispered, hoping to get her out of the bedroom, even if it was just to yell at him.

They were supposed to be taking a well-deserved vacation at the cabin as a reward for working nonstop since rescuing Ellie. Jules was busier than ever with people begging to be her clients. Everyone wanted the defense attorney who got the infamous murderer, Jason Stone, exonerated, regardless of whether he was innocent or not. That little detail didn't seem to matter. Most criminals think they're innocent of everything. He was of the mindset that most people are guilty of *something*, but Jules had gently chastised him for that.

Everyone deserves a second chance, Jay.

Jules said having a line of potential clients was a good

problem to have. She now had the luxury of picking people she thought needed her the most, and referred the rest.

Waking hours that weren't taken up by business, were spent with Nora and Ellie. Nora had been working herself to blisters lately, having taken on several different jobs while staying on as Jules's assistant. She was either helping Jules or working with victims of abuse and trafficking. If she wasn't doing that, she was at Draco's side.

Jason's heart ached whenever he thought of his former teammate and friend. He was still in a coma, even half a year later. Something about losing oxygen to his brain at some point. Each Crew member took their turn to keep the big guy company, but Nora was a permanent fixture. He couldn't tell if it was guilt or something else that kept her by his side, but Jason was glad Draco wasn't alone.

As much as it hurt, the Crew had to keep going without him. They exchanged information with ADA Aguilar to find the men who tried to murder Draco, and killed Andrew Ascot. The city was distraught at the loss of their Golden Boy, but they didn't know the whole story. The press was told he'd been gunned down as an innocent bystander in a drug deal gone wrong. No one questioned why he was at the Inland Port in the middle of the night. It was enough to blame drug dealers and mourn his loss. Andrew Wilton Ascot III, played the distraught father and demanded justice. But no other facts emerged about the alleged drug dealers and the case went cold.

Only Aguilar knew the whole truth. Jules shared everything with him, in hopes of joining forces and finding the assholes. It also helped Jules to tell someone else about what really happened to Andy. She was devastated over the Crew having to leave Ascot's body at the port. She'd wanted the world to know he was a hero, not just a victim. But they couldn't do that without blowing the future of the trafficking investigation. It was frustrating for everyone when they realized the women didn't remember anything about their captors.

Soon after their rescue, every one of the women, aside from Nora, came down with varying degrees of what they first thought was the flu. It was bizarre, until a hard truth they never anticipated hit them all in the gut.

Withdrawal.

They'd known drug addiction is often used as a means of coercion in human trafficking, but because they'd had little to no interaction with victims after they were rescued, they'd never seen the effects up close. It made a sick and twisted amount of sense, especially since none of them could remember any specifics.

The women who received injection after injection of God-knows-what for weeks exhibited signs of withdrawal less than twelve hours after their last dose. Even Ellie went through it, but to a much lesser degree. Jason hadn't understood, at first. After all, his sister was drugged for less than a week. But Dev explained that everyone's body processes drugs differently and the constant barrage of drugs—most likely highly addictive morphine or heroin—over that period of time had apparently been enough for her.

They went through hell, suffering all over again. It broke his heart to watch Ellie helpless to the sickness ravaging her body, bent sideways into a trash can by her bed. She could barely sleep, and when she did, she was wracked with chills and woke up to drenched sheets, covered with sweat. A couple of the women's withdrawal was so severe, they needed to be hospitalized. Snake had already created falsified records and fake identities for the women, just in case the traffickers were looking for them, so they were at least under the radar while they received help.

Jules and Dev were a godsend. Jules took care of each woman over the course of nearly two weeks, and seemed to be operating on autopilot. She probably had been, the memory of her mother not too far in the back of her mind. She changed the bedding, walked the women to the bathroom and bathed them when necessary, fed them when they could eat, and guided them through their aches and fears.

Dev hardly left Ellie's side, which made Jason both irked and thankful. Having a doctor as part of the Crew was an answer to all their prayers, and with his expertise, connections, and Jules's persistent ministrations, the women came out of their worst withdrawal symptoms in less than two weeks.

After that, Jules, Nora, and Ellie hit the ground running and dove headlong into rehabilitating the women. Unbeknownst to Jason, there were many different secretive organizations that specialized in different ways of helping women in terrible situations. Jules came up with a program to integrate them so the organizations could be more effective together, benefiting from each other rather than the women having to seek out the help from several different sources. They called it Sasha Saves.

The program took off, and Nora helped the women create homes and settle into their new lives. Besides Ellie, none of them had strong ties to family or friends, so they'd all decided to make a fresh start and embrace their new identities as clean slates. Sasha Saves now included local shelters, programs, and organizations across the southeast. They made sure each woman, including Ellie, was able to get some kind of substance abuse counseling and therapy. Ellie's sweet empathetic soul reached out to the other victims of her situation, but couldn't stop there. She put herself on some kind of hotline so when someone calls about being abused or scared, Ellie swoops in and figures out exactly what the women need immediately to escape. She'll be starting college soon and is planning on pursuing a degree as a counselor.

She even convinced Jason to see a therapist who specializes in veteran's issues. Before, he'd been convinced his anxiety wasn't severe enough to count as the dreaded post-traumatic stress disorder. There was also something inside him that bristled against the Army's insistence that they all be medically discharged for psychological reasons. It'd always felt like a convenient and disrespectful kick to the ass as the government shoved them and potential embarrassment out the door. But after time with his counselor and cognitive-behavioral therapy, his eyes were opened to the fact that, like everything else, PTSD has no one-size-fits-all pattern.

He still had a long way to go, they hadn't gotten to talking about his last MF7 mission, yet. It was hard work, but he was starting to enjoy going. During every session, he felt the hard boulder of guilt sink into his chest to intolerable levels, sometimes making it physically hard to breathe. But afterward, it was as if he'd chipped away at the stone, and left some of the rocks at the door as he left. The pressure in his chest would release and he could breathe easier. And damn did he enjoy the lightness of the fresh air.

He was proud of his girls, and—although he'd never admit it aloud—he was even proud of himself. But months and months of Jules saving others was starting to wear on her. Jason could see it every night when her exhausted body collapsed on their comfy couch, leading him to carry her off to their bed. There's only so long a person can ignore stress before the tension headaches and moodiness get too much to bear. And Jason, who usually thought her occasional sass was cute, was finding its constant presence less and less adorable. Jules must've realized it as well since she was agreeing to a vacation in the first place.

He was dealing with changes of his own, and not just from therapy. The day after their after-action report, Jason signed on to BlackStone Securities. Ever since, their main project was finding any leads to the thin man and the Russian from the Inland Port. In the meantime, Hawk signed them up for easy security detail, quick money with low risk and all relatively danger-free. Jules enjoyed having a built-in investigator, too. The work was innocuous enough, but being constantly busy and away from his woman wasn't sustainable. They needed the weekend away in their cozy room in the cabin. If his plan worked, they might stay the whole week.

But at the rate Jules was getting ready, they might not make it at all. He'd hoped hanging out by the door, everything set to go to the truck, would incentivize her to hurry her sexy ass up. Apparently, that was not the case.

Jason leaned against the wall beside the door and sighed. He adjusted the box in his pocket to stop it from digging into his thigh, and rested with his arms and feet crossed, glancing over the apartment one last time to make sure he wasn't missing anything himself. That would be embarrassing.

It was Jules's apartment, but completely different from the pristine, staged feeling it once had. It became a home the night he moved in, two days after saving Ellie. He dropped Jules off at her apartment and had opened the door to his own barren apartment when Jules's name appeared on his phone.

Come back, Jaybaby.

That's all she needed to say. He hung up, packed all seven things he owned, and drove back to her apartment with no intention of returning to his. He didn't even go back to break the lease. He called the next day and said something about being in the military and the rental office let him off the hook.

He hadn't provided much in the way of "stuff" for their apartment, but material things don't make a home. Love does. And he had plenty of that.

Although they were busy, he insisted on eating every meal together whenever possible. Every night, they ended up on the couch and let the stress of the day melt off. Sometimes they argued over bad TV. Sometimes they enjoyed silence as he watched the game and she leaned against him with a book until she fell asleep.

There was also much more of his favorite scotch in the liquor cabinet. He wouldn't tell her he figured out her little secret. Turns out that bottle they drank from that first night was the gesture of a hopeful romantic, and not a gift from a client, after all.

His gaze lingered over the liquor cabinet near the dining table as he debated having a much-needed drink while he waited and making Jules drive. His eyes paused on the wooden frame beside the cabinet. The new couple inside the frame was still unbelievably happy and you couldn't even see where the wooden pieces had been glued back together. The beautiful woman with honey-brown hair and sea blue-green eyes was smiling with laughter so infectious, anyone who saw the photo smiled. The man beside her, once broody and broken, was beaming as he watched her with an intense love that he'd never thought he deserved.

It was that undying, unconditional love he was trying to remind himself of as the woman in question was taking. Her. Precious. Time. She'd been awfully quiet for a while. He racked his brain over what could possibly be taking so long when he swore.

"Jules, you better not be working... shit, or *packing* anything else." He sighed at her silence, now convinced she was doing exactly that, and stepped from the wall. "Juliet, there's nothing left in your closet. This is a three-day trip and if you are unloading your drawers into more suitcases, so help me God—" He entered the bedroom only to find it empty. The bathroom light went out and the door opened.

"Jules?" His heart clenched when her tearful gaze lifted from something in her hands to meet his eyes. Without a thought, he stepped toward her, stopping when she held up her hand.

"Everything alright, baby girl?"

She nodded and gave a watery smile that did nothing for the pit suddenly gnawing in his stomach.

"Jay... I'm..." She choked out a laugh and grinned wider. "I'm pregnant."

The heaviness creeping in after seeing her tears disappeared immediately, making him so lightheaded he had to sit down on the bed.

"You're... we're pregnant?" He chuckled out a laugh and felt tears of his own prick at the back of his eyes. She continued to nod and he jumped off the bed and met her in two strides to lift and hug her. Her squeals of joy went straight to his soul, but their high pitch in his ear made him realize he was twirling a pregnant woman around. He stopped abruptly and settled her on the bed.

"Oh God, baby, I'm so sorry, I wasn't thinking. Are you alright—"

She interrupted him by covering his mouth with hers. Their kiss was deep and full of emotion, and he found himself cradling the back of her head before she gently pulled away.

"I'm okay, Jay." She giggled, caressing his cheek with her hand. "But it's gonna be a *long* nine months if this is how you're gonna act. I'm not gonna break. I haven't yet and I won't start now."

"What about what the doctors said? About not being able... I thought..."

She shrugged. "They never actually said it would be *impossible*, just very, very hard. I think I was so defeated by everything for so long that I assumed that was doctor speak for 'never gonna happen.' I guess fate loves a good technicality, too."

He huffed out a laugh. "Don't take this the wrong way. But I'm so fucking glad you were wrong."

The tears that threatened finally escaped from their stronghold and her fingers swiped them away from his cheeks. She gave him another chaste kiss and he realized he couldn't wait anymore. It was nothing like he planned, but the squeezing of his heart and the promise of their future told him it was the right move.

He shoved his hand into his pocket before bending a knee at her feet.

Jules covered her mouth and whispered behind her hand. "Jaybaby, what're you doing?" The happy lilt on the end of her question confirmed his decision.

"Baby girl, I fell in love with you once, but I was a coward and ran away. I begged you back into my life and you did more than that. You saved it. I've loved you since the day you dropped to your death on that pole" —Jules giggled and squeezed his empty hand— "and caught yourself in the end. It was then I realized that I want to be the one to catch you when you fall. You had my heart then." Jason withdrew his hand from her hold and placed it over her still flat stomach. "And you hold my whole world now." Jason closed his eyes and shuddered out a breath, nervous about what he was going to say next. He opened to find blue-green eyes sparkling with joy as tears streamed down the love of his life's cheeks.

"Will you let me love you forever, Juliet Bellerose? Will you marry me?"

Before he could pop open the box, she tackled him to the ground, smashing her lips on his and kissing him over and over with a triumphant shout of "Yes!" between each kiss. He got caught up in her embrace until she finally slowed down her assault.

She took his face in her hands and stared deep into his eyes.

"Yes, Jay. I want to be your wife—" a kiss on his cheek "—the mother of your children." A kiss on the other cheek. "I want to cry with you and I want to laugh with you, every day of our lives. Yes, Jason Stone. I'll marry you." She gave him a sweet brush of her lips.

He closed his eyes against the burn and blinked open to find her lovingly waiting. She was it for him. Jules was everything he never knew he needed and everything he never thought he deserved. He didn't know exactly what she got out of the relationship, but he would work tirelessly to make the second chance she gave him worth it. She would get everything from him he had to give. Never again would he walk away from the best thing he ever had. Now, two of the best things he'd ever have.

Because the truth was, she was his.

And he was hers.

MEANWHILE

"None of them?" he asked, careful to mask the emotion he felt from his voice. But he couldn't stop himself from tightening his hand around his phone. Not for the first time, he was glad it was military-grade. "You've been looking for months, and we haven't found a single one of them?"

"Well, there's one. But she's impossible to get close to."

"Keep trying. We have no idea how much they remember and you know I don't like loose ends. The one you know about, what's her status? Were there buyers for that one?"

"We'll work on it, sir. But the girls were drugged the entire time. There's no trace back to any of us. I—and my men—have made sure of it. That goes for the one girl, too. We had a few interested from her photo, but we've figured out that she's involved with the group that sabotaged us."

He leaned back in his chair and contemplated their options. "When you find her, maybe we should consider salvaging one of those deals. And for the others, did you try our usual channels?"

"Yes. But those private security agents are pros. They used organizations under our radar."

"So, no hope of retrieval for them?"

"Not right now, sir, no."

"This is problematic, Dmitri. We've lost business, loyal clients, and our whole operation in Ashland is compromised because of your fuckups."

He tapped his fingers against the wood veneer desk. Normally, he would've waited to take this type of call until he could work from his other office, but he couldn't leave his post at the moment. He missed the delicious chocolate gleam of his personal desk. None of this fake shit.

"I'm sorry, sir. We have time before our next scheduled auction and I'll personally ensure we are more discreet this time, starting with vetting our girls better. We were on a deadline this last time and my son didn't perform as well as he has in the past."He huffed in response. It didn't used to be this difficult to get girls. He was beginning to wonder if this side of the business was worth it.

"How's the other trade?"

"Good. We're planning on reengaging with past suppliers."

He sighed heavily and thought seriously about throwing the phone against the bulletproof window. The suppliers on the other side of the business were unsavory, to say the least. In his mind, they were all thieving scum and although the trade was lucrative, unfortunately, that was the type of employee they had to work with. He hated to put so much at risk into the side of the business that wasn't even where the true money was made. He brought the phone away from his ear and breathed out a heavy sigh. With the most recent loss, the stakes were high. They would have to make do. For now.

"Hm... alright, lay low for the time being. We didn't have anything for the last auction. We can't disappoint next time. Make sure we get that invite again."

"Understood."

-THE END-

ALSO BY GREER RIVERS

Conviction Series

Escaping Conviction

Fighting Conviction - June 13, 2021

Title- TBA - Releasing Fall 2021

Ashland County Legal Short Stories

A Tempting Motion

Thank you for reading!

Please consider leaving a review on Amazon, Goodreads, and Bookbub! Even just one word can make all the difference.

BE A DEAR AND STALK ME HERE

Be a Boss Babe and join my Facebook group Greer Rivers Babes

Sign up to become an ARC reader
Subscribe to my newsletter

TikTok
Instagram
Amazon Author Page
Goodreads Author Page
Facebook Author Page
Bookbub
Website

ACKNOWLEDGMENTS

I am super blessed y'all. My words can't possibly encompass all the gratitude I have for the following people, and so many more I can't fit here, but I'll try to do my best without gifs and emojis (although, truly, what fun is that?). Sidebar, please forgive my rambling. I'm kinda writing this like a letter so bear with me, friend.

First, and almost foremost (sorry, the hubs is always my #1), thank you READERS! The dadgum dream makers and Boss Ass Bitches. I know your time is precious, so to have you spend it on something I wrote is a true damn honor.

If you're a bookstagrammer or booktoker, holy crap, let me just tell you that you make an author's world go 'round.

Without readers, I'd just be living in my head all by myself. Been there, done that. Zero stars. Would not recommend. It's pretty lonely. Hanging out with y'all is why I do this and I love hearing from readers: good, bad, or ugly, although admittedly I'm always fingers-crossed for good. You rock my world with your encouragement. I wouldn't be able to pursue this dream without y'all so thanks for making my dreams come true!

Thank you Aleksa for my kickass logo and banner: You are awesome to work with and I apologize for using words that don't translate well into Russian. *Face palm emoji*. You did a great job and I am telling everyone who will listen how talented you are! Seriously y'all, she posts her process and everything on Insta. She's incredible.

To Jodie at Jodielocks Designs: Thank you so much for putting up with me! You were awesome and I love my cover! It's gorgeous and working with you was so great.

Many thanks to Ellie McLove, my editor at My Brother's Editor, and Rosa Sharon, the Fairy Proof Mother: Y'all are the best and I'm so thankful to keep working with MBE.

To my friends and former coworkers who have no idea I write sexy time: the only thing I miss is you. There are a few of you I wish I could name because you've been such an impact and a blessing in my life. Friday Crew, lookin' at you. Thank you for not giving me too hard of a time for quitting "to pursue a dream outside the legal field." I know a few of you are going to investigate the mystery until the day you die, but if you've made it here, congratulations, friend! You've solved the case.

To EC's alpha and beta readers:

Jessica, Emily, Kayleigh, Lee, Sav, Willow, Avie, D. Lilac, Salem, Clara, Tucker, Jennifer

This book would be an absolute disaster without y'all. Thank you for pointing out plot holes, telling me when something sucks, and telling me when it's pretty.

To the ones who don't let me quit: Jessica, Kayleigh, Lee, Emily, Sav, and Willow: I'd be chugging wine with my friendly Imposter if it weren't for y'all. Thank you so much for taking last minute requests and reading my work on the fly (some of you twice). You guys are absolute gems for constantly telling me pretty things so I can attempt to write pretty things. Our friendship has meant so much to me on this crazy journey, and I wouldn't be (nor would I want to be) on this awesome trajectory without you.

Individually: To Willow: Thank you for your tough as nails alpha/beta reading. You're truly making me a better writer. To Sav: Thank you for being all sorts of encouraging and showing me the ropes. To Lee: Thank you for being the sweetest person ever, checking in, and reading my stuff and telling me it's pretty and when it's not. Thank you also for watching almost every TikTok before it's posted to make sure it's not stupid AF, lol. To Kayleigh: Thank you for your acceptance, love of *New Girl*, and talking me through my crazy at 2 am EST. I can't wait until you talk me into getting something pierced or tattooed. To Jessica: Thank you for convincing me that others believe in me. You have no idea how important that was for me to hear. To Emily: Thank you for teaching me to believe in myself. I've never had someone push me to do that before and it's truly changed my life. Thank you to all of you for making me a better person.

To my lovely Dinner Divas: Katie the Ruthless, The Honorable Sydni, Liz the Peacemaker, and of course, last—but certainly not least—Her Majesty Wendy. You are my OG Boss Babes. I will forever be grateful for the show Dollface for convincing me I need female friends, and to y'all for proving the show was right. I love y'all so much I need to give individual shout outs:

Thank you, Katie, muh bestie, for always lifting me up when I need it, and being madder than I am when I need that, too. I'm super thankful I never have to drive anywhere and I'll always cherish our road trip talks and car hibachi.

Thank you, Sydni, for your unwavering support, never judging me, and telling me I deserve more. You're one of the few people I love to lean on and you can lean on me anytime, friend.

Thank you, Liz, for persistently and constantly inviting me to things even when I was too insecure or depressed to say yes. You're incredibly welcoming and I will always be grateful for the gift of your friendship.

Thank you, Wendy, for being a true queen, and teaching me what it is to work hard and love my work. I've never had a great group of ride or dies until y'all, and now I'll never go without. Thank God we chickened out of that stupid wine advent calendar in a 24 hour span shit. That was *definitely* one of our worst ideas.

To my wonderful family, my momma, sisters, BIL, and precious baby angel face niece: may you always be my oblivious supporters. I love y'all with all my heart and I mean it with all sincerity when I say please, for God's sake, do not read my books. If you are in these acknowledgements because you have indeed read a book or two, well, sorry-not-sorry and hope you enjoyed it, at least, lol. Keep your judgments, but I'll take your prayers. Lord knows I need them.

To Maria: because I firmly believe that when everyone is born we should be assigned a kickass therapist like you. You've saved my life in more ways than I want to count.

To Athena, you crazy bitch.

And finally, to the hubs. You are my "Mighty Alpha," first reader, favorite encourager, irl book boyfriend, best friend forever, and the love of my life. You are literally the first person to ever tell me a story I wrote was good enough to send out in the world and you selflessly read this one twice. I have to say, you shushing me because you were "in a really good part" was honestly one of the nicest things I've ever heard. I am so incredibly thankful for you believing in me and encouraging me when it was crazy and not financially sound to do so. You've saved my life and you've changed it for the better. I wouldn't want to spend a day of it without you. Thank you for making every day an HEA.

Love,

Greer Rivers

ALL ABOUT GREER

Greer Rivers is a former crime fighter in a suit, but now happily leaves that to her characters! A born and raised Carolinian, Greer says "y'all," the occasional "bless your heart" (when necessary), and feels comfortable using legal jargon in everyday life.

She lives in the mountains with her husband/critique partner/irl book boyfriend and their three fur babies. She's a sucker for reality TV, New Girl, and scary movies in the daytime. Greer admits she's a messy eater, ruiner of shirts, and does NOT share food or wine.

Greer adores strong, sassy heroines and steamy second chances. She hopes to give readers an escape from the craziness of life and a safe place to feel too much. She'd LOVE to hear from you anytime! Except the morning. She hates mornings.